To my sister, Margaret, who eagerly reads or listens to all my books!

1

January 1860

Evie Davenport skipped lightly down the stairs, a book of British birds in her hand. At the half landing, she paused and glanced out of the window at the crunching sound of a carriage on the snow-covered drive. As the woman descended from the vehicle, Evie groaned.

Mrs Myer.

A widow from the village, the woman was like a homing pigeon. The minute Evie or her papa were indoors, she arrived.

Quickly changing her mind about sitting in front of the fire with her book, Evie dashed to the cupboard by the stairs and pulled on her coat. She flung off her house slippers and hurriedly put on her boots, tying the laces around the hooks so fast she missed several.

The doorbell rang.

Evie plucked her black felt hat from a hook and squashed it on her hair with only one pin to secure it.

Fanny, the housemaid, came along the corridor that led to the kitchen, wiping her hands on her apron as she did so. 'Oh, miss. I didn't know you were going out. Shall I send for the carriage?'

'No, no, it is fine, Fanny. I'm going for a long walk, likely to Bellingham Hall.'

'The snow has stopped, miss, but it'll be deep in places.' Fanny straightened her apron as the doorbell jangled again.

'Tell my papa,' Evie whispered, fastening the last button on her coat.

Fanny opened the door and Mrs Myer sailed in with a look of displeasure on her beautiful face. Her pointed glare at Fanny spoke a thousand words, but she also voiced them. 'Dear me, girl, you are tardy at answering the doorbell. In this weather, especially, you should not keep your master's guests waiting in the cold. Punctuality is a most prized virtue and one that you should uphold in respect for this household's reputation.'

'Begging your pardon, madam.' Fanny bobbed her knees, her freckled face keeping straight though her green eyes danced merrily.

Mrs Myer turned for Fanny to help her off with her cape and noticed Evie standing by the cupboard. 'Goodness, child. What are you doing hiding there?'

'Not hiding. I was just on my way out, Mrs Myer.'

'In that state?'

Evie put a hand up to her hat and adjusted it, then checked the buttons on her coat were done up correctly. 'I was in a hurry.'

'To go for a walk in this weather?'

'It is good to walk for one's health.'

'Not in zero temperatures, surely?' The older woman slipped off her gloves, disapproval etched on her fine features.

'Papa says it is good for the lungs.' Evie couldn't help but taunt, knowing Mrs Myer would not speak against anything Major Davenport said.

'Indeed, but I am here now. So, take off your things and we shall have some tea. Your dear papa will be most pleased to have us both for company.'

Evie bristled at being commanded by this woman. 'Forgive me, Mrs Myer,' she replied with false sweetness. 'But I am expected at Bellingham Hall,' she lied.

'Gracious, you spend far too much time at that hall.' Mrs Myer swept her haughty gaze around the fine entrance as though ready to pick fault with it. Not that she could. Fanny kept the whole house tidy and clean, a large task for someone who had to be the parlourmaid, chambermaid and everything in between.

Evie smiled brightly. 'Good day, Mrs Myer.'

'Where is the major?'

'In his study.' Evie hesitated, torn as whether to stay and protect her papa from this woman's wiles or to flee and be free of her condescension. 'We were not expecting visitors.'

'But I told the major I would be calling today. I mentioned it before you left to visit your aunts last week.'

'We only returned from Bradford last evening. It must have slipped his mind.' She gave Mrs Myer a small shrug as though a visit by her was not important to them.

Mrs Myer's shoulders straightened at the slight. 'Then I shall go in and surprise him. He will be delighted to spend an hour or so with me.'

Evie stepped forward. 'Fanny, please inform my papa that Mrs Myer is waiting for him in the parlour.' She waved her arm toward the parlour's open door, indicating for the woman to enter. On no account did she want the pushy woman to invade Papa's study, which was a small room, his private sanctuary, and not where he should entertain lady visitors.

Annoyance clearly on her face, Mrs Myer swished the full skirts of her steel-grey dress and marched into the parlour.

Evie stood at the door. 'I'll say good day to you, Mrs Myer, for I doubt you will still be here when I return.' She turned away before the woman could answer and felt a flash of success at getting a small victory over the widow.

She strode down the drive, treading in the ruts made by carriage wheels, and along the road leading to the village halfway down the valley. The crunch of snow beneath her boots still gave Evie a curious wonderment. This was her second winter in England and the charm of a frozen world outside her door delighted her, at least for short periods of time. No matter how pretty the countryside looked covered in virgin white, she would rather have the bright days of sunshine, if not the energy-sapping heat, of India where she had been born and raised.

Her black boots and the hem of her thick black woollen coat were soon caked in snow. Wearing black was another thing to contend with. In India, she had only ever worn pastel colours. However, all that changed on the journey from Bombay to London. Her British parents had decided to leave India when her papa, a decorated major, retired from the British Army after the Indian Rebellion had been fought. Papa believed he was too old now at fifty-eight to be caught up in strife and didn't fancy a desk position at headquarters or in some remote village far from civilisation. So, after twenty-odd years in the subcontinent, they'd packed up, said tearful farewells to servants and friends and travelled the long, tortuous journey home to England.

Evie had been both sad and excited to be leaving India and going 'home' to England, a home she'd never seen before, but which was held in great esteem by her parents and her maternal grandmama, who lived with them. Leaving their friends and saying goodbye to servants she'd known all her life had been a wrench, but the excitement soon replaced the sadness.

England, in her mind, seemed a magical place that so many of their friends spoke about with such longing. Mama and Grandmama often wrote long letters to cousins and aunts and received packages of English treats. Papa read English newspapers; they toasted Queen Victoria at every party and dinner. To Evie, England was the home she'd never seen, and her imagination grew at how wonderful it would be.

The voyage from Bombay to Suez had been a wonder to Evie. Unlike her grandmama, she didn't get seasick on the steamer and although the boat wasn't very luxurious she had plenty of time to read and talk to the several other British passengers making the trip home. In the Egyptian town of Suez, the family had spent a few days in a hotel, waiting for the Suez to Alexandria train, which had only recently opened, meaning tickets were in much demand.

The tedious, hot and dusty train journey took them through the desert and Mama complained that they should have sailed in a ship around the Cape of Good Hope instead of taking this dirty, energy-sapping route, but Papa explained that this journey cut the six-month sea voyage to two months and was worth the discomfort. He'd read a report on how the French had managed to get permission to build a large shipping canal from Port Said to Suez. Papa said it would transform the world of shipping, even if Lord Palmerston disagreed.

Papa had arranged a short stop in Cairo for them along the way to break up the train journey and to visit an old school friend there. Evie spent the first week in Cairo in a daze of shopping in bazaars and socialising with fellow British families who lived there and who they were introduced to by Papa's friend, Mr Daintree.

It was at a Christmas party in mid-December that Papa interrupted her dancing with a young gentleman and told her Mama was not feeling well.

Four days later, Mama died from a fever brought on by food poisoning and two days after that Grandmama suffered a fatal stroke at Mama's funeral.

Within a week, Evie had lost her beloved mama and grandmama and the family number had halved. Dazed, reeling from shock, they left Cairo a day before Christmas and didn't celebrate the special day, for they were too wrapped up in their misery.

The rest of the voyage to Alexandria, then across the Mediterranean to France and another long train trip up the French countryside, before finally crossing the Channel to London, passed in a blur of grief. In the English Channel, thick fog surrounded the boat, cutting them off from the world. When they finally docked at a wharf on the Thames, Evie could only cling to her grief-stricken papa as they stepped onto a rain-washed London dock.

The cold hit Evie like a continual slap. No matter how many layers of clothing she wore, she couldn't get warm. London was bleak in winter, all grey sky, grey buildings, grey river and greydressed people. That she and Papa wore severe mourning black added to their gloom.

Papa asked her if she wanted to return to India, but she couldn't imagine being there without Mama. She knew he felt the same and as much as England was a strange place to her, she'd rather start again and make new memories living in the country where her parents had been raised.

They travelled to the county of Yorkshire in the north, the birthplace of her parents. Papa had a cousin who lived in Leeds and Mama's aunts were in Bradford. Papa deemed it sensible to find a home where they had some family, if nothing else.

Despite thick snowfalls, which intrigued and delighted Evie, who'd never seen snow up close but only from a distance one time when she saw the snow-capped Himalayas, she and her papa toured many towns in the western parts of Yorkshire looking for a suitable home.

One day in January, snow thick on the ground but with a blue sky above and the sun shining, Evie descended the hired carriage and walked up the path of High Lylston House. Immediately, the two-storey sandstone-bricked house grabbed her attention. It was situated above the village of Lylston on a slope of a hill that continued to rise behind them towards the undulating moors and the larger Ilkley Moor beyond.

The property had a few garden beds covered in snow, but several bare rose bushes stood proudly and some tall, graceful trees, their branches weighted with snow, bordered the front sloping lawn. Behind the house was a flat cobbled yard, a decent stable block and outbuildings.

'Ten acres, Evie,' Papa read from the leaflet the land agent had given him. 'We don't need ten acres.'

'You said we'd get a horse each, Papa, so we can ride together like we used to and then we need carriage horses, too. Ten acres is the least we should consider.'

He nodded and they explored inside the house, which was cold and musty and decorated in dark wood panelling.

'It needs improvements.' Papa frowned, looking about.

'We can have it done and make it our own.' Evie explored the downstairs, quickly seeing the place as it could be. The parlour, dining room and small study all needed redecorating. The kitchen needed fresh paint and she didn't dare venture down into the dark cellar. Upstairs, the four bedrooms were showing stages of damp, the wallpaper faded and old. The attic rooms were filled with unwanted furniture that needed to be sorted and cleaned, but overall, she was delighted with the house, especially the view. From every window at the front of the house you could see the rooftops of the little village of Lylston and beyond that for miles over the Aire Valley, through the centre of which ran the River Aire and the Leeds and Liverpool Canal. Behind the house, the view consisted of tree-less moorland.

Papa bought the property and High Lylston House became their home. Evie threw herself into redecorating the house over the spring and summer. As promised, Papa brought her and himself a horse each and she enjoyed exploring the moorland and the valley. Their grief gave them a bond, the house gave them comfort, but it was the new society of friends that gave them a sense of belonging, of being able to begin again.

Within a short space of time, Evie had made friends with Sophie Bellingham, a wealthy rail baron's daughter from Bellingham Hall. The large estate dominated the village, providing work and custom to the local community.

The respected Bellingham family and their friends accepted Major Davenport and Evie with open arms and that first year wasn't as difficult as it could have been. They transformed the house, engaged servants and, by the autumn of that year, they felt a part of the local society.

Slipping on some ice, Evie slowed down her strides, not wanting to fall. Papa would not cope with her having an accident. Some weeks ago had been the first anniversary of Mama and Grandmama's deaths, which had been difficult and solemn. Papa had not left his study for three days. Evie dreaded Christmas, their second without Mama, but thankfully, the Bellinghams had insisted they spend Christmas with them, and Evie had thanked the fates for giving them such good friends.

After Christmas, they had gone to Bradford for a week to spend time with the old aunts. This had given Evie the chance to attend the theatre, dine at fancy restaurants and have new dresses made. Evie had wanted to keep Papa busy, for when he wasn't busy his mind slipped into the heavy grief of losing Mama. She dragged poor Papa around the shops, doing what she could to keep him from his sorrow.

But now they were home and with the winter weather keeping them mostly indoors, she wondered what she could do to keep Papa happy. His bouts of low mood frightened her. She felt out of her depth when he refused to leave his study.

The crunch of rumbling wheels beyond the curve of the lane sent her hurrying off to the side of it. Only one other dwelling was on this lane; Lylston Top Farm was further beyond their home, and she expected it to be the farmer, Mr Lund. Only the carriage that appeared was black and shiny and nothing at all like Mr Lund's old rickety cart.

Evie smiled as Sophie stuck her head out of the window. 'Evie! You're home!'

'Yes.' She waited for Sophie to open the carriage door and climbed in. 'We arrived home last evening.'

Sophie threw her arms around her and kissed her cold cheek. 'I'm so pleased. I have missed you.'

'I have missed you, too, even though it's only been a week!' She laughed.

'Well, since we became friends, I declare this was the longest we've been apart from each other.'

'No, last summer you spent two weeks on the coast.'

Sophie scowled. 'Oh yes. We did. I was most put out that Mama wouldn't allow me to invite you.'

'We had only known each other for a few months then. I was a stranger to your mama.'

'But *we've* been close friends from the moment you arrived here last January. Gosh, it has been a year already!'

Evie nodded. 'Papa bought the house on the twentieth of January.'

'And today it's the twentieth! A whole year we have been friends, for we met straight away, didn't we?'

Evie grinned, remembering. 'Yes, you were going up to Mr Lund's farm for he was ill, and you were taking him a basket of food. You stopped the carriage and introduced yourself.'

'Well, I was so excited to see new faces come to live here, I simply had to stop when I saw you directing the men carrying boxes inside.'

'I'm terribly glad you did.' Evie didn't know what she'd do without Sophie as her best friend, despite the age difference of Sophie being younger by a few years.

'Were you *walking* down to see me in this weather?'

'I was. To take tea with you and tell you all about my week in Bradford, but it seemed a nuisance to ask Bronson to get the carriage out and I dared not ride Star in case she stumbled on the ice.' Evie's adored horse was her most prized possession. 'Also, Mrs Myer has just called, and I needed to leave as quickly as possible.'

'That woman has no manners. You are recently arrived home and she is instantly making calls. She is not family.'

'Indeed. Papa was answering his post, but he'll put it aside to entertain her. I mentioned that you were expecting me and left before tea was brought in. Papa will be cross with me.'

'Home, Jackson, if you please?' Sophie called to the driver. They lurched on the seat as Jackson turned the horses about on the driveway entrance to Evie's house.

'There's her horrid old horse and gig.' Sophie glared at the offending vehicle. 'How did she know what day you would be home? Did your papa tell her?'

'He must have done. She called the day before we left.' Evie turned her gaze away and stared straight ahead. Mrs Myer's frequent calls were becoming a habit and a nuisance.

'I wish Mama had never introduced your papa to her.'

'It's a small village; they would have met anyway.'

'Mama regrets it now, especially as Mrs Myer spends all her time visiting your papa. How does he put up with her calling every second day?'

'He doesn't seem to mind.' Evie shrugged, trying not to let it show how much *she* minded. Besides, when Papa was in one of his black moods, Mrs Myer took him out of it.

'No, he wouldn't. Mama says all the single men in a ten-mile radius are in love with Mrs Myer.'

'My papa is not!' Evie hated the thought of anyone replacing her beloved mama.

'He is sensible, then.'

Evie thought for a moment. 'Mrs Myer must have what men admire, though? She is attractive, I grant you: blonde with an enviable figure and fine features, plus she is accomplished. All the things men seem to want from a woman by their side,' Evie admitted, wishing the woman wasn't quite so gifted with exemplary features and talents. To men she was a simpering delight, fluttering her eyelashes and pouting her full lips.

'Well, if she is the perfect specimen that men prefer, I shall become an old maid for sure.' Sophie sighed deeply.

Evie grasped her hand. 'Nonsense. You are lovely.' She smiled at her friend, who was petite, shy, kind and generous, if not a little highly strung at times.

'I am a mouse. My brothers tell me often enough.' Sophie's mouth twisted in anguish. 'Dull brown hair, my eyes are no particular colour, neither brown or hazel, and I am so small most men think I am still a child.'

Evie laughed. 'They do not. Why, haven't you already got a wonderful man ready to claim you? Your Mr Lucas?'

'My *Mr Nothing* is more the answer. Alexander and I have made no promises to each other, not really, anyway. We got along extremely well then. We've danced at many a ball and have been riding together. His father and mine are great friends, they expect something to happen between us, but there is not anything put in place, if you understand my meaning.'

'If Alexander Lucas, whoever he is, does not claim you for his bride the minute he returns from America, then he is not worthy of you!'

Sophie grinned.

'And if he doesn't, you and I shall become old maids together.' Evie winked.

'You?' Sophie pealed. 'Never. You've already got half the men in the county talking about you and the other half are too old that they can't see you properly or they'd be madly in love with you, too.'

'Stop it.' Evie blushed a little.

'It's true. At every party and dinner you've attended, you've been given such attention.'

'It's because I am new to the area, and I am the girl born and raised in India. The novelty will wear off soon enough.'

'I highly doubt it. Even Mama said so. You have been here a year now. I am surprised your hand in marriage has not been asked for a dozen times by now.'

'May I remind you that I am too tall, too outspoken and not as polished as the other young ladies.' Evie gave a wry lift of her eyebrows. 'Mrs Myer has mentioned it to me already just how unsuitable I am and not to expect a decent offer of marriage. Not that I want to marry, anyway.' She constantly had conflicting emotions about marriage. Women of her society were meant to think only of getting married, of being a good wife and mother. Evie didn't really know if she wanted that. She had yet to meet a man who would make her want to give up her independence.

'Mrs Myer is a nasty, jealous woman,' Sophie declared. 'To say that to you is deplorable.'

'But what if she is correct, Sophie? Am I an oddity?' Evie dropped her voice. It wasn't often she lost confidence in herself, but the beautiful Mrs Myer had spoken those words one day during last summer when Evie had said something she didn't approve of, something about owning slaves. Mrs Myer had been alarmed that Evie not only knew about such things but dared to comment on them in public. The older woman was quite vocal about Evie's lack of qualities. In India, she had always enjoyed the freedom of doing as she pleased, of having a voice at her papa's table, but here in England she was meant to conform, to be quiet and biddable.

Since that day, Evie had disliked the woman intensely. Yet, what if the widow was right? Evie wasn't small and petite like Sophie; instead, she was tall for a woman at five foot seven. She had long, powerful legs from years of riding and swimming and playing with the servants' children in the hot, dry climate of India. Her thick hair was a mess of colours from gold to reddish brown, as though it couldn't make up its mind what colour it wanted to be. Then there was her skin... Living in a sun-soaked country had given her skin the colour of warm caramel. Mama had despaired over it, demanding she cover up, wear wider hats, use parasols for shade, but Evie had ridden and played and spent hours outside and her creamy skin would darken where it was exposed, giving her unsightly tan lines.

'Mrs Myer is not correct,' Sophie declared. 'You are simply stunning. Everyone says so. Mama says you turn every man's head, and that Major Davenport needs to watch out for you.'

'Watch out for me? Why should Papa watch out for me?'

'Because you are the daughter of a wealthy man and you are... unique,' Sophie explained as they climbed from the carriage in front of the impressive Bellingham Hall.

'Unique?' Evie followed her into the house, no longer overwhelmed by the opulence of the Bellinghams' wealth. Her papa wasn't without means – he'd invested heavily in schemes in India and earned well from them – and her two maiden great-aunts, Rose and Mary, were affluent from inheritances, but even they didn't come close to the fortune Mr Bellingham had made in the railways, carriage-making and coal-mine businesses.

'Indeed.' Sophie gave a footman her gloves and coat and waited while Evie did the same. 'What shall we do?'

'Finish this conversation?' Evie joked, admiring her friend's blue woollen dress with its red piping. Evie wore a black dress with a black lace fringe. She'd not worn a nice colour for twelve months and was itching to do so. She believed her mama would be happy to see her dressed in fine colours again.

Sophie slipped her arm through Evie's. 'We shall discuss something else. Talking about ourselves for too long is terribly indulgent.'

They went into the drawing room just as Lydia Bellingham came in through another doorway, carrying a book.

'Evie, you are returned from Bradford. How lovely to see you.' Sophie's mother was a kind woman and had encouraged their friendship, not that it was needed, for Evie and Sophie had grown close very quickly.

'Yes, Mrs Bellingham. Yesterday evening.'

'Are your great-aunts in good health?'

'They are.'

'Was Bradford enjoyable?'

'It was. I still find it surprising to be living close enough to be able to visit my great-aunts when all my life I've only ever written to them.'

'They must be delighted to have you so near.' Mrs Bellingham took a seat. 'You are staying for afternoon tea?'

'She is, Mama,' Sophie answered for her as they sat on the cream sofa.

'Your papa is in his study with Mr Guy Lucas. They will join us.'

'Aren't Paul and Helen home?' Sophie asked about her oldest brother and sister-in-law.

'No. They have gone to Bingley to visit Helen's parents,' Mrs Bellingham told them. 'I received a letter from your brother Oswald this morning. He has arrived safely back in Oxford and back at his studies.' She spoke of her youngest son. 'The Christmas holiday does seem to go by so awfully fast.'

'It won't be long until it is Easter, and he is home again,' Sophie said as her father and Mr Guy Lucas entered the room.

Evie smiled warmly at both men.

'Goodness me, such delightful company we have,' Mr Bellingham declared. Although not a large man, Jasper Bellingham had a large personality. Known for his acute business brain and his swift ability to turn a penny into a pound, he suffered no fools and was fiercely proud of who he'd become after starting life humbly as a schoolteacher's son. 'Is your father well, Miss Davenport?'

'He is, sir, and mentioned to me at breakfast that he shall call on you tomorrow afternoon.' Evie still was a little nervous talking to the man for he scowled more than he smiled, yet he'd only ever been courteous towards her, and he'd become a good friend of her papa's.

'Excellent. I shall be home from three o'clock.' Mr Bellingham took a seat by the fire, inviting Mr Lucas to do the same.

'Have you heard from Alexander, Guy?' Mrs Bellingham asked Mr Lucas about his son, giving Sophie a sideways glance.

'Not since last week. In his last letter he mentioned travelling to South Carolina.'

'Your son doesn't seem to be in a hurry to return home to York-shire.' Mrs Bellingham chuckled.

'I agree. He is relishing his time in America and learning a great deal,' Mr Lucas said in his quiet way.

'I hope he has not forgotten us?' Mrs Bellingham said lightly. 'We all miss him. Do we not, Sophie?'

'Yes, Mama.' Sophie blushed.

As maids brought in tea trays filled with an assortment of sandwiches and cakes, tea and coffee pots, Evie studied Mr Lucas, a pleasant gentleman she'd met several times at dinner parties hosted by the Bellinghams. Mr Lucas owned two mills in the area, mainly woollen textile operations. However, his only son, Alexander, had begun a cotton mill in his own right instead of working with his father. Sophie had told her Alexander wanted to create his own business empire and not be given his father's when he hadn't done anything to earn it. Evie had thought that a terribly noble idea and most unusual. Someone doing something different always caught her attention.

'He should be careful, though,' Mr Bellingham stated. 'The American states are becoming a hotbed of turmoil. The argument of freeing the slaves is gaining ground, especially in the north.'

'Do not think I am not aware of it, Jasper.' Mr Lucas sighed heavily. 'My last letter to Alexander was to ask him to return to England. He has learned enough of cotton and made many contacts. It is time he was home.'

'Does he buy cotton from the slave-owning plantations?' Evie asked. She had read much about the situation in America.

'I believe he does, yes,' Mr Lucas answered.

'And he does not care about the conditions those poor people suffer to grow and harvest that cotton?'

Mrs Bellingham gasped slightly, and Mr Bellingham frowned.

Mr Lucas gave her a polite smile. 'I will not answer for my son, Miss Davenport. His opinions are his own.'

'And what are yours, sir?' Evie asked. She and her papa had conversed greatly about slavery, amongst many other subjects. Papa supported her need to learn about the world. He regarded education as a highly admired skill, and he didn't want his only child to be an ignorant dolt.

Mr Lucas accepted a cup of tea from Mrs Bellingham. 'I have woollen mills, therefore I have no need for cotton. What happens in other countries are for those nations to contend with.'

'So, you support your son's dealings with slave owners?' Evie persisted.

'I do if it makes good business sense. I cannot change how men earn their fortunes, Miss Davenport, or the laws in other countries.'

'But you can act morally.'

He shook his head when offered a plate of tartlets. 'I do not interfere, Miss Davenport. I run my mills and see to my own business.'

'Yes but—'

'Evie, dear, allow Mr Lucas to have his tea, shall we?' Mrs Bellingham interrupted. 'We are not at a debating society.'

'Forgive me, Mrs Bellingham, Mr Lucas,' she apologised instantly.

'There is nothing to forgive, Miss Davenport,' Mr Lucas replied. 'A young woman should ask questions and be interested in the world. Only, not everything is as simple or fair as we wish it to be.'

'Of course.' She gave a tentative smile, knowing she'd gone too far, and he was gentlemanly enough to let it pass. She stared down into her teacup. There were times when she wished she'd not opened her mouth. Other people's drawing rooms were not her sounding box, and she'd do well to remember it.

Later, alone with Sophie in her bedroom, Evie flopped onto the wide four-poster bed with a groan. 'I made a fool out of myself with Mr Lucas.'

'Oh, it is fine. It is not the first time or the last, knowing you,' Sophie teased, walking to the window.

'Well, next time, give me a sharp kick.'

'With pleasure...'

Evie sat up and gazed at her friend's sad face. 'What is the matter?'

'Nothing...' Sophie stared out of the window at the white world beyond.

'Did I embarrass you?'

'Lord, no. I am used to your outbursts by now.'

'Thank you,' Evie said sarcastically. 'Then what is it? You know you will tell me anyway.'

'No, it is foolish really...' Sophie nibbled her fingernails, then quickly put her hands behind her back as though her former governess was in the room and would slap her hands away from her mouth.

'Is it foolish?'

'Perhaps.' Sophie came and sat on the edge of the bed. 'Not once did Mr Lucas mention that Alexander was wanting to come home. He has been gone for nearly two years. In all that time I have received only four short letters from him, covering two Christmases and two of my birthdays. They were such plain notes, telling me what he was experiencing, but nothing of what is in his heart.'

'And have you written to him about your own heart?' Evie asked.

'Goodness, no. That would be too forward.'

'Would it? Why would it be wrong to make it clear how you feel? You cannot expect a gentleman to write of such sentiments if you are unwilling to do the same.'

'Indeed. Only, it is such an admission, isn't it?'

'Do you want to marry him?'

Sophie blushed. 'I think I do, yes. He is older than me. He became a man while I was still a child.'

'You make him sound ancient.' Evie laughed.

'He is thirty years of age, at least. A man who knows his own mind.'

'Thirty? Hardly old. Our papas are old. Look at me, I'm twenty-three. Does that make me archaic?'

Sophie looked unsure.

Evie laughed. 'Maybe I am compared to your twenty years.'

'How can I know what I truly feel about him when he has been away for so long and before that we were simply friends?' Sophie fiddled with her sleeve, her expression full of doubt. 'Oh, I know Papa and Mr Lucas often joked about aligning our two families together, which I thought to be thrilling, for Alexander is devilishly handsome, but what if he thought it all a huge joke? Am I being a fool to wait for him?'

'You won't know until you speak to him about it. Write a letter to him.'

'I couldn't possibly.' Sophie wrung her hands together. 'I shall put it from my mind until I see him again. Once he has returned home, I shall know how the situation lies.'

'Good. Now no more talk of Mr Alexander Lucas,' Evie declared, 'for the gentleman doesn't deserve all this fuss if he hasn't made his intentions clear.'

'But he is very suitable...'

'And *handsome*, so you keep saying.' Evie chuckled.

'I think to be his bride would be a dream come true,' Sophie whispered as though afraid to even suggest such a thing. 'But he is too good for me. He is worldly, well travelled.'

'Nonsense! *You* are too good for *him* or any man.'

'As my friend, you have to say that.'

Evie scrambled off the bed. 'As your friend, I am refusing to allow you to speak of him again for the rest of the day. Now let us go down to the kitchen and ask Mrs Freeman if she will show us how to cook something.'

'Oh dear, not again,' Sophie moaned, a look of dread on her face.

'It was fun learning how to make a cake last time.'

'Mama was not impressed when she found out!' Sophie grimaced. 'I received a lecture after you went home. Mama says it is not the done thing to enter the servants' quarters for our own entertainment.'

'Then I shall ask our own cook, Mrs Humphry. She will let us.' Evie was well aware of the difference between the two houses. Bellingham Hall had a small army of servants to cater for the family, the hall and estate whereas her papa had only engaged Mrs Humphry; Lizzie, a kitchen maid; Fanny, the housemaid; as well as Mr Bronson to drive the carriage and care for the horses and his son Colin, who did all the heavy jobs around the house.

Still, the difference in their households didn't matter to her or Sophie. Evie didn't envy Sophie and she knew Sophie didn't look down upon her just because she had a smaller house and less staff. They were both young women brought up in a genteel world of the upper middle class and each in their own way needed a dear friend, especially Evie. This new stricter world could be rather stifling with all its rules for young women. After a life in India full of relaxed social gatherings, of bathing in the sea, riding her horse across the sands, of assisting in her mama's good works and being free to express herself without censure, England felt closed, limited.

'I do not want to learn how to cook. I shall have servants to do that. I want to travel,' Sophie declared.

'To where?' Evie peeped out of the window, noticing the Bellinghams' other carriage had arrived, and Sophie's eldest brother, Paul, and his wife, Helen, descend from it.

'Anywhere. I have been nowhere.'

'You have. You've gone to many places,' Evie reminded her.

'Not like you have, though. You were born in India and visited Egypt and France and you are only twenty-three. I want to see foreign countries, too.'

Evie glanced back at her. 'Maybe when you are married to Mr Lucas, he will take you to other countries.'

'I hope so if he is not too concerned with his mill. Perhaps I need to marry a diplomat and go to live in foreign climes, though I would miss you, of course.'

'I haven't seen too many diplomats in Lylston!' Evie laughed. Sometimes, Sophie sounded very young and naive.

Sophie pulled a face. 'No, it does not look hopeful for me to be introduced to one, that is for certain.'

'You and I should go somewhere!' Evie declared.

'By ourselves?'

'With a suitable chaperone, of course.'

'Mama would have a fit.' Sophie sighed. 'No, our lives are to be non-eventful, I can feel it.'

'Speak for yourself.' Evie gave Sophie a sharp look. 'I fully intend to have a fabulous life. When Papa feels the loss of Mama a little less and is more inclined to look for happiness, then he and I will keep each other company in our lovely house and, in the summer months, tour the country seeing the sights.' She longed for the days when her papa would be more his old self, when she could suggest they travel beyond Yorkshire.

'And what of a husband?'

'I have told you previously, many times, that I do not wish to marry. I wish to remain a maiden all my life, like my elderly aunts, and do as I please all my days.' In her mind, being married, keeping house and having a baby every year was not something she was willing to accept. How could such a humdrum life be her future when her thoughts were so alive with experiencing new adventures? She wanted to trek the Scottish Highlands, explore the ancient ruins of Greece, walk the roads of Rome, and so much more.

'You make it sound so simple. Papa talks of grandchildren all the time. All of us must bring forth the next generation. It's our duty.' Sophie seemed worried. 'The very thought frightens me to death. You do not have expectations placed on you as I have.'

'True. Papa just wishes for me to be happy, whatever that may be.'

'People can be happily married, Evie.' Sophie spoke as though to convince herself more than Evie. 'My parents are, as were yours.'

'Yes, and look at the pain Papa suffers now because he loved so deeply.' Evie shivered, remembering his harrowing sobs when Mama died and the change in him ever since. 'To love is to suffer. I shall do without, thank you. I am quite content it being just Papa and myself forever.'

'Unless Mrs Myer gets her way and marries your papa.'

Evie's blood ran cold at the thought of that woman snaring her beloved papa. 'Do not even mention it, I beg you.'

2

The sound of arguing drifted up the hallway from the kitchen to where Evie stood at the bottom of the staircase, sorting through the post that had just been delivered. Frowning at the noise, she marched down to the kitchen door and opened it to find Fanny and Lizzie.

'What is all this fuss?' Evie asked in surprise and with a little annoyance.

They both stared at her, red-faced from their disagreement.

'Miss, can you tell Lizzie here that I am the housemaid and therefore above her in rank as she is only a kitchen maid?' Fanny snapped, eyeing Lizzie with contempt.

'I am the senior kitchen maid!'

'The only one!' Fanny argued hotly. 'I see to the house, which makes me higher in rank than you.'

'Not in the kitchen!'

Fanny's eyes narrowed. 'You're not telling me what to do, Lizzie.'

'I need a hand in here,' Lizzie said, her hands balling into fists. 'You need to help me.'

'I have my own jobs to do.'

'Goodness, please, Fanny, Lizzie. Stop.' Evie glared at them. 'What does it matter?'

'It matters, miss, because when Mrs Humphry isn't here then one of us has to be in charge,' Lizzie defended.

'And that's me!' Fanny snapped.

'Not in the kitchen!' Lizzie argued.

Evie looked around the kitchen, a decent-sized room with a high ceiling and a large black-leaded range going along one wall. A huge window let in light over the wooden workbench, which was covered in assorted vegetables being peeled, or they had been. Steam billowed from cooking pots, and on the table in the middle of the room were two chickens in the process of being stuffed with sage and breadcrumbs. 'Where is Mrs Humphry?'

'She didn't turn up this morning. I cooked breakfast for the major and yourself, miss,' Lizzie supplied. 'But when I'm cooking, I need a hand in here. Colin helps a bit, but Fanny could do more.'

Fanny gasped. 'I can't be your skivvy and see to the dining room at the same time, now, can I?'

'You seem to think you're the only one who has to do all the jobs in this house,' Lizzie flared, hands on hips, her wispy brown hair falling out from beneath her white cap.

'Please, enough.' Evie held up her hands. 'Why hasn't Mrs Humphry arrived? She is usually here by six o'clock. And why haven't I been informed?'

'Sorry, miss, we were that busy getting the breakfast on, and the fires lit, we thought to just get on with everything until Mrs Humphry turned up.'

'But she hasn't and it is now past nine o'clock.' Evie frowned. 'I or my papa should have been told before now.'

'Yes, sorry, miss.' Lizzie bowed her head.

'Where in the village does Mrs Humphry live exactly? I know it is Meadow Lane, but what number?'

'It's the last cottage at the end of the lane, miss. Do you want me to go?' Fanny asked.

'No, thank you. I shall go and I would ask you two to get on with your duties or I will reconsider your employment here and find someone else who will work without disruption.' She turned away to the door then turned back. 'And neither of you are senior to the other. You are equal in your own domains. Let that be the end of it.'

Irritated by the interruption, Evie walked along the corridor to Papa's study and gently knocked before entering. 'Papa, Mrs Humphry hasn't arrived today, so I am going to her cottage to check that she is well.'

'Oh, right, yes.' Major Davenport took off his reading glasses and placed his pen back in its stand. 'I do hope she hasn't fallen ill.'

'I shall get to the bottom of it.'

'Do you want me to come with you?' He ran a hand over his wispy grey hair.

'No, I will go alone. I wouldn't want to embarrass Mrs Humphry by us both landing on her doorstep.'

'Indeed.'

She rounded the desk and kissed his forehead. He looked so much older since Mama died. The strong, gallant soldier had been replaced by an old man. His tall stature seemed reduced somewhat, his shoulders bowed. It was rare for her to hear his booming laugh now, which saddened her, for it was the sound of her childhood. Her papa's humour and good nature made him friends wherever he went, and Evie adored him. 'I shan't be long. Do you need anything from the village while I am there?'

'No, nothing, but you must buy something if it takes your eye.' He took a small leather purse out of the top drawer and gave it to her. 'There is enough in there to purchase something pretty. Perhaps you might want to ride into Bingley or Riddlesden?'

'I do not need something pretty, Papa.' She smiled. 'But I might go for a ride afterwards unless Mrs Humphry needs assistance.'

She changed into her riding habit of black wool with a matching hat and black veil and then went down to the kitchen to see if Mrs Humphry had arrived, but the quarrelling maids shook their heads at her enquiry and so she left them to it and exited via the scullery.

With January out of the way, February had heralded milder weather for its first week. The sun shone from a clear blue sky, melting the snow so there was a constant background noise of dripping and running water as the drains filled and the beck that ran down beside the house flowed high and fast from the thaw.

Crossing the cobbled yard, Evie sucked in a deep breath of crisp, fresh air. The stable block was hidden behind a stone wall, but the sound of hooves striking the yard's flagstone floor alerted her to the activity before she entered the archway. Mr Bronson and his son, Colin, were busy, their backs to her as she walked closer. Colin was polishing the carriage while Mr Bronson had her papa's horse, Jupiter, out of his stall and was checking his hooves.

'Good morning.' Evie smiled.

'Morning, miss.' Mr Bronson dipped his flat cap to her. 'You are wanting Star?'

'Yes, please. I am to ride down to the village and call upon Mrs Humphry; she has not turned up today.'

'Aye, the girls said when we went in for breakfast,' Colin said, going into the stables to fetch Star. He was a nice young man, just eighteen and always smiling and happy. He and his father lived above the stables.

'It's most unusual.' Evie scratched Star's long nose as Colin tied the horse to a ring in the wall and began assembling her saddle gear.

'I bet her son is about again,' Mr Bronson murmured.

'Her son?' Evie frowned. 'I didn't know she had a son, or any children. She told us at her interview that she had moved here alone, a widow.'

'Aye, she did. Her son doesn't live with her.' Mr Bronson began to brush Jupiter's flanks.

'He lives at Her Majesty's pleasure.' Colin snorted with scorn.

It took a moment for Evie to understand his meaning and then her eyes widened. 'Prison?'

Colin threw the saddlecloth over Star's back. 'Oh, aye. In and out, he is. Mrs Humphry tries to escape him, but he always finds her. She thought being up here in the village away from Keighley, her last position, would give her some peace, but perhaps he's found her again.'

'That's enough, Colin,' Mr Bronson warned. 'It's none of our business.'

Colin said no more and finished saddling Star. He took her over to the mounting step so Evie could easily mount.

Thoughtful, Evie tapped her heels to walk Star out of the stable yard and down the drive. The revelation that her cook had a son in prison was alarming. Should she have known? Would Mama have found out about her servants' past before hiring them? Had she made an error employing Mrs Humphry? Though at face value, the older woman was a decent cook and hard-working. Should a mother be punished for her son's sins? Evie thought not.

With the sun shining, the day was a beautiful, clear winter's morning. Birds fluttered between the branches in the trees, their tweets and chatter lovely to hear after the silence of the cold, snowy days.

Although wet from melting snow, the lane down to the village wasn't icy, and Evie could relax and enjoy the experience of being on horseback for the first time in weeks. She waved to Mr Lund, his ever-present pipe hanging out of his mouth. He was herding his sheep across a pasture, his sheepdog circling at his whistles.

At the bottom of the lane, Evie guided Star to the left and headed for the village, which nestled in a hollow at the bottom of the moor. The main road through the village was only half a mile long but it boasted one general shop, the public house, a small quaint church, a village hall and a little cottage school. For anything more, the villagers had to travel just over three miles west to Riddlesden or the same distance east to Bingley.

Evie preferred being in a small village rather than in a town or city. As much as she'd enjoyed her time with her aunts in Bradford, the city was dirty and noisy and crowded. The country suited her far better. She wanted to spend her days riding and walking and sitting in the garden rather than making calls and dodging traffic. At first, she'd thought she would deplore the quiet life of a village after the hustle and bustle of India, but after a few months of adjustment she'd realised the countryside had a lot to offer such as good riding treks over the moors, and seeing the same people every week became a comfort. She wasn't just a number amongst a horde as in the subcontinent. Instead, she was known, acknowledged as Miss Davenport from High Lylston House, and that didn't seem too bad.

In the village, she nodded to several people she now recognised after living here a year. Mr Butcher, who owned the public house, was outside cleaning his windows and Mrs McNally, who ran the grocer's shop and was also the woman who sorted the village's post, was sweeping her front step.

Evie turned into Meadow Lane opposite the church and carried on down its winding track to the end. A rather run-down-looking cottage sat in an unkempt garden, the front gate broken off its hinges. She hadn't expected Mrs Humphry to live in such a place, for the cook was fastidious about cleanliness in the kitchen and a stickler for rules and organisation. The cottage's appearance shocked her.

After dismounting and tying Star to a fence post, Evie gathered up the hem of her riding skirt and, dodging puddles, walked the uneven path to the cottage's front door and knocked.

It took several moments before the door opened and a man lolled against the jamb with a suspicious glare. He wore torn and filthy clothes, his hair cut very short, and sported a ragged beard. 'Who are you?'

Evie raised an eyebrow at the insolence. 'I know who I am, but who may I ask are you?'

He grinned, showing blackened and chipped teeth, and gazed her up and down. 'You're a bit of a looker, aren't you?'

She reddened. 'Is Mrs Humphry at home?'

'What's it to do with you?' he jeered, eyes narrowing, not in a threatening way but more with curiosity.

'Mrs Humphry works in my kitchen.'

'Ah, so you're the Miss Davenport.' He prized her up like she was some sort of brood mare.

'I am. And you are?'

'Hal Humphry, her son.' He bowed sarcastically.

'I was not aware Mrs Humphry had a son living with her.' She faltered; the son from prison...

'I arrived two days ago.'

Before Evie could say any more, Mrs Humphry hurried to the door and wrenched it open further.

'Oh, miss. I am that sorry.' Mrs Humphry wrung her hands together in torment. She appeared out of breath and out of sorts. Her appearance, usually always neat, was dishevelled and her grey-streaked hair escaped her white cap.

'We were worried, Mrs Humphry. It is not like you to be late.'

'My mam was unwell this morning.' Her son spoke for her. 'Weren't you, Mam?'

'Yes...' Mrs Humphry's small eyes couldn't meet Evie's questioning gaze.

'I am sorry to hear it.' Evie sensed something wasn't quite right.

'Mam will be back at work tomorrow. Won't you, Mam?'

'Yes, I will, certainly I will, Miss Davenport. It won't happen again.'

Evie nodded with understanding. 'You cannot help being ill, Mrs Humphry. Is there anything I can get for you? Do you need a doctor? I can ride into Bingley for one to call?'

'Goodness! No!' Mrs Humphry seemed to shrink at the idea. 'It's nothing, nothing at all. I'm feeling much better already. In fact, I can come back with you now and make a start on luncheon, yes, yes, I'll do that. You'll be all right, won't you, son?'

'I think not, Mam.' The son straightened, barring her way as though she was going to dash outside. 'You'd best rest for today.'

'Hal, I'm fine,' Mrs Humphry protested but she wasn't convincing, especially when she held her ribs.

'Let us leave it for today, shall we?' Evie interrupted. 'I am positive that Lizzie can cope for one day.'

'Course she can.' Hal gently pushed his mother back inside, but not before Evie saw her wince at his touch.

'I hope you are better soon, Mrs Humphry.' Evie stepped back with a smile and a nod. Something felt wrong in that house, and she was eager to be clear from it. For the last year, Mrs Humphry had been nothing but a model employee. Diligent, punctual and a fine cook. It was unusual for a house not to have a live-in cook but they simply didn't have the room. As it was, Fanny and Lizzie already shared a room in the attic.

At the gate, a hand grabbed her shoulder and she squeaked in alarm as Hal turned her about.

'Sorry, didn't mean to frighten you,' he said with a smirk. 'I just wanted a word before you go.'

'Oh?' A little afraid, Evie walked backwards towards Star, eager to put distance between them, for in the sunlight he looked worse than a beggar.

'Aye. You see, my mam keeps getting ill because she lives in this horrible place. She needs more money in her wages. You're not paying her enough.'

Insulted by the accusation, anger flared in Evie. 'If our house was larger, Mrs Humphry could live in as most cooks do, and her wage would be *less* because of that. Where your mother decides to live has nothing to do with me as long as she turns up for work every day.'

'Don't you care that my mam has to walk from here to your house on the hill every morning and return every evening in all weathers?' he sneered. 'What you pay her hardly makes it worth it. No wonder she is getting ill all the time.'

Evie saw straight through his lies. 'Your mother is never ill. She has turned up for work every single day since my papa hired her a year ago.'

'She's hidden her illness well.' His tone became sharper.

'So well that no one has ever been aware of it?'

'She needs more money.'

'She does, or you do?' Evie gave him a cutting glare. 'I find it very strange that Mrs Humphry's behaviour changes the minute her son arrives. Do not take me for a fool.'

He took a step closer, menacingly. 'Do not make an enemy of me, lovely lass. I could make your life a misery if I wanted.'

She raised her chin in defiance. 'Really? And one word from me to the right people and you'll be back in prison before the sun goes down.' He didn't scare her as much as he thought he did. He didn't know she'd been raised surrounded by the desperate men of Indian slums. Men who hated the English, men who threatened strife and trouble constantly. She and her mama had been assaulted in the street by rabble. Their carriage had been halted by thugs wanting their purses. India had not always been safe.

Hal suddenly grinned. 'You've got spirit. I like that.' He leaned forward. 'I like *you*...'

'Unfortunately, I cannot return the compliment.' In one swift move, she stuck her foot in the stirrup and mounted with ease. She gave him a haughty glare and then encouraged Star into a fast trot as his laughter followed her down the lane.

* * *

'And you didn't tell your papa?' Sophie gasped as they sat in the drawing room of Bellingham Hall the following evening. The room was full of guests for the dinner party the Bellinghams were hosting.

'No. I didn't mention it.' Evie held her glass of Madeira and with the other hand smoothed down the white lace ruffle of her pale rose-coloured evening dress. For the first time since her mama and grandmama's deaths, she was wearing a colour other than black. Surprisingly, Papa had insisted on it, telling her the time had come for them to lessen their mourning, to bury their grief and to start looking towards the future again. She'd picked her prettiest gown to please him for he seemed to be in one of his better moods and she wanted to make the most of it.

The idea of wearing pretty colours again consumed Evie. She'd been torn at first, feeling guilty for shunning her days of mourning, but Papa had said he wanted her to be happy. A year had passed, and the respect paid. Mama would want her to wear lovely clothes and get on with her life. Evie had watched with excitement as Fanny put away all the black and dark grey clothes, and unpacked

Evie's beautiful day dresses and evening gowns of subtle pastel colours, of delicate prints, stripes and patterns.

That evening for the Bellinghams' dinner party she'd selected a rose silk with white lace on the short sleeves and edging the top of the bodice. The dress had been made in India the summer before they left and only worn once at a party in Cairo before tragedy befell their family. A thin gold chain and locket sat at her throat, sent to her on her eighteenth birthday by her great-aunts. Papa had commissioned two tiny portraits of Mama and Grandmama to be done from other drawings and they were in the locket, so she always had them close.

Her tawny-coloured hair was newly washed and arranged softly about her head and held with mother-of-pearl combs. For the first time in a very long time, she felt attractive, as though she'd stepped out of the shadows and was allowed to laugh and dance again.

'Your papa needs to know,' Sophie said. 'Mrs Humphry's son as good as threatened you.'

'He was trying his luck, that was all. I've encountered worse in Bombay, believe me.'

'It sounds terrifying. You are so brave.'

Evie sipped her drink. 'Hal Humphry means nothing, an ex-prisoner who will no doubt be on his way soon enough.'

'An ex-prisoner?' Sophie bleated. 'Oh, Evie. You should never have spoken to him.'

'Let us change the subject. Is Mrs Myer attending tonight?' Evie gazed about at the people gathered. She and her papa had been invited to so many parties now that she knew a good number of the guests, which made her feel less of an outsider, but she had hoped Mrs Myer hadn't been amongst the invited tonight.

'Yes. The dreaded woman stopped Mama in the village yesterday and told her some story about it being the fifth anniversary of her husband's death next week and she was terribly upset.

Mama attempted to comfort her, but it was all very embarrassing. Mrs Myer wailed about how desperately lonely she was, and Mama's good breeding insisted she come here tonight and be with us all. Suddenly, Mrs Myer's tears dried instantly,' Sophie fumed.

'That woman is as sly as a fox in getting what she wants.' Evie watched the woman in question come into view, flirting with Mr Bellingham and Mr Lucas.

The butler spoke to Mrs Bellingham, who turned and announced dinner was about to start.

'Look, there is Mr Larry Overton, I begged Mama to put Mrs Myer between him and Mr Packwood. Two dreary old men. Your papa is free from her tonight, for he is down the other end of the table.' Sophie giggled.

'Thank you.' Evie squeezed her hand and went to find her own seat, which thankfully was placed between Mr Fairhurst, one of the family's cousins and whom Evie had met once before, and Mr Gresham, Mr Bellingham's solicitor, another man she had met on occasion.

'How are you, Miss Davenport?' Mr Fairhurst helped her to be seated.

'I am well, thank you. And yourself?' She found to her displeasure that Mrs Myer was nearly opposite her and had taken the seat between Mr Lucas and Mr Packwood. Evie caught Sophie's gaze; they knew Mrs Myer had somehow escaped sitting next to Mr Overton.

'In fine health. I have recently returned from London. The air is so much clearer in the north, despite all the factories and mills, especially if one stays in the country and out of the towns.' Fairhurst had a receding hairline, a thin face and a sharp nose on which perched steel-rimmed glasses that looked in danger of falling into his soup.

'Have you walked across the moors? On a sunny day you can see for miles.'

'Dear me, no. I fear I would become lost.' He smiled tightly. 'I would need a guide, I fear.'

'There are plenty of walking tracks.' Evie sipped at her mock turtle soup.

'Perhaps we could take a stroll together?' His pale eyes blinked behind his glasses.

Evie forced a smile, not wanting to go walking with him. 'In the summer, Sophie and I are determined to walk to the top of Ilkley Moor. You could come with us? We shall make a party of it, for I am sure we can persuade others to come.'

'Indeed, why not?' His tone seemed less enthusiastic.

Flicking a glance across the table, Evie noticed Mr Lucas watching her. She lowered her head and concentrated on her soup.

The next course had her chatting to Mr Gresham, a knowledge-able man, widely read. They talked of books, of Charles Darwin's *On the Origin of Species by Means of Natural Selection* throughout the fish course, until it was time for her to turn back to Mr Fairhurst once again as they ate their beef.

'You don't actually believe Mr Darwin's findings, do you?' Mr Fairhurst murmured quietly, as though afraid to speak of such a subject out loud.

'Indeed, I do. It makes perfect sense to me.'

'But we were created in God's image from Adam and Eve.'

'Darwin's findings are about the evolution of different species, how they evolve from the strongest line, which adapts to its environment. Religion does not play a part.'

Mrs Myer leaned forward, catching Evie's eye. 'My dear girl, I do think your conversation about this topic has come to its conclusion. I am certain Mrs Bellingham does not want her guests bombarded by such outlandish talk. Leave Mr Darwin and his book to the men of science.'

Evie stiffened at the rebuke and felt the blood drain from her face in humiliation. Thankfully, only those sitting close to them heard the whispered reprimand. Anger and shame at being told off like a child filled Evie until her hands shook. 'I will beg you to mind your own business, Mrs Myer. You are not my mother. Your advice is unwarranted and unwelcome.'

Mrs Myer's pretty face blanched. 'How dare you?' she hissed.

'Ladies,' Mr Lucas intervened. 'Let us enjoy our meal, shall we?' He gave Evie a small smile before turning to Mrs Myer and whispering something only she could hear, and which seemed to soothe the other woman.

Evie glanced down the table to see her papa was talking to his neighbour and hadn't witnessed the exchange, but Sophie had and gave her a quizzical lift of her eyebrows.

The rest of the meal passed in a tense silence for Evie; she barely spoke to Mr Fairhurst and made her excuses to leave the table as soon as possible, not even waiting for Mrs Bellingham to announce for the ladies to withdraw.

'What happened?' Sophie asked Evie the minute they were in the drawing room. 'I couldn't hear what was being said but I saw your reaction.'

Before Evie could tell her, Mrs Myer waltzed into the room, a hard look on her face. She headed straight for Evie. 'How dare you insult me in front of the whole table?'

'It wasn't the whole table, madam, and if there was any insulting it was you towards me. Who do you think you are, telling me how to conduct myself?'

'Someone had to. It is completely unladylike to discuss matters of science and breeding while as a guest at dinner. What were you trying to prove? That you have intellect? That you are equal with men of learning like Mr Gresham, a man who went to university?'

'I have had an education, madam, not that what I say or do is any of your business.' Evie's breath was constricted in her corset, such was her fury.

'I will speak to your father about this.'

'You will do no such thing, madam,' Evie retorted. 'My papa is of no concern to you, nor am I. Leave us alone.'

A devious smile twisted Mrs Myer's attractive face. 'Then you are a fool to think so. Your father and I have an under-standing.'

'You lie!' Evie said it louder than intended and drew the stares from the other women present.

Mrs Bellingham excused herself and hurried over. 'Is there a problem, ladies?'

'None at all, Lydia,' Mrs Myer answered sweetly. 'A little misun-derstanding, that is all. Evie and I are rather passionate, but we have sorted it now.' She linked her arm through Lydia's, and they returned to the other women by the fire.

'Goodness.' Sophie stared at Evie. 'How do you feel?'

'Utterly miserable,' Evie mumbled, feeling sick and in denial. 'It cannot be true. Papa would have told me if they had an under-standing.'

'You must speak with him.' Sophie took her arm and led her into the furthest part of the room where they sat on the window seat. 'Shall I fetch us a drink? Wine?'

'Yes, please.'

Sophie left her and Evie stared out at the black view of gardens hidden by a moonless night. It wasn't often she was wrong-footed by something, but Mrs Myer's words rang in her head like a doomsday bell. Would Papa have lied to her about their relation-ship? He mourned Mama deeply. Surely he could not simply forget Mama so quickly?

The door opened and the men entered, talking and laughing. Evie watched her papa, but he made no move to stand near Mrs

Myer. Instead, he moved to one side as Mr Bellingham raised his hands.

'Dear friends, we have a surprise for you all. My friend, Mr Guy Lucas, is overjoyed to find his son, Alexander, has returned safe and well from America and he has come to see us!' Mr Bellingham turned and waved in Guy Lucas and behind him his son, Alexander.

Shocked, Evie looked at Sophie, wanting to see her excitement, but Sophie stood frozen, staring at the tall man who'd entered the room. Evie turned to get her first glimpse of the mysterious Lucas heir.

Alexander Lucas stood tall, as tall as her father, and he was over six foot. His hair, cut short at the side but long on top, was raven black. But it was his handsome face that drew Evie's gaze. Alexander was one of those rare men who was clean-shaven; no whiskers or moustache covered his attractive face, which was strong and masculine. His nose was straight, his eyes not close together and his mouth, especially now as he smiled, held a hint of mischief in his curving lips.

In the space of a heartbeat, Evie's world turned, flipped and shuddered to a halt. She was absolutely captivated by him and when Sophie shook her arm, she jumped as though caught out at doing something wrong.

'Lord above! He's *here!*' Sophie continued to shake her arm. 'What am I to do?'

Blinking, taking a moment to settle her scattered thoughts, Evie took a deep breath. 'Calm down. He is simply a man, not some kind of god.' Yet, she could not deny her quickened pulse at the sight of him.

'How do I look?' Sophie panicked.

Evie gave her friend a once-over and tucked a stray curl behind her ear. 'You look perfectly fine. You are wearing your new dress.'

She admired the soft yellow Sophie wore. 'And your hair is in place.'

'I feel ill.' Sophie glanced towards the group surrounding Alexander. 'Shall I go over to him?'

'No. Wait. Let him come to you.' She stole another look at the man commanding all the attention. Just then he raised his head over the others and stared straight at her. Evie's heart plummeted to her satin slippers and bounced back up again to lodge painfully in her chest. She could not have dragged her eyes from his even under torture. Something was happening to her. She didn't understand it or identify it, but something shocking was accruing and she felt weighted down by it.

'Oh heavens. He is coming over. Do not leave my side!' Sophie gripped Evie's wrist tightly.

Like someone drugged, Evie watched the dashingly attractive man step towards them. Shockingly handsome, he also had an aura about him that made a person want to look at him, speak with him. His every movement burned in her brain as he took Sophie's hand and bent over it.

'Miss Bellingham. It has been a long time,' he said.

His deep tone sent a shiver along Evie's spine.

'I am pleased you have returned safe and well, Mr Lucas,' Sophie said in a rush, her voice high.

His smile, slow coming, revealed even white teeth and a dimple in one cheek. Evie's breath caught.

'You are looking well. You have changed somewhat since I last saw you.'

'In a positive way, I hope?' She blushed.

He gave her a slight grin. 'Be assured, you have.'

Reddening further, Sophie looked flustered. 'But where are my manners? You must let me introduce you to my very best friend, Miss Evie Davenport. Evie, this is Mr Alexander Lucas.'

He held out his hand. 'It is a pleasure to meet you, Miss Davenport.'

Stiffly, Evie lifted her hand as though dreading yet also wanting nothing more than to feel the touch of his fingers. He clasped her hand and the feel of his skin on hers affected her in such a way her legs felt weak. She forced herself to speak, to break the spell. 'I have heard much about you, sir.' To her ears her voice sounded small, surprising her. Nothing she ever did was weak or pathetic. What was happening to her?

'Really? I sincerely hope that I was made to sound interesting and not dull.' He raised a dark eyebrow, a wry smile playing about his lips.

Evie wanted to lean forward and touch those lips. The admission made her reel. She took a hasty step back. 'Yes, of course. Sophie has told me nothing that would make me not want to be your friend as you are to her.'

'It would be an honour to be your friend, Miss Davenport.'

'You must be exhausted by so much travelling?' She looked for a safe topic to discuss.

'Not at all. I can sleep well wherever I am which is helpful on ships, trains and in carriages.'

'A much-needed skill indeed,' Sophie simpered.

'And your trip was a success?' Evie asked him.

'I believe so, yes. Starting my cotton mill with limited resources hindered me. I felt journeying to America to make business contacts would benefit me greatly. Thankfully, I achieved that.'

'And so your mill will be fed cotton from the regions of America? Is their cotton a better quality than Indian?'

'I do believe so, yes.'

'And do the American mills not have a monopoly on their own grown cotton?'

'There is enough to supply all the mills both here and there.'

'And do you employ children, Mr Lucas?'

Alexander stiffened. 'Not under the age of twelve, no.'

'But I have heard it is still a common practice for mills in this region to employ young children.'

'Then they are breaking the law.'

'And what of education? Are your mill's children given time to attend school?'

'Heavens above, Evie, enough.' Sophie gave an embarrassed titter. 'Poor Mr Lucas has only just returned home. Must he have such a discussion on his first night?'

Evie paled. She had done it again, allowed her mouth to run away with her. She had been trying so hard not to focus on his charms that she had bombarded him with questions to cover her curious responses to his nearness. 'Forgive me, Mr Lucas, if I have been rude.'

'Not at all, Miss Davenport. You have shown a keen brain.'

Sophie took Evie's arm, her expression a little severe. 'Evie has such passions for diverse conversations, don't you, Evie?'

Hearing the undertone of something unpleasant in Sophie's tone, Evie had a moment of doubt about her friend's statement. Did she embarrass Sophie?

'May I fetch you both some refreshments?' he asked, his face turned towards Sophie but his sharp grey eyes on Evie, and the look spoke of things she didn't understand. Perhaps admiration but also something else, and her heart galloped in response.

'Wine, please. I was getting some when you arrived, and then it went clean out of my head, such was the surprise.' Sophie laughed lightly, nervously.

'Wine it is, then.'

When he had crossed the room, Evie sagged with relief.

Sophie's grip tightened on her wrist 'Is he not simply marvellous?'

'Yes...'

'I am so happy he is home. He has become even more hand-some than I remember. Oh, goodness, Evie. What if I could marry him? How delightful that would be. I would be the envy of every girl in the district. Are you all right?' Concern filled Sophie's expression. 'You look pale.'

'I am fine,' she lied.

'Is it that nasty Mrs Myer and her hateful words?'

Evie nodded, not able to say the truth. She didn't know the truth. 'I need some air, Sophie. I'll be back shortly.'

'But you cannot leave me with Alexander. I do not want to make a fool of myself,' Sophie whispered harshly, her eyes wide.

'You'll do splendidly,' Evie said as she fled the room. She crossed the hall and slipped out the front door, not caring for her cloak. The frigid night air stung at her bare arms, but she paid no heed. Her hot face compensated for the cold.

'Evie?' Papa called to her from the top of the steps. 'Evie.'

She turned and walked back to him, her thoughts jumbled. 'I am all right, Papa.'

'I saw you come out. What are you doing out here in the cold?'

'It was so warm in the drawing room.'

'Shall I take you home?'

'I do not want to ruin your evening.'

'Nonsense. I am happy to leave now. Come, let us say our farewells.'

Evie baulked. 'Could you do it for me, please? Can I wait for you in the carriage?'

Papa nodded, a worried look on his face that even in the muted light thrown by the lamps on the steps she could see. 'I shall tell them you have a headache.'

On the short carriage ride home, Evie sat with her hands folded in her lap.

'Is something amiss, my dear?' Papa asked.

'No, please do not worry. I am not feeling myself, that is all. I think I am just tired.' It was more than that but how could she speak of it to Papa when she hardly knew her thoughts herself?

'Then straight into bed with you.' He patted her hand in fatherly concern. 'That Alexander Lucas seems a nice chap. I shall look forward to getting to know him better.'

When she didn't answer, Papa turned his head to her. 'You are not yourself, my dear, are you?'

'Nothing a good night's sleep won't resolve.' She wanted to ask Papa about Mrs Myer but feared the answer. So she stayed quiet and wondered when she had become a coward. She'd run from being in the same room as Alexander Lucas, terrified by her reaction to him and she was now scared to ask her papa if Mrs Myer meant something to him.

As she undressed with help from a sleepy Fanny, Evie replayed the evening over in her mind. Each pocket of memory made her more alarmed at her reaction to it. Why had she reacted as she did to Mrs Myer? Why couldn't she be happy for her papa if that was what he wanted? She had to try harder to be less sentimental and emotional. Mama would want him to find happiness, and so did she, but not with that awful woman.

And as for Alexander Lucas... She would stay clear of him. She must. Her reactions to him were too extreme. Never had a man brought out such emotive responses in her as he had tonight. Sophie wanted him for a husband; the two families thought it an excellent union. All she had to do was keep a cool head and her distance from the man. Surely that was achievable?

Finally, alone in her bed with the room dark and her mind whirling, she listened to an owl hoot and knew sleep would be a long time coming.

3

The blaring of the hunting horn and the frantic barking of the dog pack echoed across the valley, spurring the horse riders on. Evie galloped on Star, jumping ditches and sailing over hedges, eating the ground up beneath them. The brilliant sunshine of a bright March morning heralded spring. Trees were in new bud, daffodils nodded their yellow heads and a gentle warmth in the air gave Evie such happiness. Winter was behind them, and the glorious days of spring and summer were about to begin.

She looked over to her right to see the hunting party spreading out over a wide field. She spotted Sophie on her white horse, but already she could tell Sophie was slowing down. The mad pursuit of hunting wasn't in Sophie's veins. She tagged along but her riding skills were lacking. Unlike Evie, who loved the excitement of hunting, of putting her wits against a wily beast. In India, she'd twice hunted rogue tigers, the ones that ventured into villages and killed people. The sight of terrified women and children, too scared to leave their huts for fear of being mauled to death, touched Evie and she had to help. They'd been unsuccessful in finding the culprits, but the thrill of the chase had been intoxicating.

Since meeting the Bellinghams, Evie had gone on shoots for game birds and a few fox hunts, but riding through sludgy fields and getting sprayed with mud wasn't everyone's idea of fun, especially not Sophie's. Besides, Sophie rode side-saddle as all the other women did, except Evie, who rode astride. They'd brought with them her hand-made saddle from Bombay where she'd ridden on the beaches or in the fields early each morning before the sun rose too high and the heat became unbearable. Riding astride was far more comfortable than side-saddle and safer. Her papa approved of her being unconventional, although her mama and grandmama didn't, but they had allowed it only because Evie rode so early before anyone 'decent' could see her. Papa said he'd rather his only child returned safe from her rides instead of falling off because she was going too fast riding side-saddle.

In English society, though, she'd caused a stir. No other women in this area that she knew rode astride. When she first rode astride in the village after buying Star, the gossip soon spread of her outlandish behaviour. Whispers abounded that she was unruly, a little strange, headstrong and, of course, Mrs Myer tutted in contempt at the very idea. Even a year later, she still caused heads to turn, but she refused to conform.

Evie wheeled Star over towards Sophie, and slowed the mare down to come alongside. 'You aren't going very fast,' she panted.

Sophie trotted along, patting her horse's neck. 'Sugar and I aren't inclined to dash across the countryside nearly breaking our necks.' She grinned. 'I know how much you enjoy galloping, though, so do not let me stop you. I shall meet you at the picnic spot. I'm going to go by the lane; it's quicker.'

'Righto.' Evie urged Star on, picking up speed as the land rolled down a valley. The dogs' barking grew louder as she caught up to the back of the party.

Suddenly, she saw a flash of rust in the thicket by the stream.

Thinking it was the fox, she veered off and went in pursuit. Star, just as fearless as Evie, clambered down the bank. Below, a narrow beck meandered through the trees. Another flash of something caught her eye.

Evie spurred Star across the stream, jumping it cleanly, but on the other side the boggy ground slowed Star. The horse jibbed when a fox darted out of the undergrowth, its eyes wild. For a second it looked straight at Evie, and she froze in the saddle. The fox's ears twitched, hearing the barking dogs coming closer, racing down the gully. It looked frightened, panting for breath. Instantly, she felt sorry for it, despite the damage they did to livestock numbers.

'Go!' Evie clapped her hands. 'Go!'

The fox sprinted away into the thicket and was gone from sight. She'd broken the code of fox hunting by letting the fox get away, but she was only interested in the chase, the joy of riding fast, not the actual killing.

'You know that isn't the aim of the contest.' A voice spoke from behind her.

Evie turned in the saddle, her skin prickling. Someone had witnessed what she'd done. Her stomach swooped even more when she saw who it was.

Alexander Lucas sat well on his horse, a sardonic smile on his face, one hand resting on his thigh.

'I never want them dead,' she confessed lamely.

'You just enjoy the pursuit?'

The pack of hounds came coursing through the shrubbery and across the beck, the riders not far behind, giving Evie time to compose herself. She'd been surprised and flustered at seeing Alexander this morning as they all gathered at the hall, but she'd stayed well away from him and spoken to other guests.

'Did you see him?' a woman rider asked, her face splattered in mud.

'He went that way.' Alexander pointed in the opposite direction to where the fox had fled.

'But the hounds are baying over that way.' The woman frowned in confusion.

'They've picked up another scent, perhaps?' Evie remarked.

'Dash it!' The woman rider jerked her horse across the beck and carried on, shouting at others to follow her.

Turning Star about, Evie edged the mare up the slope, aware that Alexander was watching her.

After meeting him at the dinner the month before when he'd surprised them all, she'd not encountered him again. Sophie had spoken of him visiting the hall only once since that fateful night when Evie had reacted so strongly to his presence. Apparently, he'd been closeted at his mill further down the valley and had barely been seen since his arrival. For that, Evie had been thankful. She needed time to understand her reaction to him.

After many sleepless nights, she decided to put him from her mind. That was easier said than done for Sophie spoke of nothing but Alexander, until Evie had snapped and said to stop. Without proof of his intentions, Sophie was making a fool of herself. They made a pact to not mention his name again until he declared himself.

At the top, she paused Star beside Alexander's horse. Despite all her rational thinking, the moment he gazed at her with his grey eyes, she was lost. Emotions and feelings unknown to her flooded through her body like a tidal flow.

She tightened her grip on the reins, fighting the inner turmoil.

'Shall we head to the picnic together?' he asked, nudging his horse forward.

She had no reason to refuse, yet her mind screamed at her to gallop away before she said or did something foolish.

They rode abreast for a few yards before the path narrowed, going down an incline. Alexander motioned for Evie to go in front, which annoyed her for she didn't want him watching her from behind. Instantly, she sat even straighter, fully aware that her skirts had ridden up over her ankles, showing her stockings above her boots. She itched to jerk them down, but pride prevented her from doing so in front of him.

At the bottom, he came alongside her. 'How are you enjoying being in Yorkshire, or England for that matter?'

'Perfectly well enough. I am glad winter is over, for I am not an admirer of snow and cold.' She felt ridiculously pleased that he knew a little about her.

'No, I imagine not. My father said you grew up in India. Major Davenport and I spoke only briefly at the Bellinghams' dinner party.'

'That is true. Papa had been stationed in India since before I was born. I've spent my whole life there.'

'This country must seem very different.'

'The sun doesn't shine as much as I am used to,' she confessed. 'But in many ways our life in Bombay is much the same as here. Making morning calls, having afternoon tea, dinners, visits to places of interest. However, here it is done mostly in the rain, not in sunshine.'

'How very English of us.' He gave a wry grin. 'I imagine India is a lot like the southern areas of America. Summer in Atlanta can be brutal.'

'Did you enjoy it very much being in America?'

'I did.' He sat relaxed in the saddle, again one hand on his thigh.

Evie glanced at that hand on his thigh and felt hot. Why was this happening to her? And why with him? She'd been surrounded by men all her life. She'd known nearly every soldier in Papa's camp and never once felt this heat, this shortness of breath and strangeness of mind with any of them. Oh, she'd had her fair share of secret assignations, the odd kiss in the bushes in the gardens at a ball or a party, but they had been a joke, a silly game, never something to make her stomach twist and her breath catch.

'My father told me you were... different.' Alexander glanced at her.

'Pardon?' She snapped back to the present.

He nodded to her saddle. 'Riding astride. No lady does that here, though I have seen it often in America, especially in the country.'

'I cannot gallop on a side-saddle. I have fallen off too many times, but never once while riding astride. It is a far more comfortable way to ride. Why shouldn't women be allowed to be safe and comfortable as men are?'

'Why indeed?' He grinned.

'I do as I please, Mr Lucas, not as old women in society dictate.'

'I am beginning to realise. You do not mind the whispers, then?'

She gave him a cool look. 'People enjoy gossiping.'

'And you enjoy giving them reason to?'

'I live my life, Mr Lucas, as I did in India. I will not change to suit some people.'

'How refreshing.'

'Really? Or annoying?'

He laughed. 'My father says you like to debate?' Alexander kept his grey eyes on her face.

'I do not debate as such. I have discussions. I have views. Does that shock you?' She became defensive. It seemed Mr Guy Lucas had said much about her to him.

'Not really. I like a lady who has a mind. Silly girls do not interest me.'

She took a deep breath, sensing a boundary, something she must not cross. But then when had she ever done as she ought? 'Do I interest you, then, Mr Lucas?'

They stopped on the crest of a hill, the picnic and riders spread out below.

Alexander watched them. 'I feel you just might interest me a great deal too much, Miss Davenport,' he murmured, and with a jerk he sent his horse trotting down the slope, leaving her behind.

Evie sat for a moment, perturbed. What had he meant by that remark?

She joined the others, giving Star's reins to a stable boy brought to the picnic to take care of the horses while the Bellinghams' guests ate, drank and chatted at several tables under an open-sided marquee.

'There you are.' Sophie waved her over to where she sat with a few other young ladies Evie had met before. 'Are you victorious over sly Mr Fox?'

'No, but the ride was good.' Evie sat down on the wooden chairs transported from the hall with all the other equipment needed to host a picnic.

'You ride ever so fast,' Susan Hearst said, nibbling at a lemon curd tart. 'I still cannot get used to seeing you riding like a man. If my mama saw you, I am certain she would faint.'

'My mama did not approve either, but she accepted it eventually.'

'You're very brave, Miss Davenport. I do not like horses, and they certainly do not like me. My pony threw me off when I was ten and I refuse to sit on a horse again.'

'Then I feel sorry for you, Miss Hearst, for riding is a joy you are missing out on.'

She tittered. 'Oh, I'm sure there are other joys I can experience.' She nudged Sophie. 'Look, there's Alexander Lucas. My, he's handsome. You must be thrilled to think one day you shall be his bride?'

Evie pasted a smile on her face but didn't turn to gawp at the man as the others were doing.

'Nothing is decided,' Sophie whispered, blushing. 'Do keep your voice down, Susan.'

Iris Owen refilled her teacup. 'Sophie, your mama was telling mine that now Mr Lucas has returned from America that you and he may finally be united in matrimony.'

Sophie glanced at Evie and back to Miss Owen. 'It is all talk at the moment. Poor Mr Lucas has only been back in the country a short time.'

'Then if you do not want him, I will have him.' Florence Davidson watched Alexander's every move as he passed their table with a nod to them all in general.

'I did not say that,' Sophie quickly rebuked, blinking rapidly. 'Joining our families would please many people.'

'Do not worry about pleasing everyone. Just concentrate on Mr Lucas pleasing you!' Florence laughed. They all had suspicions that Miss Davidson had sampled the delights of a man's touch, not that such a rumour was ever confirmed, but enough hints dropped by Florence suggested it.

Evie noticed her father leading and not riding his horse down the slope, another rider next to him. 'Papa is walking. He must have been thrown.' Concerned, Evie shot up from her chair and hurried over the grass to him. 'Papa?'

He held up a hand. 'I am quite well. Jupiter here threw a shoe and is limping. I felt it wiser to dismount.'

'Poor Jupiter.'

Mrs Myer sat upon her horse as regal as a queen. 'It was only the major's skill as a horseman that kept him in his seat, for the horse fair stumbled.'

Evie barely acknowledged the woman. It wasn't surprising she had to be close at hand. 'Papa, would you care for a drink?'

'Actually, no. I think I'll keep walking home. I want Bronson to look Jupiter over. I fear he might be lame.'

'Let me get Star and I'll come with you.'

'No need, Evie.' Mrs Myer stalled her. 'I shall accompany the major.'

Papa patted her shoulder. 'Go and enjoy yourself, daughter.'

'I think I should come home with you, Papa, and let Mrs Myer stay to have some refreshments. It would be disrespectful to the Bellinghams to take one of their guests away.'

'Really, I insist,' Mrs Myer said loudly. 'I am already seated. Do give our regards to the Bellinghams and our apologies.' Mrs Myer turned her horse about. 'Come, Major, let us see to Jupiter.'

Papa gave her a small, helpless shrug. 'Have a nice time,' he said as he turned away, giving Jupiter a rub on the nose as he did so.

Evie stood fuming at Mrs Myer's interference. The woman clearly had every intention of worming her way into Papa's affections. Evie wished she could talk to Papa about it all, but she couldn't face mentioning it in case it led to Papa acknowledging he might have feelings for the woman. Mrs Myer could not replace Mama. It made Evie angry to think of the woman wheedling her way into Papa's life, and pushing her out.

Slowly she walked back to the picnic, but the thought of sitting with the other young women was unappealing. They talked about silly things that bored Evie. They were as young as Sophie, one barely eighteen, and Evie felt not only the age difference between them of a few years, but also a maturity the other girls had not yet reached.

'The major is not hurt?' Mrs Bellingham asked, coming towards her.

'No. Jupiter lost a shoe and may be lame. Papa thought it best to continue on home.'

'Such a shame.' Mrs Bellingham waved towards the refreshment table. 'Would you care for something to eat, Evie dear?'

'No, thank you.'

'Oh look, Sophie and Alexander are having a little tête-à-tête. How charming. Heavens, they are a handsome couple, do you not think, Evie?'

Evie nodded. 'Absolutely.' Watching them caused conflicting emotions. She wanted Sophie to be happy, yet there was an awakening within Evie towards Alexander that she didn't understand or know how to control.

'It would make us all very happy to see them as husband and wife.' Mrs Bellingham leaned closer to Evie. 'As you are Sophie's best friend, I would like you to know that we, her papa and I, are fully supportive of such a match. However, I fear Sophie seems a little hesitant in making her feelings clear to Alexander, being so shy as she is. Do you think, Evie dear, that you might help her along in that regard?'

Evie blanched. 'How can I help?'

'Well, simply encourage Sophie to be a little more forward in her manner towards Alexander. Perhaps if you could persuade her to pay him more attention when they are in the same room? You are so... so... confident, and happy to talk to anyone, whereas Sophie is much shyer. Could you inspire her to be more like you and give her the confidence to attract Alexander's attention?'

'I cannot make Sophie feel uncomfortable doing something she would rather not.'

'My daughter has affection for Alexander, always has done, but he is a man, and they can be blind to a young lady's subtle interest. Out of respect for our families' friendship, Alexander may not feel easy in pursuing Sophie unless he is sure of her intentions. Sophie must be clear in what she wants. She will listen to you and try harder to capture Alexander's heart. Such a union would make us all so happy.'

'I can try...'

'We are hosting a summer ball in June, and I would very much like an announcement to be made that night. I would think it a great favour to me if you could use your guidance to steer Sophie towards Alexander more so he is in no doubt of her wishes. Perhaps suggest some outings and invite him along?'

'Mr Lucas is hardly a boy to be manipulated. He's a hard-working businessman.'

'Indeed, which is half the problem. But perhaps you could suggest a dinner party at your house, with your papa's permission of course. That way, I feel, the more Sophie and Alexander are in each other's company, the more Alexander will be drawn to her.'

'What does Mr Guy Lucas say about any of this?'

'Oh, he is all for our two families joining and I feel it is time Sophie was married.' She patted Evie's hand. 'Thank you for your help, dearest. To see Sophie happily married would be a great comfort to me.'

'I will do what I can,' Evie murmured. Of course she would help. After all, Sophie was her best friend and she'd found Alexander first... Her own response to the man, whatever that meant, must be put aside.

'I knew you would. You are such a sweet friend to my girl. And soon we must find you a beau, too!' Happy, Mrs Bellingham rejoined her guests.

Evie watched Alexander laugh at something Sophie had said and turned away. Sophie's happiness meant a great deal to her, whereas Alexander meant nothing: a man recently met and of no meaning to her.

She went to where the horses were being tended to by the stable boy and quickly mounted. She galloped away without looking back.

Not wanting to return home, not with Mrs Myer there, Evie skirted the hills around her home and headed further up on to the moor. The midday sun overhead made it a warm ride, but she slowed Star to a walk and at the top of the moor she dismounted so they could both rest.

Evie sat on the sparse grass and let Star nibble what she could. From such height, Evie could see uninterrupted for miles across the green valley. Despite the bareness of the moor, it had a beauty of its own, wild and unencumbered. This summer she would have to come up here more often. Last year, Papa had warned her of not travelling far and how easy it was to become lost on the moors. So she'd only come up once with Sophie, who had complained there was nothing to do up here and it wasn't worth the effort. The magnificent view had seemed lost on Sophie, but Evie liked the openness, the freedom to be alone.

'We shall come here every week, Star,' she said to the horse.

When she'd had enough of sitting, Evie mounted and rode down the track. She was hot and thirsty and in need of a bath. Moor farms dotted the landscape as she descended. Sheep farmers were busy lambing, and the bleats of lambs filled the air. She knew that soon the farmers would be taking the sheep up on to the moors to graze for the summer, but for now they were behind stone walls with their babies.

She steered Star to one side of the track as a man walked towards her. She didn't expect to know him and jumped in surprise when he stopped and stared up at her.

'Good day, Miss Davenport.'

For a second or two, she couldn't place him, and then she remembered his face. Mrs Humphry's son. 'Good day.'

'It's a nice day for a ride.' He came closer, his face dirty.

'Yes.' She could smell the bad odour emanating from him.

'Have you been anywhere nice?'

'Just riding the lanes,' she lied. She didn't know why she lied but he had the manner of someone untrustworthy. 'Just heading home now.'

'I should walk with you, shouldn't I? It's time I visited where me ole mother works.'

'Oh...' She didn't want to walk all the way home with him by her side.

'Unless you'd rather I didn't?'

'It's just that... Star likes to trot towards home... You'd be left behind.'

He shrugged and scratched behind his ear. He looked like he was sleeping rough but that couldn't be, for he was staying with Mrs Humphry. 'I'm in a right thirst. Do you have something to drink on you at all, miss?'

'No, I'm afraid I do not.'

'Why don't we stop by at the inn down the road?' He grinned. 'You could have a tot of something?'

'I must get back.'

Suddenly, he grabbed Star's reins, jerking the horse's head. Evie gasped in fright. 'What are you doing?'

'Listen, miss, I ain't one for messing about.' He grabbed her leg with one hand. 'Now I'm in need of a drink but I ain't got no money. Give me what you have.'

Scared of his menacing tone, she tried to pull away, but he held the reins tighter and squeezed her ankle with the other hand. 'Get off me!'

'Give me some money or you'll have to find yourself another cook.'

'Are you mad? How dare you threaten me?'

'Me mother won't be working for you for much longer unless you give me some money.'

Star skittered sideways, but Humphry held on.

'I mean it! I want money.'

'I don't carry money with me.'

'Liar, all toffs carry some coins. Now give it to me.'

'I shall tell my papa. He'll have you arrested.'

'You do that, lovely lass, and I'll make sure you suffer. I have friends everywhere, the kind of men you wouldn't like to meet. Now, give me some money or I'll do some mischief to me mother to prevent her working for you. Do you want that on your mind? That you were responsible for your cook getting hurt?'

Dumbfounded, she stared at him. 'You would hurt your own mother?'

He squeezed her ankle painfully. 'It wouldn't be the first time. The bitch has it coming to her and plenty more.'

Evie fumbled in the small pocket of her riding habit's bodice. She flung several pennies on to the ground at his feet. 'There, take it. It's all I have.'

As he bent to pick it up, she kicked Star and spurred her into a canter.

Appalled that Mrs Humphry's son was such a scoundrel, she rode all the way home in shock and disbelief. Clattering into the stable block, she nearly jumped from Star in her eagerness to get inside.

'Miss?' Colin came running out of the tack room.

'See to her!' Evie ran for the side entrance to the house that led straight into a boot room and then to a corridor behind the stairs. She prayed Papa was in his study and wouldn't see her. She hurried up to her bedroom just as Fanny came out of it carrying two empty jugs.

'Oh, miss, there you are. I've been trying to keep a bath warm for you. But I didn't—' Fanny stopped mid-sentence as Evie pushed past her and into the room. 'Miss?'

'Shut the door!' Evie barked, pulling off her riding gloves.

Fanny quickly shut the door and came back to her. 'What's happened?'

'I've just been assaulted by a man.'

'Oh, good Lord! Miss, what did he do to you?' Fanny asked frantically.

'He grabbed my leg, wanting money. I gave what I had to him and got away.' Evie's hands shook. She'd been accosted before, in Bombay: youths had surrounded her once at a market. She had thrown money and fled, but the incident had shaken her, just as this one had.

'I'll get the major.'

'No!'

'No?'

'I do not want Papa finding out.'

'But why? The man needs to be arrested.'

'We cannot do that. At least I... Heavens, I do not know what to do.'

Fanny kneeled before her and took her hands in her own. 'Now, calm down. We'll sort this out.'

'Fanny, the man was Hal Humphry, Mrs Humphry's son.'

Fanny rocked back on her heels. 'That no-good piece of filth. How dare he touch you!'

'He said if I told anyone, he'd hurt his mother.' Evie wondered if she'd heard correctly. Surely, no man would hurt his own mother?

'Aye, that'd be right, nasty toad that he is.'

'He abuses his mother?' Evie couldn't have been more shocked than if she'd seen him do it with her own eyes.

'He's a bad 'un. I've seen the bruises on Mrs Humphry since he's come to live with her. She tries to hide them but sometimes she has to roll her sleeves up when washing her hands and I see them. She says she bangs herself, but I know it's him. Once, last Christmas, she had a long day and was tired and we sat up and had a small sherry each; it's the only time she has a nip, is at Christmas. Anyway, she told me how he was always in and out of prison. He's nasty when drunk and nastier when he needs a drink and can't get one.'

Horrified, Evie paced the room. 'This cannot be allowed. Why does she let him stay with her when he is dangerous?'

'Because she's his mam, and he promises to change, and for a while he does, apparently. Then he gets in trouble and is sent down again. Mrs Humphry moves to a new village to escape the shame and then he gets out and finds her and it happens all over again.'

'It must stop!'

'It might now. Major Davenport will send for the police. Hal will be sent down again, giving Mrs Humphry some peace.'

'But Hal said he had friends that would come after me if I told anyone.'

Fanny frowned. 'He said that?'

'Yes. He threatened he'd hurt his mother, and did I want that on my conscience? Then he said his friends would hurt me.'

'I doubt he has friends game enough to come after you,' Fanny soothed.

'But do I want to take the chance?' Evie paced the bedroom. 'I do not know what to do.'

'I'll go and fetch Mrs Humphry.' Fanny was gone before Evie could utter a reply.

A few minutes later, Mrs Humphry entered the bedroom like a scared rabbit. She'd lost weight over the last few weeks and looked haggard and drawn. 'I am that sorry, Miss Davenport. I can't believe Hal would have the nerve to accost you on the road like that.' She looked downcast. 'What am I saying... Hal would definitely do something like that.'

'There is nothing for you to apologise for, Mrs Humphry, nothing at all.'

'My son is no good; that blame must land on me. Did he hurt you?'

'He scared me more than caused any harm.'

'You will have my notice by this evening, Miss Davenport.'

'Your notice?' Evie frowned. 'There is no need for that.'

'But I must move away, take Hal somewhere else far from you.' Mrs Humphry wrung her hands. 'He has you in his sights now for sure.'

Evie shuddered.

'Why should you give up a good job?' Fanny scowled. 'Send *him* packing.'

Mrs Humphry shook her head sadly. 'You know he'd never listen to me. Whatever Hal does or doesn't do, I pay the price.'

'He hurts you,' Evie stated.

Mrs Humphry nodded. 'Has done since he was a child. He stole from me, made me lie for him to the police... I try to start again somewhere new, but he finds me. He knows a lot of the wrong kind of people.'

'You must not return home. You will stay here, Mrs Humphry. Share the attic with Fanny and Lizzie. It is not safe for you to return to where Hal is living. He will hurt you again.'

'If I stay here, Hal will only turn up and cause mayhem.'

'Not if Papa threatens him with the police should he dare to show himself.' She didn't really want to involve Papa in the matter, but perhaps she would have to.

Mrs Humphry ran a hand over her face. 'When I was a cook for a family in Leeds, I lived in rented rooms just around the corner from the house. I had a visit from some of Hal's friends, pals he shared a cell with and who had been released. They stayed for three days and ate everything I had, stole anything worth stealing and then trashed my rooms before they left. They also took my house keys and went into my employer's home and stole everything they could carry. The family blamed me for bringing such disrepute into their home and I had to leave. If Hal doesn't cause the trouble himself, he has friends who will. That is my life.'

The desolation in the cook's voice and her defeated manner made Evie's chest ache for her. She couldn't allow it to continue. Mrs Humphry was a good cook, Papa praised her every meal, and the woman was kind, decent and ran the kitchen perfectly. Evie wouldn't stand by and see the woman hounded any more. 'Mrs Humphry, this pattern, this way you live, always frightened, always running away... It stops here, today.'

'Oh, Miss Davenport, you don't know what you're saying. We can't fight Hal. He's my son, and I don't like him, but I know him, know him better than anyone else and, believe me, we can't beat him.'

'We won't know unless we try, will we?' Now the shock had worn off, Evie was determined to overcome this miscreant who terrorised his own mother.

'I can't have you getting harmed, miss. I'll never forgive myself.'

'Your son is a bully, Mrs Humphry. We cannot allow bullies to win. Now, you are to live here. I know that most large houses are spacious enough to have their cooks live in, but although this house is quite suitable for Papa and me, it is not as big as some grand houses and as a result we suffer in space for servants to live in. I have always felt guilty that you had to walk here from the village in all weathers morning and night.'

'My cottage is barely a mile down the lane, miss. Not living in hasn't been a problem to me.'

Evie turned to Fanny. 'Can another bed be put in the attic? Is there room?'

'It'll be a tight squeeze, but Lizzie and me won't mind about that. There's a spare bed frame in the storage room above the stables. I'll have Colin bring it across and put it together.'

'Very good.' Evie nodded. 'Perhaps you might want to give up your cottage, Mrs Humphry? Living here will save you money.'

Mrs Humphry didn't look convinced. 'What if Hal comes here?'

'Then Papa will see him off with a threat of his own. He was a soldier once,' Evie reassured her, though Papa resembled nothing of the man he used to be. 'Now I shall have a bath and then speak with Papa over dinner. Do you need anything from your house for tonight?'

'No, I've a change of clothes in the cupboard in the scullery. I can sleep in my shift tonight.'

'I am certain we can find you spare soap and towels. Tomorrow, I shall ask Mr Bronson to take you in the carriage to the cottage and you can pack everything you need. Hal won't hurt you if Mr Bronson and Colin accompany you.'

'Thank you, Miss Davenport. It is a relief that I don't have to go home tonight.'

'This is your home now.' Evie smiled. 'You are safe here.'

Mrs Humphry's head lifted with renewed spirit. 'I'd best return to the kitchen and prepare the evening meal. Mrs Myer is... selective on what she eats.'

'Mrs Myer?' Evie paused in unpinning her hat.

'Your guest for this evening. The major spoke to me when he returned from the hunt this morning.'

Evie nodded. 'Whatever you provide will be delicious, Mrs Humphry.'

'Aye, if it's to her standard,' the cook mumbled, taking her leave.

Fanny tested the water in the bath. 'It's cold again.'

'Fanny, does Mrs Myer consult with Mrs Humphry on the menus when I am not about?'

'No, not really. She just comes into the kitchen every now and then and tells Mrs Humphry what she prefers when she is dining here, or she asks the major to hint to Mrs Humphry.'

'Does she indeed?' Evie fumed. That woman was taking too many liberties. She had to speak to Papa about her, and Hal Humphry. Neither subject was a favourable topic, and both were threatening in different ways.

4

Bathed and dressed in a lavender silk dress with silver lace, Evie headed downstairs early, hoping to speak with her papa before Mrs Myer arrived. She found him in the parlour, pouring himself a glass of whisky.

'Ah, my dear.' He glanced at her from under heavy eyelids. He looked like he'd not slept properly in weeks. 'You look lovely.'

'Thank you, Papa.' She kissed his cheek, wishing he'd perk up a little. His light mood only weeks ago when he'd suggested she stop wearing mourning had gone and been replaced with depressing moods.

'Would you care for a small sherry?' He was clean-shaven except for his moustache. Since Mama's death, his hair had turned nearly white, though he was only sixty years of age. The strong, tall man she knew him to be had crumbled slightly at the edges since Mama's death and it upset her to see it.

'Yes, please.' She spread her wide skirts as she sat on the sofa and accepted the drink. 'I am told Mrs Myer is our guest this evening?' She kept her tone light.

'Er... yes, I believe she is.' He looked guilty. 'I should have mentioned it to you, but you were out riding, and I didn't hear you come in. We should expect her any moment.'

'She is becoming a rather regular guest, wouldn't you agree?'

'Is she?' He added another log on to the small fire glowing in the grate. 'Soon we shall not bother with any fires. The weather is fining up nicely.'

'Do you have an understanding with Mrs Myer, Papa?'

His eyebrows rose. 'An understanding? That sounds very serious.'

'And is it? Serious?' Evie tried to remain calm.

'I am not sure.' He seemed confused.

'Papa, you are always decisive.'

'It is a big decision, my dear, one that I do not wish to take lightly.'

'Nor should you.' Her confidence in him that he wouldn't replace Mama waned with every second. 'Mama has not been gone long.'

'No... However, sometimes it seems years ago and other times only yesterday.' Papa sighed heavily as he sat in his chair and stared into the flames. 'I miss her so very much. Every day. There are times when I feel so hollow... Nothing makes me feel better. It is as though a part of me is missing.' He coughed, covering his emotion.

'I miss her, too.'

'Some days I do not know how to carry on without her.'

'She would want us to live and be happy, Papa.' Even if that meant Papa spending time with Mrs Myer, she supposed.

'I do try.'

'It must get easier.' She sounded hopeful, but was it true? She'd never been in love, so she had no right to speculate on the effects of losing the one person you loved above all others. The very thought of it seemed rather terrifying. To be so in love as to not be able to manage properly without them seemed so extreme and severe. She didn't think she wanted to ever feel that out of control.

'I would consider it a favour to me if you would rub along with Lavinia.'

'Lavinia?' For a moment Evie didn't know whom he spoke of as she was still thinking of Mama.

'Mrs Myer. She insists we be on first names now.'

'I do not think Mrs Myer and myself will ever be friends, Papa. I am sorry to say it, but we do not find common interests with one another. She feels it is her place to tell me what to do. Mrs Myer is not my parent.'

'I feared that would be your response. I had hope you would be company for each other. That she could be a confidante now your beloved mama has gone. You may need another woman in your life.'

'Mrs Myer will never replace Mama. Please do not feel you must entertain her for my sake. I need no one but you, Papa.'

'But...'

'I have Sophie and Mrs Bellingham, if needed. Please do not worry about me in that regard. I am happy with just the two of us.'

'Though one day you will marry, and I will be alone...' He sounded sad.

'Papa, I have no wish to marry.'

'Really?' His eyes widened in surprise.

'Absolutely. So, you have me by your side for a long while yet to keep you company.' She grinned to lighten the mood. Alexander flicked into her mind for a second only before she pushed him away. He was not the answer to her future. Sophie had claimed him.

The front doorbell rang, and Evie sighed. She'd not have time to talk to Papa about Hal Humphry. And now it would have to wait.

Fanny showed in Mrs Myer, who looked resplendent in purple velvet. 'Gosh, but I do have a favour to ask. I have brought two guests. Mr Guy and Alexander Lucas. Their carriage broke an axle right out the front of my house as I was climbing into the carriage. I insisted they come with me.' She moved aside so the two men could walk forward into the room.

Papa, who had stood on her arrival, suddenly beamed. 'Of course, of course, come in, gentlemen.'

Speechless, Evie stared at Alexander as he shook Papa's hand. The sudden intimacy of having him in their parlour flooded her cheeks with colour. This was the last thing she'd expected this evening. She took a calming breath. She would manage his unplanned visit, naturally she would. She could face anything.

'Forgive us, Major. We do not wish to impose at all,' Guy Lucas said. 'We can walk home or borrow your own carriage if possible?'

'Lord, man, I wouldn't hear of you walking home. The evening is settling in. You must stay and dine with us. I insist.'

'And then, afterwards, I shall take you home in my carriage,' Mrs Myer proclaimed like a saviour.

'Drinks?' Papa, no longer miserable, or at least hiding it well, jovially clapped his hands. 'This is a pleasant surprise, indeed.'

Mrs Myer smiled brightly. 'What an evening we shall have. I shall be spoiled for choice having three such handsome men at the table.'

'I think it is us who shall be spoiled, Mrs Myer, to have two beautiful women for company,' Alexander said with a tilt of his head towards Evie and a glint of mischief in his grey eyes.

Evie blinked as Alexander came to stand before her and offered his hand. Her breathing shortened. 'Good evening, Mr Lucas.'

'I do apologise for this intrusion, Miss Davenport.' He wore a dark grey suit and stubble was just beginning to shadow his jaw. 'Forgive me for not wearing the appropriate attire. We were returning from a meeting in Manchester when the axle snapped.'

Her fingers burned where he held them. She slipped her hand

away. 'Nonsense. We are all friends, and we must look out for each other.'

He ran his hand over his chin. 'We are not dressed for dinner.'

'You look suitable enough, Mr Lucas, do not worry. Sometimes, Papa and I do not always dress formally for dinner. It's been known for us to eat in our day clothes if we are late returning from an outing.' She smiled. 'We can be most unconventional at times.'

'That's rather refreshing to hear, Miss Davenport.' He had an intense stare that made her shiver as though he was trying to read her mind.

'Please excuse me.' Evie took a step. 'I shall inform Mrs Humphry of the change.'

'She will have cooked enough?' Alexander asked as she passed him. 'I would not like to cause her more work.'

'Mrs Humphry is a talented cook, Mr Lucas. She will cope, I am sure.' She hurried from the room and paused in the hallway to take another deep, steadying breath.

A whole evening with Alexander. Many thoughts swirled through her head. She was grateful she'd dressed with care tonight, which she'd done out of spite to Mrs Myer, daring the other woman to pick fault. Another thought pressed forward, that of her promise to Mrs Bellingham to put Sophie in Alexander's mind. Her best friend needed her help in gaining his attention. That would be her focus tonight.

Fanny came out of the dining room. 'I've just set two more places, miss. I expected the Lucases to join the meal?'

'Excellent, Fanny.' Evie sped to the kitchen. Mrs Humphry, rushing from oven to table and back again, barked orders at Lizzie, who was stirring a pot, and then at Colin, who was stoking the fire in the range.

'Mrs Humphry,' Evie interrupted. 'Can you manage? Is there enough food for extra guests?'

Her face hot, Mrs Humphry fanned herself with her apron. 'Aye, Miss Davenport. There is always enough for I cook extra to serve us lot for tomorrow's dinner. We always have what was eaten the night before if possible.'

'Then you all won't have something for dinner tomorrow?'

'Oh, don't you be worrying about that. I can knock up a meat and kidney pie in the morning for us. Go back to your guests, miss, and don't worry about a thing. It's all under control.'

'Thank you.' Evie hesitated, preferring to stay in the kitchen than return to the parlour where, no doubt, Mrs Myer was reigning like a queen. How was she to get through an evening with Alexander and Mrs Myer, especially when the other woman had the habit of irritating her?

Summoning her courage, she raised her chin and walked back into the parlour.

'Is everything under control?' Mrs Myer asked her. 'Should I speak with Mrs Humphry?'

Evie clenched her teeth. 'There is no need. Our cook and staff are very well trained and can manage under most circumstances. Mama taught me well on how to choose excellent staff.' Evie turned away from the woman and gave her attention to the men, who were discussing the distressing event of a few weeks ago regarding the paddle steamer *Nimrod*, which had wrecked off the Welsh coast, killing all forty-five people on board.

Guy Lucas sipped his whisky. 'Reports are that the captain failed to negotiate a fee with the Cork to Milford ferry to be towed when the engines failed and instead decided to sail into deeper waters along the Welsh coast, but a storm hit.'

'If he'd paid the fee, lives would have been saved,' Alexander said. 'I read in one of the newspapers how the crew and people on the rocks tried to secure ropes, but it was a failure.'

'Those poor people,' Evie added. 'And those on the shore having to watch the ship break up, people drowning.'

'I imagine those who live on the coast see shipwrecks rather too often,' Papa said sadly.

Guy nodded. 'And it comes so soon after the news of the SS *Hungarian* being wrecked on the coast of Nova Scotia. All lives lost.'

'Dear me, what a distressing topic to discuss at a dinner party,' Mrs Myer declared. 'Let us talk of something much more pleasant.'

'Indeed,' Papa agreed. 'How are you finding your return home, Alexander? Do you miss America?'

Alexander, standing by the fireplace, shrugged a little. 'There are some aspects of American life that I enjoyed very much. It is as though every nation in the world has gone to New York and so you can pass people in the street and each one might speak a different language. There are shops selling different food to what we know here and items I'd never eaten or seen before.'

'Heavens,' Mrs Myer exclaimed. 'I do not know if I would like to experience that. It is bad enough when visiting Manchester and seeing the foreigners there. Liverpool is also overrun with foreigners.'

'Liverpool is a port,' Evie said. 'Ports in every country have people there who are foreign; most are travelling through to other countries, but some stay. Bombay was a mixed bed of nationalities, and they can all bring something exotic to their new country. How dull it would be if we were all the same.'

'We are British,' Mrs Myer exclaimed. 'Therefore, we are superior, and we should not have to mix with these people in our own land.'

'It is a land that gives hope and nourishment to those who may have nothing,' Evie argued. 'How must other countries have felt when we invaded their lands?'

Mrs Myer glared at Evie. 'Am I at a university lecture or a friend's dinner party?'

Alexander coughed gently to dispel their animosity. 'In America, those foreign people have crossed the world to begin new lives. Some have terrible stories of persecution, poverty, war...' Alexander spoke soberly. 'I conversed with some men who had fled their homelands with only the clothes on their backs and a dream to find a new beginning in a new country. They had left everyone and everything they loved behind. I was there for business; they were there to survive.'

'You must have considered yourself rather alone in such a strange land with strange customs?' Mrs Myer sipped her sherry. 'Though I believe a handsome man such as yourself would never be wanting of company?' Her lips quirked in a sardonic smile.

'At times I felt alone, especially when travelling. The country is so vast. A person can ride a train all day and still be in the same state and then do the same thing again the following day to cross another state. The place is immense.'

'Did you make friends?' Evie asked, fascinated by his account of a faraway country.

He gave her his full attention. 'Some. Mainly business associates and their families. Everyone was friendly and accommodating.'

'Including slave owners who wished to impress you?'

'Some, yes.'

'It does not bother you the conditions their slaves live under?'

Alexander frowned. 'It is not for me to say.'

'But you must have an opinion?' She desperately wanted him to have the same views as herself, and the admission surprised her. She should not care what he thought or felt, but she did.

'I see a future without slave ownership. The North is leaning that way already. I fear the country will divide into two before long.'

'And you will work with the South?'

'Miss Davenport, my business needs cotton.'

'And you do not care where that comes from or under what circumstances it is grown?'

'Not every cotton grower in America is a bad person. Some growers are kind and thoughtful to their slaves. They treat them well.'

'But they still own them.'

Alexander wiped his eyes tiredly. 'This is not our argument.'

'It is everyone's argument, I would have thought.'

'Do you wear cotton?' he suddenly asked, his stare hard and cold. 'Have you cotton material within the house? Do you know if any of it comes from America? Or that if it comes from India or Egypt that the growers in those countries treat their workforce well?'

She swallowed and sighed. 'You are quite right; cotton enters our lives in many forms and unless we are very strict, we cannot be untouched by it. Forgive me. You must think of me as a hypocrite.' She was embarrassed he had won the argument, but admired the fact he was clever enough to spar intelligently.

'Let us agree to the fact we do not accept slave ownership,' he said stiffly.

Papa coughed politely. 'If war breaks out between the states, the rest of the world will be affected.'

Mrs Myer tossed her head. 'Can we please talk of something else?'

Fanny appeared at the door, indicating dinner was ready.

'Shall we go in?' Evie said, standing.

'Allow me?' Alexander offered her his arm, and she took it with a surprised look up at him.

Papa sat in his customary spot at the head of the table with Evie and Mrs Myer at either side of him. Guy sat on Mrs Myer's other side and Alexander sat next to Evie. Talk became more general as they ate the first course of asparagus soup. Mrs Myer regaled them of her jaunt into Bradford last week and how appalled she had been at the terrible state of the roads.

'I am certain now the weather is milder, the road gangs will be back filling in the ruts,' Papa soothed.

'That is not the point. One could lose their life merely for the sake of buying a new dress.' Mrs Myer pushed her bowl away as though the soup had offended her or was inedible. 'We should all write to the magistrate and declare our complaints.'

Evie noticed everyone else ate all their soup, which in her mind tasted delicious. She nodded to Fanny to clear away.

'Only one girl to clear?' Mrs Myer suddenly said to Evie. 'Two should be attending the table, surely?'

'Lizzie is needed in the kitchen,' Evie explained, not seeing the need for the woman to even mention it. Fanny had quickly taken away the bowls and spoons without an extra pair of hands to help.

'We make do with just old O'Neill, don't we, Father?' Alexander said. 'We have just the one man inside and one girl and a cook.'

'How astonishing!' Mrs Myer blinked in surprise.

'Ah, that's because we are two men who don't entertain!' Guy laughed.

'Then I pray you remedy that, Mr Lucas,' Mrs Myer simpered. 'Such fine gentlemen as yourselves should have a host of parties and dinners and then you two may not be single men any longer.'

Guy raised his eyebrows at Alexander. 'What do you think, son? Shall we begin entertaining?'

'I prefer to stay as we are,' Alexander replied, sipping his wine.

'I do not believe that for a moment, Mr Lucas.' Mrs Myer stared at Alexander. 'A young, handsome man like you should be married and raising a family by now. I hear Miss Sophie Bellingham is your perfect match?'

Evie winced and reached for her wine glass.

'The Bellinghams are old friends of ours,' Guy said as Fanny brought in the next course of mayonnaise salmon. 'We have often joked that Alexander and Sophie would be an advantageous union.'

'Oh?' Mrs Myer cocked her head to the side. 'Because he is handsome, and she is rich?'

Evie nearly choked on her wine.

Alexander softly tapped his fingers on the white tablecloth. 'I do not *need* to marry an heiress, Mrs Myer.'

'Lucky you, but I believe Miss Bellingham is in *need* to marry you. Her mother has made it quite clear to anyone who will listen that Sophie is simply waiting for your proposal. The poor girl has waited the entire time you were away.'

Having had enough of such rude talk about her friend, Evie sat forward. 'Papa, Mrs Humphry has made your favourite.' She forked up a piece of salmon.

'Indeed, she has. Not many men would own up to enjoying fish more than any other meat, but I do.' Papa scooped up some of the salmon. 'We ate a great deal of fish in Bombay, didn't we, dearest?'

'Caught fresh every day,' Evie agreed, pleased that Mrs Myer had lowered her head and remained silent. 'As a family, we'd walk down to the wharves and see the fishermen bring in their hauls. Mama enjoyed watching the gulls try to snatch the fish, didn't she, Papa?'

'It was a sight. Some men fished in boats no bigger than this table,' Papa declared, his eyes soft with memories. 'Astonishing how they didn't topple overboard.'

'I would wish to travel to India one day,' Alexander said.

Evie smiled, thrilled that he'd said that. 'India is wonderful, Mr Lucas. Such sights and sounds.'

'A honeymoon destination?' Mrs Myer giggled. 'The Bellinghams would think that a thrill for their daughter. Do you not think, Evie?'

'Sophie does want to travel,' Evie added, heeding to the plea from Mrs Bellingham to encourage Alexander to think more of Sophie.

'But the heat,' Mrs Myer grumbled. 'I should choose a softer climate, Mr Lucas.'

'I do not mind the heat.' Alexander gazed at Evie. 'Do you miss it very much?'

'I miss the life we had in India, yes. I was very happy there, but that was when Mama and Grandmama were alive.'

'Still, you would visit again if you had the chance?'

'I would, yes.' She nodded.

'My Evie was the belle of our society, weren't you, my dear?' Papa told them. 'She had all my soldiers braying for her attention.' He chuckled. 'Many would offer to ride with her at dawn, when it was the best time to ride before the heat rose. I always had to forestall them from joining her as I knew she swam in the ocean at dawn.'

'Oh my,' Mrs Myer exclaimed. 'How utterly wild.'

'You swam in the ocean at dawn?' Alexander asked, with interest and perhaps admiration in his eyes.

'I did. There is nothing like it.' She felt hot under his gaze. 'The water is cool, and I would swim from one side of the beach to the other. Sometimes, a pod of dolphins would swim with me. It is so exhilarating to see them.'

'How fascinating.' Alexander smiled.

'You would do this alone?' Mrs Myer spluttered in surprise.

'Of course. Dawn is the best time to be alone,' Evie replied.

'How did you not drown with the weight of your garments?'

Evie grinned. 'I wore only my shift.'

'Gracious. Thank the Lord we do not live near the ocean here or you'd embarrass your papa with such outlandishness.' Mrs Myer tried to make it a joke, but her tone was too hard to carry it off.

'My Evie could never embarrass me.' Papa refilled the wine glasses.

Somehow, Evie made it through the meal without wanting to throw her wine in Mrs Myer's face, but only just. The woman, for all her beauty, was an obsessive killjoy. For the rest of the courses, she dominated the conversation, eager to have the opinions of the men at the table, excluding Evie as much as possible.

Eventually, after dessert was cleared away, Evie stood. 'Papa, since there is only the five of us, should we all retire to the parlour together?' She had no wish to sit in the parlour alone with Mrs Myer.

'A sensible decision, my dear.' Papa paused in rising. 'Unless you want to smoke, Guy, Alexander?'

'No, I don't smoke,' Alexander said, rising and helping Evie with her chair.

Guy assisted Mrs Myer. 'I can forgo a cigar this one night, especially when I have such pretty company to enjoy.'

Mrs Myer fluttered her eyelashes and the small fan she held. 'We simply must do this more often, Mr Lucas.'

Evie heard Alexander groan under his breath.

On entering the parlour, Mrs Myer hesitated. 'I should thank Mrs Humphry.'

Evie swivelled her head to her. That was the role of the mistress of the house, not a guest's. 'No need, Mrs Myer. I am doing it now.'

'But as a more mature lady present, surely I should go instead?'

Annoyed and frustrated by the woman's constant interference, Evie took a step closer to her and lowered her voice. 'You may be more mature, madam, but this is my papa's house, his servants, and I am his daughter. You are simply a guest, nothing more.'

'I might be only a guest,' Mrs Myer hissed back, 'but my opinion on the quality of food served tonight should be noted. Your papa would want it to be so.'

'No, he does not, because it was all delectable.' Evie swept from the room and hurried down the corridor to the kitchen.

Mrs Humphry sat by the fire holding a cup of tea, but immediately rose on seeing Evie. 'Miss?'

'Sit down, please.' Evie smiled at her and to Fanny and Lizzie, who were washing the dinner service. They all looked worn out.

'Is there anything you want, miss?' Fanny asked.

'Nothing. I simply wanted to say that the meal was delicious, and you all did an outstanding job at such short notice. Thank you.'

Mrs Humphry relaxed. 'I'm pleased, miss.'

'And I will speak to Papa tomorrow about hiring a scullery maid to ease your cleaning duties.'

'Oh, now that would be something, wouldn't it, girls?' Mrs Humphry nodded tiredly.

'The bed is all set up for Mrs Humphry?' Evie asked Fanny.

'Aye, miss. Colin sorted it out and I made up the bed.'

'Wonderful.'

'Coffee, miss?'

'Yes, please. I hope our guests do not linger.'

Returning to the parlour, she was delighted to see Mrs Myer sitting on the sofa next to Guy and in discussion with him about something while Papa added more wood to the fire. Alexander stood by the window, studying a book that had been left on a side table. Evie joined him.

'Is this your book?' He held up a volume of *Jane Eyre* by Currer Bell.

'Yes, it is.'

'I have read this.'

She was surprised he'd done so. 'Did you enjoy it?'

'I thought it very good. Enlightening.'

'How so?'

'As a man it gives me an insight to how a woman's mind might be. What did you appreciate about it?'

'For me, it was Jane's independence, her strong character. She stood up for her principles. I admire that.'

'And what of Rochester? Was he right to lie to her about Bertha?'

'I think he struggled to be true to himself. The events had overtaken him, altered him. He loved the woman he could not have.'

He passed her the book and as she took it from him their fingers touched. A jolt went through Evie. She took a step back, alarmed at her reaction to him. It had to stop. A quick glance at him showed her that he wasn't immune to her either. His intense stare held her still, then he gave her a wry smile, which broke the spell.

Gathering her thoughts, she placed the book on the table.

'Evie, do come and sit down,' Mrs Myer called across the room. 'You cannot have Mr Lucas all to yourself. He is spoken for.'

Evie closed her eyes.

'What an odious woman. Her mouth, once open, strips her of all beauty she holds,' Alexander murmured.

She glanced at him, relieved she wasn't the only one who thought of her that way. 'Be grateful she has not set her sights on your father like she has done with mine.'

'I do not envy you that position.'

'I wish she would lose interest.'

'You may find she will cling to the idea of marrying your father like a barnacle on a ship's hull.'

'I could not bear it.'

'You may have to marry yourself to get away.' He grinned.

Evie shrugged. 'Hardly an endearing reason to marry someone.'

'I've seen worse.'

'And what of you? My friend Miss Bellingham is a most wonderful person. She thinks very highly of you.' There, she had brought Sophie into the conversation as she'd promised Mrs Bellingham she would do.

'And I her, but such decisions cannot be taken lightly.'

'Agreed. I have no wish to marry.'

'No?' He seemed shocked by her admission.

'No. My independence is not something I wish to relinquish. To be under a husband's control is not enticing enough for me to consider it.'

'And what of love? Your heart might want otherwise.'

'I have watched Papa suffer so much since Mama died. Their love was so deep... His sadness gives him days of black moods. He spends hours in his study not wanting to see anyone, barely eating. If that is love and heartbreak then I want nothing of it.' She stunned herself with the intensity of her words.

'But what of the joy of loving someone? Surely that outweighs the possible anguish later?'

'I am not an expert in such matters, Mr Lucas. However, I would be most content if you and Sophie Bellingham were happy together.' She had to believe that. Alexander, if he wanted a wife, could do no better than Sophie, she was sure of that. Any budding feelings she had for him needed to be squashed.

'Nothing has been decided yet.'

'Then what are you waiting for?' She smiled with false cheeriness and walked away as Fanny brought in the coffee.

5

Evie pulled the thread through the handkerchief and tied a knot. Rain thundered down outside, ending the short spell of fine weather, and drawing in the evening to darkness. Papa sat on the other side of the fire, reading a newspaper. He'd barely spoken two words today, giving Evie a lot to worry about. He was becoming more sullen each day.

'Perhaps we can go and visit the aunts, Papa,' she suggested, hoping to draw him into conversation. 'We've not seen them since January.'

'It is only March, my dear,' Papa said quietly.

'Yes, but they do like our visits. It gives them something to look forward to. Shall I write to them and say we will visit next Friday?'

'If you wish.' He turned the page without looking at her.

'We can watch a show at the theatre.'

'If you'd like to, dearest.'

'Was dinner satisfactory this evening? You hardly ate much.'

He frowned. 'Didn't I? I can't remember. I'm sure it was lovely.'

Evie frowned at his lack of enthusiasm. Each day was becoming as bad as the day before. Papa could not settle to anything for more than a few minutes, before he was staring out of the window in a daze. She tried to encourage him to accompany her on visits to the hall, or to go riding, but he declined more often than not.

She turned her head towards the door, hearing noise coming from the back of the house. The clock struck nine times. She waited for Fanny to bring the evening tray of cocoa and bread and butter into the parlour. Ten minutes later, Fanny still hadn't brought in the tray.

Evie rose and put aside her embroidery. 'I shall be back in a moment.'

Leaving the parlour, she headed for the kitchen. The sound of something smashing caused her to open the door with more force than she'd intended. She stared at the scene before her. Hal Humphry stood by the table, holding a bulging canvas bag while his mother, Fanny and Lizzie stood clutching each other in the corner of the room. Plates and cups were shattered on the floor.

'What is going on?' Evie glared at Hal. 'How dare you enter this house?'

'Shut your gob, lass.' He sneered, his eyes red and glassy. 'I'm only after some food.'

'You will leave this kitchen at once!' she replied in anger at his insulting behaviour.

'I'll leave when I'm ready...' He staggered from the table to the sideboard. 'Where's your money, Mam?'

'I don't have any, Hal,' Mrs Humphry told him.

'You get a wage, don't you?'

'Aye, but I've spent it on the rent of the cottage, so you have a roof over your head.'

'I don't want to stay in that stinking place.' He eyed them all broodingly. 'You need to come home and look after me. I'm your son.'

'You are not worth her care and attention,' Evie said. 'Now leave.'

'I want money.'

'You have food by the looks of it.' Evie indicated the bag he held, which had a leg of ham protruding out of the top of it. 'Your mother has no money to give you. So go.'

'You've got money, though.' His eyes narrowed. '*Get* me some money.'

'All I will *get* is my father, who will have you arrested.' She turned to go but a cup whizzed past her head to smash against the wall.

Lizzie squealed and Fanny dashed to stand in front of Evie.

Slowly, shaking with fright and rage, Evie turned back towards him and stood beside Fanny.

He took a step nearer, suddenly sober and fierce. 'You tell your father anything and I'll do you in, and before I do, I'll have my way with you, and if I can't I have friends who will. Understand?'

She nodded, terrified he'd be true to his words.

'Now, you're going to bring me two guineas tomorrow. There's an alley next to the White Horse Inn in Bingley. I'll meet you there at noon.' He glanced at his frightened mother. 'Come with me, Mam. You'll be security that the young miss does as I say.'

'No!' Evie held up her hands. 'Your mother stays here.'

Hal lunged forward and took his mother's wrist and pulled her to his side. 'She comes with me until I get me money!' He glared at Evie before pulling his mother out of the kitchen behind him.

'Oh God!' Lizzie slid to the floor, crying.

Fanny gazed at Evie. 'Are you all right, miss?'

'Will he harm her?' she mumbled, not believing what had just happened.

'I hope not. Will you meet him tomorrow?'

'I have no choice. Mrs Humphry's safety depends on it.'

'I'll come with you. You can't meet him alone.' Fanny gave her a kind smile. 'Go back to the major, miss. I'll clean this lot up and bring in a cup of tea.'

'No, not tea. Cocoa...' She ran a shaking hand over her face. 'I do not want Papa to sense anything amiss.'

'You won't tell him, then?' Fanny's eyes widened in alarm.

'No. I do not want to burden him with this. He is not himself.'

'But, miss, you can't handle this alone.'

'I have to. Papa is not up to it. I thought he might be, that he could go to the police, but the ordeal would be too much for him in his present state of mind. I shall sort it out.' She glanced around at the destruction of the kitchen. 'Hal will get his money and then he can leave us alone. Papa need not know of it, for he'll worry too much that something might happen to me, and I don't think he could take it.'

Evie went back into the parlour and sat down. Her hands shook too much to continue sewing. Hal's ugly face sneering at her replayed in her mind. She longed to confide to Papa but knew it was impossible.

'You were gone a long time, dearest. Is everything well?'

'Yes, Papa. A mishap in the kitchen. A tray was dropped and some of the tea service was broken.' She didn't look at him and instead picked up her embroidery.

'Goodness. How clumsy of them.'

'Our cocoa will be along shortly.'

'Good. It does help me to sleep, especially with a dash of rum in it. A night not broken with dreams about your mama is both a blessing and curse, for in dreams we are united again, only it is painful to wake up and realise she is not by my side.'

Evie hurried over to him and threw her arms around his shoulders. 'Papa, she would not want you to be so unhappy.'

'I know, poppet, but I cannot seem to shake this despondency.'

He sighed heavily and patted her back. 'I shall recover, I'm sure. It will simply take some time. At least I have you, dear girl. You keep me going.'

'I am always here, Papa.' She had to stay strong for him, until he was back to his old self.

'I could not live if anything happened to you, too, my daughter.'

'Nothing will happen to me.' She believed this, for once she had paid off Hal, their lives could return to normal. She kissed his cheek and returned to her chair as an idea struck her. 'Do you think that maybe we should return to India? We were happy there and we have so many friends who we could entertain. You could go back to your old club.'

'India... I have thought about it.'

Suddenly, Evie desperately wanted to return to India and the life she'd once had.

Papa sat up straighter in his chair. 'I feel as though in India I might not be so sad. I truly believe I will feel closer to your mama in Bombay. It was where we lived so happily.'

'We have so many memories of Mama there, whereas here, there is nothing,' Evie added.

'Yes, and I think that is the problem.' Papa nodded. 'This house isn't our home, not like the one we had in Bombay. I could make enquiries to buy it back.'

'It would be as though we have something of Mama with us again.'

'Exactly.' For the first time in over a year, Papa smiled properly instead of pretending. 'I shall write letters first thing in the morning.'

Evie sagged back against the sofa in relief at the change in her darling papa. If returning to India would make him happy then that was all she wanted, and if her mind strayed to Alexander, she quickly dismissed it. After all, he would marry Sophie and she wouldn't have to witness it. As much as she would miss Sophie, Papa's happiness was paramount. She could take up her mother's good works again and find her own happiness...

'Thank you, Mathers.' Alexander took the reins of his horse, Hero, from the foreman and mounted. Around him the mill yard rang with noise of industry. Wagon carts trundled in and out, bringing in bales of raw cotton and taking away the finished product of cotton cloth to be loaded on to boats on the canal and taken to Manchester or Leeds depending on where Alexander had made a sale.

He sat for a moment, watching the workers: the women and men who came each day except Sunday to work twelve-hour shifts in his mill. These people lived in cottage rows on the other side of the Lylston stream. When he'd bought Greenlee Mill, five years ago with the money he'd inherited from his grandfather, his father had said he was mad. Greenlee had been a crumbling building, outdated, using an old waterwheel and even older machines. Alexander had spent a small fortune to change the mill from a woollen weaving one to a cotton cloth mill. He saw the future in cotton, whereas his father and all their acquaintances milled wool. But Alexander wanted to be different and not simply work under his father's name and reputation.

His improvements took two years. He updated the mill to be run on steam engines, he bought new machines for cotton spinning, he added more outbuildings, bigger work areas, repaired the workers' cottages and employed and trained local people to change from working with wool to cotton.

Then he had gone to America to learn more about cotton and to make business contacts. Now he was home, and the future seemed bright. The mill was making good money; his debts were being paid. He had orders and supplies and was building his own reputation.

Now all he needed was a family of his own, or at least that was what everyone told him. He thought of Sophie Bellingham, a lovely young woman who'd make a dutiful wife. Her father was wealthy and influential and would be a great asset to him and his own business. There were many positives to marrying Sophie. Yet, instantly, his mind filled with Evie. He shouldn't think of her. It felt disloyal to Sophie to do so, but he couldn't help it. Desire flared in him every time he saw her. He recognised the same happened with her, and this intrigued him even more. Instinctively, he felt Evie was a passionate person, and also loyal to Sophie. Two women. One he should marry, the other he couldn't stop thinking about.

Annoyed with himself at such a quandary, he clicked his tongue, urging Hero out of the yard, over the bridge and down the lane. He had a meeting with his bank manager in Bradford, but had plenty of time to ride the six miles to the bustling city.

The countryside surrounding the mill included steep hills covered in woodland and winding streams. Nearing the cottage rows, he nodded to some older women, no longer of working age but who now kept house for their families and watched the younger children who weren't in school. The women inclined their heads, showing him respect, for he wasn't a bad master. He paid well and expected them to do their jobs in return. He could be tough when the need arose, though. He didn't put up with fools, or those who shirked their responsibilities. At times, he might dismiss someone who couldn't meet the standards he set, but in general he felt he took care of his workers. His mind ran to Evie Davenport again, hoping she would be impressed with how he cared for his workforce.

Leaving the steep valley, he rode across open fields, chuckling as lambs skipped and frolicked beside their mothers in the March sunshine. He raised his hand to a farmer mending a stone wall and relaxed in the saddle.

The town of Bingley, nestled between the River Aire and the Leeds and Liverpool Canal, was a hive of activity as he rode through the main street. Market day drew the crowds, and the stench of overripe vegetables and manure filled his nose. To save from weaving his way through the throng of people, he took a side street and rode away from the main thoroughfare.

A man sang a lusty song outside of a public house, spilling his drink as he swayed. Alexander steered Hero to the other side of the street so he wouldn't be spooked and noticed a man and woman in a side alley between the inn and a shop. The pair were close, and Alexander turned away, not wanting to witness an intimate moment, but then just as he did, he saw the woman's face more clearly beneath her bonnet. Evie Davenport.

He jerked the reins and twisted in the saddle to see better. Hero threw up his head in alarm, his steps faltering. 'Whoa, boy,' Alexander said without thought, rubbing his neck. He watched as Miss Davenport gathered up her skirts and walked further down the alley, the man calling after her.

Thinking quickly, Alexander heeled Hero forward, past the public house, and turned the corner on to a street parallel to the alley. At the end of it he turned on to another street where the lane came out. Miss Davenport, her head swivelling one way and then another, dashed out of the alley and into a waiting carriage. Of the man there was no sign.

Something prevented Alexander from stopping the carriage. What Miss Davenport did was none of his business. Yet for her to meet a man in an alley brought a bitter taste to his mouth. He had thought better of her. No decent young woman would meet a man alone in some backstreet. There was no possible explanation for it unless she was hiding something.

The idea sickened him. She was not the person he'd thought she was. Had he spectacularly got her wrong? He thought himself a good judge of character. Yet, how could this be explained? How could such a meeting be innocent? He had liked her uniqueness, her independence of opinion and strong will, but if she thought she could flout society's rules to the extent of a clandestine meeting with a man, then she was mistaken.

Feeling more saddened by the revelation than he cared to admit, he spurred Hero on. However, the image of her talking to the man in the alley stayed with him on the ride to Bradford and well after.

* * *

Sipping tea in the drawing room of Bellingham Hall, Evie nodded at something Mrs Bellingham had said, though she had not really heard.

'Do you not think, Evie?' Sophie said.

'Pardon?'

'Goodness, your head is in the clouds this afternoon.' Sophie laughed, holding up a swatch of different coloured material. 'I said I believe I shall choose the pale pink for my ball gown. It suits me well, do you not agree?'

'I do.'

'And what colour shall you wear, my dear?' Mrs Bellingham asked.

Evie hadn't given the ball a thought. 'My blue and white stripe, I think.'

'No, not the stripe, Evie.' Sophie's tone was full of dismay. 'That dress is more suited to a dinner party and you wore it only last week at Florence Davidson's birthday.'

'Oh...' Evie racked her brains for what she could wear, but her mind wasn't on dresses but the disgusting transaction with Hal Humphry a few hours ago. Meeting him in a dank alley had been one of the scariest things she'd done. Parting with the money, all that she had saved from her allowance, went against all she stood for, but on seeing Mrs Humphry's frightened face behind the inn, Evie knew she had taken the correct action.

She'd faced the revolting Hal and demanded the release of his mother. Thankfully, the minute she'd shown him the money he had let his mother go and the older woman had run to the carriage where Fanny waited inside.

Hal's threats still made her fearful and terribly angry. She knew his promises to stay away would be empty ones, but what choice did she have?

'You would look superb in apple green, wouldn't she, Mama?' Sophie gushed, studying the swatches.

'Indeed, she would.' Mrs Bellingham looked up as the butler entered the room and announced she had a visitor. 'Excuse me, girls, I shall leave you to your dress choices and speak to whoever has called unannounced.'

'What is the matter with you today?' Sophie asked as soon as her mother had left the room.

'Forgive me. I am out of sorts.'

'Can I be of assistance in making you feel better?'

Evie stared down at the cooling tea in her lap, her mind in a whirl, but telling Sophie the truth could not be done. 'I fear that Papa is not recovering from Mama's death as I hoped.'

'No. It is terribly difficult to see him sometimes when his face is etched in misery, poor man.'

'Last night I suggested that we return to India to see if that will make him happier.'

'India!' Sophie nearly spilled her tea. 'How utterly devasting for you to do that! I cannot lose you to India.'

'If it makes Papa better then there is no choice.'

'But do you want to go?'

'I want Papa to be happy.'

'That didn't answer my question.' Sophie frowned at her.

'Yes. Perhaps India is where I should be.' As much as she loved the country of her birth, she knew she was running away from her feelings towards Alexander. To stay would be to witness him and Sophie draw closer together and she didn't think she could do that.

'Can I be selfish and say I do not want you to go? You are my closest friend. I wanted us to attend each other's weddings, share the trials of having babies, watch our children grow and become old together when we can sit and gossip about everyone and no one minds at all.'

Evie smiled. 'How lovely that would be.'

'Then do not go to India, I beg you.'

'We can visit and write.'

'It is not the same and you know it.' Sophie pouted.

'I have to think of Papa.' Evie reached for Sophie's hand. 'If we do leave, know that I will always love you even from the other side of the world.'

'Promise?'

'Always. You are my one true friend.' Evie rose. 'I must go. Please do not mention anything to anyone about this just yet. I shall let you know when it has all been decided.'

Sophie walked her out. 'I will not tell a soul, despite feeling so wretched at the thought.'

Evie walked down the steps to where a groom held Star's reins. He gave Evie a leg up to mount. 'Goodbye.'

Evie waved and trotted down the gravelled drive. Once past the gates, she urged Star into a canter, wanting to feel the wind in her face and the freedom of being alone with her thoughts.

She rode through the valley towards Lylston Village. The faster she rode, the more her thoughts swirled in her head. Hal Humphry, Alexander, Sophie, Papa. They all became jumbled and consuming. She felt out of control with the events, something she wasn't used to.

Suddenly Star shied and stepped backwards. Evie lunged in the saddle, nearly losing her seat. 'Steady, girl.'

Whatever had frightened Star, she remained unsettled, not wanting to walk forward and instead twirling in a circle.

'There now, girl. What's the matter?'

Then she saw it: an adder. Slithering its way through the undergrowth, the adder raised its head, before deciding to escape into nearby bushes.

Star tossed her head, clearly unnerved.

'It's fine, girl. The awful thing has gone.' Evie dismounted and went to stroke Star's nose. 'You are fine now.'

The sound of hooves coming down the lane heralded a horse and rider. Evie stepped to one side, then inwardly groaned on seeing Alexander. Her pulse raced as he neared.

Alexander slowed his horse and dismounted. 'Miss Davenport? Have you been thrown?'

'No. Star saw an adder and became skittish.'

'You are both unhurt?'

'Completely.' She stared up at him, feeling the familiar tightness in her chest whenever he was close.

'It is the time for adders to be out now the weather is becoming warmer.'

'I am used to snakes in India, but not here, and Star is even more upset.' She rubbed Star's neck. 'Are you on your way home?'

'No, to the mill. I have a few hours' work in my office to deal with before I can go home.'

'I have just left Bellingham Hall. I had afternoon tea with Sophie and her mama.'

'They are well?'

'Yes. Sophie was choosing her gown for the ball. She is most excited.'

He watched her for a moment, his gaze unreadable. 'I was riding through Bingley earlier.' He paused. 'I believe I saw you.'

'Me?'

'Yes. Speaking with a man in an alley.'

A dead weight of fear settled in Evie's stomach. 'You must be mistaken, Mr Lucas. I was not in Bingley today,' she lied, feeling the heat suffuse her cheeks.

He tilted his head, clearly not believing her. 'It was *not* you?'

'Not at all. I have only been to see Sophie. We talked of dresses and the upcoming ball.' She knew she was speaking too quickly and took a deep breath.

'Then I am mistaken?' His eyebrows rose.

'Indeed, you are.'

'You were not talking to a man in an alley next to the White Horse Inn?'

'I have never been near such a place.' She turned from him, ready to mount and flee from him and his questions.

'Miss Davenport, I may not have been the only one to see you. Did you consider that when you concocted your secret meeting? A reputation cannot be easily returned once it has been lost.'

Anger flooded her. She squared up to him. 'How dare you insult me?'

'How dare *you* insult *me* with your lies? I know what I saw.'

'You were mistaken!'

'You are lying. Why is that? What are you hiding?'

'Whatever I do is none of your business.'

'But it is your father's. Perhaps I should call on him?'

'You will do no such thing. Papa is not himself. I refuse to have him bothered by anything if I can help it and you are poking your nose in where it isn't wanted!' She panted for breath, afraid he would tell Papa.

They stared at each other, each not willing to give an inch.

'Good God, you are magnificent when you are angry,' he suddenly stated, desire widening his eyes.

Evie blinked, shocked at what he'd just uttered, but she knew that look and mirrored it. In an instant she felt white-hot desire rage through her body like it was on fire.

Without thought, they grabbed each other and came together in a clash of mouths and bodies, their lips melding, their grips tight on each other. Evie had never been kissed like this before. Heat and passion and yearning pounded through her body, wanting more, demanding fulfilment.

Star snorted, breaking the moment.

Breathing deeply, Evie stepped back, staring at him. Every fibre of her being wanted to keep kissing him and never stop, not even for air. But he was Alexander Lucas, the man her best friend wanted to marry.

She spun on her heel and in one swift movement mounted Star and galloped away.

6

'*Non, non, non, mademoiselles!*' Monsieur Perritt clapped his hands in annoyance. 'Miss Bellingham, you must go the other way!'

Sophie laughed, red in the face from embarrassment and exertion. 'Forgive me, Monsieur!'

The dance teacher mumbled under his breath and clapped again at the two men he had brought with him to play the violin and piano.

Evie bit her lip to stop from chuckling.

'Really, Sophie, you must concentrate!' Helen, Sophie's sister-in-law, admonished.

'Sorry!' Sophie straightened and took Evie's hands again. 'We are ready.'

'I am going to be the girl next,' Evie huffed, as they stepped and twirled to the music again. 'I detest being the man all the time.'

'You are taller than me.' Sophie grinned. 'You have to be the man.'

They twirled the ballroom again, circling the French dance teacher as he watched them with a frown. Helen and Cynthia Fellows, a Bellingham cousin on Sophie's father's side, were the other couple learning the new dances coming out of Austria and Germany. For an hour they had learned the steps to the polka and the waltz.

'I do like this dance, though,' Evie whispered, as she easily stepped in time to the music.

'I like the polka better than the waltz.' Sophie frowned, tripping on Evie's feet yet again. 'I shall never get the hang of this!'

The music stopped due to clapping. They turned to see Jasper Bellingham, Guy Lucas and Alexander come into the room. The presence of Alexander thrilled Evie, but she strove to hide it. She had to be careful not to let her feelings show.

'Fabulous!' Mr Bellingham announced. 'But come, the ladies are short of men!' He grinned and took Helen into his arms. Guy plucked Evie away from Sophie, leaving Alexander and Sophie to partner. Poor Cynthia, a painfully shy creature, happily went and stood by the wall.

The music swelled again and around they went. Evie smiled at Mr Lucas, pleased to not be the man for once. She glided lightly in his arms around the room, feeling the music with every step and beat, her eyes half closed.

'You are very good, Miss Davenport.'

'Thank you, Mr Lucas. I learned to dance at an early age in Bombay. I do enjoy it very much.' She purposely kept her gaze above Guy's shoulder and didn't focus on Alexander dancing with Sophie.

'You are as light as a feather,' he admired. He was as handsome as his son in a more mature, aged way. 'It is a refreshing chance to have a partner who doesn't tread on my feet.'

'There is time yet.' She laughed.

'In my experience, I don't know which is worse... To have to forcibly hurl a partner along when she doesn't know the steps, which is like dragging a mutinous dog on a rope, all while keeping our dignity, or to stumble about like someone in their cups!'

Evie laughed louder.

Monsieur scowled.

Guy Lucas snickered. 'What a displeasing-looking man he is.'

'Try being his pupil!'

'Let us show him what we've got, Miss Davenport.' Guy swirled her faster and Evie laughed joyously as her skirts flew out like a sail and they twirled the length of the ballroom.

The Frenchman clapped his hands to stop the music and Evie and Guy bent over themselves laughing.

'This is impossible!' Monsieur Perritt announced.

'Perhaps the ladies could do with a rest, Monsieur?' Mr Bellingham ordered.

'Our time is up, Papa,' Sophie told him. 'Thank you, Monsieur Perritt. We shall see you next week.'

'Your mama is serving afternoon tea out on the terrace for us all.' Mr Bellingham led the way out of the French doors and along the terrace to the wide space allocated to round wrought-iron tables and chairs. Maids and footmen carried silver platters out with food and refreshments.

Mrs Bellingham straightened plump cushions an inch or two. 'Ah, here you all are.'

Such an informal setting allowed Evie to sit where she liked and she went to a chair beside Miss Fellows, keeping as far away from Alexander as possible. Every time she heard his voice, her blood ran hot and images of them kissing flashed before her eyes. He filled her dreams at night and during the day she often found herself thinking of him, wondering what he was doing.

'A cup of tea, Miss Davenport?' Miss Fellows poured her a cup.

'Yes, thank you.' Evie gave her attention to Miss Fellows. 'This is the second time we've met at dance class and yet we haven't spoken properly.'

'Forgive me, my father says I am too shy to contend with. He despairs of me.' Miss Fellows blushed a cherry red, which at least gave some colour to her pale face. 'You are a very good dancer. I wish I had your grace, but I am a dolt. The simplest steps confuse me. Did you learn in India?'

'I did.' Evie noticed that Alexander had moved his chair closer to the small round table she sat near but had turned side-on so as not to appear rude to either table. She concentrated on Miss Fellows. 'I had lessons every week. I had to learn western dances, naturally, but I so wanted to learn Indian dances, but of course that was not permitted. However, secretly I would get my ayah to teach me at night when everyone was asleep. We danced silently.'

'Your ayah?'

'My nanny.'

'How magical. And you lived in Bombay?'

'That is correct. When I was a child, we moved to wherever Papa was stationed with his regiment if he was to be there for some time. Mama didn't want to be far from where he was, but as I became older Mama stayed in Bombay.'

'Such a lot of adjustments, having to always uproot the whole household.' Miss Fellows passed her a plate of thin oat biscuits.

'Mama didn't mind. She had my grandmama for company, and me, plus loyal servants.'

'Do you miss India? I imagine it is very exotic.'

Evie swallowed a mouthful of biscuit. 'I do miss it. India can change so rapidly, the weather is hot and dry or wet and damp, the colours are brighter, the sky seems more vast than here.'

'England is soft in comparison, in every way, I suspect?' Miss Fellows smiled.

'There is a rawness to India. It can be brutal and wild, untouched yet as old as time.'

'I must visit. I have an uncle in Calcutta in the civil service and a cousin in Bombay.'

'Really?'

'Oh yes, Manfred left England about ten years ago.'

'Manfred? Not Manfred Dunlop by any chance?' Evie asked in wonder.

Miss Fellows' eyes widened. 'Why yes! Do you know him?'

'I have been introduced to him, yes, at a dinner party in Bombay. It was at least three years ago. I was twenty and Mama had asked me to accompany her to a dinner party as Papa was away.'

'How extraordinary that you have met Manfred.'

'I wouldn't forget him as he spilled his glass of wine over my dress.'

'No!' Miss Fellows gasped.

'I laughed it off, but Mr Dunlop was beside himself with humiliation. He ordered cloths to help sponge my dress. It was all very funny, but he was mortified. That is why I remember Mr Dunlop.' Evie couldn't help but smile at the memory.

Miss Fellows smiled shyly. 'I will write to him this very evening and tell him of our meeting. Shall we embarrass him again with the retelling of the story?'

'Oh yes, do!' Evie joked and took a sip of tea. Her gaze caught Alexander's. He'd been listening to their conversation with interest. She turned away slightly, saddened that she couldn't have these conversations with him. How delightful it would be to simply sit with him and talk, without the desire controlling them or the guilt plaguing her that he was Sophie's.

Sophie rose and offered a plate of plum jam tartlets to Alexander; he took one with a warm smile and murmured something low that made Sophie giggle. Mrs Bellingham stood and excused herself to check on something, and invited Sophie to take her chair next to Alexander. The joy on Sophie's face when Alexander spoke to her was hard for Evie to witness. Her friend transformed into a beauty, with her eyes bright and her smile wide. Alexander transfixed Sophie so easily, she had eyes for no one else on the terrace. Anyone looking could see how much Sophie adored Alexander and Evie turned away, ashamed she had kissed him.

* * *

With her arm linked through Papa's, Evie walked between the tables selling donated goods in the church hall, a small stone building beside the village church. It had taken ten minutes of her cajoling Papa to come with her to the village. He'd wanted to stay in his study, but she knew if he did that he wouldn't come out until dinner.

'What did you donate, my dear?' Papa asked, picking up a bottle of apple cider.

'Flower-embroidered handkerchiefs. Four in total.'

'A fair gift.' Papa dipped his hat to the woman behind the stall. 'We shall take three jugs of cider, if you please. Also, some jam. One jar of plum, one of strawberry and one of raspberry.'

Evie smiled and wondered what Mrs Humphry would say about that. She made their jam herself.

While Papa conducted his transaction, Evie wandered over to a table selling small paintings. A man sat next to the table; he only had one leg.

'Are these your paintings?' Evie admired the work of the scenes depicting the moors in various weathers, all done in watercolours.

'They are, miss.' He held his cap in his hands.

'They are very beautiful.'

'I say, very well done, sir,' Papa said, coming to stand beside her. 'Did you want to buy one, my dear?'

'I would, Papa, but I forgot my money.' She held up her empty purse. The truth was she had no allowance left after giving everything she had to Hal Humphry.

'Silly poppet.' Papa grinned. 'Pick what you want, and I will pay the man.'

'They would look nice framed in the parlour.' Evie studied each painting again, finally selecting two: one of Ilkley Moor in the summer and the same again in the winter. 'What do you think, Papa?'

'Perfect.' Papa fell into conversation with the artist, who was a war veteran, and Evie continued on around the tables.

'There you are!' Sophie came across the room. 'I have been outside talking to Miss Davidson for the last ten minutes. I was trying to get away the entire time. She does nothing but boast of her latest flirtation, some gentleman from Leeds who is in banking.' Sophie glanced around. 'A good turnout, for certain.'

'It is for a good cause.'

'Yes, the vicar does do perfectly well in browbeating us all to spend our money for the missionary in Africa he supports.' Sophie picked up a straw hat decorated in dyed bird feathers and then put it down again. 'I am not quite sure I would want any of this.'

Evie laughed. 'Do not be such a snob, Sophie.'

'I suppose it is for charity.'

'Exactly.'

'And Alexander Lucas would want his potential wife to be charitable.'

'Potential wife?' Evie swallowed back a gasp. 'Has something been agreed upon?'

'No, not yet, but Papa mentioned this morning at breakfast that it was time I was married and that he felt Alexander should do something about it. Papa may speak more seriously to Guy Lucas now Alexander has been home some weeks.'

'And Alexander is who you definitely want for a husband?' Evie felt sick at the thought of what she'd done.

'Absolutely. He is the *only* one I want. I love him.'

'You are certain?' Love? Sophie professed to *love* Alexander. Evie's mind whirled. A wave of jealousy consumed her, but she had to be happy for her friend.

'Completely. Oh, look, there's Mrs Parnell. Mama wants me to speak with her about the ball. Mrs Parnell is wanting to bring her whole family, and Mama has agreed, and I need to let her know of it. I shall be back in a moment.'

Mrs Myer entered the room and went straight to Evie's papa. Sighing, Evie went the other way and bumped into Alexander.

He held her arm to steady her although she was in no fear of stumbling.

'Miss Davenport.' He bowed his head.

She couldn't meet his eyes. Her heart thumped erratically. 'Mr Lucas.'

'Are you enjoying the bazaar?' he asked, moving aside for some ladies to pass along the aisle.

'Yes, however it is not a place where I expected you to be.' A church bazaar was frequented by the women of the area or men who had retired, like Papa. If she had known Alexander was attending, she'd have made her excuses not to come.

'I took a hunch you might be here.'

She stared up at him, alarmed. 'Why?'

'We need to talk.'

'No, we do not.' There was nothing she wanted to hear, especially not if he'd decided on Sophie. She sidestepped around him, but his hand shot out and gripped her elbow.

'I want the truth from you about that man you met, and we should discuss what happened between us.'

She jerked her elbow out of his grasp, her cheeks reddening at the memory of his kiss, the feel of his lips on hers. His touch was imprinted in her mind, driving her crazy. 'What happened between us was a mistake,' she whispered harshly, aware of women standing not too far from them.

'Was it?' His expression was unreadable.

'Yes, to be forgotten. I have. There is nothing further for us to discuss.'

'Perhaps I should call on your father, then? Ask him about the man in the alley.'

Furious at his dogged persistence, she wanted to stamp her foot in frustration. Instead, she pulled back her shoulders, eyes narrowing. 'Papa would not appreciate your interference in my business, Mr Lucas. Nor, I think, would he be happy at your conduct towards me, your advances.'

Alexander folded his arms and smiled wryly. 'We both know my advances were equal to yours.'

'Papa would believe me, not you, and think less of you in the process. Good day to you, Mr Lucas.'

'Mr Lucas,' Sophie spoke a little too loudly. 'What are you doing here?'

'Am I a disappointment?' He chuckled.

'Heavens, no. It is a delight to see you in any place,' Sophie simpered. 'Are you donating or buying?'

'Donating. I have some yards of cotton cloth that I thought might make a decent contribution. My man is bringing it in from the wagon.'

'How very generous of you. May I show you around?' Sophie blinked up at him with a shy smile.

'Of course.' He offered her his arm, but his gaze stayed on Evie.

'Would you care to join us, Miss Davenport?'

Evie saw the message in Sophie's eyes of wanting to be alone with him. 'Thank you but no, Mr Lucas. I shall return to Papa before he spends my entire inheritance,' she joked, though feeling anything but funny. 'Besides, I feel my lovely friend here wants you all to herself. I shall call on you tomorrow, Sophie.' Evie kissed her friend's cheek and left them to join Papa and Mrs Myer. A deep sadness encircled her chest. Why did she have to fall for a man she couldn't have? It was stupid of her, irresponsible.

'Those two will be married by the end of the summer,' Mrs Myer observed. 'I'll wager my best hat on it.'

'What a fine pair they make,' Papa added, nodding to Alexander and Sophie as they passed.

'Shall we take advantage of the fine day, Major, and go into Bingley and take afternoon tea at Mrs Golding's Tea Shop?'

Papa hesitated. 'Forgive me, Mrs Myer, but I promised Evie we would go for a walk after we leave here.'

Mrs Myer's expression stiffened with annoyance. 'How lovely.'

'Do you still wish to walk, Papa?' Evie asked, not wanting to stop him from doing something else should he wish it, even if it meant being with Mrs Myer.

'I do, my dear. If you have seen enough, shall we collect our purchases and make a start?'

Mrs Myer held up a hand. 'You do not want to be carrying things all the way home. Tell me what you have bought, and I shall take them home with me and bring them to you later this afternoon. Will that be suitable?'

Evie knew the woman just wanted an excuse to visit.

Papa nodded. 'A kind offer indeed, Mrs Myer, thank you. We are not as popular as Mrs Golding's Tea Shop, but we can provide an afternoon tea for you when you call.'

'I shall look forward to it, Major.' Delighted, Mrs Myer left them.

Evie looked for Sophie and Alexander and found them in the corner with Mrs Bellingham, deep in conversation. Sophie was laughing and gazing up at Alexander. Evie was glad to leave.

Strolling through the village, Evie enjoyed the sunshine on her back. 'Where shall we go? Up onto the moors?'

'We might as well. It is the perfect weather for a stroll on the moors, not too hot and not too cold.' He tipped his hat at two women walking past.

'I am so pleased it is spring and the worst of the weather is behind us,' Evie said as they headed up the lane that would take them past their own house and up near Top Farm.

'It can still snow right up until May in parts. When I was a boy, I've seen it snow in May, on my mama's birthday, which was the fourteenth.' He had a faraway look in his eyes. 'I wish you had met Mama. You are a lot like her. You have her spirits and looks.'

'I wish I had, too,' Evie replied, sad to have missed meeting the grandmother whom she most resembled.

'My mama would have told you some tales, for certain.' Papa grinned. 'Like the time she and my papa were sailing to Ireland, and they were robbed. Mama scoured the ship until she found the culprit and knocked him senseless with a piece of wood. When he came to, he found himself tied up with rope and she threatened to haul him overboard.'

Evie laughed. 'And so she should have done!'

'Then there was that time they were out riding, and a snowstorm hit and they became separated. Mama was out all night and Papa thought she'd be dead by morning, especially when her horse arrived home riderless. But no. The next day she comes walking home covered in mud and stinking of sheep. She'd only gone and huddled in a hollow with a flock of sheep and then dug herself out of the snow.'

'To be so brave. She sounds like a wonderful person,' Evie said in awe, looking up at the tree canopy hanging over their heads, blocking out the sunshine.

'My papa used to say that the woman he'd married never gave him a moment's peace, but she also gave him a lifetime of deep joy. Both he and I were spoiled to have found women who we adored with every breath. I hope you find that person, Evie.' He patted her hand where it rested on his arm. 'For you to be happy is all I want in life.'

'I am happy, right now.' She laid her head on his shoulder for a moment, but the noise of what sounded like hundreds of birds tweeting and chattering brought her head up. 'Goodness, listen to them.'

'Swallows.' Papa stopped to listen, leaning on Mr Lund's farm gate. 'You can always hear them in March. Look at them.' He pointed to some that flew overhead. 'See the forked tail, the blue on its back. Beautiful.'

'They look so graceful in flight.' Evie watched, listening to their twittering. 'It's like they are all talking to one another.'

'Perhaps they are?' Papa smiled. 'Catching up on the latest gossip.'

Walking on, Evie waved to Mr Lund, pipe in his mouth, who was walking his big shire horse through the field. She stooped to pick some wild flowers growing in the hedge. 'I shall press these and send them to the aunts,' she called back to Papa as she continued to step along the hedge, collecting the best flowers. 'Aunt Rose loves flowers and being in the middle of a large town she doesn't have much of a garden.'

When she had a handful, she turned back. Papa stood by the gate, his face twisted in agony, and a hand on his arm. 'Papa?'

He groaned as he fell, crashing on to the dirt lane like a fallen tree.

'Papa!' Evie screamed. She ran to him, dropping to her knees beside his head. 'Papa!'

He groaned again.

For a terrifying second she didn't know what to do. Then suddenly she sprang into action. 'I will get help.'

Dashing to the gate, she unlatched it and let it swing wide as she lifted her skirts and ran up the hill. 'Mr Lund! Mr Lund!'

The old farmer came out of the barn. 'What's the t'do, miss?'

'Papa! He's collapsed. Can you help me, please?'

'Aye, lass, aye. Go back to him. I'll get Flossie in the cart as quick as I can.'

'Please hurry!' She dashed back down the lane, frantic that Papa was still breathing.

Tumbling to her knees beside him, her head swam in relief that he lay wincing, eyes gazing at the blue sky, moaning softly. 'Papa, Mr Lund is getting his cart.'

'A doctor...'

'We shall get you one.'

'No time.'

Her breath caught in her throat. 'Do not say that!' She eased his cravat away from his throat. His hat had rolled away, and wild flowers surrounded him where she'd dropped her posy.

The heavy hooves of the shire horse came thumping down the farm drive. Together Evie and Mr Lund helped her papa into the back of his cart, and she climbed in after him to rest his head on her lap. 'We will be home shortly.'

'Gee up there, Flossie.' Mr Lund sent the big horse into a trot.

'I do not want to leave you, dearest.' Papa groaned with every bump and sweat broke out on his forehead.

'You shan't leave me!' Evie was determined he'd survive.

At the house, Mr Lund banged on the door until Fanny opened it. 'What you banging like that for?' she said, wiping her hands on her apron. Then, seeing the occupants of the cart, she squealed. 'Oh, miss!'

'Get Colin and Mr Bronson, Fanny, quickly,' Evie shouted, slipping down from the cart.

Mr Lund, his teeth clamped down on his pipe, helped her. 'Once your father is free from the cart, miss, I'll go into Bingley for the doctor.'

'Dr MacClay on Main Street,' Evie said as Colin and his father hurried around the side of the house.

The two men carried a limp Papa, who moaned with every step, inside while Evie and Fanny went ahead up to his bedroom.

Once on his bed, Papa closed his eyes.

'Papa, the doctor will be here soon.' Evie sat beside him, holding his hand. His pale, sweating face filled her with alarm. 'You will soon be well enough.'

'Water, miss.' Fanny handed her a glass of water.

Gently, Evie helped him to sip at the glass, but most dribbled down his chin.

'My chest, Evie,' he mumbled. 'There's a weight pressing...'

'Lie still. Rest.' She glanced at Fanny, not knowing what to do.

The ticking of the seconds on the clock was the only sound in the room as they waited. Papa lay with his eyes closed, his breathing shallow. Evie wanted to take his boots and coat off but dared not disturb him. After an hour of frantic waiting, they finally heard the sound of hooves and wheels.

Fanny raced to the window. 'It's Mr Lund and the doctor.' She hurried downstairs to let them in.

Evie couldn't find a welcome as Dr MacClay entered the bedroom. She sat frozen in fear and simply stared at him.

'Now then. What do we have here?' the doctor said in this thick Scottish accent. He glanced at Evie as he took his hat off, revealing wild, curly hair of steel grey. 'Tell me what happened.'

She told him, trying not to stutter or sound insensible.

Dr MacClay took her hand and led her away from the bed. 'A cup of tea, Miss Davenport. Wait for me downstairs.' His smile was reassuring.

'But—'

'Downstairs.' He gently pushed her towards the door where Fanny waited.

In the parlour, she couldn't sit and instead paced the floor. Fanny went to make a tray of tea, not that Evie wanted any. All she could think of was Papa dying, leaving her alone. He couldn't die. How would she cope without him? He was all she had left.

Eventually, Dr MacClay joined her, accepting the cup of tea Fanny poured for him. 'Now, Miss Davenport. The major has suffered a severe heart seizure. He is in much pain, and I have given him a draught to ease his suffering. He has survived this attack, but he is not out of danger yet.'

'He may still die?' She choked the words out.

'There is that possibility, yes, but he is in good physical shape for his age. Hopefully, with rest, he should recover his strength in time.'

She nodded, relief making her sag and reach for the back of the sofa to steady her wobbly knees. 'Thank you, Doctor.'

He sipped his tea and quickly ate a piece of fruit cake as though he was ravenous. 'I shall call again tomorrow morning. Your father is to have complete bed rest. His meals should consist of beef broths, egg custard, thin porridge, that sort of thing, nothing rich or heavy.'

'Of course.'

'No visitors at all. He must have complete bed rest, you understand?' He gulped down the last of his tea.

'I do. He shall not be disturbed.'

'Under no circumstances must he be given reason to become agitated or anxious.'

She swallowed. 'And if we do all that, he will survive?'

'God willing, Miss Davenport. However, the heart is a fragile organ, and your father is of an age when heart problems occur, that and his loss of your mother, and the stress of being a solider in battle can all affect the fragility of the one thing we need to keep us alive.' He plonked his hat on his wild hair. 'Nevertheless, Miss Davenport, you and I will do all that we can to keep the major with us for some time yet, yes?' He smiled.

'Yes...'

'Until tomorrow. Though naturally, send for me if your father takes a turn for the worse.'

Once the doctor had gone, taken back to Bingley by Bronson, Evie went up to her papa's bedroom where he lay sleeping. She quietly sat down and took his hand, watching his chest rise and fall.

'You didn't drink your tea, miss,' Fanny whispered, coming into the room carrying a teacup and saucer.

'I do not want tea, Fanny.'

'You need to keep your strength up. The major will need you to be strong and help him recover.'

'He has to get better, Fanny. He has to.' Life without Papa would be too difficult to consider. He was all she had.

'Course he will, miss.' Fanny placed the cup and saucer on the bedside table. 'Mr Lund has returned home. Mrs Humphry gave him something to eat while he waited. Such a nice old man.'

'I did not thank him.'

'We thanked him for you.' Fanny walked to the door. 'I'll bring up some soup. You must eat, miss.'

Evie reached over and softly swept back Papa's white hair. It was becoming long and needed cutting. She wanted to cry but feared to do so. Crying was weak. She had to be strong. Papa needed her strong and capable, not a weeping useless child.

Her head snapped up at the sound of the doorbell. She rose and left the room to stand on the landing. Below she heard Mrs Myer.

'What do you mean the major is not receiving callers? He knows I was coming to visit. I have his purchases from the church bazaar. Stand aside, girl, and let me pass.'

Fanny's voice was lower; Evie couldn't hear what she said.

'I insist!' Mrs Myer's louder voice drifted up the stairs. 'I will see you dismissed for this impertinence, girl.'

Taking a deep breath, Evie reluctantly went downstairs, a simmering anger coiling in her body. 'Mrs Myer.'

'This imbecile refuses to let me pass.' Mrs Myer's strident tones echoed around the entrance hall.

'Please keep your voice down,' Evie snapped. 'Papa is ill upstairs, and the doctor was strict in his instructions to keep Papa calm. You will not disturb him!'

Mrs Myer's hand flew to her throat. 'Ill? The doctor has been? What is wrong with the major? I must know.' She looked shaken.

'He suffered a heart seizure.' Evie felt the tears hot behind her eyes but blinked them away. 'He is gravely ill.'

'Dear God in heaven. I must see him.'

'No!' Evie put up both hands, barring her from taking a step towards the stairs. 'He is sleeping, and I will not allow him to be woken. His pain was severe before and while he sleeps, he is not burdened by it.'

'Then I shall wait in the parlour.'

'I am afraid that is not possible.' Evie glared at the woman. 'I have enough to do attending to my papa's needs without worrying about a guest. Go home, Mrs Myer. I shall send word to you when it is convenient for you to call.' She turned on her heel and, lifting her skirts, rushed back upstairs.

'Well, how rude!'

Mrs Myer's words followed her, but she didn't care a jot. Causing offence to that woman was the least of her worries.

She eased back on to the chair, wincing when it creaked, but Papa didn't stir. She slipped her fingers under his hand. 'Stay with me, Papa, *please*. I am not ready to be alone.'

7

'The day is fine, Evie. You must go outside for a little while,' Papa said from his bed where he was propped up on several pillows, looking wan but better than he had for days.

Evie fussed with the tea tray Fanny had just brought in. 'I will take a short stroll later when you are napping.'

'You watch me like a hawk eyeing its prey.' He took the teacup from her and sipped it. 'I am much better than I was.'

'It pleases me greatly to see you sitting up and talking, but Dr MacClay says you must have rest. I need to make sure you do that, and I know once my back is turned you will try to get out of bed!' She smiled to take the sting out of her words.

'It has been a week. I should be allowed to sit in a chair by the window now.'

'When Dr MacClay advises that is it possible for you to do so, then you can.' She straightened the blankets and folded the newspaper he'd been reading earlier.

He frowned at her. 'You'd do well in the army. Always giving orders.'

'If I was a man, I probably would!'

Papa took her hand to stop her fiddling with his pillows. 'Evie dear, right at this moment, I am perfectly well. You must rest yourself. You have been by my bedside day and night for over a week. I beg you to go for a ride or a walk, visit Miss Bellingham, anything.'

'You may need me, Papa. You tire so easily.'

'I have everything I need right here and if I do require something more, I have my bell beside me to ring for Fanny.' He patted her hand. 'Go. I insist.'

'Do you promise to not leave this bed?'

'I solemnly promise.'

She hesitated. The weather had been fine all week and a ride on Star would give her some time to breathe and ease her mind from the constant worry about Papa, but to leave him alone... She wasn't sure she was ready to do that.

They heard the doorbell downstairs.

Evie clenched her teeth. Mrs Myer had called every day but never made it past the entrance hall as either she or Fanny prevented her from entering the house. Evie didn't want to have to do battle with her again today. A week of not sleeping properly had exhausted her.

'That will be Mrs Myer,' Papa murmured.

'Fanny will see to her.'

'Allow her up, Evie. Mrs Myer can keep me company and you can go for a ride.'

'No, Papa...'

'My dear, do as I say. Do not spend the beautiful days inside when winter can be so long in this country. Take advantage of the fine weather. Go.'

'Mrs Myer will exhaust you,' she argued.

'She will not stay long. I shall take a nap shortly.' He waved her away. 'Fanny will guard me.' He smiled wryly.

Evie hesitated a moment longer and then left the room.

Descending the stairs, she heard Mrs Myer asking questions of Fanny and interrupted the answers. The woman was impossible. 'Mrs Myer. Would you care to come in?'

'About time!' The woman stormed through the front door. 'To be kept on the doorstep like a common tradesman is rather insulting!'

'We have been terribly busy with caring for Papa and visitors, although normally welcomed, can be a... distraction.'

'I am a concerned friend.' Mrs Myer's eyes narrowed in exasperation. 'To be treated so disrespectfully is a stain on your manners, not mine.'

Evie took a deep breath. 'Papa has given permission for you to go up and sit with him for a few minutes while I run some errands.'

Mrs Myer's chin lifted in triumph. 'Of course the dear major wishes to see me.'

'For five minutes only, Mrs Myer,' Evie warned. 'Then he must sleep. Doctor's orders. Fanny will be watching the clock.'

'I know how to treat an invalid. I cared for my husband until he died.' She swept up the stairs before Evie could reply.

'Shall I take more tea up, miss?' Fanny asked.

'No, Papa has a tray and I do not want to encourage that woman to stay any longer than necessary!'

Fanny grinned.

'I shall go for a walk to Bellingham Hall to see Miss Bellingham. But I shan't be more than an hour.' Evie opened the cupboard by the stairs and took out her white shawl and a straw hat she left there for when she worked in the garden.

'Very good, miss.' Fanny turned and from a small drawer in a side table by the wall she gave Evie a pair of white lace gloves. 'Do you want your parasol?'

'No, thank you. Oh, and check on Papa every ten minutes.'

'I will.'

'Send for me immediately should he need me.'

'I'll have Colin ready just in case, miss.'

Walking down the drive, Evie raised her head back to let the sun wash her face. The trees were filled with birds; starlings, wrens, robins and swallows were all busy attending to nests. They twittered and swooped above, silhouetted against the dazzling blue sky. The garden had blazed into flower with crocuses and daffodils of yellow and cream, the purple buds of violets; the elm and alder trees were bursting into full bud and at their base were swathes of yellow primrose promising to open fully. The moors behind the house were beckoning her, and she longed to ride Star up there, but that would have to wait until Papa had fully recovered.

The lane to the village was quiet. In the distance she noticed Mr Lund, smoke coming from his pipe, working in his lower fields that wrapped around her own house and acres. Mrs Humphry had baked him a fruit cake and taken it up to him as a thank you for his help the day Papa collapsed.

'Evie!' Sophie, coming up the lane, waved enthusiastically.

'This is a surprise. I was on my way to visit you,' Evie said when she reached her, and they embraced.

'I thought to come and see how you are and the major. My parents send their good wishes.' Sophie grasped Evie's arm. 'Fanny did pass my message to you the other day when I called?'

'She did, yes. Thank you for coming to see us but I couldn't leave Papa. The days after his collapse were simply dreadful. I slept in a chair by his bed, and I kept waking up and watching him. I dared not leave his side.'

'Indeed not. How frighted you must have been! Did you receive our gifts?'

'We did; thank your mama for me. The flowers cheered the rooms, and the produce was very welcome.'

'Mama said the flowers were the first ones blooming in the

greenhouse. She knew they would be happily received. How is the major?'

'Better. Sitting up now in bed. He is impatient to be moving about. He longs for his study, but Dr MacClay refuses for him to go downstairs or have his correspondence brought up to him. He must have complete rest. Papa refuses to acknowledge that he tires so easily.'

'The major might sneak down while you are out?'

'No, Mrs Myer is there. I have allowed her to see him for the first time, despite her daily harassment to get past the front door.'

Sophie chuckled. 'That woman! She is tenacious.'

'Yes, but so can I be!' Evie grinned.

'Oh, I know.' Sophie shook her head. 'The major's ill health will no doubt put off your plan to return to India?'

Evie nodded sadly. 'We cannot possibly travel for some time. Dr MacClay said Papa will need months to recover. India is something that might happen in the distant future, but it is no longer of great importance.'

'It would be best for you to stay here amongst friends.' Sophie tucked Evie's arm through her own as they walked. 'Shall we go and sit on the grass by the hedge? The sun should have dried the dew enough by now.'

'I cannot stay long.' Evie followed her friend over to an open grassy area where the lane forked between two roads, one heading to the village and one going up over the moors.

They sat down and arranged their skirts around them. Sophie wore a pale blue printed dress with a darker blue piping. Sophie's wide hat, tied under her chin with a blue ribbon, held a small bunch of artificial white roses that decorated the top of the brim. She looked glorious and her rosy complexion showed her to be in full health. In comparison, Evie felt tired and dowdy. Her dress of dark brown and tan stripes and her old straw hat that needed a new ribbon looked positively plain. Shrugging, Evie didn't care. After her chat with Sophie, she'd return home and see no visitors for the rest of the day.

Sophie plucked a grass stem. 'I am told Mrs Myer has been dining with Mr Guy Lucas recently. That woman seems to enjoy being entertained by unattached men.'

'I hope she transfers her affections to Mr Lucas and leaves Papa alone.'

'It is possible. Alexander told me that she has called at their house twice this week.'

'Alexander?' Evie had tried so hard to put him from her mind.

Sophie blushed. 'He dined with us last night. He and Papa were sorting out some business and it became late and so Mama claimed Alexander as a dinner guest. He sat beside me, and we had a wonderful time.'

Evie refused to feel jealous. He had to be forgotten. 'How lovely.'

'Oh, Evie, he is simply divine. I do think I am more in love with him now than ever before.'

'In love?' She could never forget him while Sophie raved about him constantly.

'It is true. He is the man I wish to marry and no other. He is simply heavenly. Alexander was so attentive to me, and we talked and laughed. He is everything I want.'

'How could you not be in love with such a man, then?' Evie forced a smile to her stiff face. She felt a hypocrite, and desperately lonely as though she was on the outside of life looking in at people being happy, content while she was riddled with anxiety over Papa and guilt for kissing Alexander so passionately.

'We are to go riding on Saturday and Alexander is to dine with us again next Friday. Mama suggested we, Alexander and I, join Paul and Helen when they go to the theatre in Leeds on Wednesday.

Alexander agreed. That would be three times we would see each other in a week.' Sophie clapped her hands in excitement. 'Imagine, the four of us attending the theatre. It is a step forward, do you not think?'

'Is it?' Evie summoned all her interest when her mind was screaming, *You kissed him!*

'Well, yes, silly. He is my partner to the theatre, and we shall be seen in public. Wednesday is the opening night of the play, and *everyone* will be there.'

'I see...'

'If only we could find you a gentleman as good as Alexander, then we could be so blissfully happy, all of us,' Sophie gushed.

'I have no time to entertain a gentleman, nor do I wish to.'

'I want you to be happy, Evie.'

Evie stared out over the valley. 'Happiness is not exclusive to being married, Sophie.'

'It is a great deal more agreeable than to remain an old maid!' Sophie laughed, her eyes bright with excitement.

Standing, Evie dusted off her skirts. 'I must get back.'

'Of course.' Sophie stood and embraced her. 'Send for me should you need me.'

'Thank you.'

'When your papa is fully well again, we should spend some time together before...'

'Before what?'

'Before I marry Alexander.'

The blood drained from Evie's face. 'Has he proposed?'

'No, but if he does, and I think he will, I will give my consent and so will Papa. Although Alexander isn't terribly rich, not as rich as Papa, he is a good match.' Sophie's smile was full of love and delight. 'So, before I become a terribly busy married woman, I want us to spend some time together like we did last summer. Remember when we played in the river in our undergarments?'

'You shrieked enough to scare the birds,' Evie remembered, wanting to think about anything but Alexander.

'It was cold, and we were nearly *naked*,' Sophie whispered.

'Hardly. The spot was secluded from the road, and no one would have seen us unless they came down to the water's edge.'

'Even so, I have never done anything so... so... *wild* in my life.'

Evie smiled. 'You enjoyed every moment of it.'

'I think I did, actually. Can we do something like that again?' Sophie tapped her chin. 'Let us be wild once more before I become a respectable married woman to the handsome Alexander Lucas.'

Sophie's words wounded Evie. Alexander. Why had he kissed her if he wanted Sophie?

'I shall call on Thursday, shall I? Then I can tell you all about the evening at the theatre.' Sophie kissed Evie's cheek.

'I would like that.' Evie nodded and turned away.

The short walk back to the house gave Evie little time to think of Sophie's announcement. Her best friend loved the man that Evie had kissed, the man that she felt feelings of desire for. Well, that all had to stop. She must never be alone with Alexander again and when she was in his presence, she would have to remain calm and aloof. Alexander belonged to Sophie.

* * *

Thunder roared overhead as Evie walked into the kitchen, her mind on creating a menu that would satisfy both Dr MacClay's demands and tempt Papa's tastes. She wished they were in India, where their cook would produce light, aromatic soups and delicious, delicate curries. But they were not in India and instead were in Yorkshire, where today the April rain plummeted from the sky as though in an angry spat with the earth.

Fanny and Mrs Humphry sprang apart as she entered. Fanny went to the store cupboard and Mrs Humphry to the oven, where she stirred something in the pot.

Lizzie came in through the back door, a hessian sack over her head and carrying a box of vegetables. 'By heck, it's fair thrashing it down out there.' She looked up and reddened on seeing Evie. 'Oh, begging your pardon, miss. I didn't see you standing there.'

'It is quite all right, Lizzie.' Evie glanced at Mrs Humphry. 'I understand you are busy making dinner, but I just wanted to give you this list. It's ingredients Dr MacClay spoke to me about for Papa's meals.'

'Very good, miss.'

'Now that Papa is up and about a little bit more, Dr MacClay wants to strengthen him up. Papa has lost weight.' Evie was worried that not only was it his weight Papa was losing but also his will to live. He was more down-spirited than ever before. She thought him being allowed to leave his bedroom and come downstairs would cheer him, but instead he spent long hours in his study, barely talking or eating. Evie didn't know what to do to get him out of his low mood.

'I'm sure we'll work something out, miss, to tempt the major's appetite.' Mrs Humphry carried the pot to the table in the middle of the room. 'Happen I can write down some ideas and bring it in to you in the morning?'

'Thank you,' Evie replied, ready to leave the kitchen when Colin came dashing through the back door, sopping wet, his coat dripping on the floor. 'I couldn't see nothing, Mrs H.'

'Quiet!' Fanny snapped.

Colin then noticed Evie by the door. 'Evening, miss.'

'Good evening, Colin. What are you doing out in this weather?'

'Er...'

'There was a fox, miss,' Fanny said quickly. 'It was after the hens. I saw him when I went over to the stables. I told Colin to go and see if it was still loitering about.'

'A hungry fox after our hens is something we do not need,' Evie said.

'Indeed, miss,' Mrs Humphry agreed. 'Colin, get those wet boots off my floor.'

Leaving them to it, Evie went back to the parlour. She'd dressed for dinner in a simple gown, a pale pink satin. Although the weather was frightful outside, it wasn't cold. However, she'd asked Fanny to have the fires lit to stave off any coolness for Papa as he sat in his chair reading.

He looked up as she took the opposite chair. 'I am glad that Dr MacClay is reducing his visits to once a week now.'

'Oh?' She took her darning on to her lap. Darning stockings was a boring chore but had to be done.

'I am tired of being continually prodded. It is time I returned to doing what I want.'

'Which is?'

'Spending time in my study without interruption. After weeks in my bed, I refuse to *rest* any more.'

'Dr MacClay did give permission for you to go on walks now. Soon, you shall be riding again. Your friends miss seeing you, Papa. At the Easter Sunday service they all asked after you. Would it not be nice to call on them again?'

'I am content as I am, but you, my dear, need to return to your life, instead of playing nursemaid to me day in and day out.'

'I have been only too happy to attend to you, Papa. I am your daughter; it is my duty.'

'And now I am well. Therefore, tomorrow you shall take a ride on Star and visit friends or go into Bingley and partake in some shopping.' He wagged his finger at her. 'I mean it, Evie. You are to leave this house tomorrow and not return until evening.'

'Papa, I have no wish to be out all day.'

'I want peace, Evie. Please, give me that.' He sighed heavily.

Put out, she bristled. 'I was not aware that I didn't give you peace, Papa.'

'You know what I mean. Leave me to my own devices. I can see to myself without you looking at me as if I am about to drop dead at your feet at any moment!'

'Papa!' His words upset her.

Instantly, he put up his hand and shook his head. 'I do not mean to sound harsh or ungrateful of your love and care, my dear. I know you mean well, but I am a grown man and I do not need my daughter hovering about me. Do you understand?'

She nodded slightly.

He rubbed a hand over his eyes. 'Forgive me, dearest. I just want things to be as they were.'

She didn't know how to answer that because how they were before meant that he stayed in his study for long periods of time during the day. She would have to beg him to accompany her on walks or to any dinner invitation. He only willingly went to church without argument, otherwise he was quite content to stay in his study with his books and letter-writing. She didn't want to go back to that, but what else was there? Papa didn't want her company, or anyone's.

The following morning, as Papa instructed, she had Colin saddle Star and she left the house straight after breakfast. Riding the muddy lanes could have been avoided if she took the carriage but that would limit where she could go. Besides, Star hadn't been out for a long ride in over a month and the spring sunshine peeping out between the clouds beckoned them to take to the fields.

Evie let Star have her head and galloped across the acres behind the house and up on to the lower moors. A slight breeze and Star's pace whipped her riding habit's skirt out behind her, but thankfully she'd secured her hat and its short veil with many pins.

Up high, she slowed Star down to a walk. Around her, the moors stretched higher and wider for miles and below the valley was patterned by the sun and clouds casting shadows. Although she worried about Papa, being free from the house and her responsibilities for a few hours was a welcome relief she hadn't realised she needed.

Leaving the moor, she headed down past the village and along the lane that ran beside Lylston Beck. The water gushed and frothed over stones, swollen from the previous storms. Spring grass sprouted thick and lush and Evie spotted the odd wild primrose unfurling round tree trunks.

After weeks being in the house with only the staff to talk to, Evie was eager for fresh air and time to herself. She had received the occasional visit from Sophie, who seemed busier than ever and had little time to sit with Evie lately. Not that Evie blamed her. It made her happy that Sophie was shopping and socialising and doing all the things Evie hadn't been able to do for the last month. When Sophie called, she gave Evie an hour of gossip as they ate cake and drank tea. Only, Sophie's constant references to Alexander were wearing thin on Evie's nerves. He was a saint in Sophie's eyes. Evie hoped he deserved such adoration. Thankfully, she had not seen him for some time, not that it stopped the treacherous thoughts of him entering her mind.

'Hey up, Miss Davenport.' Joe Schofield, the gamekeeper for Bellingham Hall, leaped over a narrow part of the beck and, smiling, walked over to her. 'You're a sight for sore eyes and no mistake. I've not seen you riding around the district in weeks.'

'Good morning, Mr Schofield.' Evie pulled Star to a stop beside him. 'How are you?'

'I'm fine, miss, but how's your father doing? We've not seen him since we heard of his illness.' He stood dressed all in dark brown, a rifle broken over the crook of his arm and a flat cap pulled low.

'He is much better, thank you. The doctor has allowed him to be downstairs now.'

'Then soon I hope he will be fully recovered and joining the hunting and shooting parties at the hall.'

'I would wish for nothing more; as soon as he is himself again, he'll be sure to make up a party number.'

'Would you be glad of a brace of rabbits? We have more than we need at the hall. I could have some sent up to you. Your cook can make a stew or a nice pie?'

'That would be very welcome indeed, Mr Schofield. Thank you.'

'Right you are, miss.' He waved and went on his way.

Evie clicked her tongue for Star to move on. Something caught the corner of her eye and she turned slightly to peer through the trees. Alexander sat astride his horse in the shadows. Her heart skipped and although it had been a while since their last meeting, nothing had changed in her response to him when she gazed at his handsome face.

Nudging his horse forward, he gave a nod of acknowledgement. 'I always seem to find you talking alone with men.'

'And I always find you spying on me.'

'Hardly.'

'This lane is nowhere near your home or your mill.'

'No, but it is not far from one of my father's mills.' He waved back behind him, towards the Leeds and Liverpool Canal, which snaked through the valley. 'I have just left there.'

She stared at him, drinking in the sight of his devilish good looks. His dark grey suit hugged the frame of him, emphasising his thighs. Her whole body was aware of him. She wished to God that he didn't have an effect on her. To lust, and it was lust, she admitted it, after her best friend's beau was a sordid thing to do.

'How is the major?'

'Much better. Thank you.'

'I am pleased to hear it. May I call on him, if he is well enough for visitors?'

'Yes...' Inside, she wanted to say no. Having him in her home was torture to her senses. 'Papa would like that very much. He has spent too many hours with me. That is why I am riding. He ordered me to enjoy the fresh air.'

'I heard you have been a diligent carer.'

'Why would I not be? He is my beloved papa.'

'True, but not every woman makes a good nurse. I could name a dozen of them who I'd rather not have nurse me.' His smile caught her unawares.

What he said made sense, Evie had to admit, and his smile made her stomach swoop. 'True, some women are not very charitable when it comes to the care of others.'

'Shall we ride together?' he suddenly asked. 'I fancy the idea of good gallop.'

'I do not think I should...'

'Why?' His direct look was part thoughtful and part dare. 'Do you have somewhere else to be?'

'No.' She raised her chin. God help her, she wanted to ride alongside him and so much more. 'But I have let Star have her head once this morning.'

'She looks fit enough to handle another. Shall we be daring, Miss Davenport? What say we let the horses stretch their legs and race back up along this lane and then across the lower moorland? Then we could have a steady walk back and talk some more.'

She tried to think of an excuse; however, she desperately wanted to spend some time with him. Her head willed her to stay away from him, to bid him good day and walk on, but her treacherous heart begged her to spend time with him.

He nudged his horse up alongside Star so that his leg nearly touched hers. 'Are you really as untamed as they all say?'

The challenge in his grey eyes taunted her. Her blood pumped through her veins. A rash feeling of wantonness claimed her. She leaned forward, watching his eyes widen in anticipation of something, she didn't know what, another kiss perhaps... Thrilled that he wasn't immune to her, she threw her head back and laughed. 'See you at the top, Mr Lucas!'

Evie clicked her tongue at Star, urging her into a trot and then a canter along the lane. She didn't look back, hearing him pursue her. When the lane widened on to the sheep fields, Evie let Star gallop. The wind dragged at Evie's hair, whipping it from under her hat. She bent low over Star's neck, urging the mare to go faster. Alexander's horse had spirit, though, and pace. Soon it was beside Star, its long strides eating up the ground.

They wheeled around the last tree before the moors stretched broadly before them. Both horses were going full pelt, neck and neck. The excitement made Evie shout with happiness. This was what she'd been missing. Galloping along the beaches in India had been one of her favourite things to do.

Suddenly, a rabbit popped up in front of them and ran around in a circle of fear. Alexander's horse shied violently, skidding to a jerking halt. Alexander sailed over his head and landed with a thump in the grass.

Evie, dread filling her throat, slowed Star and turned her about back to where Alexander lay still.

'Dear God!' Evie flung herself from the saddle and raced to him. She kneeled by his side, hands fluttering over him. 'Mr Lucas! Alexander!'

He lay still.

'Please God, don't be dead!' she cried out in fear and dread. 'Wake up, Alexander!'

He groaned and his eyes fluttered open.

Overwhelmed that he still lived, Evie cupped his cheeks with both hands. She couldn't take witnessing another near-death experience. 'Speak to me!'

'Bloody hell,' he moaned. 'Forgive my language...'

'Can you move?' She couldn't bear it if he couldn't. 'Where are you hurt?'

'My head took a knock, I think.'

'Anywhere else? Can you move your arms and legs? Is there pain?' She ran her hands down his legs.

'I am fine, really.'

'I shall go for help.'

'No.' He slowly sat up, drawing his knees up and hanging his head. 'I am all right. Winded more than anything. We were going at speed.' He sucked in a deep breath and exhaled.

'Are you certain?' She noticed a small graze near his temple. 'Goodness, you're bleeding.' She fished a white handkerchief out from the small pocket in her bodice. Moving closer, she dabbed at it.

Alexander didn't wince but watched her carefully. 'You have a gentle touch.'

'I often helped my mama and grandmama care for the children and elderly in the surrounding streets where we lived in Bombay.' Evie kept her eyes on the graze, not daring to look at him while she was so close.

'Tell me more,' he said softly.

'There was a slum area down the hill from our home. A small charity hospital operated there, run by two Scottish women. Mama and Grandmama would spend an afternoon there once a week, helping the Scottish nurses to heal and attend to the sick and the poor. They did it for years and I always begged to go with them, but Mama said I was an innocent. Then when I was about fifteen one of our servants, a young boy, cut himself while chopping wood. No one was at home but me and a few of the other servants, but because of the caste system they would not touch him.'

'How frightened you must have been.'

'I tended to his gaping wound. The blood was horrendous, so much of it. I could not stem it as much as I tried.' Her hands stilled. 'After half an hour he died in my arms. I was enraged at the loss, of not knowing what to do to help the boy. For days afterwards I could not sleep or eat. Mama told me it was not my fault, the wound was too deep. Papa said I was no longer a child. I had witnessed death at close hand, and it matured me overnight. The following week, Mama allowed me to help at the hospital. At first, I found it difficult. Babies died, old people suffered. It was intense and confronting, but after six months or so I found I enjoyed it.' She faltered, knowing she had talked too much.

'Nurse Davenport,' he murmured.

She had often wondered about that. If perhaps that was her true calling. Talking about the hospital resurfaced old memories. 'Maybe I should become a nurse and return to India to help the poor?'

Alexander brought his hand up to lightly touch her cheek. 'I have the utmost desire to kiss you, Miss Davenport,' he whispered.

'Shh. You have hit your head and do not know what you say,' she murmured, unable to meet his eyes as a shiver of pleasure flowed over her skin at his words.

'You have no idea how beautiful you are. No, not beautiful, exquisite. Not in a goddess way but in an unpretentious, earthy way. You are a true woman, built hard and tough and with an aura about you that sends men mad with wanting to be near you.'

Her breathing shortened. 'You should not say such things.'

'They are the truth.'

'But not what a gentleman should utter.' Finally, she looked at him and instantly wished she hadn't. His face was too close, his mouth invitingly near.

'Kiss me...' he breathed.

As though cast in a spell, she leaned forward until their lips barely touched.

'You are everything,' he whispered against her mouth.

Her lips touched his again, softly, reverently, then hungrily, demandingly. His arms pulled her into him, and she went willingly, wanting him, yearning for him to touch her, absorb her into him.

'I cannot stop thinking about you,' he murmured, nuzzling under her ear, then back to claim her mouth again. 'You fill my mind...'

'Alexander.' She sighed his name as he kissed her neck. Her body felt on fire.

Then abruptly he pushed her from him.

Evie landed on her bottom with a thud, shocking her. She blinked rapidly to clear her mind, trying to understand his actions.

Alexander heaved himself to his feet, shaking his head. 'Forgive me, Evie... Miss Davenport.' He straightened, his expression pained.

'Are you hurt?'

'No. No...' He laughed mockingly. 'Christ, I am a fool.'

'Why?' She couldn't move and simply stared up at him as he paced around the clumps of heather and gorse.

'I have made a mistake. Lord, what have I done?'

Like a slap in the face, Evie realised he was talking about her. Desire was replaced by anger and humiliation. She got to her feet and stared at him. 'Yes, kissing me like a common whore was a mistake, Mr Lucas.'

He turned in surprise. 'What? No! The mistake wasn't you.' In two strides he was in front of her, gripping her arms. 'You could never be any man's mistake.'

She frowned, not understanding. 'You are talking in riddles. Is your head hurting?'

'No... yes... a little.' He stepped away and raised his face to the sun. 'I have been a stupid fool.'

'I understand that since you keep saying it, but why?' She folded her arms in frustration.

'I did not think you were suitable. My father said you were a little untamed, outspoken. Mrs Myer tells anyone who will listen how you are uncultivated and allowed to do as you please by your father, who refuses to rein you in and indulges you.'

Evie stiffened at the character assassination.

'Then you told me you never wanted to marry. Miss Bellingham reminds me of it all the time when she speaks of you. I should never have listened to any of them, but I saw you in the alley...'

'Sophie.' A wave of guilt washed over her. Her friend's name was a slap in the face.

'I convinced myself you were not the one for me.'

'How could you assume that when we have barely spent any time together?'

'Because I thought I knew best. You were new and fresh and tantalising and so desirable...'

'But?'

'But you have a reputation of speaking your mind, of breaking the barriers of what is acceptable. The whole town finds you unusual. You ride astride, for God's sake!'

'And that makes me unworthy of you?' she asked incredulously.

'Not only that. I saw you in an alley with a man, which you denied so there must be something to hide for you will not tell me who it was and why you were there.'

'Because it is none of your business!' she flared.

'Miss Bellingham told me you long for India and you have no wish to marry. She also told me of you leading her into escapades such as swimming *naked* in the river.'

Evie laughed but it wasn't a happy sound, rather one of disbelief. 'How easily you are offended, Mr Lucas.'

'No, I am not. Your uniqueness enthrals me. I hunger for you like a drowning man needs air.'

'But I also repel you with my actions?'

He ran his fingers through his hair. 'I am not articulating my thoughts as I wish to.'

'Oh, no, Mr Lucas, you are making yourself very plain indeed. I am fully aware that I am not up to standard, not *your* standards, at least. I am merely good enough for a passionate embrace when the mood catches you.' She gave him a filthy look of contempt. 'But I *am* worthy and better than you believe.'

'Miss Davenport, please listen to me. What I mean is I have made a mistake in choosing or allowing myself to be chosen, for a better way of putting it, to be directed towards Miss Bellingham when it is you that I want. I simply didn't realise until it was too late.'

His words delighted her for a sweet second or two. *He wanted her.* 'Too late?'

Evie thought of her best friend and how she had betrayed her twice now by kissing Alexander. It was so difficult to behave around him. Her instinct was to throw away all sense and just *feel* and *act*. Only she mustn't, not with him. Instead, she spoke of Sophie. 'Sophie loves you.'

'Yes, I believe she does.'

'Do you love her?'

'No. I admire her and care for her, but I do not love her.'

He did not love Sophie. Evie clamped down on that flare of relief. 'She wants to be your wife.'

'Her whole family wants that, as does my father. And I pride myself on being an honourable man.'

'They expect an engagement announcement at the ball in June.'

'I know.' He sounded like a condemned man.

'Sophie would make a better wife than me. She knows all the right people and knows all the correct things to say. She will raise her children properly, whereas I'll let mine run wild, should I ever have any.' Evie kept her head up, back straight, despite her despair of pushing him away. 'Sophie is good and beautiful and perfect.'

'But she is not you.'

'You do not know *me*, Mr Lucas,' she whispered, forcing lightness into her voice. 'I would make a terrible wife. I do not like rules. Papa says I am too headstrong. Make Sophie happy and propose to her.' The words had to be said, but it wounded her to say them. A part of her wanted to fling herself into his arms and hang the consequences, and if it had been any other person but Sophie, she would have done and to hell with propriety.

'And what of my happiness, or yours?' He looked as wretched as she felt.

'We have betrayed Sophie twice. I shall not do it a third time. Good day, Mr Lucas.' Evie turned her back on him and walked to where Star cropped at some grass. She gathered the reins up and quickly mounted, grateful once again for riding astride and the easy way to mount. The irony was not lost on her as she rode away.

8

The cool interior of the haberdashery shop in Bingley gave a small respite from the hot May day outside. Evie studied the colourful display of bolts of materials and admired the fine lacework collars and cuffs in a glass-fronted cabinet.

The shop owner, Mrs Stewart, had her back turned to Evie as she assisted two other women in choosing yards of material. 'Oh yes, I am supplying a great many different materials to the dressmakers in this town for the Bellingham ball. It will be the event of the year.'

Evie listened to them talk as she strolled around the shop until the two other women left with their purchases and Mrs Stewart gave her attention to Evie.

'Miss Davenport, how lovely to see you. It has been a while since you were here.' Mrs Stewart smiled warmly as she rolled up a bolt of green taffeta. 'Your father is well?'

'Good day, Mrs Stewart. He is, thank you.'

'I am pleased to hear it. What may I help you with today?'

'I am in need of some embroidery thread and linen for a tablecloth. I have the measurements with me.' From her small bag she took out a piece of paper. 'One of our tablecloths is ruined with stains and needs replacing.'

Mrs Stewart read the note. 'I can sort that for you. Are you ready for the ball next month?'

'As much as I ever will be. I have been concentrating on Papa's recovery.'

'Of course you have, my dear. Is your gown ready?' Mrs Stewart pulled out a drawer of embroidery thread and selected the colours Evie had written down.

'I am wearing a gown previously bought. I have not had the time or inclination to spend hours with a seamstress.'

'That is to be expected. You will look spectacular no matter what you wear.'

Evie thought of the cream gown she hoped to wear. Sophie had wanted her to have something new made but Evie couldn't face it, not with Papa becoming more sullen and aloof with every passing day. Dr MacClay said illnesses can affect the mind sometimes, but Evie knew her beloved papa was simply missing Mama and was finding it harder each day to cope.

'Did you want lace-edged linen for the tablecloth or plain?' Mrs Stewart asked.

'I would rather the lace, please.'

'One-inch edging or three inches?'

'Three inches, thank you.' Evie stepped to the far wall where more bolts of material were on display. She ran her gloved hand across the array of wool, silk, taffeta and crêpe before scouting at the very bottom a bolt of silk whose colours danced in the sunshine streaming into the window.

Bending down, Evie pulled out the bolt a little more to inspect it. The shimmering colours of soft blues and cream in delicate swirls caught Evie's breath.

'It is beautiful, isn't it?' Mrs Stewart said, coming to stand beside her. She took the bolt out of the shelves and, taking it to a large table at the side of the room, she opened it out like a shimmering wave.

'I've never seen such a design.'

'It was a special offer I was given by a supplier, but it hasn't sold. I think it is too showy for the likes around here. Such a splendid design would sell well in Bradford or Leeds or even Manchester for evening gowns.'

'I adore it.' Evie touched the soft material.

'It would make a glorious gown with white lace, don't you agree?'

'How I wish I had seen this weeks ago. I would have had it made into a gown.'

'For the ball?'

Evie nodded. The ball had been pushed from her mind. She wasn't keen to attend. To watch Sophie and Alexander together would be challenging and if an announcement was made, she'd have to pretend to be happy for them.

'There is still time.'

'Every seamstress is busy. Miss Sophie Bellingham told me only yesterday that there is a waiting list of eight weeks at her seamstress' salon in Leeds.'

Mrs Stewart looked thoughtfully at the material. 'It has been some years since I made a ball gown, but I can do it.'

Hope flared in Evie. 'You could make a gown for me?'

'I can start on it today. I can do it between serving customers and at night. My Gerald works night shifts at the printer's, so my evenings are spent alone.'

'And you believe there is time? It is only four weeks away.'

'If I take your measurements now, I can get started this afternoon. I'd like to think I haven't lost my touch, and who knows, it might make other ladies think of me and my establishment differently if I can create such a glorious gown for you.'

'Thank you.' Evie clasped Mrs Stewart's hand, knowing that by wearing such a beautiful gown she would look her very best and that would be an armour in which to face the evening.

Later, when she left the shop and walked down Main Street, she considered her decision. For Sophie's sake she would go to the ball, and to do so she would need to guard her emotions. Alexander's words that he'd spoken on the moor, after his fall, still haunted her. She had not seen him in the weeks since that day. She called at Bellingham Hall to visit Sophie once a week and only in the mornings when she believed Alexander would be at his mill.

At church each Sunday they left immediately after service and she had refused all invitations since Papa's heart seizure, especially the two cards that had arrived recently from Alexander wanting to call.

'Evie!' Sophie called from a passing carriage window.

Walking to where the carriage stopped, Evie smiled at Sophie. 'I thought you were travelling to Keighley today?'

'Mama cancelled. She has a slight sniffle. Instead, I have been tasked to call upon the wine merchant's and give them the final order. Do you want to come with me?'

'Why not?' Evie stepped up into the carriage.

Dawson's Wine Merchant's was located on the edge of town next to the canal. Evie had never been as Papa had his order sent straight to the house.

'Shall we have luncheon afterwards at Mrs Golding's Tea Shop? I have been starving myself for the seamstress and this gown she is making. So, I fancy to treat myself with a slice of cake.'

'Lemon cake or fruit cake?' Evie chuckled.

'Both!'

'Perfect.'

'And finger sandwiches with ham and pickle.'

'With coffee!' Evie declared.

'Goodness, no. Tea is drunk at luncheon. Coffee is too masculine.'

'I drink coffee,' Evie protested.

'Yes, but you have strange ways.' Sophie grinned before giving her a playful nudge. 'I adore your strange ways, so never change.'

Evie tucked her arm though Sophie's. 'Why could your papa not make this appointment, or your brother Paul?'

'Papa is in London and Paul been dispatched to Newcastle on family business. Mama was fretting that the order hasn't been confirmed. I have never seen her so distracted over organising a ball. She has done it every year for years, yet this time she is upsetting herself over every little thing. It is unlike her.'

Evie glanced out the window at the passing people walking along the side of the road. 'There is nothing wrong with wanting everything to be perfect when so many people are attending.'

Sophie twisted her hands in her lap. 'I think she is more concerned as to whether Alexander will propose to me, and we can announce the news that night.'

'And will he?' Evie dared to ask.

'I honestly do not know.' A moment later, a large tear trickled down Sophie's cheek.

'Sophie! What is it?'

'I cannot bear to mention it.'

'What? I am your friend; you can tell me anything.'

Sophie wiped her eyes, but more tears fell. 'I believe Alexander may have changed his mind about me.'

Evie stared at her, relieved it wasn't more serious, such as an illness. 'Why do you say that?'

'He has not called at the hall for weeks.' Sophie's pained look upset Evie.

How dare Alexander play with her friend's emotions this way? He needed to make his intentions clear to Sophie one way or another. She patted Sophie's hand. 'He may be incredibly busy.'

'He does not work the whole clock round!' Sophie sighed sadly. 'How can it be that I fall more in love with him every day and yet I am not in his thoughts, or he would visit me?'

'Have you gone to call on him at the mill or his home?'

'No. It would not be seemly to do so. I cannot visit him by myself. Imagine the talk.'

'Nonsense! Heavens, Soph, it is time you stood up for yourself and what you want. You are always too worried about other people's opinions of you. An innocent visit to his mill can hardly raise a whisper of scandal. The whole district knows you are friends. You can talk to him in the mill's yard in front of people if you prefer so everything is above board.'

'Mama said I must never be alone with a man, not ever, unless he is my husband.'

'Your mama is too strict. Do you think all women who walk down the aisle are innocents?'

Sophie gasped. 'Evie!'

'Well, be reasonable and sensible about it.' Evie felt very much older than Sophie in every way. 'The mill is filled with people; you are in no danger of anyone thinking the worst of you simply because you paid a visit of a few minutes.' She noticed they had pulled into the merchant's yard. 'Dry your eyes.'

'Perhaps we should come back later?' Sophie dabbed at her eyes and adjusted her bonnet.

'We are here now. Come on.'

They were shown into the office of the owner, Mr Dawson.

'I am extremely honoured your family have bestowed this large order on us, Miss Bellingham.' Mr Dawson waved them to a seat opposite his desk.

'Your business has been supplying us for some years, Mr Dawson. It is only natural that we would continue our relationship for such an event.' Sophie, her eyelashes still wet, appeared as a tender, pretty young woman of impeccable breeding and class.

'And we thank you for it.' Mr Dawson flipped through some papers until he found what he was looking for and frowned. 'Mrs Bellingham was clear in her instructions on the types of wines she wanted to order; however, there are one or two we are having trouble acquiring.'

'Oh?' Sophie said anxiously.

'We have some alternatives. Would you care to sample them?' Mr Dawson asked.

'Yes, we would,' Evie replied for Sophie, knowing her friend would decline. She turned to Sophie with a wide smile. 'Let us have some fun and have an input over what is served on the night.'

'I could not, Evie. Mama would not want me to make such a decision by myself.'

'Blame me, then.' Evie beamed at Mr Dawson. 'What shall we start with first?'

An hour later, deep in the cellar of Dawson's Wine Merchant's, Evie and Sophie sat on a wooden bench sipping another sample of white wine. Lanterns spilled out golden light, which banished the dark into the far corners. Although it was cool in the cellar, it wasn't terribly cold. Workers rolled barrels onto trolleys, which were hoisted up to the warehouse floor above and put on canal barges.

Mr Dawson and his two sons, Bobby and George, strapping young men the same age as Evie and Sophie, were very attentive to them. Glass after glass of different wines arrived and they sipped and discussed the flavours until one wine resembled another.

'I like this one better than the last,' Evie said, feeling a little light-headed.

'They all taste the same now.' Sophie hiccupped. 'Even the red and white taste the same.' She giggled.

'They do not! One is red and one is white!' Evie suddenly found it hilarious.

Sophie laughed and held up her empty glass. 'May I have a sam... sample of that one again?' She pointed to a heavy red wine from Burgundy.

Mr Dawson Senior shook his head anxiously. 'I do believe you have had your limit, Miss Bellingham. I fear you may have sampled too many. Your mother will be expecting you home.'

Sophie stood and swayed. 'We have outstayed our welcome, Evie...' She swayed again, her eyes closing.

'Steady now, miss.' George, a large, burly young man with a pleasant face, hurried to hold her upright.

'You are terri... terribly big...' Sophie leaned close to stare up at him. 'Such arms...'

Evie stood, her focus wavering slightly. The steep staircase they'd come down would be impossible to get back up without help. The trolley was winched back down and workers, giving the two ladies a laughing glance, rushed to wheel more wine barrels onto it.

'I want to go on that!' Evie pointed to the trolley.

'Oh no, Miss Davenport.' Mr Dawson held up his hands in protest and seemed ready to pass out at the idea.

'Those steps are dangerous!' Sophie declared. 'I nearly broke my neck coming down.'

'Ladies, we will help you up the stairs.'

'No. We shall ascend on that.' Determined to climb on the trolley, Evie knocked away Mr Dawson's hand that he held out to stop her. She realised she still held her glass of wine and gulped it down in one go before passing the empty glass to an amused Bobby Dawson.

'Move the barrels, men,' Bobby instructed.

Laughing, the men removed the barrels from the trolley. 'Isn't this a sight?' one of them yelled.

Bobby gave assistance to Evie to step onto the trolley. 'Hold on to the side, Miss Davenport.'

'Sophie, hurry up,' Evie encouraged.

'Gracious me.' Sophie stepped on board, giggling. She missed the side of the trolley and nearly fell to her knees, which made her laugh even more.

Bobby helped Sophie upright. 'This is a first. Women on our trolley.'

'Good God!' Mr Dawson rubbed his eyes. 'We'll never have another Bellingham order again once this is known around the district.'

'It ain't our fault, is it? They wouldn't stop drinking.' George grinned.

'We are giving the ladies what they want.' Bobby's eyes narrowed as he stared at Evie. 'What a pair of beauties,' he whispered.

Evie heard him and gave him a saucy wink. The wine had given her normal boldness an extra lift. 'Take us up, my good man!'

'I wish I could do a lot more, miss, but up we go.'

Sophie squealed then laughed as the trolley jerked its way slowly up to the warehouse floor above.

At the top, the trolley jolted, and Evie lurched.

Bobby took her arm. He was very close. 'Steady there, miss.'

'That was enormous fun.' Sophie clapped. 'Let us do it again.'

'No, I think not, Miss Bellingham.' Bobby aided them out of the trolley while Mr Dawson waited at the carriage.

'You must go straight home, ladies.' Mr Dawson looked eager to see them gone. 'Tell Mrs Bellingham her order will be delivered two days before the ball.'

'You have been marvellous, Mr Dawson,' Sophie proclaimed, her eyes half closed.

'I'll be finished, more like,' he grumbled as George handed Sophie and then Evie up into the carriage.

'It'll be fine, Father.' Bobby slapped him on the back. 'Miss Bellingham has ordered a dozen cases more than was on the original order. Be happy.'

Evie leaned out of the window. 'Thank you, Mr Dawson, for your hospitality.'

'You are welcome, Miss Davenport.' Mr Dawson shook his head. 'Driver, take them the long way home. They have imbibed a little too much of the samples.'

Evie rested her head back against the cushioned seat as the carriage rolled away. 'That was entertaining.'

Sophie's head lolled against her shoulder. 'We did not go to luncheon.'

'Another time.'

'I have the best times when I am with you,' Sophie slurred. 'I never want to be without you.'

Evie took her hand. 'You shan't be, ever.'

'Good. I want you to be godmother to my and Alexander's children...'

Alexander. The calm happiness the alcohol had given her disappeared like mist on a summer's day. Evie sighed deeply as Sophie gave a little snore.

* * *

Evie fiddled with her lace gloves; a small thread had come loose, and she was concerned it would develop into a hole.

Papa tapped her hand gently in rebuke and nodded towards the pulpit where Reverend Peabody droned on about sacrifices God expected from his worshippers for the good of their souls.

They stood to sing a hymn and as Evie began, she noticed Sophie on the other side of the aisle giving her strange looks and nods. Evie raised her eyebrows back at her until Mrs Bellingham's stern stare made her concentrate on the hymn.

Afterwards, walking out into the sunshine, Evie shook hands with the reverend and waited for Papa to have a word with him.

Grabbed by the arm, she was wrenched away by Sophie.

'What are you doing?'

'Mama is furious.' Sophie's eyes darted about like a scared rabbit.

'Why?'

'She has found out about us drinking the samples at Dawson's.'

'And?'

'And she is livid with us for making a spectacle of ourselves in front of a warehouse full of men!'

'How did she find out?'

'Gossip, obviously! Bingley is too small to keep something like that a secret.' Sophie looked ready to cry. 'Our reputations are ruined! Alexander will not want to marry me now.' Tears ran down her cheeks.

'I am sure it is not as bad as you think,' Evie soothed.

'Evie.' Papa called for her where he stood talking to Mrs Bellingham. The expression on his face showed concern.

'Mama has told your papa,' Sophie wailed.

'United front,' Evie said, linking her arm through Sophie's as they walked to their parents. 'Let me do the talking.'

'Evie, my dear,' Papa said, his tone gentle. 'Mrs Bellingham has come to me with an alarming report. She has heard that you and Sophie were drunk, in public. This must be a falsehood, surely?'

She had never lied to her papa; it was never something she had

had to do, or wanted to do. Their relationship was one where they could speak plainly. 'Papa, we sampled some of Mr Dawson's wines to select a few different ones for the Bellinghams' ball.'

Mrs Bellingham grimaced. 'The *gossip* all over the district is that you both were so drunk you had to be aided to the carriage and not only that' – she lowered her voice angrily low – 'you made fools of yourselves by riding in the warehouse's trolley lift as though you were at some country fair!'

'Evie?' Surprise widened Papa's eyes. 'Is this true?'

Sophie stepped forward. 'It is true. We are extremely sorry, Major Davenport.' Sophie cried into her handkerchief.

'Papa.' Evie put her hand on his arm. 'We made an error of judgement.'

'It will never happen again,' Sophie added, her face pale. 'I have promised Mama that it will be my first and last time I will ever be drunk.'

Mrs Bellingham snorted in disgust at Sophie. 'See that it is, young lady, or your papa will not be kept in the dark about it next time. I will defend you this time, but such behaviour is intolerable.' She stared at Evie. 'Do I make myself clear?'

'Yes, Mrs Bellingham.' Evie nodded, then, taking Papa's arm, made a quick exit from the churchyard.

'What possessed you, my dear? To behave so vulgarly. Drunk in public!' Papa handed her up into the carriage. 'I deem it my fault.' He sighed heavily. 'I have given you free rein to do as you please. All your life you have been allowed to roam free.'

'You have a right to be disappointed in my behaviour. I did wrong. But it happened without devious intent, I promise you. We made a mistake in drinking too much. But we were having fun. You always encouraged me to have fun, Papa.'

'That is true, but you must be sensible in what you decide is entertaining, my dear. I have always trusted you to be prudent.'

Evie waved to a few people they knew as the carriage left the village and headed up the lane towards home. 'I made an error of judgement, Papa. Forgive me.'

'Of course I do.' He patted her hand. 'You are my daughter.'

'I expect there will be some scandal about it.' The whole episode made her want to giggle.

'Only for a little while until something else comes along to displace it in people's minds.' Papa gave her a small smile. 'You are a grown woman. You know that one must reap what one sows.'

'Yes, Papa.'

'The talk will circle the drawing rooms for a short time and then be forgotten.'

'It's only forgotten if the person stays quiet and good. The minute they do something unusual or speak out of turn then all the old gossip is brought out again for another feast.'

'Then you must refrain from causing any more scandal.'

'I seem to have a knack for doing the exact opposite, Papa.'

He grinned. 'And I never want you to change.' He leaned closer. 'Was it a hoot?'

She had to laugh. 'Best fun I've had in a very long time.'

Papa chuckled, a sparkle of his old mischief in his eyes. 'Then it was worth it. Though Mrs Bellingham will be sour about it for some time.'

'I feel people have lost the art of laughing, Papa, of having a good time. We used to laugh so much in India, didn't we? At the monkeys stealing food and the fabulous parties we used to attend. Remember when Colonel Finchley started to sing in the middle of a dinner that time and he made us all join in? It was hysterical because his important guest thought we were all mad in the head. And when Mama and Grandmama got lost that day and got carried home on the backs of those Indian workers. How we laughed. And that time I tried one of Cook's new curries and it was so hot I ran and put my head in the horses' water trough? You fell about crying with laughter.'

Papa chuckled.

'So many happy memories.' Evie could name so many more.

His expression saddened. 'We did have many good times, dearest. Your mama's laughter was music to my ears.'

Evie gazed out of the window as the carriage slowed, ready to turn into the drive. A man walked past and looked up at her.

Her dear memories faded as her blood ran cold. Hal Humphry.

9

Shaken by the sight of Hal Humphry, Evie caused no argument when Papa said he was going to his study. She went straight to the kitchen, where the servants were divesting themselves of their coats, having just returned from church also.

'Oh, miss, I'll be sending in a tray shortly,' Mrs Humphry said, putting on her apron. The cook seemed uneasy, troubled.

'I must speak with you and Fanny, please. In the parlour.' She turned on her heel without waiting for them to reply.

Evie unpinned her hat to give her hands something to do as the two women entered.

'Miss?' Fanny's eyes showed her concern. 'Is something wrong?'

'Indeed, very wrong. Hal has returned.'

'How did you know?' Mrs Humphry sagged.

'You knew?' Evie accused.

'The other night, in the storm. He knocked on the back door, but Fanny gave him a piece of her mind and a solid push to send him on his way,' Mrs Humphry admitted. 'He was drunk enough to be too insensible to make more of a fuss.'

'I wondered why you two were huddled together when I came into the kitchen that night.'

'Not that it worked for long,' Fanny scoffed. 'We think he's been loitering about for a couple of weeks. He stole a chicken.'

'And you blamed a fox.' Evie paced the room.

Fanny nodded. 'We told Colin and Mr Bronson about him so they could keep an eye out. They said they saw a man in the woods by the beck and someone crossing the fields behind the house a few times.'

Evie took a deep breath. 'I saw him just now on the lane.'

'Yes.' Mrs Humphry nodded. 'He's back living in the cottage.'

'But you gave the cottage up.'

'The young couple who took it over left when Hal came back. He was only gone for a couple of weeks and returned last month, before Easter. I heard he made their lives a misery, telling them it was his cottage and throwing their things on to the lane. The cottage is in a terrible state and the couple were going to fix it up, but Hal smashed the place and scared them off.'

'I told him to never come back here. I gave him enough money to start again somewhere else.' Rage burned through her at the waste of money and the man's impudence. 'What does he hope to gain by returning here?'

'To harass us.' Mrs Humphry's expression was full of remorse. 'I will leave, Miss Davenport. It's the only answer.'

'Let us not be hasty.' Evie continued pacing, thinking of the best course of action.

'You can't give him any more money,' Mrs Humphry stated. 'It doesn't work. As soon as he's spent it, he'll come back.'

'I agree, which leaves me no choice but to inform the police. I dread doing so for it will upset Papa and he is still not himself.' Evie wondered faintly if he ever would be.

'No, do not concern yourself any more, Miss Davenport. I will leave here and take Hal with me. If the police come sniffing around, it'll send Hal mad and if they arrest him, he'll tell his friends to come here and cause havoc. Leaving is the only option.'

'Will he go with you, though?' Fanny asked doubtfully.

'I have to try. He is my son, my responsibility.'

'Mrs Humphry, he is a grown man. You cannot be responsible for his actions all his life,' Evie said.

'My son is evil, Miss Davenport. Rightly or wrongly, I must have had something to do with that in some way.' The older woman's hands twisted her apron. 'With your permission, I will go to the cottage after the midday meal has been served and speak with Hal. I'll work until the end of the week and then we'll be gone.'

Evie felt out of her depth. 'Is that the correct thing to do?'

Fanny stepped forward. 'If you go, Mrs Humphry, you'll be walking the roads looking for work.'

'And there is no assurance that Hal will not cause trouble for you, no matter where you are,' Evie added.

'What else can I do?' The older woman looked defeated.

'You are to stay here, where you are safe,' Evie decided. 'We shall inform the police that Hal is a menace to us and take it from there.'

'Hal will go mad, Miss Davenport.'

'Then the police can deal with him.'

'They can't watch him every minute of the day and night.'

'I shall go and speak with Papa. He will know what to do.' She left the room and went along to the study. She knocked once and entered. 'Papa, may I have a moment, please?'

He looked up from the letter he was writing. 'My dear, I was just writing to Captain Fitzgerald. You remember him?'

'Of course. He is in your former regiment. Isn't the captain stationed in Calcutta now?'

'Yes. We have been corresponding since I left the regiment. I received a letter from him yesterday. He writes that he has sold his commission in the army and has taken up a position in the Bellingham Railways office.'

Evie sat on a chair by the desk. 'Bellingham Railways? The captain has returned to England?'

Papa tapped the letter. 'No. He is staying in India. Bellingham Railways has recently established an office in Calcutta and is set to build railways on the subcontinent.'

Evie took a moment to process such news. 'Heavens. I did not know that. Sophie never mentioned it.'

'She may not be aware for it is all rather recent and I rather doubt her father informs her of his business choices. Jasper Bellingham has great business sense and the courage to back his decisions. His company's expansion needs good men to steer the progress. Fitzgerald is just the man for the position. I am pleased Jasper took my advice.'

'It is an honour to you that Mr Bellingham listened to what you had to say.'

'And on that note, I shall tell you now that Jasper Bellingham invited me, and others, to buy shares in this business to build those railways in India. I accepted.'

'You have bought into Mr Bellingham's railway business?' The news shocked her. 'You never told me you wanted to invest in our friend's business. Is that wise?'

'Why wouldn't it be?'

'Mixing friendship with business.'

'It is done all over the world, my dear. The deal was all finalised a few days before my heart seizure.'

'You have gone into business with Mr Bellingham.' Evie was surprised. 'I never expected that, Papa. You seemed content to simply be a retired army major.'

'Bellingham convinced me otherwise. I will admit that such business doesn't enthuse me with passion as it does for Bellingham, which is why I remain a silent partner. However, Bellingham is keen to be educated on India using my knowledge, which I am happy to give him. To me, the investment seemed a wise one. So, I invested and hope to see dividends, that is all. If the scheme becomes a moneymaker then your future is set. If not, and I do not forecast that happening, then you will have only a small inheritance from me, and this house. You may want to consider a suitable marriage as your best option.'

'This house is enough for me, Papa. I do not wish to marry.' Although it had always been something she said offhandedly, this time she knew she meant it. Meeting Alexander had changed her. If she couldn't have him, then no other man would come close, so why bother?

'That is your choice, my dear, and one I respect, but it does baffle me as to why. However, that is a discussion for another day. Mr Enoch Latimer is calling tomorrow at one o'clock and will have luncheon with us. He has written to me and said he can call. I know it is short notice, but it is manageable?'

'Indeed, yes. I shall tell Mrs Humphry. Why is your solicitor coming here? You usually meet with him when we go to visit the aunts.'

'With my investing in Bellingham's company, I need to sign some papers and make certain everything is in order.' Papa suddenly appeared tired; the lines on his face were more prominent and his colour pasty. 'I think I should go and lie down for a short time.'

'You are feeling unwell?' She instantly went to his side.

'Do not fuss.' He patted her arm. 'I will rest. Wake me in an hour for luncheon. We shall talk more then.'

She watched him leave the room, slow and shoulders bowed.

Where had her tall, strong papa gone? With each passing day he seemed to shrink before her eyes and grow old.

Without a doubt, she knew that telling him about Hal Humphry would be too much for him. She would have to deal with the man herself. How she would do that, she didn't know.

While Papa slept, Evie took a turn of the garden. Colin worked in the vegetable patch as one of his numerous jobs and had made a fine effort of growing delicious vegetables and herbs for the kitchen. Evie watched him hoe the soil between rows of young potato plants.

'I'll be able to cut some of the early roses for the house, miss,' Colin said.

'I noticed that some are blooming in the front garden by the drive.'

He straightened. 'I prefer vegetables to flowers, miss, but I'll do my best to keep the front gardens flowering. Good manure on them helps.'

'Thank you. Mama loved roses. I would like to plant more.'

'Well, you order the roses, miss, and I'll make another garden bed for them.'

Evie smiled. 'Thank you. I shall send for a catalogue and make an order. Tomorrow I shall need Star saddled in the morning after breakfast; could you tell your father, please?'

'Very good, miss.'

Evie turned away and walked across the lawn to the trees edging the main garden. She stopped at the fence, searching the fields for any sight of Hal Humphry. In the morning she would go to the police. Something had to be done about the man. His reign of terror had to be stopped.

'Miss Davenport.'

She turned and her stomach swooped at the sight of Alexander strolling across the lawn towards her. 'What are you doing here?'

'That is a pleasant greeting.' His wry smile mocked her.

She clenched her teeth. 'Well?'

'I have called to speak with your father.'

'He is napping.'

'Napping?'

'Papa tires easily since his heart seizure. You must return another time.'

'I cannot wait until he wakes? Perhaps have some light refreshment?' His eyebrows rose and his eyes held laughter. 'I would like us to talk awhile.'

'It is not possible.' Looking at him, she soaked in his presence, his handsome face. A gripping need to touch him overwhelmed her.

'Why? Explain why we cannot talk and drink tea?'

Her mind whirled for a decent excuse. 'You know why!'

'Remind me.'

'Please, Mr Lucas, just leave. We cannot be friends or anything else.'

'You refuse to talk to me, but you are happy to get drunk with warehouse men and be the point of scandal in the district?'

She gasped. 'How dare you?'

'How dare I? I speak the truth, do I not? Once again you are the talk of the area. Do you not care that your reputation is unravelling?'

'Actually, no, I do not care and what I do has nothing to do with you.'

'But when you bring Miss Bellingham down with you, then that does affect me for I have to keep it a secret from her father, and he is a good friend.'

She turned away and started back for the house. 'I think it wise for you to leave. I shall tell Papa you called.'

He touched her hand to stop her. 'Miss Davenport... Evie.'

'Do not!' She knocked his hand away. 'Do not call me by my first name. We are not friends.'

'You are rejecting my friendship?' He scowled.

'I am rejecting everything about you, Mr Lucas.' She summoned all her strength to put him from her life. What she wanted she couldn't have, and it was torture to think otherwise.

'Is that so?' He took a step nearer, anger emanating from him. 'I recall how not so long ago you very much accepted anything I was willing to give.'

Her corset felt tight under his scrutiny. 'We were very wrong to do what we did.'

'We cannot be friends?'

'No.' It pained her to say it, but she knew it was for the best. 'Please, Mr Lucas, do not come here again.'

'Tell me the truth, do you feel nothing for me?'

Evie sucked in a deep breath. 'I feel nothing for you,' she lied.

A muscle in his jaw twitched. 'How brutal you are, Miss Davenport.'

'It is for the best.'

'For whom?'

'Everyone.'

He bowed. 'Then I shall take my leave. Good day.'

She sagged as he walked away. She watched him go, his long strides, his straight back. She wanted to yell for him to stop, to return and hold her, kiss her, but that could never happen.

* * *

Evie waited for a gentleman to hold the door open for her as he exited the Bingley police station, and she went in. The stark reception area held a few chairs and a high partition, behind which a policeman sat. An old woman leaned against the far wall, hunched over and muttering to herself. Evie had never been in a police station before and wasn't sure what to expect. Obviously, she hadn't thought it would be a homely type of place, but nor had she thought it would be a cold, stone-walled dungeon of bleakness.

The policeman glanced at her as she approached. 'May I help you, miss?'

'Yes. I wish to speak to someone about a man who is harassing me and my staff.'

'Wait there, miss.' He climbed down from his position, which seemed to be built on a higher floor than that out the front. Behind him were several doors and he disappeared through one.

Evie moved to one side as the front door opened and a man was roughly ushered in by a policeman. The pair argued their way to a far door near the old woman. A scuffle broke out with the old woman lashing out at the policeman and the man he held.

Darting further away, Evie thought to leave and come back another time, but on the other side of the room, an officer came out and beckoned her to him. She gladly fled the warring threesome.

'Good morning, Miss...?' The officer waved her to a seat in a small box room with a narrow window high in the wall.

'Davenport. Miss Evie Davenport.'

'I'm Sergeant Coleridge. How may I help you?'

'There is a man, Hal Humphry. He is the son of my cook and recently freed from prison. He has been causing trouble for his mother and has been stalking around my home. I was hoping the police could see him on his way?'

'Miss Davenport, has the man broken the law?'

'He beats his mother. He accosted me while I was out riding.'

'Why hasn't his mother laid charges against him? Or you for that matter?'

'His mother didn't want to cause a fuss. She is frightened of him. I did not report his assault because my father is ill. I was hoping one of your men could speak with him, tell him to move on and that would be an end to it?' This was one of the times she wished she was a man so she could take care of such issues herself. If she'd been a man, she'd have squared up to Hal and given him a good thrashing!

The sergeant shook his head. 'Unless the man has broken the law, Miss Davenport, there is nothing we can do. What did he do to you?'

'He grabbed my leg and demanded money.'

Coleridge took a notebook out of his pocket and started writing. 'Did he have a weapon?'

'No, not that I am aware of.'

'And his beating of Mrs Humphry. Were there witnesses?'

'No... He has come to my home and threatened me and his mother.'

'Trespassing.' Coleridge nodded. 'Has he stolen anything from your property?'

'A chicken.'

'Is there proof? Witnesses?'

'No.'

'So, it could have been a fox?'

'Well, we believe it was him.' She felt useless at failing to build a proper case against Hal. It all sounded feeble even to her ears.

'Will his mother come and make a claim against her son?'

'I believe so, yes. She would not at first, but her feelings have changed since he has begun harassing me.'

'If you and Mrs Humphry make formal complaints, we can speak with Hal Humphry, which could lead to his arrest and trial. Are you both aware of that?'

'He is evil, Sergeant Coleridge. Mrs Humphry wants him gone from her life. We all do. I gave him money to go away, but he's returned.'

Coleridge stared at her in surprise. 'Miss Davenport, giving money to an ex-prisoner is not something I would recommend.'

'It was foolish of me, I know that now, but at the time I thought it would put an end to his harassment.'

'Where does he live, do you know?'

'He's been staying in a cottage in Lylston Village that his mother rented, but she gave it up and came to live in my home.' She gave the address and a description of the miscreant.

'Very good.' He wrote a few more lines. 'I shall send one of my men over to pay him a visit and that may make him mend his ways, but I highly doubt it. Unless you or his mother make a formal complaint, there is nothing else we can do without proof.'

'Then I shall make a formal complaint,' she decided.

The sergeant gave her a fatherly smile. 'Are you sure you want to go through a court hearing regarding this matter?'

'A court hearing?'

'Once Mr Humphry is arrested, you, his mother and any other witnesses will be summoned to the court to give your stories before the judge.'

Evie blanched. She could not do that to Papa. He couldn't take such a public demonstration of her being in court, or his staff. He needed a quiet life until he was fully recovered.

'Miss Davenport?'

'I... my parent is unwell and to put him through the embarrassment of his daughter and his household going to court...' Papa's heart would not handle that.

Sergeant Coleridge closed his notebook. 'I understand. I will have one of my men speak to this Hal Humphry.'

'Thank you.'

'I warn you, though, it may not do any good at all.'

Evie stood. 'Anything you can do will be something. It might be enough to scare him and send him on his way.' She didn't believe her words but had to hold on to something positive.

Coleridge escorted her out to the front door. 'If anything else happens, come to us straight away.'

'Thank you, Sergeant.'

'Do you wish for me to report back to you after we have spoken to him?'

'I shall come here next week. I do not want Papa disturbed about this issue.'

'As you wish, Miss Davenport.'

Frustrated, she left the building and walked along the street to the stables where Star was being cared for. What more could she do? A court hearing and all the scandal associated with it would be ill-timed with Papa's illness. If he was strong like he had been in India, then she knew he'd be right beside her, demanding justice. He'd likely want to shoot Hal himself! However, Papa wasn't the man he once was, and she had to protect him. She couldn't live with herself if her actions made him more unwell.

A carriage stopped beside her, and Mrs Myer poked her head out of the window. 'Did I just see you leave the police station?'

Evie sighed. 'You did, Mrs Myer.'

'What on earth possessed you to enter such a place alone? Where is the major?'

'At home, resting. He had a bad night.'

'And he allowed you to go there unaccompanied? What reason would you have to do so?'

'Mrs Myer, what I do is none of your concern. Good day.'

'I insist you tell me, or I shall report this meeting to your father, for I am guessing he has no knowledge of it. You are determined to lose your reputation.'

A wave of rage flowed over Evie. The woman was impossible.

'Papa is not well enough to be bothered about this, Mrs Myer, and it is *none* of your business.'

'Your father is my friend, so I shall make it my business if he is unable to do so for the good of *his* reputation. Is it not enough that he has a daughter who gets drunk in public, but who now frequents such establishments as police stations? The poor man doesn't deserve such a child.'

Evie wanted to climb into the carriage and slap the woman senseless, but of course she couldn't and instead she tried to remain calm. 'I was simply reporting a sighting of a poacher, Mrs Myer. We have lost some chickens and it wasn't a fox.'

The statement took the wind out of Mrs Myer's sails, and she appeared disappointed. 'A poacher? That is all?'

'Indeed.'

'Well, why did you not say so? And forgive me for wanting to protect the major from wagging tongues but I sincerely beg you to be more circumspect. Such a report to the police can be given by you in a letter, or you could send a servant. There was no need to go there yourself and mix with the degenerates of society.'

'I was passing. It saved time.'

'A piece of advice, if I may,' Mrs Myer continued. 'Your reputation is suffering at the moment. You need to be diligent, or it will be ruined beyond repair.'

'I do not welcome your advice. It may be kindly meant but it is unwarranted. Good day, Mrs Myer.' Evie regally bowed her head and walked on.

'At this rate you will have difficulty finding a decent husband,' Mrs Myer called out.

Evie ignored her and walked into the nearest shop, a bookshop. She closed her eyes and took a moment to breathe.

'Miss Davenport,' Mr Fairhurst declared, coming over to her. 'Are you ailing?'

Surprised to see him in Bingley, she forced a smile. 'No, Mr Fairhurst, I am well, thank you. I did not know you were back visiting the Bellinghams.'

'I arrived last night and will stay until after the ball.' He pushed his glasses further up his nose. 'You are attending the ball?'

'I am.'

'Then I must beg a dance from you, if I may?'

'Certainly.'

'My cousins are most excited by the upcoming event. Lydia is all aflutter that an engagement will be announced between Sophie and Mr Alexander Lucas. An excellent match, do you not agree?'

'Absolutely. Excuse me, I must be getting back.' She turned and opened the door.

'But you have not bought anything?'

Evie shrugged one shoulder. 'I have forgotten an appointment, silly me. Must hurry. Goodbye.'

She wondered if this day could get any worse as she rushed to the stables and ordered Star to be brought out. Was it possible to have one day without thinking of Mrs Myer or Alexander or Hal Humphry?

10

'Well, Miss Davenport. I can affirm this is the most beautiful dress I have ever seen.' Mrs Stewart twitched the lace and adjusted the small blue-ribbon bows attached on the short sleeves of the ball gown.

Evie stood facing the cheval mirror and took in the dress – the part she could see, anyway, for the dress spread out over the crinoline cage in all its magnificent glory.

'You look beautiful, miss,' Fanny said in awe. She'd spent an hour arranging Evie's light brown hair into an elegant halo of loose curls secured with mother-of-pearl combs, hairpins and small white rosebuds.

'You will outshine every other young lady there,' Mrs Stewart stated, standing back to check the gown was correct in every way.

Evie smoothed the silk, acknowledging the woman's handiwork and skill. The blue and silver swirl pattern suited Evie's colouring. The off-the-shoulder design enhanced her delicate collarbones and graceful neck while the tight, fitted bodice sculpted Evie's slender waist. 'Thank you, Mrs Stewart. The gown is perfect.'

'I enjoyed creating such a dazzling gown.' Mrs Stewart packed away her tools of trade. She'd brought the dress to the house that afternoon for the final fitting and adjustments, then stayed to help Evie don the gown after her bath. 'But I'd best be getting home before my husband thinks I'm not returning.'

'I shall call in and see you tomorrow and let you know how the evening went,' Evie said, slipping on silver elbow-length gloves.

'I look forward to it, miss.'

Alone with Fanny, Evie scrutinised her reflection. The gown was perfection. Wearing it gave her the confidence to face an engagement announcement between Sophie and Alexander.

Going downstairs, she paused as Papa stood at the bottom dressed in a splendid black suit.

He gave her a wide smile. 'You look glorious, my dear.'

His appraisal meant the world to her. 'Thank you, Papa. I want to do you proud.'

'My dear, you always do me proud. That gown is stunning. You will outshine every woman there. How beautiful you have become. It saddens me that your poor mama is missing such a night, but more so that she has not witnessed the woman you have become.' He draped a navy-blue velvet cape edged with white fur around her shoulders.

'Mama is always in our thoughts. For her we shall have a pleasant evening,' she told him, walking out to the carriage.

'And so we shall.'

She glanced at him and noticed he seemed lighter of mood this evening. His face wasn't creased with pain or exhaustion. The summer sun had set an hour ago, but full darkness hadn't enveloped the land just yet despite the late hour. Pinks and orange hues streaked the sky. Birds dived and soared on the air currents of a warm June night.

At the hall, they waited in the line-up to enter through the front doors. Evie grew nervous about seeing Alexander, which was silly really. She had told him to leave her alone and he had done. To that end, in the last two weeks she had only seen Sophie a few times and believed Mrs Bellingham had orchestrated for the two of them not to spend as much time together as before, which was sad but understandable. The episode at Dawson's hadn't been forgotten by Mrs Bellingham, but Evie refused to change who she was to please others.

Still, tonight Evie wanted to dance and have a lovely time, and she could keep a smile on her face when the announcement came and give nothing away of her true feelings.

'Ah, Major!' Mrs Myer pounced on them immediately after they had removed their outerwear and before they were able to move into the ballroom.

'Good evening, Mrs Myer.' Papa bowed over her hand.

'So formal, Major?' the woman tittered. 'I thought we were past formalities?' Her eyes narrowed with appraisal at Evie. 'Goodness. What a gown.'

'Is she not beautiful?' Papa asked proudly.

'The pattern is charming.' Mrs Myer's face froze on the compliment as though it pained her to utter it. 'Now, Major, I insist on a dance, several in fact.'

'If I am feeling up to it, I may honour your request. However, first, I have promised my daughter the first dance and I will see how I get on after that.'

'Papa, if you do not feel ready to dance, you mustn't do so.' Evie gripped his arm that she held.

'One dance will be fine.' He gave her a wink, to prove he was feeling well. 'Shall we?'

'You must be delighted for Sophie?' Mrs Myer said, trailing after them into the ballroom.

Evie ignored her remark and turned to greet Mr and Mrs

Bellingham, who stood at the entrance to the large ornate room and welcomed their guests.

'You are a stunning picture, dear Miss Davenport,' Mr Bellingham said, bowing over her hand. 'Major, your daughter is glorious.'

Papa grinned. 'Indeed, Jasper, she is.'

'Your gown is superb, Evie.' Mrs Bellingham kissed her cheek. 'I have never seen a pattern like it, at least not around here. Is it from London?'

'I shall tell you all about it later, Mrs Bellingham, as I am holding up the line.' Evie noticed the stretch of guests behind them.

'Go and find Sophie. She is in the dining room checking the refreshments for me.'

Evie nodded and moved away with Papa, who was conversing with Mr Gresham, the Bellinghams' solicitor. The three of them stepped to one side of the ballroom as people chatted and greeted each other.

The musicians, situated on a raised dais at the end of the room, played a final soft note and then paused for a moment before they began again, signalling the start of the dancing.

'Evie.' Papa held out his arm and led her to the middle of the dance floor. They were soon joined by others.

The swell of the music lifted Evie like nothing else as Papa swirled her about the ballroom.

'You are as light as a feather, my dear.' Papa grinned. 'Your lessons have paid off.'

'Do you feel well?'

He nodded. 'At this moment, I feel the best I have in a long time.'

Relieved, Evie relaxed and enjoyed the waltz. She noticed the admiring glances from the men in the room and the whispers of the women as they studied her and Papa dancing. The dress she wore was the best in the room, she knew that without any false modesty, and that was down to Mrs Stewart and the unique colours and subtle pattern. She had never looked as good as she did tonight and Papa was feeling better, which meant she could cope with anything the evening brought.

Once the dance ended, Evie declined more dance offers from young men. 'Papa, I shall find Sophie.' Evie left him and Mr Gresham and circled around the swiftly filling ballroom towards the dining room. The path between the two rooms was thronged with people and so Evie slipped out of a French door and along the terrace that went the length of the hall.

'Miss Davenport.' Alexander walked the garden path below the terrace.

Evie stopped and clutched her hands together. He looked so handsome in his black suit and crisp white shirt. She wanted to run down to him, but knew it was impossible. 'How are you, Mr Lucas?'

'Well, thank you.'

'Are you coming inside to dance?'

'As much as I would wish to dance with you all night, Miss Davenport, it is not to be. I am just leaving.'

'Leaving?' Shocked, she stared at him. 'The night has only just begun.'

'I feel it would be more… agreeable if I left.'

'Oh.' She didn't understand and he clearly wasn't going to tell her why.

'You look divine. I knew you would.'

She blushed at his compliment because she believed he meant it and wasn't simply being polite. 'Thank you.'

'From where I am standing, you appear as brilliant as any portrait. I wish I could dance with you.'

Unable to stay away from him, she went to the steps and walked down to the garden below.

He met her halfway. Another couple walked past them, and Alexander held out his hand in a proper greeting as though they had just met by chance. 'Good evening, Miss Davenport.'

She slipped her gloved hand into his. The touch even through the material sizzled up her arm and straight to her heart. 'Good evening, Mr Lucas.'

His eyes devoured her. 'You are magnificent,' he whispered.

Her body swelled in delight. 'Do you have to leave?'

Instantly, his gaze lowered to the ground, and he dropped her hand. 'I do. Tonight... Let us just say that tonight will be remembered for all the wrong reasons.'

'That sounds intriguing,' she murmured, memorising every detail of his face.

From the open doors and windows, the sound of music drifted out, accompanied by laughter and talking.

Every ounce of her wanted him to say something more, to take her hand again. 'Then I will say goodnight, Mr Lucas.'

He bowed, a look of regret in his eyes. 'Goodnight, Miss Davenport. Enjoy your evening.'

When he had gone, she went up onto the terrace and into the dining room. There was no sign of Sophie. She entered the ballroom and failed to see her there either.

'My dear?' Papa came beside her. 'Are we to dance?'

'Again?' She grinned. 'You will tire yourself out.'

He tilted his head. 'Listen, it is your mama's favourite piece of music.'

'Oh yes, it is. Chopin.'

'We must dance to it.' Papa took her elbow and guided her into the middle of the room. Filled with nostalgia, Papa closed his eyes briefly and waltzed Evie around the room. So many times, in the past, she had watched her parents dance to this music. Unlike the first dance, Evie couldn't relax and enjoy this one as much. Alexander's early departure caused her to dwell on the reason why. With Alexander not at the ball, there could be no engagement announcement. She was both curious and worried by the thought.

When the notes drifted away, Evie kissed her papa's cheek, noticing a glistening in his eyes. 'I was a poor second to Mama.' She smiled.

'No, it was exactly what I needed.' He squeezed her hand lovingly.

'Major! Major!' Mrs Myer came up to them. 'What a lovely sight I just witnessed. I implore you to waltz with me next.'

Papa bowed, but the light died from his eyes. 'I think one more dance is all I have left in me. Then I shall rest.' He touched Evie's cheek tenderly. 'I am fine, before you ask.' He took Mrs Myer's hand and led her into the middle of the room.

Evie, holding on to the delicious feeling of dancing the waltz not once but twice with her papa, left the ballroom and went in search of Sophie again. She finally found her in her room, alone and sobbing on her bed wearing a gown of pale yellow silk.

'Sophie! Goodness. What on earth is wrong?' Evie kneeled before her. 'Are you ill? Shall I fetch your mama?'

'No!' Sophie straightened and wiped her eyes. Tears had streaked through her face powder and Evie went to the dresser and took a damp cloth from the basin. 'What has happened?' she asked, sitting beside her and gently wiping Sophie's cheeks.

'There is to be no announcement tonight.' Sophie hiccupped. 'Or ever, I shouldn't wonder.'

Evie felt the blood drain from her face. She had suspected correctly. 'Why?'

'Alexander came to see me before everyone arrived.' Another tear rolled over her lashes. 'He confessed that my, and others', expectations of him had given him much concern lately. Papa had spoken plainly to him a few days ago, asking him to make tonight the time when he was to formally ask for my hand.' She screwed up the handkerchief in her hands. 'Alexander said that Papa's words had shocked him. He was not ready to make any such announcement or promise to me or anyone. He realised the hopes I and my family had about us had gone on for long enough and had to be put to an end before my reputation was damaged and I was hurt.' She gave a long, wavering sigh. 'He does not want to marry me.'

'Then he should have said so before now!' Evie blasted, angry at Alexander for causing Sophie pain. This was exactly what she hadn't wanted to happen. Sophie was never to be hurt.

'It is not Alexander's fault. My wishes and my family's wishes were not his. I truly believe that Papa's comments surprised Alexander. He did not think as we did.'

'How could he not when the idea of you two marrying had been mooted for years, before he went to America and more so since his return?'

'Well, none of it matters now, does it?' Sophie's face twisted in agony. 'He does not love *me*, Evie!' She wailed, heartbroken. 'And I love *him* so very much. How will I *bear* it?'

Evie hugged her tightly and let her cry. 'You will bear it because you are stronger than you know.'

'No, I am not. He is everything I wanted, *everything*.' Her sobs grew louder.

'I know you are hurting but you will overcome this, and life will go on.' Evie stroked her back. 'You are good and kind and wonderful, and some other gentleman will love you completely.'

Sophie sat straighter and blew her nose. 'I want Alexander. He has been in my heart for years, more than I realised. I waited for him. Every moment we have spent together since his return I have fallen more in love with him.'

'I know.'

'How foolish was I?' More tears fell. 'So utterly foolish. The whole district believes we shall be married and now...' Her face twisted in horror. 'Lord, I will be a laughing stock!'

'No, you will not!' Evie snapped. 'If I hear one person say anything about you, they will receive my wrath!'

'Everyone will laugh at me, think of me as a fool. I cannot face them all downstairs. I have flaunted my smugness at gaining Alexander's attention.' Sophie closed her eyes, her face awash with tears. 'I have built up a whole life in my head of being his wife, the mother of his children.' She moaned softly. 'It was so real to me, so obtainable. Tonight... tonight was the night when all the people I knew would find out that he had chosen me.' She sprawled across the bed, sobbing.

The door opened and Sophie's lady's maid entered. 'Oh, miss, the mistress is looking for you. Are you unwell, miss?'

Sophie sat up and turned her face away from the maid. 'Quite well, Doyle.'

Mrs Bellingham charged into the room, her face like thunder. 'There you are!' She clicked her fingers at Doyle, who instantly fled, then came to her daughter's side. 'Your papa has only just now informed me that Alexander has refused to propose!'

'Mama!' Sophie cried and threw herself at her mother.

Mrs Bellingham held her tight. 'There now. Hush, sweet little one. It is not the end of the world.'

'It is!' Sophie's wail was full of hurt and anger. 'I love him!'

'Shush now. Everything will be fine. But I do not understand Alexander. He gave us every signal that he was interested in you. He took you to the theatre. What has changed his mind? Did you two quarrel?'

'No.' Sophie wept.

'Do you know anything, Evie?'

Evie stood, feeling sick. 'No, Mrs Bellingham.'

'Fetch her a glass of water, dear,' Mrs Bellingham instructed.

Evie went to the dresser and poured a glass of water from the jug and gave it to Sophie, who sat dejectedly on the bed.

Mrs Bellingham sighed deeply. 'What a mess. I am furious at Alexander, truly I am. So is your father, though not as much as I would like him to be. He says he will speak to Alexander. Give him some incentive to go through with it.'

'No!' Sophie shot to her feet, spilling the water. 'I will not be humiliated further. Papa is not to beg Alexander to take me. If he does not want me then that is an end to it.'

'Dearest child, your papa can make Alexander see sense if he is a little wary of becoming married. Some men are, you see. They do not want to give up their freedom. Alexander has had years of living a bachelor life. Taking a wife would seem a huge step to him at first. Perhaps he simply needs time to adjust to the idea.'

'Time?' Sophie nearly screamed. 'Time? He has had plenty of time to consider the idea. It's been nearly six months since he returned from America.' Sophie wiped her eyes. 'No. He does not want me. It is clear that I am not the wife he wants.' Her chin wobbled.

'I fail to see why he should think so. There is no one better than you for him to take as his wife. You have breeding and wealth and position in the community. Who else is better?' Mrs Bellingham embraced her daughter. 'Let Papa talk to Alexander tomorrow. Nothing needs to be decided this evening.'

The misery in Sophie's eyes was hard to witness. 'I am not goods to be bartered for, Mama. Alexander either loves me or he does not. He clearly does not love me.'

Evie stepped forward and placed her hand on Sophie's back. 'You would make any man a wonderful wife. There will be some other gentleman who will adore you.'

The miserable expression on Sophie's face matched her dull tone. 'But not the man I wanted.'

'Will you come downstairs?' Mrs Bellingham asked.

'No. Everyone will be expecting an announcement. Say I am unwell.'

Mrs Bellingham nodded. 'Indeed. It is probably for the best. However, your papa will have words with Alexander, and make it clear this is not the behaviour of a gentleman and a friend. If Alexander refuses to marry you then he will not be invited here again.'

'Mama! No. Alexander cannot be blamed for not loving me.'

'Then he should have made that plain months ago!' Mrs Bellingham paused and controlled herself. 'He has brought my child pain and that is unforgivable. I will not have that man in this house. Does he think he can treat you so abominably and still be our friend?'

'Mama, please...'

'You will stay with her, Evie?' Mrs Bellingham asked.

'Of course.'

'I shall send up a tray and return in an hour to check on you.'

Left alone with Sophie, Evie was at a loss to know what to say or do. How did you comfort someone who had expected such a bright and loving future only for it all to be ripped away? And how much of a part had she played in it?

Sophie walked to the window, but not close enough for anyone below to see her. 'How I have been looking forward to this evening.' She touched her gown. 'I spent hours agonising over this gown, wanting it to be spectacular for Alexander...'

'It is his loss, dearest,' Evie murmured.

'What a fool I shall seem to everyone for pinning my hopes on him.'

'No one will think you a fool.' Evie's heart broke for her friend. They both knew the gossip would do the rounds of the drawing rooms for weeks to come.

'I only have myself to blame. Mama and I were so sure he would ask Papa tonight for my hand.' Despondency entered Sophie's voice. 'I made more out of our friendship than was warranted. I made his every word and gesture mean something. I believed in signs that were not there. Every gathering, every event we attended, I made it a courtship.'

'Sophie, do not torture yourself.'

'Why should I not? I did this to myself. I gave in to my imagination, my emotions, my dreams without any true facts.' She laughed bitterly. 'Standing before you is a stupid, pathetic girl.'

'Enough now!' Evie hated to see the loathing in her eyes. 'You are better than this. You will recover from the disappointment and live your life in happiness.'

Shoulders slumped, Sophie turned away, but not before whispering, 'I doubt it.'

11

For a week, Evie visited Sophie each day and stayed for hours, making sure she was never alone with her thoughts. She encouraged Sophie to walk the hall's grounds while the weather was nice and when inclement Evie would sit beside Sophie and they would embroider, flick through the pages of Paris fashion catalogues or press flowers or sew ribbons to hats; all the while, Evie would talk non-stop. Telling Sophie about India, her childhood, all the stories she had told before and those she hadn't. Mrs Bellingham thanked her for her efforts, but Evie knew guilt played a huge part in her daily ride to the hall.

However, none of it made any difference to Sophie's state of mind. She was withdrawn and barely ate. Dark shadows formed under her eyes and often Evie caught her staring at nothing. Visitors, mainly Mrs Bellingham's friends, would want to talk of the ball and Sophie couldn't bear it and would look at Evie in panic. These women brought the rumours with them about Alexander and Sophie and likely took away more gossip after seeing the sad figure of Sophie.

Mrs Bellingham grew angrier at Alexander, whispering to Evie when Sophie wasn't listening that she'd told her husband that Alexander wasn't welcome at the house, and he had agreed and said he would only meet with him at their club in Bingley.

'Another cup of tea, dearest?' Mrs Bellingham encouraged Sophie when the last of their afternoon visitors had left.

'Thank you, Mama,' Sophie replied softly, although they all knew she'd not drink it. Her last cup of tea had gone cold, untouched.

Evie smiled and took a plate of coconut puffs from the tray and offered it to Sophie. 'Your favourites.'

'Maybe later.' Sophie suddenly stood. 'Forgive me, Evie, Mama, but I have a slight headache. May I be excused?'

'Of course, child. Would you like for me to send for the doctor?'

'No, no fuss, Mama.' Sophie turned to Evie, her expression full of apology. 'Would you mind if I went up?'

Evie rose and embraced Sophie, feeling the thinness of her. 'Go and lie down. I shall return tomorrow.'

'Actually...' Sophie couldn't meet Evie's gaze. 'I am not in the mood for entertaining or company... You have been my constant companion all week; I shan't take up any more of your time. Could you come next week instead? Maybe next Friday?'

'Absolutely.' Evie squeezed her hands. 'But send for me if you wish to talk.'

Sophie nodded, tears filling her eyes. She hurriedly left the room.

'I do not like this at all,' Mrs Bellingham muttered. 'I had an aunt who was rejected, and she pined away and died within six months. She was only young.'

'That will not happen to Sophie. We will not allow it.'

Mrs Bellingham sadly shook her head. 'How do we bring her out of this?'

'Papa, as you know, has had low moods since Mama died. I find he copes better when he is busy. He is currently compiling notes for Mr Bellingham on India, for the railway business. Despite my worry he is overtaxing himself, he does leave his study in a more contented mood at the end of each day.'

'So, you suggest we keep Sophie busy?'

'Yes, wallowing will not help her. I have tried all week to keep her entertained, but I am not enough.'

'I shall take her away.' Mrs Bellingham nodded fiercely and rose from her chair. 'That is the answer. London. She enjoys London. We shall visit friends and attend the theatre and go shopping.'

'I am sure that will make her happy.'

'Thank you, Evie. You are a true friend. Would you care to come with us?'

'I wish I could, Mrs Bellingham, but I cannot leave my papa.'

'No, indeed.' Mrs Bellingham grasped Evie's hands in gratitude. 'We shall depart for London in the morning. Sophie will call on you when we return.'

'I hope the trip is successful.'

Leaving the hall, Evie had witnessed enough of Sophie's suffering and rode to Alexander's mill a few miles away. His treatment of her best friend was deplorable, and he had to be held accountable.

The beauty of the countryside was lost to her as she rode Star down the lanes towards Alexander's mill. She hoped he'd be there. With every stride she grew angrier, recalling the hopeless image of Sophie. How dare he treat her so badly, humiliating her in front of all their society?

She cantered into the mill's yard, scattering workers out of the way. Flat-cap-wearing men, pushing wheelbarrows or rolling bales of cotton, glared at her but she didn't care. The heavy sound of whirling machinery filled the air as she pulled Star to a halt before the steps of a red-bricked building, which above the door said *Office.*

Not waiting to be shown in, Evie strode straight through the outer office, past a shocked clerk and into the main office, where through a window she saw Alexander sitting at his desk.

'Miss Davenport!' Alexander frowned as she stormed in. He left his desk. 'Has something happened?'

'Oh, yes, something has happened! You have humiliated Sophie!'

Alexander grimaced and stepped to the door and spoke to the clerk. 'Phillips, take a tea break, will you?'

'Yes, Mr Lucas.'

Alexander closed the door. 'It was never my intention to make Miss Bellingham suffer.'

'Well, you have, deeply. She is barely eating or sleeping! That is your fault,' she snapped. 'I visit her every day and each time I see her she is worse!'

'She will recover from this disappointment.' Alexander walked back behind his desk. 'I am sorry to have caused her upset, but I never gave her any promises.'

'Upset! You have ruined her happiness, which she had completely pinned on you!'

'That is her doing.'

'You led her to believe you were going to offer for her hand.'

'I never once mentioned marriage to Miss Bellingham, not once!'

'But she believed that was your intention. She thought you were paying her special attention.'

'I was included in certain parties and entertainments. Never once did I single her out to give her some hope that I wanted her as my wife. I never spoke of love or a future together.'

'You paid her attention; you gave her hope. That is all a girl needs.'

'That wasn't my intention, I promise you. I like Sophie Bellingham a great deal, but I do not love her. It is impossible.'

'Why is it impossible? She is pretty and kind and good. She would make you a wonderful wife. Please, Mr Lucas, please consider her.'

He frowned. 'Would she thank you for coming here to *beg* on her behalf?'

'Absolutely not. But I have to do something for her. Her suffering is breaking me.'

'Better that she hurts for a short time than she weds a man who does not love her and endures a loveless marriage for the next forty years or more.'

'That is so cold.'

'It is the truth.' He shrugged. 'I am not a monster, Miss Davenport. I did not set out to raise her hopes. Miss Bellingham's feelings for me are her own responsibility. If you and no doubt others feel I am to blame, then as a gentleman I will accept it. But I gave her no encouragement to think of us as anything other than friends.'

His argument took the heat out of her anger. 'She is miserable.'

'She will very soon recover.'

'She loves you.'

'I am sorry for it. Yet, I cannot return her love for I love another.'

Evie stiffened, a stab of pain spearing through her chest. *He loved another?*

Alexander strode around the desk and took her in his arms. 'You, Miss Davenport, darling Evie, you since the minute I first saw you.'

She sagged against him, revelling in his admission. Her body responded to his, but she fought for control of her scattered wits.

'You are the only woman I want to marry,' he said softly.

Evie stepped back in surprise. 'Marry me?'

Alexander looked quizzical. 'You seem shocked.'

'We... that is I...' She took a steadying breath.

'Do you deny that there is an attraction between us?'

'No...' She gazed up into his eyes and felt the pull of desire, the need reflected there.

He lowered his head and his lips gently brushed hers. 'You are all I think about.'

His touch melted her insides, teasing her body into wanting more. Yet this seemed worse than before. Now she had witnessed Sophie's devastation and knew she couldn't add to it. Evie stepped away. 'We cannot be together.'

'We can. In time. I understand Miss Bellingham is your friend, but we can go slowly. Take the time she would need to accept us.'

'She would *never* accept us, Alexander.'

'Evie, please, listen to me.' He reached for her, but she spun away.

At the door, she held on to the knob. 'I cannot hurt her more than she is already. Imagine the gossip! It would be the ultimate betrayal for me to be with the man she loves.'

'We can be discreet. Let her heal and then gradually be more open.' He ran a hand through his hair. 'Evie, I will wait for as long as it takes, but I will not give up on the chance for us to be together.'

The heady glimpse of being with him filled her brain but the reality cut deep. 'And I cannot hurt my friend. Not now or in the future.'

'What about us?'

'There is no us and never will be.' She left him.

In a daze, she mounted Star and rode out of the yard.

* * *

In front of a long garden bed under the parlour window, Evie kneeled on a piece of canvas and sniped at the dead flowers and pulled out numerous weeds. At the other end of the bed, Colin did the same. The warmth of the June day brought out a great many butterflies, which hovered and fluttered around the garden, landing on the flowers blooming in the sunshine. Bronson had brought the horses on to the front lawn to eat the lush grass, which had grown too long.

Papa sat at the garden table, the newspaper spread out before him, and read interesting reports out to them. 'I fear there is so much strife going on in the world that there is nothing but doom to read about. There's conflict in Italy, America and New Zealand.'

'I am pleased you are no longer a soldier, Papa,' Evie said, placing a handful of weeds into a basket. 'This is pretty.' She pointed to a tall pink flower and looked at Colin. 'Foxglove, yes?'

'Yes, miss.' Colin beamed, for he knew a lot about flowers and vegetables and gardening and had been teaching her since last summer to know all the names of the plants and trees. 'And the one next to it?'

Evie studied the purple flower. 'Iris.'

'Excellent, miss.' Colin carried on digging with a trowel. 'The strawberries are in flower; we'll soon have tasty strawberries for the table.'

'I noticed the honeysuckle had become rather wild near the stables.'

'Yes, I'll see to that tomorrow, miss.'

She moved along the bed, wiping her forehead as she went, for the heat was building. 'I cut some of the briar roses this morning. Enough to fill two vases.'

'Watch those forget-me-nots, miss, they have burrs, remember? They'll stick to your clothes.'

'Oh, yes.' Evie gave the little blue flowers more respect.

'There is a fair coming to Bingley next week, miss. Will you go?'

'I am not sure.' She smiled, then thought perhaps Sophie would enjoy it if she had returned from London by then.

In the two weeks since Sophie had been whisked away to London by her mother, and she had confronted Alexander, Evie had stayed close to the house, not wanting to meet anyone who would want to discuss the ball, or accidentally see Alexander.

Her only outing had been to call in at the police station, where she was told that there had been no sighting of Hal Humphry and the cottage had been relet to a family.

Luckily, after that visit, they had been plagued with thunderstorms, so Evie had the perfect excuse to stay home. She spent her time by starting with the organisation of the linen cupboards with Fanny. Next, they inspected all the dinner service and drinking glasses for cracks and chips. They took down the curtains and sponged the dust off them, rugs were beaten, glass lampshades washed, picture frames dusted, the silver polished.

Keeping herself busy kept her sane, when all her mind wanted to do was think of Alexander, and she fully understood the mental torment Sophie was enduring. Only, Evie's conflict was created by Alexander's lovely words and her guilt over Sophie. Whereas Sophie was plagued with pain and humiliation.

Often in the quiet of the night, Evie lay listening to the odd owl hoot, or the call of the cuckoo, and relived the moment when Alexander said he wanted her for his wife. She knew he meant it. She was both thrilled and alarmed by the declaration.

Her heart and mind warred. She wanted Alexander. Her body throbbed whenever she thought of him. But there could never be anything between them. How would she live with the guilt of being with the one man her best friend wanted? She'd been wracked with remorse over a few kisses, but to actually marry him would sever her friendship with Sophie. She had no doubt about that.

She couldn't have the two of them in her life. No matter what her feelings for Alexander were, Sophie had loved him first. To take him from her was unthinkable.

She dug into the soil with force, hating that her mind always strayed to Alexander. Until meeting him, she'd had no thoughts of marriage. Was completely against it, in fact. She had seen successful women who had rewarding lives without the trappings of marriage. Her two aunts were a perfect example. They did whatever they pleased and were content. In India she had known an older friend of Mama's, Mrs Gilbraith, who had sufficient means to live by without the need to marry a rich man. Mrs Gilbraith laughed and had the most fun Evie had ever seen any single woman have, throwing parties and dinners, and had been the darling of most events, enjoying a wide circle of friends. She travelled and explored and sat on charity boards, all the while giving her time to her friends whenever they needed her. That was the kind of woman Evie aspired to be.

So, she didn't need to marry Alexander Lucas and pour more misery on Sophie's fragile soul. She didn't have to forsake her special friendship with her dearest friend. Alexander, as handsome and eligible as he was, had never belonged in her life. The sooner she put him from her mind, the better she'd feel.

'There's someone arriving, miss.' Colin nodded towards the end of the drive, where a carriage was turning in.

Evie recognised Mrs Myer's coachman and groaned under her breath. 'Looks as though my progress here has been curtailed for the day,' she murmured, standing up and taking off her gloves and apron.

Colin grinned. 'Shall I take those into the scullery for you, miss?'

'Thank you, and can you ask Mrs Humphry for tea?' Evie walked over to Papa. 'Mrs Myer is here.'

Papa turned his head to acknowledge the carriage. 'Our peace is shattered.'

'Hopefully, she won't stay for long.'

Evie sat next to Papa to prevent the other woman doing so and waited for her to approach them.

'Why, is this not the prettiest scene?' Mrs Myer declared, descending from the carriage. She wore a cream dress of superior quality edged with inches of gold tassels and gold ribbons. Her hat was a vision of perfection with cream roses and feathers on the side of the upturned brim. 'What is more delightful than enjoying the English summer?'

'Welcome, Mrs Myer.' Papa stood and bowed over her hand and guided her to another chair.

'You have a stain on your skirt, Miss Davenport.' Mrs Myer tutted.

'I was gardening.' Evie brushed away the offending stain from her old green and white print dress.

'Do you not have men to attend to the grounds?'

'Yes, but I enjoy the exercise.'

'Really, Major, you must curb your daughter's enthusiasms.'

Evie clenched her teeth and gave a tight smile as Fanny and Lizzie brought out the tea trays.

'I have added a jug of elderflower cordial, miss,' Lizzie said quietly.

'Goodness.' Mrs Myer baulked. 'Are we farm labourers now? Next, we will be eating raw onions and offal.'

Evie went to speak but Papa placed his hand on her arm. 'Are you planning on visiting the coast this summer, Mrs Myer?'

'Well, I had thought to, but decided against it. I do prefer staying in Brighton rather than the north, but the travelling is very tiresome.' She accepted the cup and saucer from Evie. 'The Bellinghams are in London, I believe. Why on earth anyone would want to visit London in the summer is beyond me. The heat and dust are indescribable.'

'You would not like India, then,' Evie muttered.

'Indeed, I would not!' Mrs Myer rejected the plate of sliced cake. 'I understand why Lydia has taken dear Sophie away, though. The poor girl must be feeling horrendous after the ball.' She stared at Evie. 'Did you know that the engagement announcement would not be happening?'

'No, I did not.'

'I dined with Guy Lucas last evening and he says Alexander refuses to talk about it.'

'It is none of our business,' Papa said, taking a triangle of bread and butter and spreading marmalade on it.

'They say Alexander Lucas has his attentions on someone else...' Mrs Myer sipped her tea carefully. 'I thought with you and he being such friends that you would know?'

'We are not friends,' Evie murmured as casually as possible.

'Really? I simply assumed, what with you calling in at his mill office the other day.'

The colour drained from Evie's face.

'Did you, my dear?' Papa asked innocently. 'You never mentioned it.'

'It was a short visit.' She glared at Mrs Myer. The woman must have spies all over the county.

'Still, the damage is done, isn't it? Poor Sophie is rather pathetic now. Tossed aside so carelessly.'

Evie seethed. 'I would rather not discuss my friend, if you do not mind, Mrs Myer.'

'Guy told me that he is perplexed at Alexander's behaviour. He assumed, as we all did, that it was rather a done deal between Sophie and Alexander. We must know what changed his mind.'

'Why must we?' Evie snapped. 'It is none of our business!'

Mrs Myer smirked. 'Young love can be such a tortuous path. Perhaps they will find each other again soon and make up.' She eyed Evie with a tilt of her head.

Evie gripped the teacup handle so fiercely she was afraid it would shatter and so gently replaced it on the saucer and decided to turn the tables on the woman. 'You seem to spend a great deal of time with Guy Lucas. Is there something we should know about?'

'We are indeed great friends. I hold him in high esteem, as I do the major.' Mrs Myer smiled sweetly at Papa. 'One can never have enough friends, isn't that so, Major?'

'Absolutely.' Papa frowned as sweat broke out on his forehead and he lost all colour. 'Evie...'

She shot up from her chair. 'Papa! You must go to bed and rest.'

'Yes, I agree...'

She helped him up slowly, taking his weight as the strength seemed to have gone from his legs.

Mrs Myer hovered about like some tedious fly. 'Shall I call someone, a servant?'

At that moment, Alexander rode up the drive and Fanny came out of the house with a fresh pot of tea.

'Fanny!' Evie yelled. 'Fetch Colin, hurry.'

'Miss Davenport?' Alexander threw himself down from his horse and ran to them. He took Papa's other arm and most of his weight. 'There now, sir, that's it. Nice and steady.'

'Upstairs to his bedroom if we can.' Evie concentrated on getting Papa inside.

'Miss?' Colin came rushing along the corridor.

'Help us.'

'Evie.' Papa winced. 'Dearest, sit... me... down...'

'In here.' Evie instructed Alexander and Colin to move Papa into the parlour and lay him along the sofa. 'Ride for the doctor, Colin. Hurry! Papa, just rest now. The doctor will soon arrive.' Evie kneeled beside him. Papa's face now had a pasty colour and a sheen of sweat coated him. 'Fanny, a damp cloth.'

'Evie, his cravat and shirt buttons, undo them.' Alexander kneeled beside her. 'It will make him more comfortable, easier to breathe.'

'Yes.' She did as he said with fingers shaking so much, she could barely use them.

'Evie...' Papa croaked.

'Yes, I am here. Rest now.'

Mrs Myer collapsed into a nearby chair. 'This is all too much. I feel faint.'

'Then I shall escort you to your carriage, madam,' Alexander said, rising to take her elbow. 'Home is the best place for you to recover.'

'No, I must stay! The major needs me!'

'The major needs rest and the doctor, Mrs Myer,' Alexander said. 'You can provide neither.' He propelled a protesting Mrs Myer out the door.

In other circumstances, Evie would have laughed. Instead, she held Papa's hand and prayed he would recover. He'd done it before and would do so again. He must.

12

Evie woke with a start, blinking rapidly, disorientated for a moment. Then she focused on Papa lying in bed, sleeping, and relaxed. A lamp shone a soft golden glow over the bed, leaving the corners of the room in muted light. On the bedstand sat a silver-framed portrait of Mama and Evie gazed at it, missing her mama more at that moment than at any other.

The small gold clock on the mantle chimed gently twice. Outside the drawn curtains, all was quiet. The middle of the night was a strange time. Nothing stirred, no animal cry or bird call. Just silence.

Carefully, she slipped her hand under Papa's, ready to go back to sleep, but he stirred and opened his eyes.

Evie leaned forward. 'Papa?'

Slowly, he turned his head and the corners of his mouth lifted slightly. 'My girl.'

She brought up his hand and kissed it.

'You are... the most... precious thing... to me...'

'As you are to me,' she whispered.

'I... do not... want to leave you...'

'Then do not,' she tried to joke but the words caught in her throat.

He winced, pain written over his features.

'The doctor left a draught for you. I shall get it.'

'No...' He barely had the strength to squeeze her hand. 'I am done for now...'

'Papa, no.' Tears burned hot behind her eyes. 'You must fight. You are a soldier.'

'I go... be with...' His eyes closed and the words faded away.

'Mama,' she finished for him as he took his final breath. 'Go to Mama. She's waiting.' Evie's chin trembled and the tears fell one after the other as though in a race.

Stunned by her loss, she bowed her head and held his hand and let the pain wash over her.

Her mind emptied of all thought as she sat beside him until the birds began their morning chorus and Mr Lund's milking cows bellowed for attention.

She remained holding his hand as noise above her head heralded the movements of Fanny, Lizzie and Mrs Humphry waking and dressing for the day.

A sliver of light bordered the curtains as night turned to morning. Beyond the bedroom, life was going on, people were eating breakfast, going about their tasks, walking to work, yet Evie couldn't contemplate any of that. Her beloved papa was gone. She was alone in the world. The pain of not having either of them built in her chest like a heavy weight pressing hard.

The door opened quietly, and Fanny came to stand beside her. 'Morning, miss. How was your night?'

Evie raised her head, feeling dazed. 'Papa has gone, Fanny.'

The maid's eyes widened in surprise. 'Oh, miss. You should have called for me. I'm so sorry. The poor major. He was such a good and kind master to us all.'

'Will you send for the doctor, please?'

'Immediately, miss.' Fanny ran from the room.

Minutes later, Evie heard the sound of hooves drumming on the drive. Colin had gone to fetch Dr MacClay. She didn't have long with Papa. She leaned forward and kissed his cool cheek. 'I hope you are at peace, Papa.' Her voice broke, but she controlled it. The fear of breaking down and sobbing kept her eyes dry, for she believed if she started, she would never stop.

Instead, she crossed the landing to her own bedroom, washed and changed into the black mourning she'd worn for Mama. She shivered as the cool material touched her skin. Black. How she hated the colour. In the mirror, she transformed from the fun-loving Evie to a grief-stricken shadow of herself.

Fanny came in carrying a cup of tea. 'I thought you might need this, miss.'

'Can you fix my hair, Fanny? I cannot get the ribbons right.'

'Yes, miss. You should have waited for me; I would have helped you dress.'

'I managed.' She bit her lip. 'There is much I have to manage on my own now, Fanny.'

'You're not alone, miss. You have me. I'll not leave your side, not ever.' Fanny brushed Evie's long hair and twisted portions of it to arrange it into loops, which she secured with combs and tied with black ribbon.

Evie gave her a thankful smile. 'One day you will marry and then you will leave.'

'Not me, miss. I have no intention of dying in childbirth like my mam did.' Fanny bowed her head. 'Forgive me, miss. I should not have mentioned that.'

'Death touches us all, Fanny. We cannot escape it.' Evie sighed, tilting her head in the mirror, content with her appearance. She looked tired and pale, but there was nothing she could do about that. 'We have a lot to do today.'

'Yes, miss. Whatever you need.' Fanny put away the box of ribbons into a drawer.

'When Colin returns, I will need him to make several errands on my behalf. Tell him to take Papa's horse...' She swallowed the lump in her throat, determined not to cry. 'Jupiter will need the exercise.'

'Will you sit with the major for a bit, miss?'

'Yes, I will. Then I must begin writing letters.'

Evie sat with Papa until Dr MacClay arrived an hour later and made a quick examination.

'Ah, Miss Davenport. I am afraid his heart was simply no longer strong enough to carry on. The second seizure was stronger than the first and weakened him considerably. I believe the organ would have been severely damaged. My sincere condolences.' He shook her hand. 'Your father was a gentleman that I respected.'

'Thank you, Doctor.'

'He spoke to you before he went?'

'Yes, a little. I think he knew time was running out.'

'I am pleased you had some final words.'

She blinked back hot tears. Not now.

The doctor packed away his bag. 'I will take care of the paperwork. Do you have an undertaker in mind?'

'Rogers and Sons in Bingley? They are the only ones I know of.'

'An excellent company. Mr Edwin Rogers will take care of your requests with much consideration.'

She walked downstairs with him where Fanny waited with the doctor's hat and coat.

'Thank you, Fanny,' Dr MacClay said before turning to Evie. 'Would you care for me to stop in at the rectory? I can inform Reverend Peabody of what's happened and save you the trouble.'

'Thank you. That would be very agreeable. Also, thank you for your service to my papa. I truly appreciate it. Please send your bill to me when convenient.'

'Indeed, and do inform me when the funeral is to take place. I would like to attend if I can.'

Evie nodded. The word *funeral* made her shake.

'Now, miss,' Fanny said after closing the door on the doctor. 'Colin is ready to do whatever you bid.'

'May I have a cup of tea, please?'

'Of course, miss!' Fanny dashed down the hallway to the kitchen.

Feeling as though she was in a dream, Evie went to her small writing desk in the parlour and sat down to write.

Dear Aunt Rose and Aunt Mary,

It is with deep and utter sadness that I write to inform you both that my dearest papa died this morning. His heart could not continue on.

I shall have him buried in the Lylston churchyard. I will send word on the date of the funeral once I have conferred with Reverend Peabody.

Sending warmest regards,

Your devoted niece,

Evie Davenport

Taking a long breath, Evie folded the note and placed it in an envelope and addressed it. The following note was to Rogers and Sons, explaining the situation and asking for them to call on her at their soonest convenience and then she wrote to Mr Latimer, Papa's solicitor, and a quick note to Sophie, though she wasn't sure if she had returned from London, and finally to Mr Bellingham since Papa was invested in his business.

Fanny brought in a tea tray, which held a plate of buttered toast. 'You need to keep your strength up, miss.'

'Thank you, Fanny.' Evie noted Fanny had quickly changed her grey uniform into her black one. Fanny drew closed the curtains and lit the lamps about the room despite the brilliant sunshine outside. The customs of someone dying had to be done correctly.

'I'd put the black ribbons on the front door, too, miss, but I can't seem to find any. Shall I send Colin to the shops to buy some?'

'Yes, he can do that when he posts these envelopes for me. He is to post the letters to my aunts and Mr Latimer and then call in at Rogers and Sons Undertakers in Bingley and then ride to Bellingham Hall. At the shops I need him to buy me a bundle of black-edged cards for the funeral invitations.'

'Very good, miss.'

'Papa's coffin shall be put in here.' Evie gazed about the pretty parlour. 'So, the furniture needs pushing back.'

'Mr Bronson and I can manage it, miss.'

'And flowers. We need lots of flowers and candles.'

'Colin will cut the flowers from the garden.'

'Oh, and food for the funeral. I shall speak with Mrs Humphry.' Evie put a hand to her forehead in weariness. There was so much to think about.

'Mrs Humphry has it in hand, miss. She's already started planning, knowing you'd have a lot of other decisions to make today.'

'She is good, as are you, Fanny. What would I do without you?'

'We are all here for you, miss. We want to make it easier for you in any way we can.'

'I shall go up and sit with Papa until Reverend Peabody or the undertaker arrives. Send them straight up, will you? But no one else. I cannot face anyone else today.'

Fanny's expression became fierce. 'You'll not be disturbed, miss. Don't you worry about that.'

As Evie took the first step on the staircase, the doorbell jangled. 'It might be the reverend. It was very fast of him to come.'

Fanny glanced through the narrow window at the side of the door. 'Mrs Myer! Go on up, miss. I'll send her away sharpish!'

Evie paused on the staircase as Mrs Myer's strident tones filled the house.

'No visitors, Mrs Myer,' Fanny instructed.

'The major is my very good friend; I must see him.'

Sighing, Evie turned and went down to the front door. 'Mrs Myer.'

'Your maid is better than any guard dog!' she huffed in annoyance.

'Papa died this morning,' Evie told her bluntly. 'I do not wish to see anyone.'

'Oh!' Mrs Myer's face drained of all colour. 'Oh, no.' She looked ready to faint.

Evie wiped a hand over her face, not wanting to witness the woman's sorrow, but she'd been brought up well and so nodded to Fanny. 'Come inside, Mrs Myer.'

Fanny frowned, but said nothing as she opened the door wider, and Mrs Myer stumbled in.

Evie grabbed the woman's elbow and guided her to a chair in the hallway. 'Fanny, fetch some water. Mrs Myer, take a deep breath.'

'I was not expecting him to die.' Tears filled Mrs Myer's eyes and she dabbed at them with a white handkerchief. 'He has recovered before.'

'But his heart weakened each time.' Evie gave her the glass of water Fanny brought.

Sipping the water, Mrs Myer's hands shook. 'Why are you not inconsolable? Yet you stand before me as though we are talking of nothing more alarming than the weather.'

Insulted, Evie strove for patience. 'I will thank you to not make assumptions about me. I have too much to do to wallow in my own grief just at the minute. The undertakers and Reverend Peabody are due any moment. So, I shall bid you good day.'

'I'll see you out, Mrs Myer.' Fanny plucked the glass from her hand and strode to the front door and opened it wide.

Evie paused on the first step. 'I shall send you word of the funeral date.' Without waiting for a reply, she hurried upstairs, but standing in the doorway to Papa's bedroom, seeing him lying there pale and still was too much. She quickly went back downstairs and out a side door to the garden on the other side of the house.

She gulped in large gasps of air, leaning against a tree for support. She wanted to scream and shout at the unfairness that her beloved papa was gone, but she couldn't do that. Today wasn't about her. Today she had to make Papa proud and endure the necessary visitors with composure.

The morning slipped by so fast Evie wondered where the hours went. Reverend Peabody arrived and prayed over Papa for some time, then took tea with Evie and discussed the funeral, which he could arrange in three days' time for Thursday morning at ten o'clock.

No sooner had the reverend left than Mr Rogers came: an old man, older than Evie expected, for he looked about seventy with grey hair and a stooped back. His wife, also elderly, was shown upstairs as she was to lay out the body and prepare it for the coffin. Mr Rogers spoke to Evie at length about what her wishes were regarding the funeral. Evie wanted the very best for Papa and settled on a fine mahogany coffin and Rogers and Sons' glass-sided hearse. Papa would be buried wearing his military uniform.

As the afternoon sun began to descend, Evie's eyes grew heavy with tiredness. She sat at her desk writing letters to Papa's friends.

Fanny came into the parlour. 'Miss, Mr Bronson and Colin are waiting in the kitchen to come and move the furniture, when you are ready.'

'Let them come in. Mr Rogers will be here again shortly. He said before six this evening. He had a burial to do this afternoon.' Evie stood. 'Mr Rogers is bringing the trestle legs for the coffin.'

'Colin has cut a good number of flowers. Lizzie is arranging them now.'

'Fill the room with them, Fanny. I want the parlour to look the best it ever has, surrounding Papa with colour and scent.'

'Yes, miss,' Fanny said as the doorbell jangled. 'It's bound to be Mr Rogers.' Fanny went to answer the door.

Mr Rogers arrived with his wife and two strapping young men, who turned out to be his grandsons. Evie stood to one side in the hall as Mr Bronson and Colin went into the parlour and moved furniture to the sides while the grandsons carried the coffin upstairs.

The sight of the coffin tightened Evie's chest with pain. She turned away and walked out of the side door and into the garden. The sky was shredded in pink and purple hues so magnificently that she just stood and stared at the beauty of it. It hurt that Papa would never see such a sunset again.

'Evie.'

She closed her eyes at the sound of her name on Alexander's lips. His footsteps sounded soft in the lush lawn. Then his hands were on her shoulders. She sagged and he pulled her back against him.

'You are not alone,' he whispered.

She rested her head back against his chest. Why did it feel so right to be in his arms when it was so wrong?

'How did you know?'

'I did not know. I came to call, wanting to know how the major was, how you were coping. I would have been here earlier but there was an accident at the mill and my day was swallowed up. Then, when I rode up the drive, I saw Rogers and Sons' cart and my stomach sank.'

'He died this morning,' she whispered, staring at the distant valley, the pink sky. 'Already it seems a long time ago, and yet I still cannot believe it is true.'

'There is no right or wrong way on how to cope when a loved one leaves us forever. We just try to do the best we can.'

'It was hard enough when Mama died, then Grandmama, but I fear that Papa's death...' She could barely get the words out. 'I fear I will simply collapse under the weight of my sorrow.'

'Then lean on me.' His hold tightened.

For a brief moment she allowed herself the luxury of being in his arms, having his strength to comfort her, but then she stepped away, knowing she wasn't entitled to it, and that's when the tears spilled, as though the loss of Papa and Alexander was too much to accept.

'Evie.'

'No! No, do not come near me, Alexander.' She held up both hands. 'I cannot bear it. I cannot!' A sob broke from her. 'You cannot comfort me.'

'I can. I will. Let me.' His anguish was evident on his handsome face.

Tears ran down her cheeks quicker than she could wipe them away. 'Is this my punishment? To lose Papa because I wanted you, the one man I could never have?'

'No, Evie, please!'

'Go away, Alexander, I beg you. I need you to leave me alone. Do you not see? The pain is too much. Papa is gone. He was the only one I could depend on. I have lost my beloved papa!' She cried, heartbroken. 'Papa will never again hear the birds' chorus, or ride Jupiter or taste his favourite foods. He and I will never laugh together again, or dance.' An ache in her throat dried up her words, but the ache in her heart was overwhelming. She fell to her knees, sobbing, wailing in anger that her papa was dead.

Alexander dropped to his knees beside her and held her tightly to him. 'Cry, my darling. I have you.'

She raged against him, pushing him away. 'No, you don't have me!'

'Evie!' Sophie's yell split the air.

Eyes red and swollen from crying, Evie couldn't focus clearly, but she was pulled up from the ground by Sophie.

'Get away from her, Mr Lucas,' Sophie snapped. 'Evie, dearest.' Sophie crushed Evie into her embrace.

The familiar smell of Sophie's floral scent gave Evie a sense of comfort and she cried into Sophie's shoulder, not knowing how to stop.

'Come, dearest. Let us get you inside.' Sophie pushed Evie's hair away from her face where it had fallen out of the combs and ribbons.

Inside, Sophie led her into the parlour, where Sophie's parents stood looking at Papa in the coffin.

'Oh, my dear girl.' Mrs Bellingham embraced her. 'How sorry we are. We only arrived home this afternoon and did not read our letters immediately.'

'I am sorry, Evie. I should have done,' Sophie added. 'But Helen announced she was having a baby and we all celebrated. Now I feel ashamed for doing so when you were enduring all this.'

'You were not to know. I am happy for Helen and Paul,' Evie murmured. She went to stand beside the coffin. Seeing Papa in it for the first time took her breath away. He looked so young, free from pain. He had returned to the papa she adored. Gently, she touched his folded hands.

'He was the best of men,' Jasper Bellingham said. 'I am grateful to have called him a friend.'

'He thought well of you, too, Mr Bellingham.'

Jasper smiled and nodded at that. 'If you need anything, anything at all, you send word to me, understood?'

'Thank you.'

Sophie came to stand next to Evie. 'I can stay the night if you wish me to?'

'No, it is fine. I am fine. You have been travelling and need your own bed. Besides, I am not much company right now.'

'You do not need to be.' Sophie squeezed her hand.

Evie looked at her properly. Shadows bruised under Sophie's eyes. The visit to London had not helped her. She was terribly thin, pasty and there was a dullness in her eyes that hadn't left since the ball.

Evie gazed back at Papa; she could not deal with Sophie's pain as well as her own. 'I shall be fine.'

'I think an early evening is called for,' Mrs Bellingham said, coming to kiss Evie's cheek. 'We shall go, Evie. Have your maid lock up for the night and go to bed.'

'Yes, Mrs Bellingham, I think I will.'

'I shall return tomorrow.' Sophie kissed her.

'If there is anything you need, remember, do not hesitate to send for me.' Mr Bellingham nodded to her and then escorted his women out of the room.

After Fanny had shown them out and locked the door, she came into the parlour. 'Do you wish for some supper, miss?'

'I feel I have drunk tea all day.'

'What about some hot chocolate and some shortbread?'

Evie smiled. 'Sounds perfect.'

'I'll take it up to your room, shall I? You can have it in bed.'

'No, I shall sit here beside Papa. Keep him company.'

'Miss, you need your sleep.'

'I can do that after the funeral.' Evie pulled a chair closer to the coffin. From a shelf in the glass bookcase, she took a volume of *Jane Eyre* down. She recalled talking about it with Alexander. Tears rose but she blinked them away and returned the book to the shelf. Instead, she selected Elizabeth Gaskell's *Cranford*. 'Shall I read to you, Papa? Mama enjoyed this book. It has been a few years since I read it, too. Mama said it was one of those books that everyone should read and no one did. How excited she was when it arrived from London in that chest with all the other things she had ordered for Christmas. Do you remember?' She stopped to think of her dear mama, recalling her happiness whenever they received a crate of items ordered from England. They'd sit together and open the boxes, marvelling at everything British, the dress patterns, the tins of fruit cake, boiled sweets, lace collars and cuffs, the latest books and newspapers and paintings on cards of snow scenes to give to friends and which were so out of place in the hot, sticky heat of India.

Taking a shawl from the back of the sofa, Evie wrapped it around herself and settled on the chair with a cushion. She smiled sadly at Papa, lying so still. 'I will be all right, Papa, for I have my memories and no one can take those from me.'

She shut her mind off from everything, Alexander, Sophie, the impending funeral, the future of being alone, and turned to the first page. She and Papa could share this night together.

13

Evie descended the stairs, having finished bathing and dressing in fresh mourning clothes. She'd slept fitfully in the chair during the night, listening to the rain outside and talking quietly to Papa, reminiscing about their life in India until the morning chorus of birds and the rooster's loud crowing heralded the dawn.

After breakfast she'd asked Fanny to draw her a bath, knowing she needed to be fresh for visitors today. Mr Rogers would be coming to place the lid on the coffin later. An ordeal Evie wasn't sure she was ready for.

Fanny came along the corridor from the kitchen carrying a pile of envelopes on a silver tray. 'Post, miss.'

'Goodness, there is a lot.' She took the pile of black-edged envelopes, used when signifying a bereavement. 'Word has spread.'

'Aye, miss. It doesn't take long.'

Evie had used all her sheets of paper and needed more. There were some in Papa's study. She glanced at the closed study door. She'd not been in there since he died. It was his room, and she didn't have the strength to venture in just yet.

The doorbell clanged and Fanny went to open it, muttering

about people having no respect for a house in mourning and what was the point of her tying ribbons on the front door if no one took any heed of it.

'Ah, you must be Fanny, the housemaid, or are you the house-keeper now? Evie did say they didn't have one, did she not, Mary?' Aunt Rose asked, entering the house.

'See to the luggage. The driver has been paid,' Aunt Mary instructed Fanny.

Stunned, Evie stared in surprise to see her great-aunts waddle through the door. Both were short and round as pennies and the best aunts anyone could wish for.

'Oh, dear girl!' Aunt Rose, the younger of the two spinster sisters, came straight to Evie and held her tightly. 'We are here, dear child, to help you through it.'

'Let her go, Rose, so I can see her,' Aunt Mary demanded. 'Dearest girl, come and give me a kiss.' She gazed deeply into Evie's eyes, which was a feat since Evie stood inches taller than her. 'You must lay your burdens on us now. We are here to ease your suffer-ing, if such a thing can be achieved.'

'I never expected either of you to come,' Evie said, finally finding her voice.

'As if we would not?' Aunt Rose cried. 'Poor dear Max was a true gentleman and took care of our darling niece Caroline since the day he married her, and our dear sister Lucinda when she was widowed. How could we not admire and respect him? He was like a son to us, was he not, Mary?'

'The best of men.' Aunt Mary nodded sagely. 'We could not leave you to face this tragedy alone. We are family and we are not so frail we cannot make the journey when the need is important.'

Evie gave a small smile in gratitude. 'Papa is in the parlour.'

Aunt Rose took Aunt Mary's hand and together they shuffled slowly into the parlour. Aunt Rose sniffed her tears into a handkerchief while Aunt Mary patted Papa's hand. 'God go with you, Max Davenport. You will join your beloved wife, our beautiful niece, Caroline, and our much-missed sister, Lucinda.'

The sight of her elderly aunts paying their respects gave Evie a sense of calm. Their presence in the house made her feel less alone.

'Miss, shall I take their luggage up to the spare room?' Fanny asked.

'Have Colin see to it, Fanny. We shall take tea.'

'The sun is shining, Evie,' Aunt Rose said. 'Shall we not take it outside and enjoy it?'

'We had rain overnight, Aunt. The grass will be damp underfoot.'

'We brought house slippers. We can change our boots when we are finished. We have been in a carriage all morning and I would like some fresh air.'

Aunt Mary scowled. 'Then go and take a walk, sister. This is a house of mourning. We cannot sit outside like a band of gypsies.'

'But nor can we sit around Max drinking tea. It is unsightly,' Aunt Rose argued.

'Shall we go into the dining room, then?' Evie offered the alternative. 'Mr Rogers will arrive later to secure the coffin.'

'And the funeral is tomorrow, that is correct?' Aunt Mary asked, following Evie into the dining room.

'Yes. At ten o'clock.'

'Do you need assistance with managing the particulars?' Aunt Mary asked, sitting down.

'I have it all taken care of,' Evie replied as Fanny came in with a tray. 'Most of Papa's friends are in India. But some of the village people may come and then there are the Bellinghams, Papa's solicitor, Mr Latimer, and other acquaintances. It will not be a large gathering.' Evie felt sad at that. In India, Papa would have had his regiment and so many of their friends and neighbours.

'Still, it will be well attended, more so than Caroline and Lucinda's funerals in Egypt.' Aunt Mary sighed as she took her cup and saucer from Aunt Rose.

A large crash sounded from the back of the house.

'Goodness, what was that?' Aunt Rose exclaimed.

'Likely the demise of a tray of china by the sound of it,' Aunt Mary answered.

Evie put down her cup and saucer. 'I shall go and see.'

Entering the kitchen, Evie found Lizzie on her own on her knees, cleaning up broken crockery and spilled food. 'Where is everyone, Lizzie?'

'Oh, er...'

The back door opened, and Mrs Humphry came in, puffing; behind her was Fanny. They jerked to a halt on seeing Evie in the kitchen.

'Fanny?'

'Miss, there is nothing for you to worry about.'

'Let me be the judge of that.' Evie turned to Mrs Humphry. 'Well?'

The cook lowered her head. 'Hal was here. Colin has seen him off, the brave lad that he is. Threatened him with the fire poker.'

'Has he gone now?' Alarmed, Evie wasn't prepared to deal with Hal, not with her papa lying in the parlour and her aunts sipping tea in the dining room.

'He took some food, miss,' Fanny said. 'He looked starved, as though he's been sleeping rough. As soon as Colin came in, he took off.'

'Aye, I don't think he'll be back today, miss,' Mrs Humphry answered.

'But Hal seems to think he can enter this house when it suits him.' Angrily, Evie went to the back door and opened it. There was no sign of Hal or Colin. 'What would Colin do if he caught Hal?'

'He said he'd tied him up and drag him to the police for stealing. We'd back him up,' Fanny told her.

'Colin is no match for Hal.' Mrs Humphry's bowed shoulders told of her defeated manner. 'Forgive me, miss. To have this worry at such a terrible time for you...'

'We cannot have Hal just walking into the kitchen whenever he pleases,' Evie said, glancing at each of them. 'From now on the back door must be locked at all times. Give Mr Bronson and Colin a key so they can let themselves in whenever they need to, but I do not want Hal to feel he can come and go as he pleases.'

'I'll see to it, Miss Davenport.' Mrs Humphry nodded.

Shaken that Hal had once again decided to terrorise them, Evie returned to her aunts and gave them an excuse of a clumsy kitchen maid. After the funeral she would call in at the police station again and ask them to search for Hal. With Papa gone, she no longer cared about her reputation and if she had to go to court about Hal, she would. The man was a menace and needed to be dealt with.

Sophie arrived before Mr Rogers and while the aunts were resting upstairs.

'Are you all ready for tomorrow?' Sophie asked as they walked around the garden. Today, she wore a dove-grey and soft-pink striped dress, which was superbly made, but it couldn't hide the fact of Sophie's thinness, or detract one's attention from the shadows beneath her eyes, the hollowed cheeks.

'As much as I can be.'

'Do not be afraid. You have people who care for you. Your great-aunts have shown that by travelling here at their age.'

'I know and I am grateful.' The soft twittering of the birds and the warm sunshine soothed Evie's soul.

'And you have friends.' Sophie stopped walking. 'I must ask it, Evie.'

'Ask what?'

'Why was Alexander here yesterday? Why was he holding you?'

Evie momentarily closed her eyes. How much had Sophie seen? 'He was giving me comfort. I was upset.'

'I saw that. I could not hear what was being said but something unpalatable was said because you pushed him away and yelled at him. What did he say to you?'

'I cannot remember.' Surprised that Sophie had seen so much, Evie thought quickly. 'Forgive me. My reactions were raw and uncivilised. Mr Lucas was offering me comfort, but I rejected him harshly. My grief comes in waves and unfortunately Mr Lucas received a taste of my bad manners.'

'But for him to hold you? He is not family.'

'No, but he is a kind man. He saw me in distress and acted without thought.'

Sophie walked on, frowning. 'Alexander can be impulsive, it seems.'

'I was rude to him. I shall have to apologise.'

Putting her hand on Evie's arm, Sophie shook her head. 'No. He should have been a gentleman and left you in peace or called for your maid to take you inside. He forgot himself to hold you so intimately.'

'I barely remember it,' Evie lied. She remembered every word and touch. She always would.

'You... you do not see him as a...' Sophie looked away. 'Never mind, I know you would not. You have no wish to marry and especially not someone who treated me so carelessly.'

'Sophie, you wear your sadness like a cloak, enveloping you. I am worried about you. I thought your time in London would have given you some happiness.'

'How could it?' Sophie groaned. 'Mama says I should stop thinking about Alexander. It is impossible. My head is full of him day and night. I had foolishly planned my future with him and I cannot see one without him. I know he is not all to blame. I became fixated on the man, expecting more than he was prepared to give.' She took a deep breath. 'The humiliation is too much, Evie. Everyone sees me as someone rejected, foolish.'

'They do not.'

'They do! Before I left for London I received letters from Florence Davidson, Susan Hearst and Iris Owen. All three of them wrote nearly identical letters. I swear they must have sat together to compose them; all sent their sympathy in my shame.'

'You have nothing to be ashamed about. We both know those three are little witches.'

'I deserved their gossip. I crowed like a rooster to all who would listen about how much I esteemed Alexander. I know I brought his name into conversation as though something had been promised between us. My embarrassment is total, and I can only blame myself.'

'You will get through this. Time will heal you.'

'No, I do not think I will. In London we attended a wedding of a distant cousin of Papa's. I cried the entire day as I kept imagining my wedding, my husband looking at me with love as my cousin's new husband did. So many times, I dreamed of being Alexander's wife, especially after we attended the theatre together in public. I assumed he had chosen me. Pride is a dangerous thing, Evie.'

'Your day will come, dearest.'

'Oh no. I shall not ever put myself in such a position again.'

'Sophie, do not say such things.'

'Why? You do.'

'But I have never coveted marriage. You are the opposite to me.'

'And look where that got me? No, I was a silly girl before but now I am much changed.' Suddenly, what little colour Sophie had drained from her face as Alexander rode up the drive. 'Oh, my Lord. No. I am not ready to face him.'

'Go inside. I shall not let him in.' Evie gently pushed Sophie towards the house. She lifted her skirts and strode to the end of the garden as Alexander dismounted.

'Evie, can we talk?' he said.

'No, Mr Lucas, we cannot and please do not use my Christian name in public.'

He let out a breath. 'Was that Miss Bellingham?'

'She is here, yes; so are my aunts. I must return inside.'

'I did not mean to hurt Miss Bellingham. I never had intentions to wed her or make her fodder for gossip. I hope you believe me.' Misery shadowed his grey eyes. He looked as tired as she felt.

'I believe you would never purposely hurt anyone, but your actions, or lack of them, have given Sophie a great deal of pain.'

'I understand that. Her father has written to me, detailing how extremely angry he is with me and that I am to stay away from the hall until his daughter has recovered her disappointment. Naturally, I agreed, but I replied that I had never played my hand at intentionally choosing Miss Bellingham.'

'Perhaps you could have been a little more careful towards her...' Evie rubbed her forehead in weariness. 'The truth is, I warned you that Sophie thought highly of you, and you ignored it.'

He nodded. 'I did. I never realised her interest in me was so resolute. Miss Bellingham was not the woman I was thinking of.'

'Maybe not, but the damage is severe on her part.'

'Do you forgive me?'

'It is not my forgiveness you need.'

'Then I shall speak to Miss Bellingham.' He took Hero's reins.

'No, she has been humiliated enough. Write if you must, but please be sensitive to her feelings.'

'Of course.' He took a step closer, his expression tender. 'You would reach out to me if you needed anything, wouldn't you? I am at your service.'

'I doubt I would, Mr Lucas.' She turned away with a heavy heart.

The stone church in Lylston held a small number of people for the funeral. Evie was proud that Papa had made such good friends as the Bellinghams, but his low moods and long periods of time spent in his study had not allowed him to gain a wide circle of friends. If they'd been in India, the church would have been full. Men from his regiment would have given a guard of honour. Instead, only a little gathering of people stood by the grave after the service. Mrs Myer leaned heavily on Guy Lucas' arm; next to him stood Alexander and Mr Latimer, Papa's solicitor, who'd arrived just as the service started.

Evie stood between her aunts, and close by the Bellinghams gathered as a family. Behind them, Fanny, Mrs Humphry, Lizzie, Mr Bronson and Colin stood with bowed heads. Even Mr Lund had taken time away from his farm to attend.

As Reverend Peabody finished his last words, he nodded to Evie.

Taking a steadying breath, Evie stepped forward, grabbed a handful of dirt and threw it on the coffin. The thud of it hitting the wood made her shudder. 'Sleep well, Papa,' she murmured.

She watched as others did the same, then they departed for carriages. Evie didn't want to leave. To do so would signal the end of it all. Leaving Papa would begin the next stage of her life, alone, and she feared the future.

'Dearest.' Aunt Rose touched her hand. 'Shall we go back to the house?'

Evie noticed the gravediggers waiting under a tree near the church. How she longed to stay, but her role as hostess came before her own wishes. She thanked the reverend, inviting him to come back to the house if he had the time.

She caught Alexander's gaze as she waited to climb into the carriage after her aunts. He gave her a small smile, then mounted Hero and rode away. She was torn with relief that he wasn't coming to the house and disappointment that he had left.

Walking into the parlour, Evie realised the furniture had been put back in its rightful places by Fanny and Lizzie after the coffin was taken to the church. Making sure her aunts were comfortable, she smiled and said the odd word to the Bellinghams and ignored the tears from Mrs Myer, who was being comforted by Mr Lucas.

'Is there anything I can do for you?' Sophie asked her, looking ill.

'No, nothing, but thank you.'

'How pleased I am that Alexander did not return here with us.'

'Indeed. He had the good manners not to make it awkward.'

'I had hoped he would not attend at all. I could barely cope with him being in the opposite pew. Has he no consideration of what he has done to me?'

Evie frowned at the selfish comment. 'He came to pay his respects to Papa, as he should have. They were friends.'

'Yes, of course...' Sophie's wan smile faltered.

'I shall check on the kitchen.' Evie escaped before she uttered something she would later regret. Sophie's wallowing was becoming self-indulgent, and Evie was starting to tire of it.

Evie stayed in the kitchen as long as she could without being rude to her guests. Fanny and Lizzie were busy filling trays with plates of food, fresh pots of tea and jugs of milk.

Reluctantly, she returned to the parlour and sat next to her aunts as they conversed with Mr Bellingham and Mr Lucas. Evie stayed away from Mrs Myer, who still dabbed at her eyes, where she sat with Mrs Bellingham and Sophie.

'Miss Davenport.' Mr Latimer came alongside Evie. 'May I have a word with you once all your guests have departed?'

'Yes, absolutely.'

Mr Bellingham turned towards them. 'The reading of the will, I take it?'

'That is correct.' Mr Latimer nodded.

'Would you like me to stay, Miss Davenport?' Mr Bellingham asked. 'I can advise you? Your father had invested in one of my businesses.'

'Yes, I am aware.'

'You are?' Mr Bellingham's eyebrows rose in surprise.

'Papa talked to me about such things.'

'How astonishing. I would never imagine speaking of business with my daughter.'

'Then that is a shame, sir, for how is a woman meant to control her future if she is ignorant of important factors such as money?'

'I expect her husband or brother to take care of that for her.'

'And what if, for instance, like me, she has neither brother nor husband? She is left in a state of flux and ignorance.' Evie shrugged. 'That may suit some women, but it would never suit me. Knowledge is power.'

'You are an extraordinary girl.' Mr Bellingham scowled.

Evie didn't know if that was a compliment or a failing; by the offended look on his face, she took it to be the latter.

Eventually, her guests said their farewells and left, much to Evie's relief.

'I shall come and see you tomorrow?' Sophie said, kissing her cheek.

'Shall we go for a ride?' Evie was desperate for a good gallop on Star.

'No, I am not up to such exercise.'

'It might do you good, Soph. We can ride over the moor to Ilkley, make a day of it.'

Sophie winced. 'Forgive me, but no. If you desire a ride, then I shall call the day after, yes?' She left before Evie could reply.

The last to leave, Mrs Myer paused in front of her. 'I will never forget the major. He was an excellent man.'

'He was.'

'Now you are all alone.' Mrs Myer gripped Evie's hands. 'You must come to me for comfort and advice.'

Evie pulled her hands out of the hold. 'Thank you, but I believe I will be fine, Mrs Myer. I have my aunts should I need comfort or advice.'

'But they do not live close. I am in the village.' She tilted her head. 'And we all know how liable you are to saying or doing things you shouldn't.'

Bristling at the reprimand, today of all days, Evie lowered her voice. 'Papa is dead, so you and I have no need to ever speak to each other again. Good day.' Evie stared at the woman, daring her to speak.

Mrs Myer huffed and stormed from the house.

'What is wrong with that woman?' Aunt Mary asked.

'I do not care, Aunt.' Evie turned her attention to Mr Latimer. 'Is now a good time to discuss the will?'

'Indeed, if you are ready.' Mr Latimer fetched his leather satchel from the table in the entrance hall.

'Should we stay?' Aunt Rose asked nervously.

'Of course we stay,' Aunt Mary barked. 'Evie may need us if the news is not good.'

'Not good?' Evie spun to her aunt. 'Is that what you think?'

'I have no idea, child.' Aunt Mary sighed. 'Whatever happens, Rose and I will never see you go without. If you cannot stay here, then you are to come and live with us.'

A tingle of dread shivered along Evie's skin. Not once had she thought she would have to leave this house. Papa had said it was hers. She gripped her hands tightly in her lap, bracing herself for what was to come.

'Shall we start?' Mr Latimer sat down and pulled out some papers. He read the usual words declaring it to be Papa's final will and that he was of sound mind when writing it. 'I witnessed it,' Mr Latimer told them. 'Everything is above board and legal.'

'I should hope so!' Aunt Mary glared at him.

Coughing over his embarrassment, Mr Latimer shuffled the papers. 'This is a transcribed copy of the will. The original is held in a safe in my office. Major Davenport's bequeaths are simple. Everything he owned now belongs to his only child, Miss Eveline Lucinda Caroline Davenport. That includes this property in its entirety, the house contents, the money in the major's bank account, which currently stands at three hundred and five pounds, four shillings and sixpence. Also, his shares in investments, which I have listed on a separate page for you to read. They are not extensive.' He glanced over his glasses at Evie. 'Five per cent in Bellingham Railways India, some bank bonds and a fifteen per cent stake in a tea plantation in Darjeeling.'

'A tea plantation?' Aunt Mary's tone held admiration. 'Max always was a clever man. Tea, like property, will always be a worthwhile investment.'

Mr Latimer nodded in agreement. 'Miss Davenport, the dividends from your father's investments are sent by cheque. Your father would then deposit them into his bank in Bingley. I can instruct for those cheques to be sent to me and I can deal with that banking for you, if you wish?'

'No, thank you, Mr Latimer. I shall see to it myself.'

'Is that wise, dearest?' Aunt Rose asked worriedly. 'You are young to be taking on such a responsibility.'

'Do be quiet, Rose,' Aunt Mary muttered. 'Evie is a grown woman and needs to take care of her own financial concerns, such as I do and always have done. She is not a fool.' Aunt Mary folded her arms. 'Evie takes after me. Clever, and I thank God for it.'

'I am careful with money, Aunt Rose,' Evie said soothingly. 'Both Mama and Papa instructed me on how to be wise with whatever money I was given. After Mama's death, Papa gave all housekeeping money for me to deal with because there were times when Papa was low... and he could not manage household accounts.'

'He took your mother's death far too keenly,' Aunt Mary said.

'How could he not?' Aunt Rose rebuked. 'He adored our dear niece.'

'Yes, and look where it got him. Caroline's death left him half a man. He was once a strong, strapping soldier who led men into battle. Yet, his wife dying nearly killed him, too. I truly believe his grief killed him. Weakened his spirit.' Aunt Mary sniffed with disapproval. 'I thank the fates for never allowing me to fall in love and suffer so severely as Max did.'

Evie thought of Papa's suffering for the last two years and also of Sophie's misery over Alexander's rejection. Love had a lot to answer for.

'Ladies, if I can conclude?' Mr Latimer interrupted.

'Please finish, Mr Latimer.' Evie smiled.

'I do understand that Major Davenport's investments will be a continued income, albeit a small one, which you need to keep your current lifestyle. However, my advice is that, until you marry, to live within your means.'

'I do not plan to marry, sir.'

He blinked at the unusual admission. 'Then I advise you to cut any costs that may be extravagant.'

'Yes, I understand.'

'There may be a reaction to you, a young woman, holding

shares in those companies and shareholders might approach you to sell. I would strongly advise you to contact me and we can discuss it should that arise.'

'I will, Mr Latimer.'

'Very good. Do you have any questions?'

'No, I do not think so. Thank you for everything, Mr Latimer.'

'If you do, simply write to me. I will have the deeds of the house transferred into your name and inform the companies of your intention to hold on to the shares.' Mr Latimer rose and took off his reading glasses. 'I shall leave you, ladies. I can make the train back to Bradford if I hurry.'

'I shall have the carriage brought around for you.' Evie rang the bell pull by the fireplace and informed Fanny when she entered that Mr Latimer was leaving and needed the carriage.

'I think we need another cup of tea,' Aunt Rose said when the solicitor had left.

Aunt Mary stared at Evie. 'You plan to stay unmarried?'

'I do, Aunt.'

'Then you need to be intelligent regarding money, as I was. It is not easy, mind.' Her tone was full of warning. 'You have to think ahead. Household economy is the easiest way to lose a fortune. You must account for every penny, trust me.'

'I do, Aunt.'

'I am happy to go over the accounts with you tomorrow and we can investigate where savings can be made?'

'I would like that, thank you.'

'Max's horse is the first thing that can go. That will be a saving and he should fetch a good price.'

Evie's heart tumbled. 'Jupiter?'

'Who is going to ride him now? He's in his stall eating his head off! Keeping him will be a waste of money. Remember, you must think smartly about this type of thing.'

'Or you could sell up and come and live with us?' Aunt Rose interjected.

'There is that, of course,' Aunt Mary agreed as Fanny brought in fresh tea.

Evie's mind whirled with the hidden dangers of being solely responsible for her own money, and not just the housekeeping money but everything Papa had.

'You would have your own room,' Aunt Rose added, pouring tea for the three of them.

'May I think about it?' Evie asked. 'It is a big decision and I do love this house, and the garden, and riding Star over the moors.'

Aunt Mary took a slice of apple tart. 'There is no rush to make any decision. Take your time.'

'I do wish you would reconsider your resolve to never marry,' Aunt Rose said with a deep sigh. 'I would so adore it if you did, and we would have babies in the family again.'

'I do not wish to marry, Aunt.' She thought fleetingly of Alexander, but even her desire for him had caused her heartache; why would she want to suffer more than that?

'But, my dear—'

'Rose!' Aunt Mary scowled at her sister. 'Leave Evie alone. She has no wish to lumber herself with a man and that is the end of it.'

'Just because we did not marry does not mean Evie should forgo it. Many people are happily married. Why should she miss out on the chance of that?'

'The odds of being happily married are very slim, sister.' Aunt Mary shook her head in annoyance. 'We have had this conversation for sixty years or more, since we were young women ourselves.'

'I wanted to marry!' Aunt Rose answered passionately.

'No one was stopping you! But did you find a decent man? No. Every suitor was some jumped-up snape looking for an easy life living off our father's money and then my money.'

'You are cruel,' Aunt Rose said sullenly.

'But honest. Lucinda, our own sister, married a useless man that left her destitute. She had to beg her daughter to go and live with them in India. The shame of it.'

'Mama and Papa were happy, though,' Evie murmured.

'An exception,' Aunt Mary snapped. 'And look what happened when one died: the other couldn't continue living. I rest my case.' She took another slice of tart. 'There is more to life than marriage and babies, Evie dear, when you are an independent, wealthy woman. That is the truth of it.'

'Yes, I expect so, Aunt. I just have to find a way to give my life meaning and fullness.' Evie stared down into her teacup. She had no idea how to achieve it, but she was going to try.

14

Alexander closed his ledgers and pushed them away. His desk was strewn with paperwork and accounts, but his head refused to work on the numbers before him. He checked his fob watch and decided it was time to ride to Bellingham Hall and attend the meeting.

'Are you off, sir?' his clerk asked as he walked out of his office.

'I am. I'm expected at Bellingham Hall for a shareholder meeting in an hour. I have left those papers you wanted me to sign on my desk.'

'Very good, sir.'

'Until the morning, then.' Alexander nodded his goodbye and went down the steps and across the yard to the small stable where Hero spent the day. The stable boy had got him out of his stall and saddled him in preparation.

Riding through the yard, Alexander nodded to his employees who passed him. Noise and industry went hand in hand and so, once clear of the yard, he felt the silence of the wood more clearly. Low clouds forecasted rain but as yet it remained dry.

His thoughts turned to the upcoming meeting as he rode up out of the small valley where his mill was nestled between the River

Aire and the Leeds and Liverpool Canal. He'd been surprised to
receive a note from Jasper Bellingham inviting him to the hall for
the shareholders' meeting after being advised to stay away. Why
hadn't Jasper held the meeting elsewhere, perhaps at his club in
Bradford?

Had he been forgiven for his actions of not asking Sophie to be
his bride? Had Sophie forgiven him? She'd never answered his
letter that he'd written, not that he had expected her to. Her feelings were still raw from the disappointment and his apology would
not be the salve she wanted, but he wanted to show her that he'd
never meant to cause her any hurt. She was a fine young woman
any man would be happy to marry, just not him.

Still, for the first time since the ball last month, he was visiting
the hall and he hoped Sophie would not be there. He did not want
to be the reason for Sophie to feel awkward in her own home.

On Bradford Road, he saw the sign for Lylston and wished he
could ride up the other side of the valley to visit Evie. It had been
two weeks since the funeral. Two weeks since he'd seen her. As
desperate as he was to speak with her, he had to give her time. He
knew Evie couldn't deny the attraction between them, for she
responded to his touch as much as he did to hers. Her eyes would
watch him, sending him silent signals only he could read whether
she knew it or not.

He had never been in love before, never expected to be so, for
most marriages were a meeting of two like-minded people, a
shared understanding that the other might make a reasonable
partner. He had expected to marry to produce an heir for his business, a companion, a wife to run his household. All men were
brought up to think of such things. However, he'd never expected
to be hit in the gut with such power of emotion and attraction
whenever he thought of, looked at or touched Evie. In the past, he
had shunned reading the romantic poets and love sonnets,

believing them to be melodramatic. Yet now he understood. Now he realised the excitement, the absorbing passion a man could feel for a woman.

But Evie was in mourning, and she was loyal to Sophie. Neither of which he could do anything about just at the moment, but he was determined to not let Sophie's misplaced emotions for him get in the way of a future with Evie. Deep in his soul he recognised Evie as his life partner; no other would do.

He hoped one day soon Sophie would meet a new man to adore and he'd be off the hook and life could return to normal, where he could gently pursue Evie, show her his admiration, his devotion. Was he asking for too much?

A pheasant ran out in front of Hero and the horse shook his head in alarm but soon settled. Alexander patted his neck and picked up the pace. Turning the corner in the tree-lined lane, Alexander pulled Hero to a halt as ahead a farmer ushered his flock of sheep from one field into the opposite one across the lane. A black and white sheepdog ran frantically around the flock, expertly guiding them through the open gate in the stone wall.

Behind Alexander, a carriage pulled up and also waited. On the other side of the flock, a man walked towards them. Alexander watched him, noting his scruffy appearance. At last, the final sheep jumped and bleated its way across the lane and into the field.

'Thank ye for waiting, sir.' The farmer held up his hand in thanks.

Alexander touched the rim of his hat in acknowledgement and walked Hero on past the unkempt and grubby man, who scowled up at Alexander.

'Got a penny, sir?'

Alexander reached into his waistcoat pocket, pulled out three halfpennies and tossed them to him.

The man caught the three coins with lightning speed and pocketed them instantly. 'Most kind, sir.' The ruffian's grin revealed blackened and chipped teeth.

Alexander rode on, not wanting to hold up the carriage behind him. Moments later he rode down the long, winding drive to Bellingham Hall. The impressive greystone country house stood among lush lawns and graceful trees.

A groom came through a stone arch to take Hero's reins as Alexander dismounted, and led the horse away. The front door opened as Alexander reached the steps and a footman welcomed him in, taking his hat and gloves.

'The master is in his study, Mr Lucas.'

'Thank you.' Alexander turned to cross the entrance hall when his eyes caught movement on the stairs. Sophie stood at the top of the landing. She looked as white as a sheet; the cream day dress she wore bleached further colour from her face.

'Good day, Miss Bellingham.' Alexander gave a bow of his head.

Slowly, Sophie descended the staircase and, as she came closer, Alexander was shocked at her thin frame, her frailness.

'Mr Lucas.' Even her voice was weak. 'I... I did not know you were coming here today.'

'Your father invited me. A meeting. Business.'

'Business.' The light died from her eyes.

He winced. Had she thought he was coming for her? 'How are you?' He thought she must be ill by her appearance.

'I am well. And you?'

'Very well, thank you.' The awkwardness was everything he had wished to avoid.

'Thank you for your letter... Forgive me for not replying.'

'I did not expect you to. I simply wanted to convey my apologies for any misguided expectations you may have felt.'

Sophie's bottom lip wobbled. 'How foolish you must think I am.'

'Not at all.'

'When your letter arrived, I hoped you had changed your mind. Silly of me, I know.'

'I am sorry. You deserve a man to love you unconditionally.'

'So everyone tells me. Yet, it is you I love.' She shrugged terribly thin shoulders. 'I can tell you this because I have nothing to lose. My humiliation and embarrassment are total.'

He felt sick at her admission. 'You must put me from your mind and live your life.'

'I have tried, Mr Lucas. I seem incapable of it. Some days I believe I am getting better, then, like now, I see you and I am adrift again...'

'I am not worth such devotion. Please do not waste another moment thinking of me.'

She bowed her head. 'You make it sound so easy.'

'Miss Bellingham, please.' Mortified by the depth of her despair, Alexander didn't know how to react.

'I shall not hold you up a minute longer, Mr Lucas. Enjoy your meeting.' She slipped away into the drawing room without looking up.

He stood frozen, unable to understand how she could feel so deeply about him when they had done nothing more than attend a few social gatherings and chat about things of no consequence.

'Alexander.' Jasper Bellingham came down the hall. 'We are waiting on you.'

'Coming.' He walked forward, feeling confused and heartily sorry for Sophie Bellingham.

When he walked into the study, he faltered on seeing Evie sitting near the desk. Her small smile gladdened his heart. He shook hands with Bellingham's solicitor, Mr Gresham, and then the other investors in Bellingham's business: Mr Crompton, Mr Overton, Mr Wilkinson and Mr Evans.

Alexander took the chair near Evie. 'I did not expect you to be here.'

'It was a last-minute decision. Papa's shares have been bequeathed to me, so I convinced Mr Bellingham to include me in the meetings from now on, so I can learn what my shares stand for.'

'Very wise.' Alexander was proud of her being so sensible.

'Indeed,' Jasper Bellingham said, sitting behind his desk with a frown. 'I have to admit I do not approve of women being in business and tried to deter Evie from attending. Any pertinent information she needs to know I can send to her solicitor, who can instruct her on what to do with it.'

'How can you not approve of women in business, Mr Bellingham?' Evie sat straighter. 'Many women control their own businesses. Who do you think dresses your wife and daughter? Where do they buy their hats from and so forth? Such businesses are run by women for women all over the country. It is ignorant to imply business is not something women should be involved with.'

Jasper's eyebrows rose. 'I see mourning has not stilled your tongue, girl,' he murmured in exasperation.

'My tongue will never be still, Mr Bellingham, when something needs to be said.'

Alexander hid a grin. How wonderful was this woman!

'Shall we get on?' Jasper shuffled some papers. 'With poor Max's demise, we obviously have a duty to allow Evie a chance to know what she is involved with. The railways in India are gaining popularity and notice. Max was to educate me on what pitfalls we could run into and also what advantages we could use to our benefit.'

'I can still help you with that,' Evie butted in. 'I also lived in India.'

'But your father was a solider, a leader of men. He visited a great many regions of the country.'

'True, but I also visited those regions with Papa. Often Mama and I would go ahead of Papa. I may be of some use to you.'

Jasper nodded. 'Then let us begin. Now, the East Indian Railway, the Great Indian Peninsula Railway and the Madras Railway have all achieved a great deal in networking railroads across the vast country. However' – Jasper stood and pointed at a large map of India on his wall – 'there are still large tracts of land to be joined. I want my company to be at the forefront of not only building railways but providing the infrastructure to do so. You see, the locomotive engines and carriages are all built in this country and shipped to India, at immense cost. I propose to build ironworks in India and construct the carriages and engines there. To do that, we need to raise more capital. What are your thoughts on such a scheme?'

'It seems a worthwhile opportunity,' Mr Overton agreed.

'Why has no one thought to build ironworks in India before now?' Mr Evans asked.

As Jasper continued talking, Alexander turned his head slightly to gaze at Evie. She looked beautiful, even in full black mourning. She had a presence about her that made men want to watch her, be near her.

Feeling his eyes on her, she glanced his way and his heartbeat skipped rapidly. She focused her attention on Jasper again, but he noticed the blush colouring her cheeks and it thrilled him that she wasn't immune to him. Now all he had to do was convince her to let him court her properly.

* * *

Head down against the rain, Evie spurred Star into a trot. She cursed herself for not taking the carriage this morning, but she'd thought her few errands would be done in a timely fashion and then she'd ride over the moors to give Star a chance to stretch her legs. But the sudden change in weather while she was in Bingley shopping had caught her out. The moors had disappeared in a low mist and home was the only place she wanted to be.

The lane went through a tunnel of trees, showering her with large drops of water from the saturated branches. She thought of the welcoming fire at home and a nice cup of tea and maybe a slice of Mrs Humphry's jam sponge.

Suddenly, something hit her in the chest. With a scream, she fell backwards over Star's rump and landed on the lane with such force it took the wind from her lungs. Bewildered, she lay in the mud not knowing which part of her hurt the most.

A weight landed on her back, snatching her hands behind her and tying them together before she could gather her wits. Rough hands grabbed her, hauled her up.

Coming to her senses, Evie screamed and struggled.

A hand clamped over her mouth, a snarl in her ear. 'Be quiet!'

Frightened, she squirmed and wriggled to be free as she was dragged into the thicket at the side of the lane. She tried to see who had captured her, but he kept her in front of him, his face averted, and his hat pulled down low.

'Let me go!' she yelled, furious and scared. The rain came down faster as the man pulled her through the trees. She gasped as they crossed a narrow beck. Cold water splashed over her boots, wetting her stockings and the bottom of her riding habit. He dragged her up the opposite bank. Evie tripped and fell, but he yanked her up again with a filthy curse.

On and on they trudged, through trees and undergrowth. Evie tried to get her bearings until he stopped, turned her around and pulled a hood over her head.

Evie shrieked at the darkness. The air seemed trapped in her lungs as the material clung to her face. She was going to die. It was all she could think about. This monster would kill her, suffocate her and leave her in the woods never to be found.

Tripping often, she blindly staggered where the man guided her. The rough hessian over her head had a few tiny holes, enough to give a distorted view of a hazy world, but she knew nothing of where he was taking her. Then, when she thought she could walk no more, he yanked her to a halt.

She heard the sound of a door being opened, the squeak of the hinges loud. He thrust her inside and she fell to her knees with a cry.

Manhandling her, he pushed her on to her bottom, and she felt something solid behind her. Abruptly, the hood was ripped off and she blinked in the dim light. A hut. She was in a wooden hut. And there, snarling down at her, stood Hal Humphry, grinning.

'Let me go!' she yelled, trying to get her hands free.

He kneeled in front of her, grabbed her face and kissed her hard, bruisingly. His foul breath made her retch.

Affronted, he slapped her face. 'Bitch! Think you're too good for me, hey?'

Whimpering at the assault, Evie jerked her head away as he leaned closer.

Hal, filthy and wearing clothes not fit to be seen in, laughed and sat back on his heels. 'Don't be so fussy, missy. You'll be getting more of that, a lot more by the time I'm done. You need taking down a peg or to, for sure, and when I'm finished with you, your high and mighty attitude will be gone forever.'

A shiver of dread snaked through her body at the thought of him touching her. 'Please let me go, Hal.'

'Not a chance. When I'm done having some fun, I'll squeeze the life from you and bury you somewhere no one will find you.' He chuckled as though he'd told a joke. 'Now, I'm off to celebrate.' He stepped towards the door, then thought better of it and returned to her. Hal checked her hands were tied tightly.

'Hal, no, please.' She cried out as the rope cut into her wrists.

Ignoring her, he pulled off her hat, painfully tearing the pins out of her hair. She yelled and jerked away but he grabbed her shoulders and hauled her closer to him. Panting, he tore at her bodice, ripping the buttons off the material, exposing her chemise and corset beneath.

Evie screamed and Hal slapped her face so hard her head snapped back.

'Shut your mouth, you stupid bitch!'

'Please, let me go. I'll tell no one, I promise.'

'Really? You'll not go to your friends the police?' One hand gripped her chin. 'I know all about your visit to the police station. Did you think I would let you get away with it? I've been biding my time for the right moment to teach you a lesson.'

'I am sorry. I will not do that again. I promise.'

'I know you won't,' he scoffed. 'Because I am going to kill you.' He ran a dirty hand down over her breasts. 'But not yet, definitely not yet. Soon, though.'

He pushed her on to her back and lifted up her skirts.

She shouted for help until another slap shut her up. She tasted blood on her lip.

Hal, clumsy in his haste, fumbled with his trousers, freeing his erect penis. He leaned over her, his eyes narrowing in excitement, exposing her thighs. He fell on top of her.

Evie screamed and squirmed underneath him. The horror of what he was about to do gave her strength to fight. She bucked and twisted, shrieking for help.

Hal held her under him, thrusting to get closer to her flesh, but she fought and strained to not let him defile her as he wanted to. Then, suddenly, he moaned and stilled. He quickly rolled off her.

Evie felt wetness on her thigh. She stared, not understanding, before scrambling backwards into the corner of the hut as far away from him as possible.

Adjusting his clothes, Hal spat on the ground. 'I'll be back.' He walked towards her, and she shrank away from him while he searched her riding habit. Finding her small leather purse tied to her waist, he laughed, revealing his black and chipped teeth. 'Perfect!' He left the hut and shut the door, locking it.

'Hal! Let me out!' Evie clambered to her feet and ran to the door. She barged against it, but it held fast. 'Help! Someone help me!'

Leaning her head against the wood, she screamed until she ran out of voice and her throat hurt.

Drained, she fell to her knees. She had to think, be smart. Hal would come back and want a repeat performance. This time he might actually succeed and rape her.

Shaking, she tried to think clearly. Star would have made her way home, Evie was certain of that. Star knew the way and would want the warmth of her stable in this weather. As soon as Colin or Mr Bronson saw Star without Evie, they'd raise the alarm. The police would be summoned, and the search would begin.

Tears burned hot behind her eyes, but she wouldn't cry. Such weakness wouldn't help her. She needed to be strong to outwit Hal.

She twisted her hands, wincing at the pain the tight ropes caused on her wrists. How was she to get free?

The hut held no window and only one door. The wooden sides and roof had tiny gaps between the slats; the hut could only be used for farm animals or storage. Straw and manure littered the floor.

She stepped closer to a narrow gap halfway down a wall and peered out. Disappointed she could only see grass and trees in the distance, she leaned her forehead against the wood. Hal had taken her somewhere remote; of course he would. They might have walked in any direction. She couldn't recall much of the journey, just walking across a shallow beck.

She shivered. Now the immediate danger had lifted, the coldness of her wet boots, stockings and the bottom of her dress made her aware how chilly she was. Cold and sore. Her whole body seemed battered.

Closing her eyes, she slumped to the ground. Physically, she couldn't beat Hal, not with her hands tied behind her back. All she could do was reason with him, if such a thing was possible. Talking to him might buy some time until the police or someone found her.

Rain pounded on the roof harder than before. Water dripped through the cracks above her. She huddled in the corner. There was no point in yelling for help. No one would be out in this weather.

Miserable and frightened, she drew her knees up against her chest, trying to keep warm, and thought of the heat of India before her mind slipped to Alexander. How angry he would be to learn of her abduction, but he wouldn't hear of it for hours, maybe even days.

When she'd left Bellingham Hall yesterday after the meeting, he'd asked her if he could call on her, but Sophie had come out of the drawing room to say goodbye to Evie and so she'd stepped away from him and shaken her head. Sophie was barely clinging on to her health and her sanity, and Evie refused to be the one to cause her more upset. Sophie was simply deteriorating before everyone's eyes. Mrs Bellingham had spoken to Evie in worried tones about Sophie's state of mind, asking Evie for any help she might give, but Evie didn't know how to heal Sophie. Her friend was eating less and less and becoming more reclusive, convinced society was talking about her.

A crack of thunder made Evie jump. Her heart raced as the hut grew darker. She put everything from her mind, except how to escape. When nightfall came, she'd be in complete darkness unless Hal had a lamp. How was she to outwit him? Would he listen to her calm reason? Or was she soon to join her papa in Lylston's churchyard?

She sat waiting for the night to arrive, and Hal.

15

'What do you mean she is missing?' Alexander jerked up from his chair as Colin stood in his office and told him the news of Evie's disappearance. 'When did it happen?'

'Miss Davenport never returned home from her shopping yesterday.'

'*Yesterday?*' Alexander shouted, sick with worry.

'Aye. Mr Lund, the farmer next door, spotted Star, Miss Davenport's horse, in the bottom field around six o'clock last evening. He thought it strange, her being saddled and left in a field in the rain. He came and told me and my father about it. Naturally, we knew something must have befallen Miss Davenport.'

'She's been out there all night?' Alexander strode out of his office to the coat stand by the door to grab his hat and coat.

'Fanny, Miss Davenport's maid, sent me for the police once night had fallen and Miss Davenport hadn't returned. I went and reported her missing. The police came around and asked questions, and said they'd do a search of the lanes and ask at Bellingham Hall. But no one had seen her and there wasn't a trace of her in the village,' Colin told him, following him out of the office and to the stable. 'My father and me have been out all night, and Mr Lund, looking for Miss Davenport. A policeman is asking people in the village this morning. But Fanny said we needed to do more and what with Hal nosing about as always, we thought—'

'Hal?' Alexander frowned at Colin as Hero was led out of his stall. 'Who is Hal?'

'Hal Humphry, a right nasty piece of work, he is. He's Mrs Humphry's son and in and out of prison, he is.'

'What does he have to do with Miss Davenport?' Alexander mounted Hero as Colin mounted Jupiter, Max's horse.

'Hal's been a menace since he got released and been tormenting his mam. Miss Davenport stood up for Mrs Humphry and said she could stay at the house instead of living in a cottage in the village and being at Hal's beck and call, and at the receiving end of his fists. Hal didn't like Miss Davenport interfering.'

'Do the police know this?' Alexander couldn't hide his shock. He couldn't believe Evie hadn't told him any of this.

'Aye, sir. Miss Davenport has been to speak with them, not that they could do anything as Hal is clever and comes and goes like a ghost in the night. Hal keeps hanging about the house, stealing chickens, causing problems, entering the kitchen to torment his mam and so on.'

Alexander tapped his heels to spur Hero into a fast trot. 'We'll start a search with more men. I'll go to Bellingham Hall; you go to the Lylston pub. Get as many men as you can. I'll pay them if need be.'

'Aye, sir.' Colin peeled away at a fork in the road and headed back up towards the hills on the other side of the canal.

Riding fast now, Alexander's head spun at the thought of Evie being missing, perhaps in pain and terrified. He had to find her.

On the hall's drive, a carriage came from the other way and slowed down as he reined in Hero.

'Oh, it is you.' Mrs Bellingham did not look pleased to see him. 'Jasper is not at home. Have you heard the news about Evie Davenport?'

'I have. Just now. I have come to gather men for a search.'

'Jasper has already begun a search. We were told last evening and when Evie had not returned home by midnight, Jasper and the estate men took lamps out and searched the grounds until dawn.'

'I wish I had known.' Alexander cursed under his breath.

'Jasper sent a note to your father, and other friends, this morning, asking for help.' Mrs Bellingham clutched a handkerchief to her chest. 'They are going to search the canal and the riverbanks next.'

His blood ran cold. 'Evie swims excellently.'

'But if she hit her head...' Mrs Bellingham waved her handkerchief weakly. 'Sophie has taken the news badly and collapsed in fear for her best friend. I am fetching the doctor personally.'

'I must go and search.'

'You have nothing to say about Sophie?' She tutted. 'You caused her health to suffer when you embarrassed her in front of all our society, and now this with Evie! My daughter cannot bear much more.'

He gritted his teeth, tired of being the talking point in society simply because he hadn't asked Sophie to marry him. After seeing her weak-willed manner, where any disappointment could lead her to ill health, he was very glad to not have properly courted her.

'Good day, Mrs Bellingham.' He touched his hat in acknowledgement before turning Hero around and cantering back to the road.

He refused to think that the worst might have happened to Evie. In no possible way could Evie be dead and he not feel it. His soul would *know* it.

Alexander rode into Bingley, needing to speak to the police for any updates. In the yard beside the police station, he tied Hero to a post and went inside the station. The reception area held an assortment of men, some drunk, others sourly cursing their fate and others resigned. Chaos reigned supreme and Alexander had to fight his way to the desk to speak to someone.

'Sir, now is not a good time,' a sergeant said, writing quickly on some papers. 'We are full to bursting, as you can see.'

'I am Alexander Lucas and I wish to know if there is any news on Miss Davenport's disappearance?'

'Not that I'm aware of, sir. A constable is doing his rounds in Lylston and asking the villagers for any sightings.'

'One man!' Alexander fumed. 'One man is not enough!'

'Sir, look around you. Does it seem as though I have men to spare?' The sergeant glared at a dishevelled man who, despite having his hands and ankles chained, managed to lumber up to the desk. 'Sit down! Constable Scott, get this vagrant into a cell!'

The filthy, unkempt man leered towards Alexander. 'You asked about the Davenport girl?' he sneered, then laughed. 'Are they all out looking for her?'

'You have seen her?' Alexander wanted to grab the man's shoulders but refrained as a constable roughly took the man's arm and dragged him away.

The man laughed dementedly. 'Aye, I've seen her,' he called over his shoulder.

'Ignore him, sir.' The sergeant sighed. 'We found him drunk this morning in the High Street. He's only just woken up from his stupor.'

Frowning, Alexander felt he'd seen the man before. 'What's his name?'

'No idea. I've not got to him yet. He resisted arrest and tried to get away; that is why he's in chains.'

'Get him back here and ask him what he knows.'

'He's a drunk, sir. He won't even remember his own name, never mind seeing a lost woman.'

Alexander leaned forward, frustrated. 'Ask him, for God's sake!'

The sergeant raised his eyebrows in annoyance, then turned to the constable, who waited by the steps that led down to the cells. 'Constable Scott, bring him back.'

Standing with a surly look on his face, the scruffy man stared at Alexander. 'I ain't telling you nothing.'

'Have you seen Miss Evie Davenport?' the sergeant asked.

'I said, I ain't speaking to any of you.'

'What's your name?' The constable roughly jerked the man's shoulder. 'Name!'

The man laughed.

Alexander clenched his fists. 'If you do tell us, and the information is found to be true…' Alexander thought quickly. 'I shall pay your fine for being drunk and disorderly in the street.'

'Is that so?' The man rubbed his chin, making the chains jingle.

'I promise you.' Alexander nodded. 'There are witnesses. I will pay.'

The fellow grinned, revealing several black and chipped teeth. 'I think I'd rather do the time.'

The urge to hit him swelled in Alexander until he had to clasp his hands together to stop him from doing just that.

'He knows nothing, sir,' the sergeant said with a wave of his hand. 'Dregs of society, they are. Time-wasters.'

'Hal Humphry,' the vagrant suddenly admitted with a grin.

Alexander's head snapped around at the felon in shock. 'You are Hal Humphry?'

'Hal Humphry?' The sergeant pushed back his chair. 'Miss Davenport reported you for being on her property and causing mischief. She claimed you accosted her on the road and stole a chicken.'

Hal's grin widened. 'That's not all I've stolen.'

Heart thumping, Alexander grabbed Hal's shirt. 'You filthy scoundrel! What have you done with Evie?'

'Wouldn't you like to know?' Hal chuckled. 'But boy, didn't I have fun!'

Alexander punched him hard on the jaw. Hal stumbled back, laughing.

The sergeant came around his desk as the other prisoners erupted with jeers and calls for a fight. Mayhem broke out in the reception area. Whistles were blown as those arrested barged each other and tried to flee through the front door.

Alexander grabbed Hal and punched him again.

'Sir, enough!' The constable tried to break them apart, but rage fuelled Alexander, overriding his good manners. He hit Hal in the face again. Bone on bone. Alexander ignored the pain in his hand as blood spurted from Hal's nose.

'You'll never find her!' Hal taunted.

'You bastard. Where is she?' Alexander grabbed Hal by his shirt, hearing the material tear. 'I will see you hang if she is harmed in any way.'

'You have to find her first!' Hal laughed like a maniac.

Alexander flung him away with such force Hal landed on the floor. 'Hanging is too good for you,' he panted.

'Sir, please. Calm down. We'll get the information out of him.' The sergeant called to another officer to grab Hal.

'Do it now!'

'Sir, I have my duties.'

'A woman is missing! Let me speak with Humphry. I shan't touch him, just talk to him.'

'Men like him won't answer to you, Mr Lucas. They take great delight in causing mischief. He knows you want this information too much. He won't tell you a thing and he'll revel in that.'

'This is a woman's life at stake.' Alexander took his hat off and ran a hand through his hair. 'We must find her.'

'I'll send more men out to search and speak with Humphry once this room is under control.' The sergeant went behind his desk. 'We'll spread the word.'

'This is not good enough,' Alexander fumed. 'Not at all. I shall offer a reward. Ten guineas to the man who finds her.'

'Very good. I'll let my men know. Good day, Mr Lucas.'

'I want them all out searching.' He turned on his heel and marched out of the building, wondering if he should have offered more for the reward. Who knew what the going rate was for a missing-person reward?

At pace, he cleared the town and rode up into the hills towards Lylston. Once in the village, he saw a group of men standing outside the public house.

'Mr Lucas,' Mr Butcher, the landlord hailed him. 'We are going out to search for Miss Davenport.'

'A man called Hal Humphry has taken her, hidden her somewhere.'

'That blackguard. He was in here last night drinking. I wondered where he had got his money from, but men like him, who are quicker with their fists and even quicker with a knife, I don't like to engage with.'

'He's in a cell now. They picked him up this morning in Bingley, drunk.'

'And he's definitely taken Miss Davenport?'

'Yes, but won't tell anyone where she is.'

'A filthy specimen such as him will think it funny to keep us all guessing.'

'Which is why we must keep looking for her. I shall join you and your men.'

'Actually, sir, could you ride up on to the moors? On horseback you can cover that area quicker than we can walk. Mr Bellingham's party are searching south of Otley Road, and we'll search all the woods around Lylston.'

Alexander nodded and spurred Hero on.

A stiff wind met him on the road as he climbed higher, away from the village and on to the lower moorland. Rising above him was the wide, treeless Ilkley Moor, turned brown by the summer sun.

A hare darted out of a gorse bush near the track, sprinting away in panic. Alexander squinted into the horizon, looking for anything that would be a sign of Evie. The flatness of the moor would show a person standing, but if she was lying somewhere in the bracken and heather, how would he or anyone ever find her? She'd been out all night. His stomach flipped at the thought of her alone and scared. Yet, she was tough, brought up in the harsh environment of India. Evie wasn't some little drawing-room mouse, too frightened to leave her mama's side like most of the young women Alexander knew. No, Evie had wits and strength. She wouldn't let someone like Hal Humphry win.

Pacing the hut, Evie would often stop to peer out of the gaps between the wooden slats. She'd seen nothing but a rabbit and a pheasant in the grass near the hut and no movement in the distance. She'd slept fitfully, jerking awake at every sound. When dawn broke through the gaps, lighting the gloom, she scrambled up off the dirt floor and started pacing to warm her stiff legs.

Hunger made her stomach rumble, and thirst dried her mouth. She was glad but also surprised Hal hadn't returned. Her purse had contained several shillings and pence, so he'd obviously spent the night enjoying himself at her expense. Not that she cared about that. The few shillings were worth losing to keep him from tormenting her. However, he was bound to turn up soon and she had to be ready.

The rope around her wrists, after hours of pulling and twisting her hands, was loosening, to the detriment of her skin, which she could feel was raw and sore. She kept tugging, wincing in pain but determined to be free. After several minutes she paused to rest, her wrists throbbing.

'Help!' she screamed, as she had done at intervals all morning, hoping a passing farmer or someone out for a walk would hear her. Only her voice was becoming hoarse and the screams weaker.

Despite the agony, she twisted her hands, pulling and tugging to free them. Tears of pain and rage filled her eyes. How had her life come to this? What had she done to deserve such torment? Surely people were looking for her? Or were they? Had Fanny raised the alarm only to find people didn't care enough to come looking? Panic reared up in her chest, threatening her sanity. She kicked at the door repeatedly until her boots were scuffed and toes hurt. Her whole body ached. So many hours of having her arms behind her back had stiffened her shoulders. Hunger and thirst vied for supremacy.

Exhausted and frustrated, she slumped on to the ground and closed her eyes. She was desperate to empty her bladder but had no possible way of doing so unless she wet herself, and that was an indignity too far.

Falling down on to her side, she closed her eyes to rest, praying like she'd never prayed before that someone would find her before she was dead.

* * *

Alexander dismounted, tired and thirsty. Lit lanterns stood on tables around the front of the public house and barmaids were bringing out jugs of beer to the men returning from searching all day. The sun had set an hour ago, streaking the sky in orange, but all beauty was lost to him as the word spread that Evie hadn't been found.

'The poor miss is likely to spend another night in the open,' one man said, supping his tankard of beer.

'Thankfully it's not midwinter,' another said.

The landlord's wife came out with a tray of meat pies for the men. She spotted Alexander and walked over to him. 'Are you hungry, Mr Lucas?'

'I honestly do not know, Mrs Butcher.'

'Sit down and I'll fetch you a pint of ale.'

'Are men still out searching?' he asked, sitting on a bench near the door. From inside, he heard men talking.

'Yes, another group have gone over to West Morton and are looking there. My husband's cousin lives near the Bingley Five Rise Locks, and he's gathered a group of men to search along the canal. Mr Bellingham's estate men came through here about an hour ago. They've been searching since first light and looked done in. They've gone home for a rest.'

'Gone home?' Alexander reared up. 'We cannot waste time resting.'

'Sit down, Mr Lucas. You'll be no good if you fall asleep in the saddle, will you, and neither will those men if they don't rest. It'll be full dark soon and what can you see in that?'

'She cannot spend another night out there,' he murmured, filled with dread.

'Everyone knows Miss Davenport is fit and healthy. She'll survive this.' Mrs Butcher gave a small smile. 'We'll find her. Now,

I'll have young Robbie go and see to your horse. I bet it could do with a feed, too.'

'Thank you, yes.'

Alexander had thought he wasn't hungry, but the pie Mrs Butcher left him barely touched the sides. The tankard of ale followed suit and a barmaid brought out another for him. The food and drink brought him awake, sparking his energy once more. Nightfall wouldn't stop him from searching.

He was ready to head to the stables when a group of men rode in. He recognised his father and hailed him.

'Ah, Alexander. I have been wondering where you are.'

'I stopped for a drink and for Hero to be fed.'

His father glanced around. 'We have just returned from searching around Bingley. Mrs Myer insisted I take a party of men out.'

'Did she?' Alexander was surprised at this, for Mrs Myer and Evie did not get along.

'Yes, she is at Bellingham Hall with the other women. Sophie Bellingham has taken it badly. A policeman called at the hall to ask her some questions. They wondered if she knew anything about Hal Humphry, but she didn't.'

'If Miss Davenport isn't found by the morning, I shall get my workers out looking for her. Losing a day's production is not as important as finding her.'

'She could be anywhere, son.'

'Hal Humphry had to walk her somewhere, so he couldn't have managed too far.' Alexander's mind continued with the thoughts that had been plaguing him all day.

Guy rubbed his chin. 'Word is that she left Bingley after shopping. The police think Mrs Stewart's shop was the last one she visited before getting Star from the stables. Humphry must have taken her on the road home, but before the village as no one saw her pass through here.'

'Then the search must be centred on the road between Bingley and here, but we've found nothing.' Something wasn't sitting right with Alexander.

'He could have walked her ten miles in any direction.' Guy sighed.

'That's too far without anyone seeing them. Evie would have struggled.' He felt sick at the thought of Hal touching his precious girl.

'Lad.' Guy gave him a fatherly look. 'Does Evie Davenport mean more to you than she should?'

'Is that a problem?' he snapped.

'Not to me, but, well, the Bellinghams won't feel too favourably about it. You rejected Sophie and now want her best friend.'

'What I feel for Evie Davenport is no one's business.'

Guy shook his head. 'You know it's not that simple.'

'Let us just find her, shall we?' He turned away to fetch Hero, not caring in the slightest what people thought about him. Once Evie was found he'd do his best to make her happy and to convince her that they should be married. Sophie would just have to live with it.

16

Rain woke Evie the following morning. She lay on the dirt, not caring to get up. She had wet herself during the night, the humiliation barely registering, such was her apathy. Tired, cold, hungry and thirsty, she no longer cared about dignity. Her throat was raw from screaming, her voice horse and croaky. The skin around her wrists wept blood, for she felt it drip down her hands. She had no energy to tug at the ropes any more; the pain cut too deep.

A sudden rustle in the grass next to the hut lifted her head to hear properly. A grey gloom had banished the darkness of night, and the constant drum of rain on the roof was the only sound. Forcing herself to scramble up, she shivered in the dampness. Her habit now was to peer through each gap in the slats, going from wall to wall, checking for any sign of someone passing.

At the right side of the hut, she stared in surprise at seeing a small herd of brown and white cows grazing close by. This was the first time she'd seen cows so near to the hut. She watched them for a short time. One cow turned and she noticed the branding on its flank. L in a circle. Lund! Mr Lund's cows!

Excited, Evie watched beyond the cows for any glimpse of the old farmer. His cattle herd grazed on the hills around his farm-house, unlike the sheep, who were taken up on to the moors in summer.

She studied the trees in the distance, harder to see today because of the rain. She couldn't identify them. They didn't look like the trees that bordered Mr Lund's farm and her own home. They had crossed a beck, she suddenly remembered. Mr Lund's farm had two becks running through it; both came down from sources higher up on the moors. One beck flowed past the village; the other ran south-west towards Riddlesden on the far side of the farm. Evie had never seen that part of Mr Lund's farm, but the old man had once told her that he bred pheasants in the small wood there. Evie had told him she wouldn't ride in that wood for fear of scaring the young pheasants. Now she knew why she hadn't recognised her surroundings.

Although relieved she knew where she was, it didn't alter the fact that she was trapped in this hut. She wondered why Hal hadn't returned. Had he thought to leave her here to die of starvation? How much longer could she survive without water and food?

A spurt of anger at Hal flared for a moment only to die shortly after. To be angry, she needed energy. She had none. Misery returned quickly. Why hadn't anyone found her? Surely, if people were searching for her, they'd search in this area, too? Mr Lund was a nice man; he'd give them free access to his farm. Where were they? Did no one care? She thought of Alexander. Did he not want to find her? What of the Bellinghams? Had anyone informed her aunts? They would be distraught.

Her head pounded, her body ached, and her wrists were too painful to move now. She leaned against the wall, fighting the urge to cry. She missed her papa and mama, but she was glad they weren't alive to witness her disappearance. How upset they would have been.

A cow bellowed and she jumped. She peered through the crack again. Then blinked, wondering if she saw correctly. Mr Lund's dog, Poppy, bounded through the grass, circling the cows, who eyed her with disdain. Eagerly, Evie pressed closer to the gap. There, coming out of the trees, was Mr Lund, walking with his long staff in one hand and his pipe in his mouth.

'Mr Lund!' Evie's voice came out as a croak, and she whimpered at the frailty of it. He would never hear her.

The empty hut had nothing to help her make a noise. She watched him walk along the edge of the wood, whistling to Poppy, who responded with sharp movements, sprinting across the field. Another cow bellowed its disapproval of Poppy wanting to herd them.

Evie swallowed painfully; her voice couldn't shout. Instead, she kicked at the wall. She kicked and kicked, wincing at her bruised toes.

'Help!' she moaned, slamming her boot into the wall. 'Please help me!'

She paused to peer again through the gap. Mr Lund had walked closer but stopped. Poppy ran into view, close to the hut.

'Poppy!' Evie yelled brokenly. She started up the kicking again. Poppy turned and barked. The nearby cows lumbered away.

'Poppy!' Evie cried, letting the tears fall finally. She continued to kick, and Poppy barked in reply, backing away as if unsure of what was going on.

'Here, girl,' Mr Lund called and whistled. The dog darted back to him.

'No!' Evie yelled, her voice barely a weak screech. She barged the wall, hurting her shoulders, and then kicked as hard as she could. 'Help!'

Poppy's barking grew closer. Evie squinted through the gap. Mr

Lund was only twenty yards away. She kicked again, not caring she was losing feeling in her toes.

'Who is in there?' Mr Lund shouted, the rain dripping off his hat. 'Come out or I'll send my dog in.'

'Mr Lund!' Her voice squeaked. She banged her head against the wall, willing him to come closer.

'I said come out,' Mr Lund demanded, waving his pipe in the air.

Evie watched him walk out of sight. Faint at the thought of him leaving her, she ran to the other side of the hut and slammed her body into the wall.

The lock on the door rattled.

'Mr Lund!' She hurried to the door and kicked it. She heard the old man on the other side grumble and the lock rattle again. Then suddenly there was silence.

Evie stood, panting, wondering if he'd left her when a shadow passed one of the gaps and then blocked it.

'Who is in there?' Mr Lund yelled.

She ran to where he peered in so he could see her. 'Me! Evie Davenport!'

'Jesus Christ Almighty! Miss Davenport!'

'Yes...' She fell to her knees and remembered no more.

When Evie came to, she was in an unfamiliar room. She lay on a dark green chaise longue with the stuffing poking out of several holes. A grey blanket lay over her and a roaring fire blazed in the fireplace. She closed her eyes as exhaustion washed over her in waves.

A sound woke her, but her eyelids seemed too heavy to lift. Pain wracked her body as though she'd been run over by a carriage.

'Miss, oh my God, miss.'

Evie blinked and Fanny came into focus, crying fit to break.

'Now lie still, miss. The doctor is on his way. Mr Lund has gone to fetch him, but he came and told us first that he'd found you. Lord, what did Hal do to you? Look at your wrists.'

'Fanny.' She winced at her sore throat.

'I'm here, miss. I'll never leave you.' Fanny wiped her eyes.

'Water?'

'Yes, yes. I'll get some.' Fanny ran from the room.

Staring at an etching of a portrait on the mantlepiece, Evie couldn't work out who the person was. Her brain didn't want to concentrate.

'Here, miss.' Fanny kneeled beside the chaise longue and helped her to drink.

The cool refreshing taste of water soothed Evie's throat. She drank the entire glass. 'Where... am I?'

'In Mr Lund's house. As soon as the doctor has been, we'll take you home. Mr Bronson has the carriage outside waiting, and Colin is here to carry you.'

Evie gripped Fanny's hand and moaned as pain shot up her arm.

'Keep still, miss. Your wrists are badly damaged.'

She must have slept for the next thing she knew Dr MacClay was bending over her, the blanket gone and most of her clothes.

'I'm finished my examination, Fanny. Cover your mistress now,' he instructed.

Fanny leaped to his bidding, wrapping a blanket around Evie.

'Now, Miss Davenport. You're awake, I see.' Dr MacClay smiled down at her. 'What an ordeal you've been through. Can you tell me what happened?'

Slowly, her throat on fire, Evie recounted the kidnap, the days and nights in the hut until her voice grew too squeaky to continue.

Dr MacClay nodded and finished taking his notes. 'We shall get you home, if you think you can be moved?'

She nodded, desperate for the safety of her own bedroom.

Colin was called for and, red with embarrassment and something else Evie couldn't work out, he lifted her up and carried her outside to the carriage. Fanny fussed around her, still crying, while Mr Lund held the carriage door open.

Evie looked at the dear old man. 'Thank you, Mr Lund.'

'Nay, lass.' He waved away her thanks. 'Take care now.'

Evie rested against Fanny, who, drying her eyes, held her tightly. The short journey from Lund's farm to her own drive didn't give her time to prepare to see the amount of people lining the drive up to her home. In front of the house, carriages lined up, allowing a small, narrow opening for Mr Bronson to drive the carriage to the front door.

Cheers filled the misty air as Mr Bellingham opened the carriage door. 'Miss Davenport, welcome home. The whole district has been looking for you.'

'Evie!' Alexander came thundering up the drive, galloping past the onlookers. He jumped off Hero and ran to the carriage to embrace her tightly. 'I am so happy you are safe.'

She smiled into his eyes, seeing his love there so clearly.

'Alexander,' Mr Bellingham interrupted them. 'Miss Davenport needs to be inside.'

'Of course.' Alexander took her in his arms and carried her inside as more cheers rang over the valley.

'Oh, miss. We're so happy to see you home.' Mrs Humphry stood in the hallway, wiping her face with a handkerchief. Lizzie stood beside her doing the same.

'Pleased to be home,' Evie croaked.

Aunt Rose and Aunt Mary kissed her, and both looked so much older than they had when they'd left after Papa's funeral.

'Shall I take you straight up to your room?' Alexander asked.

She nodded and rested her head against his chest.

'I am never letting you out of my sight again.' He kissed the top of her head when no one was looking as they climbed the stairs. Gently, he laid her on the bed. 'Your wrists.'

'I am fine,' she lied, wanting to wipe the worry from his face.

Fanny and Dr MacClay followed them in with her aunts right behind them. 'Right, now, thank you, sir.' He frowned at Alexander.

'I am waiting outside the door.' Alexander hesitated.

'There is no point.' Dr MacClay ushered him away. 'Miss Davenport needs rest and plenty of it. There shall be no visitors for days.'

'Evie.' Alexander paused by the door. 'I shall wait. Even if I have to sleep in the garden.'

She smiled. 'Go home. Fanny will send word,' she murmured.

He stayed a moment longer until Dr MacClay scowled and forcibly closed the door on him. 'Fanny, a hot bath for your mistress.'

'The water is already heating up, Doctor.' Fanny took a fresh nightgown out of a drawer. 'Mrs Humphry has soup warming. I'll bring up a tray in a moment.'

'A bath first, Fanny,' Evie whispered, desperately wanting to get the dirt and the stain of Hal off her body.

Dr MacClay began inspecting the wounds on her wrist more closely. 'These need a good wash, Miss Davenport, then I shall bandage them.'

Aunt Mary and Aunt Rose came closer to the bed.

'Dearest child,' Aunt Rose wept. 'We were mad with worry.'

Aunt Mary nodded in agreement. 'When we received Fanny's note, we could not believe it. We came straight away.'

'We are so thankful for your safe return,' Aunt Rose added.

'And we'll make sure that horrid man is dangling from a rope!' Aunt Mary fumed.

'Where is Hal? Does anyone know?' Evie asked.

'In a cell,' Dr MacClay told her. 'He was found drunk in Bingley.'

'That is why he didn't return to the hut.' Evie understood now.

'Did he...' Aunt Mary swallowed. 'Did he damage you, dearest, you know what I mean?'

Evie wiped a tired hand over her filthy face. 'He tried, Aunt. Then he went away and said he'd return and, well... I was scared the entire time. Waiting for him to come back and attack me.'

Aunt Rose whimpered into her handkerchief, but Aunt Mary glowered with anger. 'I shall not rest until he has paid for what he has done to you.'

'Ladies, please,' Dr MacClay soothed. 'Your niece needs rest.'

'Indeed, Doctor. Come, Rose, we shall go downstairs.'

Evie held out her hand to Aunt Mary. 'Will you thank everyone for me?'

'Absolutely, my dear, leave that to me. I shall come up and see you later.'

Eventually, when MacClay had attended to her and left, and the crowd outside dwindled away, Evie soaked in a relaxing bath while Fanny washed her hair. She fought to keep her eyes open so she could enjoy her soup later, but the effort was proving difficult.

'I never want to experience anything like that again, miss,' Fanny said, rinsing the soap from Evie's hair. 'None of us have slept properly and worried ourselves silly with what might have happened. I swear Colin nearly fainted when Star came home without you.'

'Is Star hurt?' Her voice still cracked a little, but a cup of tea with honey had helped the scratchiness in her throat.

'No, she's fine. Colin looked after her. At first, we all thought you had fallen from Star, so Mr Bronson took the carriage out to look for you. When he returned and it was near dark, we began to worry you were lying in a ditch hurt somewhere. Colin and Mr Bronson spread the word you were lost and possibly injured. Everyone rallied to find you.'

'I hoped they would, but as time passed, I fretted no one cared.'

'Nonsense, miss. Everyone around here likes you. And poor Mr Lucas. He lost his head about it all. He wouldn't rest.'

Evie's heart swooped at the image of Alexander looking for her, never giving up, then carrying her upstairs in front of everyone.

'Mr Lucas has shown his feelings for all to see, miss. How do you feel about that?'

'That is something for me to think about another time, Fanny. Help me out, please. Dr MacClay says I mustn't wet the bandages on my wrist.' Knowing that Fanny would be distracted in helping her, Evie cleverly changed the subject. What Alexander had done would be the talk of the village and beyond.

'Make sure my aunts are comfortable, won't you?' Evie asked as Fanny helped her to dress in her nightgown.

'Yes, miss. I have been, especially your aunt Rose; she has been so upset. Mrs Humphry has cooked up enough food to feed an army. She's had Colin taking it down to the village to feed the men searching.'

'Poor Mrs Humphry.'

'Aye, she feels responsible.'

'What her son does is no fault of hers.' Evie climbed into bed, wincing at the aches and pains in her body.

'I told her that, but she still feels that way. Cooking has kept her sane.'

'I think I shall have my soup and bread and then sleep, Fanny. Will you tell my aunts, please?'

'Aye. I think we will all have an early night tonight, miss.' The maid gathered up the filthy mourning clothes and underwear.

'Burn those,' Evie instructed with a shudder. 'All of it. I never want to wear them again. I have others I can wear instead.'

'Yes, of course, miss.'

Left alone, Evie rested against the mountain of pillows Fanny had placed behind her and felt an overwhelming need to sleep. Dr MacClay had said to eat as she'd sleep better and for longer if she did, so she fought her eyes closing.

A knock at the door heralded Aunt Rose slipping into the room. 'Dearest, I shan't disturb you for long, but I wanted to give you this.' She passed to Evie a folded piece of paper.

Opening it, Evie read the words: *I love you. A. x*

'A not-so-secret admirer.' Aunt Rose grinned. 'He is a lovely man.'

'But he can never be mine, Aunt, not without hurting Sophie even more than she is.'

'So, you are going to sacrifice yours and his happiness for your friend's? Is that why you say you will remain unmarried?'

'What else can I do? To acknowledge my... feelings for Alexander will cause so much pain to Sophie. She loves him. If I had never come here, I believe Alexander would have married her, but he met me...'

'If...' Aunt Rose smiled. 'It is such a strange world where one little word, two letters, can change so many things. Fate decides what happens, or God if you're a believer.'

'I never wanted to hurt Sophie or fall in love. I was happy to remain ignorant of a man's love, to be an independent woman.'

Aunt Rose nodded. 'Sometimes in life we have to make sacrifices. When I was younger, I had a bevy of charming young men vying for my hand.' She paused to remember. 'But my parents believed them not to be suitable for one reason or another. In the end I never married, and I regret that to this day. I should have taken charge of my life, but as a dutiful daughter I listened to others, even Mary, and allowed them to alter my path in life. Do not do that, Evie dear. Do not allow others to make you walk a road that is not yours to walk. Understand?'

'Yes, Aunt.'

Aunt Rose kissed Evie's cheek. 'I shall tell no one about the note.' She quietly let herself out again.

Evie gently touched the words on the paper. A rush of emotion filled her. Alexander. Staring at the words, she wondered how she could ignore him after all this.

17

After Dr MacClay's visit the following morning, Evie, who had slept for twelve hours straight, rose and asked Fanny to help her dress.

'But, miss, Dr MacClay said you must stay in bed.'

'Nonsense. I have slept hours, eaten all my breakfast and, apart from some aches, a scratchy voice and my sore wrists, I am well. I need to get back to doing normal things. I am not the kind to wallow in bed.'

'If you say so, miss.' From the wardrobe, Fanny took out Evie's mourning clothes. 'Will you be staying home or venturing elsewhere, miss?'

'Staying home. I am content to spend the day with my aunts.'

Dressed, her hair combed and arranged neatly up into soft curls, Evie took a deep breath and walked downstairs. Both her aunts were still in the dining room eating breakfast. They rose late in the mornings and breakfast was a leisurely affair of eating, drinking cups of tea and reading the newspapers.

'Good morning, my dear,' Aunt Rose gushed, rapidly folding the newspaper away.

'Dr MacClay was most happy to see you recovering. Did he

allow you to leave your bed?' Aunt Mary asked, with a scowl at Rose.

'He did not say I couldn't.' Evie kissed her aunts in turn and noticed that Aunt Rose clamped a hand down on the newspaper. 'I wanted to spend time with you both.'

'As we do with you,' Aunt Rose gushed.

Evie felt something was not quite right. 'What is it?' She stared at Aunt Rose, knowing she would break before her sister.

'It is nothing,' Aunt Mary said. 'Do you want some tea?'

'Do not lie to me, please.'

Aunt Rose blushed. 'Dearest, it is nothing at all.'

Sighing, Aunt Mary tapped the newspaper. 'Your kidnap was reported in the newspapers and today they have reported your safe return.'

A wave of humiliation washed over Evie. 'Everyone will be reading about me over their breakfast.'

'And tomorrow those newspapers will be in the fire,' Aunt Mary said. 'In a day or two it will all be forgotten.'

She glanced out of the window, knowing that really wasn't the case. People had long memories. Her ordeal would be gossiped about for months to come. Still, what did it matter, really? With Papa gone, she had no one to please, no one to behave for. Suddenly, she had the urge to ride Star, to gallop over the moors, to feel the wind on her face, but her body couldn't take that today. Still, she felt the need to bask in the sun, to have her body warm and to be free to move about.

'You will recover from all of this,' Aunt Mary said.

Evie gave her a reassuring smile. 'I know. And today the sun is out. It is a beautiful day.'

'Maybe a stroll around the garden this afternoon?' Aunt Rose suggested.

'I think you should rest,' Aunt Mary muttered. 'Have you had enough to eat? Your voice is still husky. You might have caught a chill.'

'Please do not worry. I am fine.' Evie stepped to the door. 'I shall attend to my mail while you finish your breakfast.'

Fanny had placed all the post on a silver platter that stayed on the sideboard in the hallway. Taking the bundle, Evie went straight to her papa's study. For a moment she hesitated, for walking into the room she still expected to see Papa sitting behind his desk.

With determination, she opened the door and walked in. Sun shone through the window. Papa liked this room for its morning sunshine. Evie stood still, soaking up the smell of books, Papa's cigars and the beeswax polish Fanny used on the furniture.

Going to the window, she unlatched both panes and swung them open. The scent of fresh air and the fragrance of the roses in the garden bed next to the window drifted in. Swallows twittered in the trees and a robin hopped on the thin branches of the white lilac near the house. How pretty the garden looked, the grass lush and green, the garden beds in full summer flower.

Evie shivered at the sudden thought that Hal could have killed her and she would have never seen another pretty day such as today. Why had he not come back and finished what he started? Was he arrogant enough to think that after his drunken stupor, he'd be able to take his time in defiling and then killing her before she was found? Her luck had changed when Hal had passed out in the street and was then found by the police constable.

A knock on the door interrupted her thoughts. Fanny entered. 'Miss, the police are here.'

'Tell my aunts.' Evie left the study and went into the drawing room. Sergeant Coleridge and another younger policeman stood waiting.

'Miss Davenport. I am pleased to see you safe and well,' the sergeant said, taking off his hat.

'Thank you. Please, be seated.' Evie sat on the wing-backed chair as her aunts entered the room and came to sit on the sofa near her.

Sergeant Coleridge looked uneasy. 'May we ask if Mrs Humphry is able to join us?'

'Yes, of course. I should have thought of that. Fanny, ask Mrs Humphry to join us, please, and bring in some tea.' She smiled gently at the two men. 'Naturally, Mrs Humphry needs to hear whatever you have to say. Hal is her son.'

Mrs Humphry hurried into the room, nervously wringing her hands.

Sergeant Coleridge cleared his throat. 'As you are aware, we took Hal Humphry into custody after finding him drunk on the street outside of the Black Hen public house in Bingley. At the time we did not know of his involvement in Miss Davenport's disappearance. We only later learned that when he had an altercation with Mr Alexander Lucas.'

Evie frowned at the news. She hadn't been aware of that happening.

'Mr Humphry refused to tell us where he had imprisoned Miss Davenport. He admitted to taking you, but nothing else.' Sergeant Coleridge rubbed the back of his neck tiredly. 'Thankfully, Mr Lund found you.'

'Yes, I am lucky Mr Lund did because Hal threatened to return to the hut and attack me,' Evie said, suddenly angry. 'He told me he would do unspeakable things to me and then kill me and bury me where no one would ever find me!' She jerked to her feet, unable to sit still.

'Dearest.' Aunt Rose reached out a hand to her.

Rage burned in Evie. 'I have done nothing towards Hal Humphry and for him to kidnap me and keep me locked in a hut for days is... is...' Her voice broke, cracking once more.

Furious, Aunt Mary smacked her hand on the arm of the sofa. 'I want this man swinging from a rope. He is a menace to society, a repeat offender, I am told. How has he been allowed to roam the countryside capturing people to torture?'

Sergeant Coleridge held up his hand. 'I understand, ladies. However, kidnap is not a capital crime. He cannot hang for it.'

'What a disgrace!' Aunt Mary fumed.

'But murder is!' Evie snapped. 'If I was dead, he would hang.'

Aunt Rose started crying.

'Has my son been charged, sir?' Mrs Humphry asked quietly.

'I need a statement from Miss Davenport and then, yes, he will be charged with what he is accused of. He will be taken to Leeds Gaol and await trial. Miss Davenport will be called to give her account of what happened.'

'But he has confessed,' Aunt Mary said. 'Why does my niece need to be there?'

'Indeed, he has, but he will still go to trial and be sentenced. Miss Davenport will stand witness.' Sergeant Coleridge stood. 'May we go somewhere quiet for you to give your statement, Miss Davenport, another room perhaps?'

'Come into the study.' Evie led the way; being in the study, she would feel like Papa was there, guiding her.

When the police had left, Evie needed to go outside into the sunshine for some air. The sun on her face helped her to forget the last hour, reliving the attack at Hal's hands. She walked across the damp grass, stopping to admire the roses. She was about to venture over to the stables to check on Star when the sound of carriage wheels caused her to stiffen. She had no wish to socialise today.

Through the trees, she watched the Bellinghams' carriage come into view. It stopped at the front of the house and Mrs Bellingham, Sophie and Mrs Myer climbed out and went into the house.

Reluctantly, she turned back to greet them, entering through the side door. Inside, the women's voices reached her from the drawing room. Evie smiled at Fanny, who was coming down the corridor. 'Is Mrs Humphry coping?'

'Aye, miss. She has plenty of food made. She's been up since dawn baking.'

'I mean about the news of Hal.'

Fanny sighed. 'She knows her son is a bad 'un. She's just thankful you are home safe. Hal belongs in prison and this time he'll be in there for a very long time, which means Mrs Humphry is also safe.'

Evie nodded. 'Try and make her rest a bit. She mustn't carry all the guilt for Hal's actions. She will become ill.'

'I'll try, miss.'

When Evie stepped into the drawing room, she blinked in surprise at Sophie. Her friend looked devoid of all colour expect the blue shadows beneath her eyes. She was skeleton-thin and frail. Evie went straight to her and embraced her, feeling the bones through her dress.

'How happy I am that you are safe,' Sophie said. 'I had to come and see you.'

'I am so pleased that you did.' Evie smiled. 'How are you?'

'Me?' Sophie laughed gently. 'I am perfectly well. It is you who I am concerned about. What an ordeal you have endured. Oh my, all those bandages on your wrists. How brave you were.'

'Not really, I was very frightened.'

'But fought to be found. I heard Mr Lund nearly had a heart attack on hearing the banging coming from what he assumed was an empty hut. You did brilliantly to survive such torment.'

'I feel it has been an age since we spent any time together.' Evie brought a chair over from the window for Sophie, for she looked ready to fall.

'I see you are recovered from your ordeal?' Mrs Myer said loudly to Evie.

'I am, thank you.'

Mrs Myer dramatically clasped her hands together. 'How your poor papa must be turning in his grave at such a spectacle. His only daughter to be taken by a ruffian and kept prisoner in a hut for days. The whole area is agog with the news of it. That he dared lay his filthy hands on you. How degrading. Such an insult!'

Evie cringed.

Aunt Mary eyed Mrs Myer with distaste. 'You must forgive us, but Evie shall need to go up for a nap soon. The doctor insisted on no visitors, you do understand?'

'We shall not stay long,' Mrs Bellingham said. 'We only wanted to pay our respects and give our good wishes to Evie. Sophie was eager to see her friend.'

'Shall we take a walk in the garden?' Sophie stood, taking Evie's arm. 'I saw you out there as we came up the drive and we have brought you inside. I know how much you enjoy being in the sun. We shall only be a few minutes.'

Evie nodded and with arms linked they went out through the front door and around the side of the house to the widest part of the garden.

'Mrs Myer needs to hold her tongue,' Sophie said as they strolled.

'Or have it cut out altogether,' Evie muttered.

'Or wear a scold's bridle.'

'It's good to see you.' She squeezed Sophie's arm. 'I have missed you dreadfully.'

'I feel the same. When I heard you had gone missing, I was beside myself. I would have gone searching for you, too, if I had the strength. Forgive me for not joining the men to search.'

'There is nothing for you to be sorry for,' Evie reassured her, but a little voice in her head said that if it had been the other way around, Evie would have been the first one on a horse looking for her friend.

'Well, you are home now, and it is all in the past. What a wretched man to do that to you.' Sophie stared off into the distance. 'Papa says that Alexander arrived when you were brought home. Papa told us that Alexander was... distressed. He carried you into the house, up to your room.'

'He was concerned for me, as many people were. I was weak and couldn't walk. He was there...' Again, guilt flooded Evie.

'So, there is nothing more to it than that?' Sophie probed.

'No,' she lied, yet trying to make it the truth.

'I have tried so hard to stop loving Alexander.' Sophie took a deep breath. 'However, the more I try, the more he is on my mind. Papa has allowed him back at the house and I see him occasionally. I feel the humiliation every time I see him. Oh, he is kind and polite but we both know how awkward it is when we are in the same room together.'

'You must forget him.'

'But I cannot, Evie.' Sophie frowned and then straightened her bowed shoulders. 'I am going to write to him and ask him to reconsider having me as his wife.'

Shocked, Evie spun to face her. 'Why?'

'Because I cannot live without him.'

'But he has made it clear that a marriage between you both is not what he wants.'

'Doesn't he, though? Has he truly considered it? Papa can advance him greatly. Alexander can be more than simply a mill owner. I would be a wonderful wife to him. I would help him in everything he does. I will give him children, create a beautiful home for him. I have been trained all my life to be a man's wife.'

'Pick another man, then!' Evie cried in frustration. 'Alexander

Lucas is not the only man in society, Sophie. Any man of your acquaintance would be honoured to have you on his arm.'

'I want Alexander. Papa said he would help me.' A fierce glare lit Sophie's eyes. 'If Alexander is smart, he will reconsider and know his future is going to be wonderful. With Papa's help he could become very wealthy and very influential and powerful. Papa said Alexander could enter politics, and Papa would back him all the way.'

'Alexander does not want to be a politician.' Evie couldn't believe what she was hearing.

'How do you know?'

'He has never once mentioned in conversation that he wants to be in public service.'

'Some men do not realise what they want until it is in front of them. Papa believes he would enjoy entering politics. He went to rallies in America. He has spoken to Papa at length about the situation in America, the states fighting for supremacy to govern their own lands as they see fit. I have heard them discuss it.' Sophie turned back towards the front of the house. 'Alexander will soon see that marrying a Bellingham can alter his life.'

Floored by Sophie's convictions, Evie didn't know what to say.

'I shall call again tomorrow afternoon,' Sophie said, standing by the carriage. 'Perhaps we can devise a plan together to make me more agreeable to Alexander. New clothes, perhaps? I cannot ride as well as you, but when you feel up to it, you might give me some lessons so I can become more comfortable in the saddle?'

'Sophie, if he wanted to make you his wife, he would have done so by now. You do not have to alter for him.'

Sophie's manner changed. She stiffened and her expression hardened. 'I *will* change. I will transform into whatever he wants me to be. You do not understand the desperate need in me to be his wife. You do not wish to be married, but I do. I always have done.

Alexander is the one for me. I waited for him while he was in America. All that cannot be for nothing. He simply needs to see me as the best possible wife. I beg you to help me.'

Mrs Bellingham and Mrs Myer came out with the aunts following.

'Are you ready, daughter?' Mrs Bellingham asked Sophie.

'Yes, Mama. Evie and I had a lovely talk.' Sophie kissed Evie's cheek and climbed into the carriage.

Mrs Myer paused by Evie. 'Do take care of yourself. I do not think any of us could withstand another incident concerning you. Do give the gossips the chance to whisper about someone else for a change.' Her gaze swept over Evie before she stepped up into the carriage.

Evie raised her head at the remark. That damned woman always had to have the last word.

Her aunts came to stand on either side of her.

'Was that Mrs Myer the woman who wanted to marry Max?' Aunt Mary asked. 'The one you told me about last year?'

'Yes.' Evie gladly watched the carriage trundle down the drive.

Aunt Mary huffed. 'Thank goodness your papa had the sense to repel her advances. I would rather suck a bag of lemons than spend an hour in that woman's company!'

Evie grinned, but it faded quickly as she thought of Sophie and her pledge to claim Alexander.

* * *

The following day, Evie stood with Colin and Mr Bronson in the stables, all three studying Jupiter.

'It makes sense to sell him, miss, but I'll be sorry to see him go.' Colin rubbed his hand over Jupiter's flank.

'We have no need for him,' Evie admitted. 'He is an expense I can forgo. Feeding and caring for four horses requires a huge sum of money.'

'I was thinking about that, miss,' Mr Bronson said, scratching his whiskery chin. 'At the moment you have four horses, but we could get that number down to two.'

'How so?'

'As a lone woman, perhaps you don't need a large carriage? A smaller one, that requires only one horse to pull, could mean selling Jupiter and Copper.'

'Oh, I never thought of that,' Evie mused, liking the idea.

'Sell the carriage, Jupiter and Copper and buy a smaller vehicle that Blacky can pull, and you have Star to ride. You would make considerable savings.'

'Absolutely, Mr Bronson. An excellent idea.'

'Would you like me to make some enquiries, miss? I can visit the market and spread the word at the wainwright's and blacksmith's as well. Usually someone knows someone who is looking to buy a carriage or horses.'

'And I shall put an advertisement in one of the newspapers, too. Thank you.' Evie gave Star another pat where she stood in her stall before leaving the stables.

Another beautiful day would have seen her riding Star but the wounds on her wrists bled easily at too much movement and needed more time to heal. Dr MacClay had told her she'd have scars for life, and she had sent word to Mrs Stewart asking her to call. Evie would have long sleeves added to all her summer dresses that only had short sleeves to cover the scars until they faded somewhat.

'There you are.' Alexander came around the path bordering the vegetable gardens. 'Your aunt told me you were in the stables.' He stopped only inches from her. 'How are you?'

'Much better.' She took a step back from him, knowing her aunts might be peering out the windows somewhere.

'I know you said you would send a note, but I could not wait another day without seeing you.'

'Alexander...'

'No, Evie!' he said sharply. 'Please do not put me off with some excuse as to why we cannot see each other. I am tired of it.'

'Yesterday, Sophie came. She wants my help to win you back in her favours. She is determined to have you as her husband.'

'That is insane. I have made it clear I do not want Sophie.'

'She says you will change your mind this time. Mr Bellingham is to aid in this endeavour as well.'

'How?'

'By furthering your advancement in the world.'

'My advancement?' Alexander frowned in confusion. 'I do not understand.'

'Apparently, they think you would be keen to enter politics. Mr Bellingham will back you.'

He walked away, under the beech trees on the other side of the stables. 'How utterly absurd.'

'You do not wish to enter politics? They feel it is a great interest to you, though I have never heard you mention it.'

'I have spoken about the politics in America, and how interested I am in that simply because it affects me and my mill. I buy cotton from America. Any threat of war there impacts me.'

'What of local politics?'

His expression was of surprise. 'I have no interest at all.'

'Sophie and her papa believe that they can raise you up to be a powerful man, a rich, powerful man.' Evie watched his reaction. 'Something most men would grab at with both hands.'

'Not this man.' He marched back to her and took her in his

arms. 'You are all I need. I am a simple mill owner, Evie. Is that enough for you?'

'Of course it is enough.' She sighed, relaxing in his arms, tired of fighting their attraction. Life could be over in an instant. Her parents' deaths had shown her that. Surely, she could claw back some happiness and, for her, that meant being with Alexander. Yes, it would hurt Sophie, but she had tried to push Alexander away for the sake of her friend and nothing had come from it but misery for them all.

'Then marry me and let us get on with our lives.' He kissed her tenderly, lovingly.

A loud gasp broke them apart. Evie swung around and froze as Sophie glared at them, her hands over her mouth.

'Sophie!' Evie ran towards her.

'Do not come near me! You Judas!' Sophie screamed.

'Listen, please. I can explain.'

'Explain what? I have eyes!' Pain etched Sophie's features, draining them of colour. 'How foolish was I to believe you when you said you were only friends?'

Alexander stepped forward. 'Miss Bellingham, let us talk sensibly.'

The look she gave him was full of loathing. 'Twice now you have humiliated me. Papa will *destroy* you this time.' She spun on her heel and ran down the path beside the house.

Evie ran after her, calling her name, and managed to grab her arm at the carriage. 'Sophie, stop. Let us talk.'

'There is nothing you can say that I want to hear.' Sophie yanked her arm free. 'I wish you had died in that hut. Humphry should have finished you off.'

Evie blanched. 'What a horrid thing to say.'

'Is it? Is it as horrid as you stealing the man I love behind my back?'

'I never stole Alexander. He was never yours to take away,' Evie argued.

'How dare you!'

'I fought my feelings for him out of respect for you!'

'Oh, you were doing a grand job of it from what I could see,' Sophie sneered, wrenching open the door before the groom could do it for her. 'Our friendship is over.'

'Sophie, please.' Evie hurriedly stepped back as the door was slammed in her face. The groom jumped up beside the driver and the carriage rolled away.

'What is all the noise?' Aunt Mary asked from the top of the front steps.

Alexander, standing beside the house, walked slowly to Evie. 'I did not want it to happen that way, but I am glad Sophie knows.'

'Will you be happy when Mr Bellingham ruins you?'

'Why would he? He is a man of business and I have done him no harm. Sophie has it in her head that I am hers and she is wrong.'

Evie shook her head and took a deep breath. 'I have just lost my best friend.'

'When she has calmed down, she will want to talk.'

'You do not know her as I do. She may be mild-mannered and sweet, but Sophie also knows what she wants. Her forgiveness will take a long time to earn, if ever.' Devastated at their falling-out, her shoulders slumped. How had it all come to this?

'Then you must forget about her and concentrate on us.'

'Us?' Evie walked away, wishing it was so easy. 'How can I think of us right now? Sophie is in pain, and I caused that, *me*! The one person she trusted and depended on outside of her family. We were as close as sisters. I have destroyed that.'

He grabbed her arm and stopped her. 'And what of me? I have done as you asked and held back, waited, stayed quiet. I did what you asked and tried to not love you.'

'I needed more time!'

'For what?'

'To allow Sophie to accept a possible union between us.'

'She never would have.' He scoffed. 'How long were you going to keep me waiting? A month, a year, two?'

'I do not know!' she yelled, hurting her throat.

'Enough!' Aunt Mary marched over to them as fast as her stumpy legs could carry her. 'You, Mr Lucas, leave at once. My niece does not need this upset.'

Alexander threw his hands up in the air. 'I love your niece! Why am I the one in the wrong?' He stormed off to where Hero grazed near the drive. Seconds later he was thundering down it.

'Heavens, girl.' Aunt Mary tutted. 'What hard work you make of life.'

'I do not mean to, Aunt.' She stared after Alexander and wondered if she had lost both her best friend and the man she loved.

'Sometimes you have to make difficult choices in life.'

'And sometimes they are made for you,' Evie murmured, her heart heavy with sadness.

18

'I do not like to leave you,' Aunt Rose cried, slipping on her gloves in the hallway. 'We should stay another few days at least.'

Evie kissed her cheek. 'You have kept me company long enough, Aunt. You have your own life in Bradford.'

'We have no life there.' Aunt Rose sniffled.

'Speak for yourself, Rose!' Aunt Mary snapped. 'We have things to attend to at home and Evie has recovered well from her ordeal.'

'You will return soon, though?' Evie said, suddenly wanting them to stay longer.

Aunt Mary took her hands. 'I was thinking perhaps you could come to us? A change of scenery for you might be nice?'

Evie nodded happily. 'I would like that very much.'

'Come next month, yes? When you have finished sorting out the sale of Max's horse and the carriage.'

'I will.'

'Good.' Aunt Mary kissed her. 'Take care of yourself.'

Crying quietly, Aunt Rose embraced Evie. 'Do not wait a month if you would rather not. You are always welcome. In fact, you can come with us now.'

'Rose!' Aunt Mary beckoned from the front steps. 'Evie has much to do. She has her own household to run, as do we. Come along.'

Evie waved them off and closed the door. The house grew quiet. A pile of mail needed reading and the accounts reconciling, but the August sun streaming through the windows beckoned her outside. Soon it would be autumn, and the cooler weather and grey days would be aplenty.

'Fanny,' Evie called, grabbing her hat and gloves and a small leather purse of coins from the cupboard.

'Yes, miss.' The maid came rushing up the corridor from the kitchen.

'I am going for a walk.'

'Will I come with you, miss?'

Smiling, Evie was so grateful to have such a devoted maid. 'Thank you but I shall be quite all right.'

Fanny didn't seem so sure.

Evie pinned on her black straw hat. 'I need to stretch my legs, Fanny. I may only walk into the village and back.'

Leaving the house, Evie delighted in the blue cloudless sky, the warmth on her body. Today would have been perfect to go swimming in the river, or have a picnic, but she was in mourning and such activities were frowned upon when wearing black.

Strolling into the village, she nodded and smiled to those she passed. Several older ladies were chatting together outside of their cottages, a man whistled as he hoed his vegetable plot and a young mother with three small children who ran about her skirts as she struggled with her shopping nodded to Evie as she passed.

Outside of the public house, two old men sat on a bench supping ale and smoking pipes. They touched their foreheads in acknowledgement as she went inside the taproom. It took a moment for her eyes to adjust to the dimness after the brightness outside.

'Miss Davenport?' Mr Butcher wiped his hands on a cloth.

'Good day to you, Mr Butcher. I do not wish to disturb you. I simply wanted to give my thanks to you and all the men who went out searching for me. I have been terribly remiss in not coming sooner, but my aunts have been staying with me for weeks and—'

'No thanks are needed, miss. We were happy to do it. We look after our own hereabouts.' The big man grinned and put his arm around his smaller wife, who'd come out of a doorway to join him behind the bar. 'Love, Miss Davenport has come to say thank you to us for searching for her.'

'We are just pleased you are safe, miss.' Mrs Butcher nodded.

'And that the scum who took you is in gaol,' Mr Butcher added.

Evie drew out her leather purse and shook all the coins into her palm. 'I would like to buy the men a drink as a thank you.' She handed the money over to the landlord. 'I do not know how much it would cost, but if it is more than I have given you, please send word to me.'

Mr Butcher glanced at the coins. 'That'll be enough to wet their throats, miss, don't you worry about that, and they'll be grateful.'

'As am I. Thank you again. Good day to you both.' She gave them another smile and stepped out into the sunshine.

She walked to the churchyard and entered through the gate to wander the path that led to where Papa was buried. She cursed herself for not bringing flowers, but fresh ones had been laid by his headstone by her aunts only yesterday.

She stood thinking of Papa, remembering the times they'd laughed, the times they'd sat reading in companiable silence by the fire, of the times they'd ridden fast along the beach below their house in Bombay. The dances, the theatre plays, the dinners they'd attended. After Mama's death it had been just the two of them and she missed him sorely.

Turning away, she waved to Reverend Peabody, who was talking with a young couple. Evie hoped they were discussing a wedding. The loveliness of the day was perfect for planning a wedding.

The idea made her think of Alexander as she left the church-yard and walked down the valley. She ached to see him. For a fleeting moment she thought to walk to his mill, but what would that achieve? No, first she must put things right with Sophie.

It took her ten minutes to walk to Bellingham Hall and she was hot and thirsty by the time she rang the doorbell. A footman let her in, and she waited in the drawing room until he returned and said that Miss Bellingham wasn't at home.

Frowning, Evie didn't believe him. If Sophie wasn't at home, he'd have said so when he answered the door. Sophie was within the house but simply didn't wish to see her.

Annoyed, Evie lifted her chin. 'Kindly tell Miss Bellingham that I shall not leave until we have spoken.'

She paced the drawing room, growing angrier by the second.

The footman returned. 'Forgive me, Miss Davenport, but Miss Bellingham is indisposed and cannot see you.' He couldn't meet her eyes.

'Indisposed?' Irritated, Evie swept past him and up the stairs before he could protest. She ran along the gallery to Sophie's bedroom and flung open the door.

Sophie, standing by the window, spun with a gasp. 'Get out.'

'I will not. We must talk.'

'I have nothing to say to you. Get out.' Sophie glared at her, looking like death; her hair hanging lank and loose, her skin blotchy.

'We need to talk this through, Sophie. I value our friendship and want to save it.'

'You did not value it while you were sneaking behind my back meeting Alexander,' she choked.

'I never meant for any of this to happen. I denied my feelings for months. I fought all attraction to him, but it was impossible not to fall for him.'

'Even when you knew he was mine.'

'He was never yours, Sophie,' Evie said quietly. 'If he loved you and wanted you for his wife, he would have told you before now.'

'His head was turned by you!' Sophie sneered. 'You dazzled him from the very first moment. No one can compete against you. You're clever and knowledgeable about most things women don't care to know. You challenged him with your outspokenness, your physical attributes. In comparison I was a pale shadow.' Sophie's shoulders slumped.

'I did not purposely try to win him over. It happened on its own.'

'So you say.'

'It is the truth. I constantly told Alexander that we must ignore our feelings because of you. I never wanted to see you hurt.'

'Did he tell you he was going to embarrass me at the ball?'

'No! I had no idea what he'd planned. I had told him I wanted nothing to do with him. I wanted him to propose to you.'

Sophie laughed softly. 'What a martyr you are.'

'I am nothing of the sort. I simply wanted my best friend to be happy.'

'To the detriment of your own happiness? How noble,' Sophie mocked.

'Please, Sophie, let us put this all behind us.'

Sophie glared at her. 'How can we possibly? We both love the same man, but he only wants one of us.' She sagged and held on to the windowsill. 'You have won, Evie.'

'How have I when I have lost you?'

'Alexander more than makes up for it.'

'It is not the same,' Evie murmured, her chest hurting. 'You are my best friend.'

'I was.'

'We can be again.'

'Are you saying you will give up Alexander for me?'

Evie hesitated, but it was enough for Sophie to huff condescendingly.

'I thought not.' Sophie stared out of the window. 'You can go now. We are done. Do not come back. There is no friendship in this house for you.'

Evie placed her hand on the doorknob. 'I hope in time you will forgive me. We do not control where love strikes, Soph, and I love you.'

Leaving the bedroom, Evie walked downstairs. Coming in through the front door, Mrs Bellingham and her daughter-in-law, Helen, both greeted her.

'Have you been to see Sophie?' Mrs Bellingham asked. 'I am glad. She needs cheering up. I have decided to take her to Cornwall, to the sea. I think it would help her a great deal.'

'Cornwall is lovely, I am told,' Evie answered, desperately wanting to get away.

'Will you stay for tea?' Mrs Bellingham walked into the drawing room.

'No, thank you. I must be getting back.'

'How are your injuries?' Helen asked, her stomach clearly showing her advanced pregnancy.

'Much better, thank you.'

Mrs Bellingham pulled the bell rope by the fireplace. 'When you feel up to it, you must come for dinner.'

Sadness welled in Evie. She would never have dinner here again. Sophie might not have told her family about their quarrel yet, but she was bound to soon. 'Thank you. Now, I must be going. Good day.'

Walking down the drive, Evie glanced back behind her up at Sophie's bedroom window. Sophie stood behind the lace curtains like a ghost. Evie waved, wishing with all her being that Sophie would reconsider their friendship, but instead she turned away from the window and was gone.

* * *

Giving her parcels to Colin, Evie left Mrs Stewart's shop. 'Mr Bronson said to meet him at Holden's Blacksmith at eleven o'clock,' she said to Colin as they walked up the street.

'Yes, miss. Father said the buyer for the carriage, Mr Formby, wants to view Jupiter, too, and since Father was taking Jupiter to the farrier, he thought meeting in town would be more suitable for everyone.'

'But why at the blacksmith's?'

'The farrier is working in the field behind the blacksmith's, miss.'

'Oh, I see. Does this Mr Formby seem a decent fellow, do you know? I only want Jupiter to be sold to someone who will take care of him.'

'Father says Mr Formby is a decent gent. Made his money in Australia with sheep. He's originally from around here, a Yorkshire-man, and he's returned home to buy goods to take back to Australia.'

'How fascinating.' Evie crossed the road, sidestepping a pile of manure. 'So, Mr Formby, if we come to an agreement, will ship the carriage and Jupiter to Australia?'

'Aye, miss.' Colin grinned. 'Jupiter will be taken care of, for no man willing to spend all that money on shipping will want his goods damaged, will he?'

'That is a good point.'

'Miss Davenport!' Mrs Myer came out of the bookshop as they passed.

'Good morning, Mrs Myer.' Evie was forced to halt.

'I am pleased to see you,' Mrs Myer gushed.

'Oh?' Evie didn't know why.

Mrs Myer flashed her hand in front of Evie's face. 'I am engaged.'

Evie blinked in surprise. 'Goodness. Congratulations.'

'Mr Lucas asked me last evening.'

Evie's heart flipped. 'Mr Lucas?'

'Mr Guy Lucas, yes.' Mrs Myer giggled like a young girl. 'I am so delighted, of course. At my age, to remarry is a blessing indeed.'

'Indeed,' Evie echoed, not all that concerned about Mrs Myer's affairs. Though she did wonder if the woman had ever been in love with Papa or if it had all been superficial.

'And Guy is such a wonderful man.'

'He is.'

'You simply must come to the wedding.'

'Really?' Evie blurted out. 'Well, yes... Thank you.' She couldn't think of anything worse.

'The wedding is in three weeks, when the banns have been read.' Mrs Myer flapped her hands in excitement. 'My betrothed is away at present, left this morning with Alexander to Manchester on business. I told him to buy a new suit while he is there as Guy insists we marry before Alexander leaves for America for good.'

Like a bucket of cold water had been thrown over her, Evie gasped. 'Alexander is going to America?'

'Is it not thrilling?' Mrs Myer's eyes narrowed. 'He is selling his mill and emigrating. Guy is unhappy about it, of course, but no father can stand in the way of his son wanting to seek his own path.'

Evie had nothing to say. Her stomach churned with the thought of Alexander making such decisions without telling her. Had he given up on them? Had she told him one too many times to stay away? She had no one to blame but herself.

'I am in a terrible rush. So much to organise.' Mrs Myer laughed gaily. 'Must dash!'

'Absolutely.' Evie walked away, towards the blacksmith's at the end of town. Her head whirled with the news. She had lost both Alexander and Sophie. What did she have left?

She pushed those thoughts aside as she did business with Mr Formby. He agreed to her asking price on the carriage and hardly haggled with her over Jupiter and Copper's prices.

'I will come and collect both on Thursday, Miss Davenport. Is that agreeable?' he asked.

Evie shook his hand. 'It is, Mr Formby.' She liked the tall thin man with a shaggy beard and wide-brimmed hat.

'My business is all concluded, so I am sailing back to Australia next week. I miss my family, but I've bought them enough fine goods to keep them happy for years.' He beamed.

'What an extraordinary life you must lead on the other side of the world, Mr Formby,' Evie said where they stood in the field behind the blacksmith's.

'It is hard work, I won't deny it. But my life is good, Miss Davenport. We have plenty of land, our own, mind you, not tenanted, fresh air, good food and a steady income. None of which I had here in England. I left Yorkshire with a few shillings in my pocket and have returned ten years later with a thousand times that.' He tipped his hat at her. 'If you're ever in the southern land, Miss Davenport, do look me up. The area is called the Illawarra, south of Sydney, on the coast. Until Thursday, then.' He nodded and walked away.

Back home, Evie wrote to her aunts telling them the carriage, Jupiter and Copper were sold and she would come and visit them on Friday week and, while there, she would purchase a smaller vehicle.

Tapping her fingers on the desk, she had the idea to learn to drive herself. A small buggy of some sort would be easily managed. But then if she did that, she would have no use of Mr Bronson. She couldn't get rid of the coachman. He was a loyal and good servant.

Pondering on the dilemma, she didn't hear Fanny enter the room.

'Miss, there is a letter come in the last post.'

'Thank you, Fanny.' Opening it, she didn't recognise the handwriting, but her breath caught as she began to read,

Darling, Evie,

I am travelling to Manchester on business and will return in a few days. There are things I would like to discuss with you. I shall call on you on my return. I am planning for the future, a future I hope you will share with me.

With eternal love,

Alexander

Evie pressed the letter to her chest. He wanted her to be with him in America. She hardly dared believe it. She would go, of course she would. What did she have to stay here for?

Movement outside of the window caused her to stand up and take a closer look. Sophie? Amazed, Evie rushed out of the house to meet her along the drive. 'Sophie?'

'Did you know?' Sophie swayed as though drunk. She was dressed in a day dress without a hat or gloves and wearing house slippers, not shoes.

'Know what?' Worried, Evie walked closer. 'Is something

wrong?' She looked behind Sophie for the carriage. 'Have you walked here?'

'Did you *know*?' Sophie screamed. She brought one hand up and waved a letter in the air above her head. 'This is from Alexander!'

Her heart dropped to her toes and bounced back up again to beat painfully in her ribcage. Why had he written to Sophie, of all people?

'Did you compose this letter together?' she accused, red blotches covering her cheeks.

'No, not at all.'

Sophie held the letter in one hand, which shook slightly. '*Dear Miss Bellingham, I am writing this letter to once again apologise for any pain I may have caused you. I am going to truthfully tell you that I am in love with Miss Evie Davenport. She rejects me out of respect for your feelings and does not want to cause you further pain. However, I beg you to consider Evie's happiness, if not mine. As a decent lady of good birth, I would hope that you wish us both happiness. To make this easier for you, I have decided to emigrate to America, and I wish for Evie to come with me. I know she would want your blessing, but if you feel you cannot do that then we shall go quietly, and you will never have to see either of us again. Sincerely, Alexander Lucas.*' Sobs wracked Sophie's thin body as she finished.

Shocked, Evie clasped her hands together, trying to work out what to say.

'So, there you have it,' Sophie said matter-of-factly, tears streaking her face. 'He asked for forgiveness and my blessing, then you two can sail to America with clear consciences.'

'I had no notion he was going to write that. I only received a letter from him just minutes ago.'

'Will you go with him?' Sophie's deadpan expression frightened Evie.

'I haven't decided. There is much to discuss.'

Sophie's peal of laughter was high-pitched and false. 'You lie to my face. Again! Of course you will go with him!' She brought her other hand around, which she'd had hidden behind her back, and dangled a pistol.

'Sophie!' Evie yelled, stunned with fear that her once-best friend was going to shoot her. Backing away, she whimpered as Sophie raised the pistol.

'Miss!' Fanny shouted from the front steps.

'Put the gun down, Sophie,' Evie begged, never so scared in her life as she was facing the pistol. 'We can talk.'

'You want what is mine,' Sophie said calmly.

'No! No...' Evie pathetically put her hands up to ward off the bullet.

'You can have him. Have the future with him that I should have had, and you can also have my death on your mind forever!' The gun went off, a spark of light, a boom, then Sophie dropped to the ground.

Evie screamed. She stared at the bloodstain spreading around Sophie's dark brown hair, soaking into the dirt.

The world around Evie spun and tilted, before springing into sharp focus. She ran and fell beside Sophie, her hands hovering over the mass of blood and damage done to her head. 'Sophie! Oh, no, Sophie!' She kneeled over her, pain and shock bending her double.

Sophie stared at her with wide, accusing, dead eyes.

19

In the misty drizzle, Evie stood beside the newly dug grave, not caring that the water ran down her dress, her face, the back of her coat's collar to touch her neck with icy fingers. Nothing mattered but the deep sorrow reflected in the faces of Mr and Mrs Bellingham, Sophie's brothers and Helen, their friends and extended family.

In the days since the accident, Evie had withstood the overwhelming grief and shock, the tortuous cries of Lydia Bellingham when she'd arrived to see her daughter dead, the disbelief in Jasper's eyes, the questioning by the police sergeant, the wounded silence of her servants.

Dr MacClay's draught had brought her some sleep the first night, but since then her eyes refused to close and her mind continually flashed images of the scene until she thought she'd go mad.

The tragedy of Sophie's death had rocked the district to its very core. Hundreds of people turned out for the funeral, regardless of the thunder and rain. Evie knew of their whispers. How could a lovely young miss such as Sophie Bellingham kill herself?

Jasper Bellingham, cold and detached with grief, had silenced the rumours and said it was a shooting accident. Sophie had gone to Evie's house to practise for the upcoming grouse season. Whether people believed him or not, Evie didn't know, but the police had filed it as an accident, and it had been kept out of the newspapers.

But Evie knew the truth. It was written in her memory in blood, a reoccurring nightmare she couldn't wake from.

Reverend Peabody concluded the service, his clerk covering him with an umbrella. As others drifted away, Evie stared down at the polished mahogany coffin with its brass plaque on top. Flowers were thrown onto to it by Sophie's family and Mrs Bellingham cried into her husband's shoulder.

Evie couldn't turn away. It was as though her feet were lead weights keeping her to the spot. It was too painful to accept that Sophie was down in that box. She would never hear her laugh again or tease her about her terrible swimming ability. Never again would they enjoy a picnic or discuss dress patterns. No more would Evie be able to ride to the hall and beg Sophie to do something that she knew Sophie thought was not *the done thing*, such as asking the cook to teach them to bake, or flirt with the stable grooms. How she would miss Sophie's giggles when they gossiped about young men trying to impress them at dinner parties, or when Sophie would act out a scene in a play to make Evie laugh.

It was all gone. The tragedy of Sophie not marrying, having children or growing old rendered Evie weak with anguish.

The rain fell harder, the sky grey and low.

Mrs Bellingham, helped by her husband, stepped to Evie's side. 'Do not come back to the hall.'

Surprised, Evie looked at her.

Lydia Bellingham lifted the black lace veil from her face. Her eyes bored into Evie's. 'You are not welcome. My daughter is dead because of you. I knew she was suffering because of

Alexander, but I did not realise that it was *you*, her best friend, who had replaced Sophie in *his* affections. I know all about it now. Last night while in her room I found her diary and read it. Suddenly it all became clear. Sophie detailed your treachery.'

Shaken, Evie's mouth gaped. 'Mrs Bellingham, I—'

'Do not speak. I will not listen to your excuses. You killed my daughter as good as if you'd pulled the trigger yourself.'

Evie swayed, destroyed by her hateful words.

Jasper Bellingham stiffened. 'And *he*' – he pointed a finger at Alexander, who stood a few yards away with his father and Mrs Myer – 'he will feel my vengeance. I will ruin Alexander Lucas, as God is my witness.' He marched his wife away.

Those that had heard the exchange hurried away, heads close, whispering.

Every part of her shook with shame. Evie stared across Sophie's grave at Alexander and her broken heart shattered into sharp, jagged pieces. She turned away, but he raced around the grave to grasp her arm.

'Evie.' He looked as devastated as she felt.

'Go away, Alexander. I can deal with no more.' She walked through the soaked grass, ignoring the glares and glances thrown her way.

Mr Bronson took her home in the carriage and then dealt with Mr Formby, who came to collect it and the horses.

Crying into Jupiter's neck, Evie said goodbye to him, feeling as though she was saying goodbye to her papa all over again. Misery weighted her shoulders like a heavy cloak. She quickly made her excuses to Mr Formby and dashed into the house.

Fanny helped her to change out of her wet things, keeping silent, but the kindness in her eyes made Evie cry.

'You cry, miss. It'll do you good.'

Sobbing, Evie buried her head into Fanny's shoulder and cried for those she had lost until she was spent and weak.

'There now, have a little nap, miss.' Fanny settled her on the bed and placed a blanket over her. 'I'll wake you this afternoon.'

Evie didn't think she'd sleep, but she did and was surprised when Fanny woke her a few hours later.

'It's still raining, miss, and it's come over cold.' Fanny fussed around her. 'So, I've lit the fire in the drawing room. I know we shouldn't, it still being August, but it's cold enough for it.'

'Thank you, Fanny.'

'Mrs Humphry has made you some beef broth to help you get your appetite back. She's made fresh bread, too, knowing how much you like it straight out of the oven with butter.'

'What would I do without you, Fanny?' Evie said, going downstairs to the drawing room.

'Well, miss, let's hope you never have to find out.' She grinned.

After a bowl of broth and two slices of bread and butter, Evie felt somewhat revived in body if not spirit. Her mind couldn't concentrate on anything. Instead, it replayed the scene with Mrs Bellingham. Such humiliation still made her shiver, and her cheeks turn red in mortification.

Hearing voices in the entrance hall, Evie sighed, not wanting to be disturbed. She'd taken up her embroidery, but it lay untouched on her lap.

Fanny opened the door to Alexander and showed him into the drawing room, where Evie sat by the window to make the most of the grey afternoon light. Surprised to see him, Evie could only stare and try to calm her rapid breathing.

'I had to come,' he said, coming to kneel by her side. 'I know you said not to, but I could not rest.'

She placed the embroidery in the basket at her feet. 'I need some time alone.'

'What will time bring you?' he asked, taking one of her hands.

'To understand all that has happened. Not that I ever will, I don't think.'

'You are not to blame.'

'Yes, I am. We both are.' She rose and stepped past him. 'We caused Sophie so much suffering that she had to end her life.'

Alexander ran his hand through his hair. 'I will not have that. Not at all. Sophie was selfish. She killed herself to punish you, and me, but mainly you; that's why she did it in front of you.'

Evie winced. 'And I deserved it.'

'No, Evie!'

'Her friendship meant a great deal to me. She became my instant friend when I arrived here. Through Sophie's kindness I was able to survive the grief of losing Mama and moving to a strange country. Sophie's generosity made my life here so much better. To lose her, to have caused her such misery is something I cannot even comprehend.'

'Do you love me, Evie?'

She thought hard about the answer. She did love him, but she had lost Sophie because of loving him. 'My feelings are no longer important.'

'They are to me.' His expression was full of anguish. 'Let me take care of you. We can leave here. Get married and sail away.'

'You believe it is so simple?'

'We can make it easier for ourselves by being far from the memories of this place. We also need to live *our* lives.'

Exhausted from thinking, Evie wanted nothing more than to return upstairs and curl up in bed and forget everything. She was heartsore, weary of grief. But more than that she carried a heavy weight of guilt, which bowed her back. The burden was so great she doubted she would ever be able to stand straight again.

'Darling.' Alexander came to her side and folded her into his arms. 'I love you. I will make you happy, I promise you that.'

She stepped back enough to reach up and kissed him tenderly, lovingly. 'We lived in a dream, Alexander. One where we thought we could be together and love one another.'

'We can!' he said desperately, kissing her, holding her tightly.

'No. Our time has come and gone.' She pushed him away. 'We messed it all up.'

'We can make it right again, Evie, please.'

She gently cupped his cheek, loving him so much it was a physical pain. 'Our love is tainted. Our happiness forever stained.'

'No. I won't let Sophie's madness ruin our future.'

'But she already has. I cannot be with you.' Evie lifted her shoulders in despair. 'Sophie's shadow, the memory of her shooting herself right in front of me will never be erased. Every time I look at you, or want to make plans with you, I will see her. Sophie's ghost won't let me rest and be happy with you. Guilt will be my constant companion in our lives together. I cannot live like that. It is best we part now and make a clean start of our lives.'

'I cannot and will not accept that.' His voice broke.

'We are not getting the happy ending as in *Jane Eyre*, Alexander.' Tears blurred her vision. She straightened her spine, daring to say the words that would separate them forever. 'My love for you will die, Alexander, and I hope it does very quickly, for we will never be together.'

'Evie, no, please!' His grey eyes were bleak with agony.

'Goodbye and good luck in America.' She left the room and went upstairs to her bedroom and closed the door. Leaning against it, she wondered if her heart was as fragile as Papa's. She hoped that it was, and that it would stop instantly to end her suffering.

* * *

Standing in the midst of the drawing room, surrounded by boxes, Evie wrote on labels and then passed the label to Fanny for her to glue on to the correct box.

'Another box complete,' Fanny said, wiping the label flat.

'I cannot leave Papa's books behind.' Evie wrote another label.

The idea to sell the house had been an easy decision. Within a week of Sophie's death, the invitations had stopped arriving. Society turned their backs on Evie, for she meant nothing to them, whereas a falling-out with Lydia Bellingham would not be considered. The news of the Bellinghams' wrath reached far and wide and their friends knew which side to take. She understood their reasons, and having no friends made the decision to leave much simpler.

The time had come to start a new phase of her life. The house sold within ten days to a family who wanted to take it furnished. Evie agreed. It was less work she had to do to sell it all. The new owners had also bought Blacky and asked for the servants to remain. Again, Evie agreed, except for Fanny, who would be going with her, and Star. Mr Bronson had ridden Star to Bradford and had her stabled there. Evie could not sell her beloved horse.

Of Alexander she heard nothing. Whether Mr Bellingham had made good his threat to ruin him or whether Alexander had sold the mill and sailed to America, she did not know. Selling up kept her mind occupied and she refused to think of anything but the future. For her to be without Alexander now was too painful to consider, but the independent side of her forced her to carry on, to make a life alone. She could do it. She *would* do it.

'What time are the new owners arriving tomorrow, miss?' Fanny placed another label on a different box.

Startled out of her thoughts, Evie continued writing. 'One o'clock. I want the rest of the packing finished today. Mr Bronson has borrowed Mr Lund's cart and he will take us and all the boxes to my aunts'. We shall leave mid-morning tomorrow.' She paused. Through the window she saw Sergeant Coleridge riding up the drive. A shiver passed over her. She'd seen too much of that man recently. 'Fanny, the sergeant is here.'

'Now what?' Fanny huffed, rising from her knees and straightening her uniform.

Evie waited for Fanny to show the police officer into the drawing room.

Sergeant Coleridge's eyebrows rose when he noticed all the packing. 'You are leaving, Miss Davenport?'

'I am. The house is sold. I am going to stay with my aunts in Bradford until the trial. I was going to write to you and inform you.'

'Ah.' He glanced around. 'Is Mrs Humphry still here?'

'Yes.'

'Would you be so kind as to fetch her for me, please?'

Fanny scooted out of the room.

'Is this about Hal Humphry and not Miss Bellingham, then, Sergeant?'

'Both. I can tell you that Miss Bellingham's case has been declared an accident. The investigation is closed.'

Bowing her head, the misery rose once more. Whenever she thought she might manage to move forward, something happened to slap her with it again, whether it be a mention of her name in the village or Evie finding some item that Sophie had given her in the past.

Mrs Humphry came in, wiping her hands on her apron. She looked worried and glanced between the sergeant and Evie.

Sergeant Coleridge cleared his throat. 'Perhaps we could sit down?'

Fanny rushed to pull off the dust sheets placed over the chairs and sofa.

'Mrs Humphry,' the sergeant began as they sat, 'this morning, information came to me concerning your son.'

'Lord above, what has he done now?'

'He was involved in a fight with fellow prisoners.'

Mrs Humphry sighed deeply, the wrinkles on her face pronounced, showing the hard life she had lived.

'I am sorry to tell you that your son was stabbed by another prisoner. He died during the night in the gaol's hospital.'

Fanny put her arm around Mrs Humphry's shoulders.

'I'm fine.' Mrs Humphry lifted her chin. 'To be honest, it is long overdue. I don't know how he kept alive as long as he had with the trouble he got into and the people he associated with.'

'His body can be released to you for burial.'

Mrs Humphry shook her head. 'I have no money to bury him. He took everything I had, always did. It's only been since his arrest that I have managed to keep my wages to myself. Before that, he'd come to the back door and demand them and if I didn't give the money over, he threatened to come inside and terrorise everyone.'

'Why did you not tell me?' Evie asked, shocked.

'You had enough to deal with, miss. It was easier to give him money and keep him away; that was until he decided to kidnap you.' Mrs Humphry clasped her hands together. 'Will the prison bury him?'

'Yes, but in a pauper's grave,' Sergeant Coleridge told her.

'That is all he deserves.' Mrs Humphry nodded once. 'That is an end to it.'

'I can pay to bury him,' Evie decided. 'For you, Mrs Humphry.'

'No, miss. I'll not hear of it. After what he did to you? Not a chance will you spend a penny more on him. Let him lie in a pauper's grave with no one to mourn him. You get out of life what you put in, and he wanted to only harm. I'll shed no tears. Now, if that is all?'

'Yes. I will write to Leeds Gaol and tell them to deal with his body.'

'Thank you.' Mrs Humphry left them, her eyes dry.

'Go to her, Fanny.' Evie walked with Sergeant Coleridge to the door. 'Thank you for coming.'

'There will be no court case now regarding Humphry snatching you.'

'I am pleased I do not have to partake in such a spectacle,' she said, relieved. The thought of appearing in court at Hal's trial had been another burden keeping her awake at night.

'Then this should be the last we see of each other, Miss Davenport.'

'I mean no disrespect, Sergeant, but I sincerely hope so.' She shook his hand and wished him good day.

When Evie turned around after closing the door, Fanny and Mrs Humphry were standing in the corridor. 'Yes?'

'Miss.' Fanny licked her lips anxiously. 'Would it be possible for Mrs Humphry to come with us when we leave tomorrow?'

'I can speak for myself, Fanny,' Mrs Humphry said sharply.

'Is that what you want?' Evie asked the older woman. 'I am simply staying with my aunts until I decide what to do.'

'I would like to go with you, miss, if there is room. If not, I'll stay in lodgings somewhere.'

'You have no money!' Fanny blurted out.

'Mrs Humphry, you are very welcome to come to Bradford. My aunts' house is large enough to accommodate a small army,' Evie soothed.

'Thank you, miss.' Mrs Humphry let out a relieved breath. 'Lizzie said I should stay here as she is doing, and Mr Bronson and Colin, but there are too many memories. I need a fresh start.'

'I understand that all too well. The new owners did say they would employ you as well as Lizzie, Colin and Mr Bronson, so the decision is yours.'

'And I've made it. Wherever you set up home, miss, I'd like to be the cook there.'

'Good. Then it is settled.'

The following morning, Evie took a last walk around the gardens. The trees were beginning to change colour, the breeze a little cooler. She hated the thought of another cold winter, of ice on the inside of the windows, damp on the walls.

Above her head came the cry of geese flying south in an arrow formation. She watched them until they were small specks in the overcast sky. Suddenly, she knew where to go. Home. India.

The thought grew enticingly real. Yes, it made sense. She would return to the place she'd been happy.

Lifting her skirts, eager to be on her way, she hurried into the kitchen. 'Come, it is time,' she told Fanny.

Mr Bronson and Colin were there, standing next to Lizzie and also Mr Lund. Evie shook hands with them all. At breakfast she had given them their wages and a bonus amount in gratitude for their service.

'You've been a good mistress, Miss Davenport,' Mr Bronson said. 'I hope you will be happy in your new life.'

'I hope so, too, Mr Bronson.' Evie smiled. She turned to Mr Lund and gave him a parcel she had put to one side.

'I don't need a gift, Miss Davenport.'

'It is a small token of how much I have valued our friendship, Mr Lund. You have been a wonderful neighbour and friend.'

He opened it to reveal a leather pouch filled with expensive tobacco and a shiny new pipe made of polished briar wood. 'Gracious me.' He sniffed emotionally. 'I shall treasure it for the rest of my days.'

Pleased he liked it, Evie looked at Fanny and Mrs Humphry. 'It is time to go.'

Rocking down the drive on Mr Lund's cart, Evie glanced back over her shoulder to the house and silently said goodbye to it.

In the village, she stopped to visit Papa's grave and place the last of the summer flowers near the headstone. 'I know you want me to be happy, Papa. That is why I am going home, to India. It is where all my happy memories are, and they will give me comfort.'

'Miss Davenport?' Miss Fellows, the Bellinghams' cousin, walked across the grass to her.

'Miss Fellows,' Evie said in acknowledgement. She was the first member of that family she'd seen since Sophie's funeral and didn't know what to expect.

'I am glad I have met you.'

'Oh?'

'I heard in the village that you are leaving. Your house is sold.'

'Yes, that is correct. I am leaving for Bradford now.'

'Bradford? That is where you will be living?'

'Only until I sail for India.' Saying it out loud made it even more real.

'India? By yourself?' Miss Fellows' pale red eyebrows rose in surprise.

'Yes, with my maid and cook, too,' Evie added, knowing the other woman didn't mean servants.

'How I envy you,' said Miss Fellows wistfully.

'Me?' Evie scoffed. 'No one envies me, Miss Fellows. I am without friends and very little family.'

'But you have spirit and are courageous. I have never met anyone as adventurous as you. Again, you are proving it by going to India on your own.' Miss Fellows glanced away, towards where Sophie's fresh grave was covered in dying flowers. 'I do not blame you for Sophie's accident. She knew what she was doing. I have spent a good deal of the summer at the hall and witnessed Sophie becoming obsessed with Alexander Lucas.'

Evie winced at the mention of their names.

'I tried to talk to Sophie, but she would shout and rage at me that I did not understand her pain, her humiliation. She did not realise that I, too, know what it is like to be miserable. I am the unseen, forgotten cousin, the one no one really cares about, and most of the time they forget I am even in the room, never mind the house.'

For the first time, Evie truly saw Miss Fellows, and felt ashamed she had been one of those people who didn't take her seriously or pay her much attention. Miss Fellows had been at all the balls and parties that Evie attended and not once had Evie sought her out.

Miss Fellows fiddled with the black tassel on the cuff of her dark grey dress. 'So many times, I have wished to end my life. But I am a coward. So, I suffer in silence and pretend to be a part of a family who has no time for me. Helen gave birth to a baby boy last night.' She suddenly changed the subject. 'Aunt Lydia is overcome with joy.' She bowed her head. 'I would give anything to travel to India and experience new things, meet new people.'

'What is stopping you?' Evie blurted out, then remembered that Miss Fellows might be poor, which was why the Bellinghams had taken her in.

'Nothing is stopping me but cowardice. I have the funds to be independent, but I could never do it on my own.'

'Then come with me.' Evie shrugged. 'You have your cousin over there, Mr Dunlop, as well. So you are not without family, or a friend if you include me in that sphere.'

'When do you sail?' A light of interest entered Miss Fellows' eyes.

'I have not made arrangements. I only decided this morning to go. But I can write to you and let you know what my plans are?'

Miss Fellows gripped Evie's hand. 'Please do. I will buy a ticket on the same ship.'

'The Bellinghams will not like it.'

'There is no need for them to know. I shall simply say I am visiting my cousin.'

'Very well.' Evie glanced down at Papa's headstone. 'I must go.'

'Then I shall leave you and await your letter.' Miss Fellows hesitated a second longer. 'I could never replace Sophie in your affections, nor do I wish to, but one cannot have enough friends.'

Alone, Evie placed her hand on the headstone. 'Goodbye, Papa. I love you.'

She walked over to Sophie's grave, the headstone not erected yet. 'Goodbye, Soph. I hope you are resting in peace.'

20

'India?' Aunt Mary's voice cracked on the word, such was her shock. 'Oh no, dear. That cannot do.'

'Why?' Evie sat at the breakfast table. She had arrived the evening before and with all the fuss and unpacking, she had not told them about her plans until now. 'It was where I was the most happy, Aunt.'

'Dear girl.' Aunt Rose placed her hand over Evie's. 'You cannot go back and think it will be the same. When you were in Bombay, yes, you were happy but that was because you had your parents there and lived a lavish life provided by Max's position. All that is gone.'

'I have wonderful memories there,' Evie defended, ignoring the small voice that murmured that none of it would be the same India she'd known with her parents' love to surround her.

'That is all they are,' Aunt Mary said, folding her newspaper in half. 'Memories are not the same as picking up the old life you had there. It does not exist any more, dear girl. Rose and I are not being cruel; we are simply alerting you to the fact that your old life stopped the moment you boarded the ship and left Bombay.'

'But I can get it back again,' Evie persisted.

Aunt Rose shook her head sadly. 'All that will be there are ghosts of what you once had, dearest. Nothing will be the same because Max, Caroline and Lucinda aren't with you. Not having your papa and mama there will make you miss them even more. You cannot live in the past, dearest.'

Evie felt a panic rise in her, rebelling against the food in her stomach she'd just eaten. 'I do not wish to be rude, but you are both wrong.'

'Have you kept in touch with your old friends in Bombay?' Aunt Mary asked.

'I did, yes, at first, not so much lately...' Evie tried to remember the last time she'd written to any of her friends in Bombay and realised it had been many months. Having Sophie as her friend had pushed them out of her mind, not purposely, but slowly by degree.

'We appreciate you wish to begin a life somewhere new but going back to India to try and recapture the life you once had there is not the answer.'

'Then what is?' Evie asked dully.

'We would like you to stay here with us,' Aunt Rose encouraged.

'At least think about it,' Aunt Mary suggested. 'There is no hurry to make any decisions. You have only just arrived.'

Evie wiped her mouth and rose. 'I think I shall walk to the stables and check on Star.'

Aunt Mary waved her fork at her. 'Take Fanny with you. Bradford is not Lylston. It is a busy town filled with undesirables.'

'And you may get lost,' Aunt Rose added.

Escaping the house, Evie strode down the street with Fanny hurrying to keep up with her. Her aunts' words about India and trying to recapture the past niggled her. She knew they were right but that didn't make her feel any better. She was so sure India was the answer. She'd even encouraged Miss Fellows to travel there.

'Miss!' Fanny suddenly pulled Evie back from the kerb before she stepped in front of a hansom cab going at speed.

'Goodness,' Evie breathed.

'You're in a headlong rush to get to those stables, aren't you, miss?' Fanny joked.

Sagging with hopelessness, Evie fiddled with her gloves. 'To tell you the truth, Fanny, I do not know what I am doing or where I am going.'

Frowning, Fanny gave her a comforting smile. 'Who says you have to know right now, miss?'

'I thought going to India was the answer, but maybe it is just a silly dream.'

Fanny's mouth dropped open. 'We were going to go to India?'

Abruptly, Evie realised that she had not mentioned it to Fanny. 'I would not have made you go, of course.'

'I said I'd never leave you, miss. I would've gone with you, though I'm not sure about Mrs Humphry.'

'No...' Evie started walking, slower this time. 'But I do not think I want to live with my aunts for the rest of my life, either.'

'You're young and not without means, miss. What is to stop you buying a little house somewhere? You can meet new people, learn about a new place.'

'But where, Fanny?'

'That's for you to decide, miss, but it doesn't have to be as dramatic as India. Take some time to think it over.'

When she returned home to her aunts' house, a letter was waiting for her from Mr Enoch Latimer, the solicitor.

'Why is he writing to you?' Aunt Mary asked as Evie sat down opposite her in the drawing room. 'The house sale has gone through smoothly, has it not?'

'Yes. The money is in my account. I have signed the papers.' Evie pulled out the letter and read it twice.

'Well?' Aunt Mary scowled. 'Do not keep me in suspense.'

'It is concerning my shares in Mr Bellingham's business, his railway scheme in India that Papa bought into. He has offered me above price to sell the shares to him.'

'Ahh,' Aunt Mary murmured.

'They blame me for Sophie's death.' Evie passed the letter to her aunt.

'My advice is to sell.' Aunt Mary removed her glasses after reading it. 'Cut all ties with them.'

'Yes, I will. I hurt their daughter and it is only natural they want my name removed from all association.'

'Sophie Bellingham killed herself, Evie,' Aunt Mary stated. 'Her actions were selfish and cruel to do it in front of you. I will not let you suffer years of guilt because that girl could not accept a rejection.'

Aunt Rose entered the room and stopped. She looked cagey, twisting her fingers together, and two spots of colour stained her cheeks.

'Rose?' Aunt Mary snapped. 'What are you standing there like that for?'

'We have a visitor,' she exclaimed, and stepped to one side.

Alexander walked in, holding his hat.

Evie thought her heart would actually stop this time. He looked dashing in a black suit, his hair a little too long to be tidy, but Evie noted the bruising under his beautiful grey eyes, the thinness of his cheeks.

'Well, this is a surprise, Mr Lucas.' Aunt Mary stood slowly, her knees creaking. She offered her hand and Alexander bowed over it. 'I was not aware that you knew our address, sir.'

'Forgive me for arriving unannounced,' he said, his gaze straying to Evie.

'It was me!' Aunt Rose gushed. 'I could not let another moment go by without these two young people conversing.'

'Rose!' Aunt Mary said furiously. 'It is none of your business.'

Evie blinked in confusion at her aunt. 'I do not understand.'

Aunt Rose looked pleadingly at her sister as though asking for forgiveness. 'Last week, Monday it was, I received a letter from Mr Lucas. I lied and told you it was a note from Bradford Orphans' Charity.' She sucked in a gasp of air, her cheeks flaming red. 'In Mr Lucas' letter he confessed his deep *love* and *admiration* for our great-niece.' She waved her hand towards Evie. 'He begged me to inform him that should Evie ever need a... a friend, or...'

Alexander stepped forward and gazed tenderly at Evie. 'I asked Miss Rose to contact me should you ever speak of me in a way that perhaps might mean you wish things had turned out differently between us.'

'But I have not said any such thing,' Evie whispered, still overcoming the shock of seeing him in her aunts' drawing room.

'You did not have to.' Aunt Rose dabbed at her weeping eyes. 'I took one look at you, Evie, and I knew.'

'Knew what?' Aunt Mary snapped at her sister.

'That Evie needed Mr Lucas. I saw the note Mr Lucas asked me to give Evie telling her he loved her, and I saw the same look in Evie's eyes when she read that note. I refuse to allow all that has happened to keep them apart from each other. Mr Lucas' declaration is proof that they are meant to be together, and I *will not* let Evie suffer a lifetime of loneliness as *we* have done, sister, because of circumstances beyond her control!'

'How dare you interfere?' Aunt Mary bristled.

'I dare! And I am glad of it.' Aunt Rose waddled out of the room, crying.

'I shall have words with her.' Aunt Mary stormed from the room as fast as her short legs could carry her.

Amazed, Evie stared at Alexander. All the emotions and feelings she'd fought so hard to bury rose to the surface again.

'I will fight for us, Evie,' he said, not moving, but his expression was full of love. 'You can keep sending me away and I shall keep returning for as long as it takes for you to love me.'

'I do love you,' she whispered. 'You know I do.'

He released a long sigh. 'Then we are halfway there.'

'But nothing has changed, has it? Sophie will always be there between us, robbing me of happiness because she will never experience what I have.'

'So, you will be a martyr?'

'Do not be so blind or flippant, Alexander,' she said harshly.

He grabbed her to him, holding her tight when she pushed away. 'No, do not fight what we have. Do not sacrifice us.' He bowed his head to touch hers. 'I do not believe for a minute that this will be easy. Demons will ride our backs for a while, but together we can support each other. We can hold each other when the past rears its ugly head and threatens us.'

'How I wish to believe you.' She closed her eyes, revelling in the feel of his body against hers.

'Sophie was not herself at the end. Something had triggered a disease in her brain, which changed her, we all know that. But before that time, I remember her being happy, laughing, dancing. That is the Sophie I think we should honour. Live for that Sophie, my love, because I think that Sophie, the one who loved you, would be happy for us.'

'How can I be happy with you when she is dead?' Tears spilled over her eyes and Alexander wiped them away with a finger.

He cradled her to him. 'All I ask is to give it a try, my darling. Can you do that? For me?'

She nodded, tired of hiding her love. Maybe she would never be truly happy, maybe the ghost of her best friend would always haunt her, but denying a life with Alexander hurt him, too, and she wasn't strong enough to cause the man she adored pain.

The door opened and her aunts entered the room. Alexander released Evie but kept hold of her hand, not caring what her aunts thought.

'Am I forgiven?' Aunt Rose asked timidly.

Evie nodded. 'Of course.'

'Shall we ring for tea?' Aunt Mary said, sitting in her favourite chair between the fireplace and the window.

'First I must seek your permission,' Alexander said to the aunts. 'I adore Evie and wish to marry her with your blessing.'

Aunt Mary stared at them both for a long time. 'You have our blessing.'

Alexander squeezed Evie's hand gently. 'And I must tell you that I wish to take Evie to America to live.'

'America!' Aunt Mary barked. 'What on earth will you do there?'

'I have sold my mill. I shall either buy another there or some other form of business. I have the means and the intellect to succeed. Evie will want for nothing.'

Evie stepped forward. Alexander's announcement gave her hope for the future, not in England with its ghosts nor in India with the old memories, but somewhere new, fresh. 'America is the answer, Aunt Mary.'

'I do not know what to say.' Aunt Mary scowled.

'But I do,' Aunt Rose said. 'America sounds exciting, Evie dear, and if you are willing, we shall come with you.'

'Have you lost your mind?' Aunt Mary banged her hands on the armrests.

'No, not in the slightest.' Aunt Rose grinned and turned on her sister. 'All my life you have told me what to do. Not any more.'

'We are old!'

'Then let us try and be young again, before we die, Mary. I wish to go to America. We shall buy a house near Evie and Mr Lucas. I want to hold Evie's babies in my lap.' She turned to Evie. 'Unless you would rather we did not join you?'

For the first time in a very long time, Evie felt a wave of joy flow over her. 'I would like nothing more, Aunt.' She turned to Alexander and saw the love and happiness in his eyes. 'America shan't know what has hit them.'

He raised her hand to his lips. 'As long as I have you, that is all that matters.'

'You have me.' She reached up and kissed him. 'Always.'

ACKNOWLEDGMENTS

Firstly, thank you to all my readers. Where would I be without you all? I appreciate each and every one of you. The messages I receive from people around the world telling me how much they have enjoyed my stories is something I will always treasure and never take for granted. Being an author is hard work, but it is also extremely rewarding, especially when readers take the time to contact me, or leave a lovely review. Facebook groups, such as the saga groups run by Deborah Smith, that champion my and other authors' books are wonderful. Thank you.

Another thank you goes to the writing industry friendships I have made over the years. Writing brought us together but it's genuine caring that keeps us all strong. I'm so grateful to have many friends, too many to name, but I must do a shout-out to Lynda Stacey and Maggi Andersen. Those two ladies keep me sane when sometimes it's touch and go!

A huge thank you to all the team at Boldwood Books. What a great bunch of women they are – all striving to produce excellent books in a friendly environment. They deserve all the success they achieve.

Finally, once more I must reserve the biggest thank you to my family. My husband, Mark, who works so hard and is so supportive of my career. (He doesn't read my books, but I don't hold that against him as he's there every step of the way!) To my children, Jack and daughter-in-law Bec, Joshua and Ellie (and grandsons

August and Cillian), thank you for the support and for asking when I am getting a Netflix deal. Love you all.

MORE FROM ANNEMARIE BREAR

We hope you enjoyed reading *The Soldier's Daughter*. If you did, please leave a review.

If you'd like to gift a copy, this book is also available as an ebook, digital audio download and audiobook CD.

Sign up to AnneMarie Brear's mailing list for news, competitions and updates on future books.

https://bit.ly/AnneMarieBrearNews

ABOUT THE AUTHOR

AnneMarie Brear is the bestselling historical fiction writer of over twenty novels. She lives in the Southern Highlands in NSW, and has spent many years visiting and working in the UK. Her books are mainly set in Yorkshire, from where her family hails, and Australia, between the nineteenth century and WWI.

Visit AnneMarie's website: http://www.annemariebrear.com/

Follow AnneMarie on social media:

 twitter.com/annemariebrear

facebook.com/fenella.miller

 bookbub.com/authors/annemarie-brear

instagram.com/annemariebrear

Sixpence Stories

Introducing Sixpence Stories!

Discover page-turning historical novels from your favourite authors, meet new friends and be transported back in time.

Join our book club Facebook group

https://bit.ly/SixpenceGroup

Sign up to our newsletter

https://bit.ly/SixpenceNews

Boldw∞d

Boldwood Books is an award-winning fiction publishing company seeking out the best stories from around the world.

Find out more at www.boldwoodbooks.com

Join our reader community for brilliant books, competitions and offers!

Follow us
@BoldwoodBooks
@BookandTonic

Sign up to our weekly deals newsletter

https://bit.ly/BoldwoodBNewsletter

Printed in Great Britain
by Amazon

22787566R00175